Also by James Barlow

James Barlow

ONE MAN
IN
THE WORLD

SIMON AND SCHUSTER
NEW YORK

LIBRARY OF CONGRESS CATALOG CARD NUMBER: 67-10521
DESIGNED BY EDITH FOWLER
MANUFACTURED IN THE UNITED STATES OF AMERICA
BY H. WOLFF BOOK MFG. CO., INC., N. Y.

ACKNOWLEDGMENTS

Before I could become emotionally involved in a novel about UNO and Portugal in Africa I had to understand the nature of the problem and seek a very elusive truth. In this I received help of various kinds and am grateful to Gustavo Duran, Michel and Verdalee Tombelaine, Brian Urquhart, Professor Ritchie Calder, Professor Conor Cruise O'Brien, Lieutenant Colonel V. de Guinzbourg, Colonel Chuck Whitehead, Lieutenant Colonel Bob Renneissen, Tom Ditchfield, Antonio de Figueiredo, Mrs. M. Teitelbaum and Amnesty International, Oxfam, and members of the Secretariat of the United Nations in New York and London who must remain anonymous. The views expressed and conclusions made are, of course, my own and are subject to the structure of fiction.

Part One ▪ ▪

Tired
And lonely,
So tired
The heart aches.
Meltwater trickles
Down the rocks,
The fingers are numb,
The knees tremble,
It is now,
Now, that you must not give in.

1 ··

THE CLERK led the way along the heated corridor, fumbled at the door of the freezer and inquired for the second time, although he had the key in his hand, "What number's she in?"

"Seven," McQuade said.

"And the name's McQuade?"

"My mother—"

"Jeez cripes," protested the clerk, opening the seventh tray, "I'll leave you to it. Too cold to hang around. I want to go to the john already. Just push the tray back until it clicks. That'll lock it. Automatic. Everything's automatic these days," the man said in resentment. It hadn't helped *him*.

McQuade waited for the clerk to go away, but the man lingered despite his complaint.

"Aren't you Mr. Shaun McQuade?"

"Yes, I am," acknowledged McQuade. He felt a flash of irritation, having mentioned his name three times.

"Heard about you," the clerk claimed. "You work at United Nations, that right?"

"It's true."

"Pretty important, I guess. Can't say I understand it myself," the clerk said with disapproval. "All them niggers and Europeans making trouble. It's in the papers—often," he told McQuade, like a claim of literacy. "When'll you bury her?"

"When the ground's softened."

"We'll get a rush then. Have to be late March or April."

"Okay," agreed McQuade.

"Well, I'll leave you," the clerk said in McQuade's condemnatory silence. "Just push the tray till it clicks. Automatic."

The room was as cold as McQuade could bear. He pulled the tray out to its limit and stood humbly by the corpse of his mother. She'd been dead a week, but the ground was already too hard in the early Canadian winter to allow digging. April. He'd have to pay a

9

rental. There was a big, ugly cemetery outside—fluorescent lighting illuminated an untidy pattern of gravestones. But it was where his mother belonged. A hick town. There was money here—in the pulp mills, oil refineries, supermarkets and garages and timber companies. Don't despise it, McQuade reminded himself. Most of the world lives in hick towns or the bush or desert or jungle or industrial hells. The untidy small city of fifty thousand people was pretty now in the deep, unexpectedly early snow. Drunken, stunted poles along the highways were burdened and festooned with as many as twenty heavy wires. Square wooden or brick buildings, few of them handsome, whose ugliness was aggravated by the exterior iron staircases—useless, surely, in this weather. There were some mighty poor people in this town of Saint John—down there by the harbor, for instance. Education in the whole province of New Brunswick was twenty-five years behind the times under a frustrating system that looked good on paper but had problems, some of them ugly.

But it was, or had been, his town. He belonged now to the Boeings and international airports; to Ottawa and New York: to the delegates' lounge and the lobbying in Ferdi's Restaurant across First Avenue; to missions in the Pfizer Building and Rockefeller Center and on Third Avenue and 42nd Street; and to committees and interviews in the big glass house by the East River. He was part of the system of telephones and the delegates' aides and Telex messages and the five-language translations, the pinpricks of fierce light in the General Assembly, and the Canadian Mission up there on the twenty-eighth floor in a Third Avenue office. But he acknowledged his beginnings here. And you did not have to go far outside this small city to be among picturesque forests and lakes that stretched a thousand miles beyond. He had a view of the world, a cosmopolitan pity, that took no notice of the color of skin, the degree of ignorance. He believed in what he was doing. The clerk in this mortuary was no more intelligent or worthwhile than the people of Ruanda, who voted for freedom with bits of colored paper to indicate the candidate of their choice. Both were worthy of equal consideration. They didn't start the wars or manufacture the machine guns. Time. It was a race against time. A race of education and freedom, inch by inch, with a billion injections on the way, against the final loss of temper, the refusal to lose prestige, and the fool who committed the irretrievable act of turning experiments with kiloton bombs on silicate into megaton bursts on granite bedrock and destroying the cities.

His mother was small and plump, with a lined face and gray hair. He had a youthful face and light auburn hair, cut close in the American style. His mother's neck was creased and tallow with fatigue. She was, or had been, seventy-four. He was forty-seven years old, five foot ten, healthy, and good humored, with a temper that was slow to come. What had she done in the world? You could say nothing. But the lines showed differently: work and illness, strain, marks of weather, and types of food—it was all written there. She was his mother. Any mother had his pity. The things that happened to their children—he had seen it. The dead Canadian infantrymen in slashed heaps in Italy, the starved bodies in Africa. He remembered a riot in Lahore, blood running across the station yard, bellies ripped open . . . and when the stunned, hot silence had stayed for a few minutes and the hoarse breathing and the thousand trotting feet had moved on to wreak other havoc, a sound had ended the silence, a sad sound terrifying him as he sat there untouched in a Jeep, the sound of women wailing. Love and stupidity. They went hand in hand. As fast as men were born and cherished in love, they thought up some other thing to kill for. . . .

He felt near despair and tears and stayed awhile to recover himself. Then he pushed the tray back into the freezer and, sure enough, it clicked. He went out along the slippery illuminated paths into the roar of vehicles and the changing traffic lights and the world to which he belonged.

In the warm hotel bedroom Kristan said guiltily, "We're going to a party tonight."

"Tonight?" protested McQuade, shocked.

"Don't be mad, Shaun. I know it's your mother, but she's been dead a week and she was very old anyway. And there's a lot of people I—we—want to see and won't for *years*."

"We'll be here in the spring for the funeral."

"I know, but a funeral's *serious.*"

"All right, all right! You want to go to a party. You're just a hicktown girl at heart. Whose party?"

11

"Emelda Routtu."

"Do I know her?"

Kristan laughed. "You knew her when she was Emelda Sisk."

"I don't remember."

"You'd say that anyway, wouldn't you? The perfect diplomat! I'm going to change. The taxi's coming in twenty minutes."

Emelda and Wendell Routtu lived ten miles out of town, in a long, white-painted wood bungalow with picture windows, some of which overlooked Lake Kennebecasis. The taxi smashed its way through the snow and slush, banged its springs in potholes. McQuade was a little tired and apprehensive. There'd be nobody he knew. He would stand around talking, becoming facetious as the drinks went down, and at two in the morning have four or five new friends. Seventeen hours later he'd be in New York and they'd merely be a headache. It was cruel but true: as a delegate he already had too many friends and acquaintances, so that life was too fast. He could not commit himself deeply to anyone, only to an idea and an organization and a committee which had twenty-three other members. Kristan complained all the time about it, but not too sourly: "You *used* to take notice of me when we were in Ottawa." "Ah," he'd counter, "that was a long time ago." It had been three years, in fact, since he had been accepted for duties at the Canadian Mission to the United Nations.

He recognized no one at the party, and it was hard to let go of the deep seriousness in him.

Ten or twelve people were there at the moment, more were coming, the snow-laden automobiles like cream cakes outside. They all knew each other. He didn't know anybody. Kristan identified a few. Kind, careful remarks to test him, see if he was good humored or a stuffed shirt. A certain caution, recognized after two or three introductions. They were in mild awe of him! He was a diplomat, had climbed in the world while they had stayed behind. And made three times as much money, he thought cynically. The drinks and his good-natured answers put it right. A sprinkling of attractive girls of the thirty age group—interesting to look at for him who was forty-seven. Bald heads and shining faces that stared over glasses and tried to get in the quick remark or comment to prove that they were politically informed, too. An Englishman who started off very bit-

12

terly with his opinions of Saint John and Canadians, but mellowed as he poured down beer, and began to recite poetry and pinch girls. One girl was drinking too much vodka and was obviously going to be the problem of the evening.

It thinned down to five or six people, ultimately—the ones who would be submerged reluctantly in the reality of tomorrow. Three younger men, one wife, and two of the unmarried girls eventually sat on the carpet and pounded their way verbally through the problems of the times, through art and love with increasing frankness. They shouted confidences while around them people stood or moved, other conversations went on in an uproar and sweet music trickled from somewhere.

The girl who'd had too much vodka was becoming amorous. She had a new technique and would say simply, "Catch me!" and fall like a pole. Shouts of laughter as someone missed and she fell on a chair. The first glasses broken.

The noise was too much and McQuade found himself talking, face to face, within inches of each other, to one of the girls.

She was talking fast, unburdening herself to a stranger. She kept leaning on one elbow, then the other, and her hurt eyes smiled now and again.

"You're different," she claimed with approval. "Not like a politician at all."

"Is that good?"

She blundered on clumsily. A wise man, she'd found a wise man and a kind one. Talk, plead, see what *he* says. McQuade could see it in her face, overlaid by the flush of alcohol. "Well, you're so easy to talk to. All the important people I've met have been so *cold*. We went to New York, Pollyann and me—" McQuade recalled now that Pollyann was the plump, curvaceous, cheeky girl full of vodka, who could be heard now saying frankly, "I want to be kissed," which evoked a response of *"Wow!"* from two or three husbands and angry stares from middle-aged wives.

The girl whose name McQuade didn't know moved to rest on her left elbow and shifted her legs so that McQuade saw a slender thigh with repairs to the stocking. She didn't care about his brief scrutiny, and he knew that she was starved, in need of love to the point of carelessness. It was not a new problem in girls of thirty,

13

but he was anesthetized enough to listen as if it was rare. And the girl's face was desperate enough. He *had* to care, he reminded himself.

"What's your name?" he asked.

The girl laughed—a small mouth, creased bad skin, but she was attractive for all that. "That's another thing," she confided. "Jane Brown. Can you imagine? My grandfather was de Bruin, but he wanted to be the same as everyone else. Nothing. You know? So he changed it to Brown. I even have to sign my Christmas cards Jane D. Brown."

"What's the D.?"

"Debbie."

"You do have problems!" he said.

"Listen," Jane D. Brown pleaded, holding his hand on the floor. "I mean, when you were talking to Wendell you—well, you seemed to understand."

He sensed the impending hard-luck story or the sentimental advances of the unhappy and looked at her. He wanted to deal with every problem of humanity that he encountered. You could say that compared to Ali Shadhi (who'd had his bowels cut open on the street, and who'd had tuberculosis in the first place, not to mention being illiterate and living on the pavements of Lahore, wet or shine) Miss Jane Brown had no problems. She was thirty and had good health and a life expectancy of seventy years or so, whereas Ali's life expectancy (if they hadn't gutted him with a sword) had been thirty-seven years and two months, according to the World Health Organization's statistics. But this was no solution for Jane Brown. She was *here*. Punjab was in the atlas or on TV. She would express sympathy and acknowledge that there was always someone worse off, but the fright and loneliness and disappointment in her blue eyes would still represent what was gnawing at her. If he could help. . . . She could claim about half an hour, after which he'd be outside her life forever. She talked rapidly as if sensing this, and he put an arm around her for physical support and to prove his sympathy. A package deal for Miss Brown. That's what was required. Love. He couldn't give her that sort. He had to let it go with sympathy and understanding. The point was that she *believed* him.

14

"Where d'you work?" he asked.

"At the blood bank in the hospital. You know," said Jane Brown shakily, "I saw one of my friends shot? I mean he was brought in. You know when they tried to rob that bank by the bridge? He was shot." The blue eyes met McQuade's brown ones and told him everything. "And one of the fellows that did it—we had him there too. I never smelled so much garlic on a man's breath in my life," she said with a return to the shaky laughter. "Oh, Jesus, I was scared. The only time I was scared worse was three weeks ago. I went blind in one eye. I was scared skinny," she said with huge relief. "Because my mother went totally blind, you see."

"It's not hereditary," McQuade comforted her.

"It's okay now," Jane Brown told him. "Now my only problem's the usual one. He died, y'see—my friend, I mean, not the garlic character. He just went to prison. . . . We're going to Montreal, Pollyann and me."

Over heads and through thick smoke McQuade caught Kristan's eye. Glasses and heat and people talking. . . . An older woman standing by the seated McQuade, confiding deafeningly, "Y'know what marriage is? It's fractional death . . ."

The girl called Pollyann came over and complained, "You haven't kissed me," and that was the end of all possible seriousness for the day. People were beginning to leave. The two girls had an escort who offered McQuade and Kristan a lift in his automobile. McQuade sat by chance in the rear of the Rambler, and for half an hour, while the station wagon made its way along the highway, skidding slightly now and again, he had one girl leaning on his left shoulder sighing with drunken amorousness, giggling, and the other holding his hand fiercely and whispering her problems: "I'm old. Thirty. We're going to Montreal. We're fed up with this dump. I'm Irish really. Irish. Is that good? Oh, thank you! I'm sick of blood. I want something nice to happen. A tourist agency, that's where we're going. Over Niagara in a barrel, that's about my luck! You're nice, y'know that?" And the alcoholic Pollyann urged, "Kiss him then, if he's nice." The small mouth met McQuade's—a taste of gin and lipstick.

When he stepped out of the car, assisting Kristan, the girls insisted on final kisses. Pollyann said, "Wish me luck," and Jane D. Brown qualified, "Wish me love. . . ."

Silence. Resentment sensed. Oh, shoot, McQuade thought, she's angry. But Kristan at least withheld it until they were in the hotel bedroom.

"*That* was a stupid party."

"Oh, I don't know—"

"Sure. *You* were enjoying it."

"Isn't that the idea of parties?"

"It was humiliating. Right there in front of people. Just as if I wasn't there at all. People were laughing. Bernadette said—"

"But she didn't mean—"

"Oh, yes, she did."

"No. The other girl had had too much vodka."

"What other girl? You mean that floozie you were necking with in the car?"

"Oh, for heaven's sake!" he protested. "We were having a ball, weren't we? You wanted to go, not me."

"Next time I'll let them get fresh with me. I'll find a man."

"You do that," he shouted in frustration. "You find one. Jeez, all I did was talk."

"Oh, sure. We could all see that. You snubbed a whole heap of people so's you could sit on the floor necking with some girl. Why didn't you take her to a bedroom and finish it off there?"

"What the hell's the matter with you?" he bellowed, angry now. "Do you want a mouse for a husband?"

"Don't make excuses. It was embarrassing to watch. Ridiculous and humiliating. Only next time I'll do it and see how you like that."

"You do that."

"I will. Don't think I won't. What do I care? I've nothing to live for."

This was too much and McQuade grinned.

"What the hell's so *funny?*" Kristan cried. The tears were coming and it'd soon be over. "What would you do if I messed about with some half-drunken man?"

"You wouldn't—"

"Who says I wouldn't? Are you so perfect I couldn't bear to?

16

Suppose I did. Not that anybody'd be interested, but suppose they were? And you found an affair going on?"

McQuade said, "Then I'd kill him."

"And me? Would you kill me?"

He managed to smile. "I don't know. I'd have to think about you."

"You mean you'd devise something special?"

"Oh, hell, shut up. You know I wouldn't hurt you."

"You just did."

"Well, not on purpose. I was sorry for the girl. She has problems."

"You're not the answer to them. Okay. Subject closed. You've got a kind heart. You're a big sentimental slob. When do we get out of this hick town?"

"About twelve hours from now. This afternoon's plane."

"Any other girls you want to see?"

"A few, but it doesn't matter!"

Kristan was undressing and McQuade embraced her in reconciliation, felt the bones of her thin structure under the nylon.

"What did you mean when you said you'd nothing to live for?"

"I was hurt," she admitted.

"Live for me," he pleaded.

"Don't I always?"

"Don't you trust me?"

"I love you. So it hurts, see?"

"If you trust me you should never be hurt."

"All right, so I was embarrassed."

"I trust you," he said calmly. "When I'm on the other side of the earth I never have any doubts at all about you."

"That's because you know I'm forty-three and no one looks at me."

"Don't be silly."

"It's true. It's my problem, isn't it, my condition? It's a little frightening that no one does care—only superficially—when you're no longer beautiful."

"I care," he insisted, "and you *are* beautiful . . ."

17

2 ▪▪

THE AIRPORT LOUNGE was stifling hot. There were even tropical plants among the marble mosaics. Outside, the snow lay a foot thick.

"Air Canada," the voice announced. "Flight 427 to Fredericton, Quebec and Montreal . . ." and the thirty or so passengers walked out to the waiting Viscount. "You can sit by the window," Kristan told McQuade. The businessmen in fur hats and coats relaxed in boredom or fetched magazines from the rack, but McQuade stared along the port wing and watched the mechanic signal with his hands, saw a flurry of snow as the first engine fired. "Rolls-Royce" was printed on each engine cover, but on the wing near McQuade was stenciled the instruction "Walk here." McQuade was amused—a whole crowd of people ascending several miles into the atmosphere in freezing temperature and relying on wings which a kid could poke his finger through! Or his shoe anyway.

The engines had a satisfying sort of scream. As soon as all four were roaring the aircraft taxied, thumped over lumps of snow, turned, and without a pause raced down the short runway which ended between two hillocks and lifted effortlessly in one thrust to a thousand feet or more. Out of the window, five or six miles away, McQuade could see the clumsy sprawl of Saint John—the steam belching out of the pulp mill across Reversing Falls, a ship in harbor with the yellow insignia of Canadian Pacific, even the tall structure of the hospital where a jaded Jane D. Brown would be working in the blood bank right now. And as they climbed in a wide circle he observed, a mile away, a cloud sagging onto the Bay of Fundy, collapsing in a white column of snow and hail. The low winter sun, a red ball in a white sky, like the flag of Japan, glistened on the edges of this column and gave it the illusion of moving upward like some almighty depth charge.

The stewardess, leaning over his wife (thinking, because of their silence and because he looked the younger, that McQuade was on his own), startled him. "Don't you want a newspaper, sir?" And

18

the beautiful, meaningless face, so nearly perfect but marred by the heavy makeup on the curiously dead skin (the crazy hours they worked tired the flesh?), slightly shocked, mildly excited in the small encounter—a thousand male faces stared a week, but such was vanity that it wasn't a surplus. While her eyes acknowledged communication and her perfect mouth talked about coffee and biscuits, she passed over the local newspaper, and on the pages unfolded with the skill of one who often reads papers in confined spaces, was the world the attractive young woman in her green uniform could ignore.

> Washington. The United States Government has asked Congress for 7.8 million dollars to build seven underground command posts throughout the country for civil-defense organizations in case of enemy attack . . .
>
> Police Clash with Lisbon Students. Lisbon, December 11. Many arrests were reported today when a crowd of about a thousand students demonstrated in Lisbon. They were protesting outside the Boa Hora political criminal court against the trial of three art students on charges of subversion. . . . Police in steel helmets . . . shoppers and workers rushed down side streets and into open shops. Many store owners locked their premises or pulled down steel shutters . . .
>
> Malawi had 150,000 Africans working in Rhodesia while Zambia was entirely dependent on Rhodesia for coal . . .

Not quite relevant.
But another item caught McQuade's eye:

> . . . that the Maori Bishop of Arrowtown might give evidence which would indicate what was happening in the Portuguese Overseas Territories and in particular the abuses in the territory of Angolique. . . . The Bishop, a New Zealand subject, complained of treatment he had received in a New York City restaurant and at Kennedy International Airport, and while agreeing that the incidents were relatively trivial, he suggested that they indicated the position of the colored man in the United States irrespective of his status and profession . . .

19

There was a tendency among some journalists—and even among some of the older politicians—to believe that the best men were no longer sent to the United Nations as delegates. This was strictly a white problem—the colored nations were short of politicians—good, bad, or indifferent. The belief died hard in these older European politicians, who had been in the League of Nations before World War II, that anyone except the men who'd inaugurated the UN—themselves in fact—could run it. McQuade was not an important figure in Canadian politics. He had sat as number two to the Canadian Ambassador in the General Assembly without anyone noticing it. Not many people lobbied him in the corridors or the delegates' lounge. But in committees where he'd been number one, his straightforwardness and honesty and obvious belief in the UN's field work had attracted the attention of various people, although McQuade was not aware of this. Currently he was a member of the Committee of Twenty-four, which dealt with the so-called colonial problems. The committee had the lengthy title of The Special Committee on the Situation with Regard to the Implementation of the Declaration on Granting of Independence to Colonial Countries and Peoples. The declaration concerned dated back to 1960, and the remainder of the title had been taken from a request made by the Soviet Union for inclusion of an item in the 1961 Assembly agenda.

As a member of subcommittees of the Committee of Twenty-four McQuade had been to Swaziland, Fiji and Malta and had heard petitioners from South-West Africa, Aden, Rhodesia, Basutoland, Oman, British Guiana and Singapore. When he'd heard what these petitioners had to say and had been to some of the places where they lived—or wanted to live—an honest, good-natured man like McQuade could never again feel quite the same about anything. But whereas some of the African and Scandinavian delegates were overwhelmed with frustration and anger, McQuade, who'd done an earlier tour of Italy with the Canadian Army and knew that things *could* be worse, kept calm. You could not alter the nature of man in ten minutes—people had been trying for thousands of years and there had been little progress. Nor did McQuade take the easy way out and despise his own civilized society. He liked New York and did not cry out in despair at the flagrant wealth which bludgeoned the eye and ear.

The old face on the tray and the tiny lined hands had been his mother's. This frustrated him. He had not done enough. He had failed her. He didn't know how, except that even if he became Prime Minister of Canada (which he did not think likely) he'd still not have given the devotion in the world that she had. Why were women so powerless in the world when they had so much of the goodness? They accepted all the madnesses of man without a qualm. Jane D. Brown's thin Irish face and nervous eyes flickered in his mind, the small mouth talking fast, the nails digging into his hand for love. Montreal, a travel agency . . . Why should a Maori bishop from New Zealand be in Portuguese African territory? He'd never know. Who'd paid his fare? Where did he eat? Where had he been educated? What long process of fifty-five years had brought him to a New York hotel to complain on behalf of the indigenous people of Angolique? Was he a nut case? Was he a Communist of some kind? McQuade would never know much about the bishop unless the bishop wrote a book, and he wasn't the book-writing kind of bishop. It didn't matter. Do what was relevant. McQuade was like a man waiting for a situation: when it became possible for him to put his tough sympathy into action he would do so. He would still be limited very largely to words, although he might operate within circumstances that could kill him. The UN lived on words. Millions of them were translated, printed, spoken and mimeographed each year—the thin line of blood that went in and out of the brain. Only a handful really altered the world. The world waited sadly for its quota . . .

An hour and a half in Montreal's elegant airport buildings. A couple of gin rickeys to work up an appetite for chopped tenderloin steak smothered in onions, and half an hour in which to digest it all. Kristan, pink in the face, complained without emphasis, "I'm tired." A remarkable silence—for an airport—during which aircraft to Paris, Düsseldorf, Calgary, Vancouver, Toronto and Edmonton were announced and departed in the falling snow. Then their own announcement, and Kristan, enjoying the little game of walking through electrically operated doors, asked, "Do we alter our watches?"

This was McQuade's world. Airport lounges and the foreign languages over loudspeakers; cigars and acres of linen and unfamiliar foods; the tired photographers and reporters who'd been there in

21

the rain for five hours, not moving away for a second. Strange faces which probed yours. Was this man a fool, honest, a cunning enemy, a hypocrite? Did he have humor, pomposity, integrity? Shall I admit, ask, persuade? If we agree this, surrender that. Words. The strain of words and the body and mind operating in unfamiliar densities and temperatures in conditions of comparative or complete exhaustion. And never to lose your temper or forget protocol. The men from the little countries were the touchiest of all. Why was I not met at the airport? Why, when I am here, did you speak, drink and eat with *him* first? It was a kind of battle—long silences while you waited, traveled, ate and tried to sleep, and then, at any hour of the day or night, you were hurled into an intellectual debate—but not a debate any undergraduate would understand. A debate or discussion in which the nuances of foreign languages and previous lies, later disowned, had to be remembered . . . "I am tired." But you could never be tired, or, if you were, must not allow it to throw a strain on intelligence, temper or sympathy or ultimate causes. And he had to *care*. Intellectually, the civilized Western man was fully aware that the doctor who examined him had one eye on his watch. The people who greeted him at parties might like him but would be fascinated by his death or misdemeanors found out. They wrote "Yours Sincerely" at the foot of letters, but had lost sincerity. The colored man did not have this curse of the pressure of sophistication yet and did not understand the effort required by the white man—who often seemed harmless and kind enough at face value—to rise above it.

The airplane flew for an hour and a half through absolute darkness outside, not a pinprick of light on the ground below. The Appalachians—seen in daylight three days before as a vast pale-blue landscape that merged into the sky and snow, with clouds poured among the mountains like cream from a jug—were unseen, thousands of feet beneath. The spatial blackness put New York into perspective—a whole hour and a half at 350 m.p.h. and *nothing* seen proved that even this giant of a city was a mere dot on the world. But now here it came—slowly at first, villages and small towns upstate, illuminated highways. Then the descending Viscount, with its sixty or so passengers, came into the world of sophisticated man. It seemed to crawl like an animal in pain, in the wrong ele-

22

ment, engines audibly reluctant to leave the rarefied air of 17,000 feet and creep over these miles of buildings, highways and water. Blinking red lights: those were other aircraft. A fault now, any failure and the impact was obvious—it had seemed remote and impossible higher up. They were over Bridgeport then Yonkers, losing height. Even the most seasoned passenger could not resist craning his neck to see this fairyland of lights—more illumination, surely, than any other city in the world. Over Westchester now— some of the UN's top politicians lived there—and the Bronx. They were above water and Randall's Island and Ward's Island, flying so low that it seemed possible to touch things. Welfare Island and Queensborough Bridge—all lights off in the Secretariat Building, McQuade could see. No crisis this week. The myriad lights swung as the horizon tilted and they skirted Queens and Brooklyn, with the lights of automobiles racing along the expressways, and then, all remoteness lost, at 170 m.p.h., they zipped in over lights and small buildings and the wheels touched and that was it. In the darkness the Viscount followed its lane of blue bulbs to the Air Canada buildings.

It was cold in New York and raining heavily.

"Oh, I'm tired *now*," Kristan said as McQuade fought in a sea of trunks for their cases. "Let's get a taxi."

The taxi took them out of the mess of Kennedy International Airport, raced in the rain up the Van Wyck Expressway and Grand Central Parkway and now, on his left, McQuade could see the most famous skyline in the world. As they went across the Triborough Bridge he looked and there it was—the great chunk of masonry and steel from about 106th Street to about 34th. There was more of it far downtown, where East River meets North River, but this was what you, a foreigner, meant when you said Manhattan— everything, from the hotels, doctors' offices and museums along Fifth Avenue up to 86th Street, to the shops, banks, hotels, office blocks and airline terminals midtown. You tended to disregard the warehouses and shipping berths on the West Side altogether.

They lived in an apartment, rented for four hundred dollars a month, on the East Side, where all the UN personnel tended to find accommodations, but rather far up—on 96th Street, in fact, which was practically in Harlem. It was a new block, very handsome, and

23

the rent would have been higher but for the Negro and Puerto Rican population density. The building had an impressive lobby and a uniformed doorman who acknowledged them. "Good evening, Mr. McQuade. Cold tonight?"

"It's chucking it down out there."

"Well, it's better than that white stuff."

"Lots of that in Canada."

"Some upstate, they tell me."

There were letters in their box. A few invitations. There'd be a lot more at the office. The season of the General Assembly, not yet over, was also the season of parties. One of the nice things about being a delegate at UNO (as distinct from the Canadian Embassy in Paris or Moscow or anywhere else) was that you were not obliged to go to all these parties. No one was offended, no protocol damaged if you didn't. The smaller nations tended to give the most lavish parties— usually held in the UN buildings or hotels—in the hopes, presumably, of making political progress. But the noise in the delegates' dining room was so tremendous that it was quite impossible to hear a thing unless one shouted. The richer nations tended not to give parties—the United Kingdom never bothered at all. An amusing aspect of the dinners given as UN functions was that the protocol was very simple compared to that of normal embassies and consisted simply of alphabetical arrangement. Thus Kristan found herself all too often next to the delegate from the Cameroons and over a period of time had talked herself dry about Canada and listened until she felt she knew more than enough about the Cameroons. And McQuade chatted regularly above the noise of knives and forks and others' conversation to a rather delightful lady on the perhaps limited subject of the Central African Republic.

There was an invitation from his old regiment, and he was thinking about it in the ascending elevator as Kristan said with pleasure, "There's a letter from Peter. He's in a new squadron. They fly Starfighters on photographic-reconnaissance work. He's going to France soon. Lucky boy!"

McQuade commented, "They make the Starfighters in Canada. Does he know that?"

"He doesn't say so. It shifts along at Mach 2.2, whatever that means, but only for short bursts, so not to worry."

24

"About 1600 m.p.h.," McQuade told her. "But he knows his stuff, our Peter, so don't brood. If it was something you should worry about he wouldn't be telling his parents about it. Right?"

"You're a real psychiatrical comforter. Very convincing."

"I took a course. How to make friends and influence diplomats."

"I wish he'd get married."

"Don't wish that on him! Let him play with his airplane first."

McQuade sat in a chair and read the other letters. He wondered who Reg Dobell was. Mr. Dobell had sent the invitation from the Canadian tank regiment and underneath the print had written in ink, *"Oh, for a tin of bully!"* This meant something—things past, a war shared—but McQuade couldn't place it.

He, too, was tired now.

Kristan inquired, "Do you want anything to eat?"

"What? After all that in Montreal?"

"Just coffee?"

He felt something sad and terrible, half forgotten, gnaw at him. He never thought about the war—or not often. Many of the politicians at UNO came from countries not directly involved in it or were young men—especially the Africans—with burning problems of their own. They were not interested in contemplating the tragedies of Europe. McQuade had fought as a tank sergeant in the disaster of Dieppe, and later, as an officer, in Italy and Normandy. There had been bad moments. He had been very lucky indeed to get back from Dieppe, for most Canadians didn't. But he suffered no nightmares. The periods of fighting had been widely spaced and there'd been many boring months in England. He had been invalided out of the Canadian Army while it was still exploiting the chaos of the Falaise Gap and had missed the rest of the Normandy advance. He had the scars of burns even now. Reg Dobell meant something—not that McQuade would get to the reunion, for he had only just been to Canada and now had his part in a big work program. Pity and idealism do not come in a moment to a man—except, perhaps, when he is witness to some cataclysmic event such as the A-bomb on Hiroshima—but McQuade had found his way into politics while the war was still on and into the diplomatic service as a tough, sympathetic, fairly well-educated young man who had had the advantage at that moment of no longer being able to fight, but of being able to speak French, Spanish and German.

25

Kristan said, "You're thinking, aren't you? Your coffee's gone cold."

"About the war."

She said flippantly, after a pause, "I wouldn't have met you if there hadn't been one."

He smiled and chided, "I hope you don't think they organized that little epic just so's you could meet me!"

She countered, "Oh, I'd have met someone else. You just happened to be around!"

What she meant was quite different, and he caught the vague, loving restlessness of her eyes and movements. They'd make love, ignoring travel fatigue and postparty tiredness, and it'd be one of those special times. He wanted instantly to begin. But she had her own small routine of surrender and he acknowledged it.

"I'm going to bed," he announced in a difficult voice.

"What are you telling me for?"

"Just in case you're interested!"

"You eat too much steak!"

McQuade lay in bed and thought about his wife. What is marriage? he wondered. A lot of events endured together? The tolerance of shabby things, your secrets shared, pain and distress and bitter disappointments and failure dissipated by the love of this other person? A woman who washed your dirty socks and cleaned up when you or your kids were sick? Passion conveniently handy? Someone who saw you at your worst and tolerated it—even went on loving in spite of your tempers, swearing, farting around the place, your reckless driving or your occasional heavy drinking? A woman who'd stand anything except the success of another woman? McQuade didn't know. It was all of these things, but still undefined. At times he felt pity for Kristan, at times love or compassion, or he would marvel at her humanity; occasionally he'd feel nothing at all; and quite often he'd experience with her sexual completion that was raw and perfect and violently crude.

Some women knew the weaknesses of their husbands and sneered about them, gently or not, in front of others, humiliating them. There were things even a big man like McQuade was afraid of. They came around once in a while—the particular pains, the setups—and he bore them or lived through them. Kristan never mocked him. Equally, there were many things she feared and he treated them with care. Marriage was a private institution in which no one else was interested.

In the darkness or under the pink light, bodies smashed into each other so hard that he wondered, when it was over and she gave a long sigh, "Was it ever?" why physical injury never resulted. Her small voice would ask him, "Why do you love me?" And he'd say awkwardly, "You know why," and she did—they both did—a long chain of small things shared, pains and passions, embarrassments, tenderness and absurdities.

No one could know as Kristan went down in the elevator, or went shopping anxiously in an area with too many Puerto Ricans, or sat quietly when others talked big, or ate a meal, or wrote a letter, or moved slowly across a room, that she was so full or capable of love. She looked—an impartial piece of McQuade knew it—like someone who'd been dark, slender, quite tall and possibly attractive a long while before (ten years before and meaning you couldn't tell now). . . . Now, in others' eyes, she was just someone with good clothes, graying hair, who was too slender and looked a bit bad-tempered or sad—not sexy, not physically powerful.

She would come in ten minutes and present herself naked. She would leave the small pink light on because she was ashamed of herself white—the truth of white light or day was unbearable for her. So she had to have partial illusion. She liked to start love naked, to give herself. Deep in McQuade was the masculine urge to humiliate and overcome by exploration. She'd understood this a long time ago—frantic loving, half dressed, in an afternoon, with interruption all too possible—or, perhaps, not understanding, had conceded love this way because of his desire. He loved her because she was so straightforward, so direct in her surrender, so total and human. It was possible to forgive her for anything, for she loved him so devotedly. If she really knew me . . . he qualified in thought, but, then, she believes she does.

Is this marriage, when the beautiful girl you scarcely knew twenty-two years ago but married believing you did still stirs you although the beauty is different, has gone perhaps, and you yourself are lazy or dirty or greedy or have acquired middle-aged intolerance?

It does not matter.

27

Nothing matters.

They can't hurt me while I have her.

She came, left the pink light on, made sure the curtains were drawn, pretended, as usual, that this was something he wanted; she'd come to *sleep* . . . She touched his face and arms and genitals in her usual tender way and they both began to breathe faster. A quarter of an hour? Half an hour? He wasn't counting. It was violent and lasting, the slap-slap of thighs that couldn't grind hard enough, so that he grasped her buttocks near the climax. And then, finished, he lay with his hand in her hair and felt an absurd pity, as if he had deceived or robbed her. And, as usual, Kristan whispered a sincere "Oh, Shaun, was it ever?" and kissed his face and neck in what seemed like gratitude. Seconds passed and practicality returned and she commented humorously, "I sure am hungry," and his skin tightened in shock and he remembered Dobell . . .

Stunned with tiredness, unshaven, dirty from days of fighting, withdrawing, halting to fight, advancing, faces caked with layers of mud and dirt which blew into the tank whenever it moved. Bloody cold, especially in the mornings. And plenty of rain. The smell of cordite in the turret and the shattering noise when the 75mm. fired. Lousy little villages in the rain, mined to hell. Eyes bloodshot with fatigue. But this was a bigger town, with cobbled streets and balconies and people standing around staring and waving. Out of a barber's shop had come a German officer. He'd had an Italian girl on his arm so the gunner had had to wait until he ran before shooting him down. Farther in the town were some Mark VIs which hadn't been expecting Canadians. One had gone around and around in a circle, burning. Some of the crews had been caught standing in the square. The others had fought a point-blank fight, with civilians scattering. Later McQuade had counted eleven hits on his tank, all in ten minutes. Hot oil had poured down his leg from the power traverse. He'd thought it was blood. Shells from the German tanks had screeched by, sounding like saws cutting steel. Smoke and dust from smashed buildings had soon filled the square, but in ten minutes it was over. They'd moved out of the way until a burning Mark VI had exploded.

The commander of the other Canadian tank involved had been Dobell, and with Italians gathering around in a frenzy of excitement, he'd said to McQuade, "I sure am hungry." They'd had a rich and greasy Italian meal within the hour. All next day their bowels had been uneasy and they'd groaned with stomach-aches. They'd had to climb out of their Shermans and crouch where they could. At camp that second night Dobell had said wistfully, "Oh for a tin of bully!"

McQuade had been through a hundred smashed towns and villages in Italy and France, concerned with the day-to-day problems of keeping alive, dealing with antitank guns and armor and infantry. (His worst memory was of the time his gunner hadn't been able to depress the 75mm. or machine-gun barrel down far enough and he, McQuade, had had to command, "Over them, then," and they'd crushed half a dozen screaming Germans to death.) Rain, cold, mud, noise, death. But his heart must have noticed the misery of those villages and his hope must have grown that other villages and towns around the world should be spared it. They had troubles enough already.

Other memories related to tank fighting returned . . .

The medic who did not have the respect for death that the fighting man did. He was on a good number in Cairo—did any fighting soldier recall Cairo with anything but contempt? McQuade wondered. This medic would join a group of wounded men at lunch outside, eating from a trestle table, and he'd sit opposite the newest invalid—just out of bed and battle, shaken still, and finding his way back to courage and health—and while the man was eating, this medic would bring out of his pocket a handful of human eyes and play with them. After a while the wounded soldier would leave his food alone or rush away to be sick. Everyone would laugh, including the earlier victims. When McQuade's turn came, he hit the sniggering face so hard he smashed the medic's nose . . .

And the badly wounded Italian just in from the infantry sorties lying on a stretcher. He'd found a knife somewhere, and when the doctor bent over, he stabbed the doctor in the throat, killing him. A British Guardsman grabbed a rifle and beat his face in with one blow. The ethics of this episode had been beyond McQuade's comprehension. Presumably the Italian knew he was dying and wanted to "take one with him" . . .

You had to remember these things now and again.

29

He, McQuade, hadn't screamed with the burns, but had groaned and thrashed about, remembering this later with humiliation . . .

Like pictures in an album.

Kristan at twenty walking along a river bank. How innocent. Youth that was, in both of them, despite war, that of children. It didn't make sense. He saw the same kind of innocence in Peter, but all too often other young people seemed as if they'd lost the quality of innocence. Youth was no longer sacred, words had no meaning for the young. They were old at nineteen now, had screwed around at parties, notched up abortions like the score in a game. God was a fool, patriotism made them heave. What would they have to value as they grew old?

He looked at his wife, who was asleep under the pink lighting.

I am human.

We had something special.

Words have meaning.

Pity and love.

I was scared skinny.

He wanted to be the same as everyone else. You know? Nothing.

Words, words. Tread carefully through the pounding millions that assault the delicate instrument that is you, that seek to enter along the eyes and ears and alter it.

God (if there is a God), give me something to do in the world that rises above the claptrap of words.

3 ▪▪

THE GENERAL ASSEMBLY was welcoming a small new Asiatic nation into the United Nations Organization. The Prime Minister of that country, a little shaken by the size, not to mention the December temperature, of New York, had been invited by the President of the Assembly to take his seat, and now, escorted by the Chief of Protocol (a Secretariat official of the middle-brass category and inevitably American), he and five of his ministers marched in among the thousand and more seats to take theirs. There was applause and the speeches began. There could not be 117 speeches of congratulations, so a limited selection of countries and blocs relevant to that country, or wishing to be, or anxious to make a speech anyway, were allowed to take the floor. The speeches were each of about a quarter of an hour's duration and the morning passed away pleasantly. Finally, the colonial power which with reluctance and under pressure had conceded the independence wished the new country well. The Prime Minister (who had been given plenty of time in jail to think up speeches) stood and, as the distinguished delegate from an undistinguished country, began his own speech. He made references to ancient gods and philosophers which caused strain among the translators who were following him gesture by gesture, sometimes improving his phraseology. It was a question of how long a speaker could stand and how long he could hold his water, and this one could evidently do both for a long time . . .

In the Trusteeship Council it was the second day of the hearing by the Committee of Twenty-four on the subject of the Portuguese African territory of Angolique. On the first day the committee had read letters and cables from petitioners in that territory. A cable from Eduardo Marum, a schoolteacher, informed the committee that Agusto Cabral, a political refugee from Angolique, had been detained by the immigration authorities in Johannesburg, whose intention it was to hand him back to the Portuguese. Before the committee was able even to consider this petition it learned that Mr. Cabral had in fact been taken to Vila Lobanda. . . . A letter from a Mr. Bajune, also a schoolteacher, explained that he had fled temporarily from Angolique during recent disturbances and had now formed the Tando Party, which would attempt to negotiate with the Portuguese authorities, although he, Mr. Bajune, was very much of the opinion that they would, if they could, exterminate the Tando or any other political organization, and this letter was to prove the party's existence. Mr. Bajune hoped he would be able to meet any member of the Committee of Twenty-four who came to the territory, although he doubted sadly if the committee or any member of it would be allowed anywhere near Angolique which the Portuguese regarded as part of Portugal and beyond the jurisdiction of UNO.

31

By letter Chief Junqueiro informed the committee that he alone was responsible for the views of the OOP. By separate cables Mr. Iena and Mr. Luchazes dissociated themselves from any statements made by Chief Junqueiro and informed the committee that they alone were responsible for the policy of the OOP and a statement made by Chief Junqueiro in Dar es Salaam was to be ignored. By cable the Secretary General of the APP affirmed that José Ahmad was in New York and was authorized to speak on its behalf. A similar cable said that Henri Arroio was in New York on behalf of the ANP. By letter Mr. Hoxico, Chairman of the Board of Directors of the Porto Girassol Publishing Company, complained that the Portuguese authorities had forbidden publication of his weekly newspaper *African Affairs* on the grounds that it was pornographic and harmful to the moral welfare of the people. He had transmitted copies of this paper, which had had only three issues. It was now learned that Mr. Hoxico was in prison on charges of corruption and subversion.

"In theory," the Bishop of Arrowtown was saying now, "the indigenous person has the right of complaint and petition at all administrative levels, and especially in regard to the administrators of indigenous affairs. In fact, he knows nothing of the apparatus of governor general, district governors, or municipal assemblies. He only sees the *regedor,* or chief, who is responsible to the district *administrador* and takes orders from him. In fact the *indigena* only sees the *chef de posto* and he all too often has a *chicote* in his hand.

"The *indigena* has no political status in actuality," the bishop continued, "although all things are possible in theory. If he is educated and has acquired basic habits, if he is over eighteen and speaks Portuguese properly, if he has a trade or craft, and if he has a certificate of the criminal registry 'showing that the person concerned has never been sentenced to imprisonment and has not been sentenced to detention on more than two occasions,' *then* he can consider himself a Portuguese citizen, although he is hardly likely to be accepted on the next plane to Lisbon. In the Statute of 1954, in Articles 60 and 61, some exceptions were made. For instance, provincial governors could grant citizenship to an individual who had performed considerable service to the State. And if this happened his wife and all children under his direct control who were less than eighteen years old and could speak Portuguese correctly and had adopted the customs of the Portuguese could also become citizens with a vote . . .

"The ideal of a multiracial society is eroding, and the armed settler, backed by the military and prisons, has come to stay. Lack of education does not make for a supply of politicians, and thus the politically minded have had to flee the country with a view to being educated, both literally and politically, before returning with armies to remove Portuguese rule.

"In this way," continued the Bishop, "while on the one hand the *indigena* who has gone through the ordeal of fleeing from a vast and inhospitable country—his own—is grateful to those who are anxious to grant him asylum, scholarships and the sort of help which may be given by the bodies of this organization, on the other hand he seeks the help of those—ignoring for the time being their politics—who will help him throw out the Portuguese. There seems to be no possible meeting ground with the Portuguese. But I believe that, as with other African territories, there is the third alternative—namely, that this organization demand entry into the territory of Angolique and with the cooperation of Portuguese and African begin to work out a policy of independence.

"As a final, more personal plea," the small, bony Maori bishop concluded wearily, "I must ask this organization to do its utmost to recover from jail two party leaders who happened to be in Vila Lobanda at the time of the disturbances outside the police station. There was no evidence against them, and they were arrested in the atmosphere of alarm. But while that precaution did not seem too unreasonable at the time—although it was still not justified—there is no reason for them to be kept in the fortress of São Damba. I refer to Mr. Andrade and Mr. Maúa."

The twenty-four members of the special committee sat in their horseshoe of blue leather chairs and listened in silence. The Trusteeship Council room was like a theater—a very expensive and fashionable theater in which were put on rather inexplicable plays, with the members on stage and the lighting and curtains controlled from the sides, where, in glass-enclosed booths, were verbatim reporters, a few interpreters and sometimes (but not today) news-

33

reel, TV and radio announcers. Today, in the entire slope of several hundred seats which looked down onto the delegates' area, there were four public spectators, and there was only one interpreter on duty. In the several rows of seats at each side of the delegates' horseshoe of chairs were half a dozen interested Secretariat officials and two members of the Portuguese Mission to the UN. Once, a party of children came along the corridor behind the seats and in fact filled half the public gallery, and McQuade, seated almost underneath Starcke's statue, heard in the hot, hushed air the American guide's voice, saying, "People have got to eat . . ." And from a second party, conducted by a Spanish-speaking girl, he heard "Are there any questions?" A silence. No questions. Were the party dumb, or indifferent, or tired, or had the girl explained it all so well that there was nothing left to say? "Sure, you can take pictures," the first guide was saying, and there were a few electronic flashes. The bishop's voice continued, and the other three men, seated and waiting to speak, did not look around; they'd come a long way and were not likely to be distracted by trivialities.

On the bishop's right sat José Ahmad of the APP group in Angolique. Ahmad was twenty-two years old and had been a railway worker in Porto Girassol. He was almost illiterate. His recent history was interesting. He had become a member of the APP because someone had suggested he should. His job had been to grease the wheels of railway locomotives and to stack eucalyptus logs at specified places—for the trains in Angolique had been manufactured years ago in the industrial city of Birmingham, England, for use with coal, but had been adapted easily enough to eucalyptus logs. Ahmad had also had the occasional task of cleaning out Pullman compartments and lavatories. Perhaps he had found copies of Rhodesian newspapers (for the trains ran to and from Salisbury in God's good time), with drawings and advertisements, or had picked up a real treasure, a copy of *Life,* which had suggested pictorially that somewhere there was a place where black men drove automobiles, sat in restaurants, had their shoes polished and received salutes. Ahmad was good humored, lazy and talkative, and he hadn't given a damn about politics. Life in Porto Girassol was not bad. He was not married but had two children.

But somewhere along the line José Ahmad had gotten the urge

34

for freedom. He was not brave and had been badly frightened four months before by the events in Vila Lobanda which he had witnessed in part from the mere accident of being in that city. He had been so alarmed, in fact, that he had decided he would be killed by someone—Portuguese or African—if he stayed in Angolique, and he had set out on foot in merciful ignorance to cover the four hundred miles to its northern border. He had never seen a wild animal in his life, nor much of the jungle, and it took him six alarming weeks to get to the Congo. He came over the border with some wounded refugees, and when he saw how interested the Red Cross and others were in him, he became drunk on self-importance. He found it hilariously funny to have survived, and he was bursting to tell the world what had been going on in Angolique.

Two fascinating months of hanging around New York—for the special committee sat when it was convenient—had cooled his imagination, but here he was, in a badly fitting suit, unable to speak English, rather alarmed and thinking perhaps of the good old carefree days when he had oiled those big wheels and made love to cheeky girls on Lobanda Island. He spoke in a husky voice—for tuberculosis was raging within him, although he did not know this yet, and his life expectancy was two years.

Ahmad told the committee, "I have come a long way to tell you these things. I am a member of the Angolique People's Party. There has been much trouble in that country and I saw some of it. On that day I saw the people attack the prison at Vila Lobanda. The policemen say there were weapons, but there were no weapons. Later there were weapons—but we did not understand them. These weapons were taken from a police jeep which was overturned at that time. It saved nobody. I saw hundreds of our people lying in the street—this was the Rua do Passeio—and all were bleeding. *Why* did we attack the prison?" asked Ahmad, who had stared in terror at these events from a signal tower half a mile away. "It was because there were important journalists there— some from America—and we wanted them to know the people were oppressed.

"It was very frightening afterward, because the Portuguese gave weapons to their people. We had no weapons. A campaign of killing was carried out by the Portuguese in Vila Lobanda, and without doubt the police were glad that this was so. Many were arrested for information, and in this way Mr. Andrade and Mr. Maúa were taken, being important members of our party. They had killed no one because this was not the matter of the APP. Bodies lay in the street for days and no one dared to move them.

"It is true that some policemen were killed. Seven," explained Ahmad, "on that day. Five more at the funeral, but they were trampled when the crowd ran about all ways. I saw two policemen lying in the road by the broadcasting station.

"I was working on the railways then," continued Ahmad, "and saw many thousands of Portuguese soldiers arrive. Others came in ships. And the ones on the trains talked very big of the killing they had done in villages. I heard them say that the town of 31 de Brasilia had been burned down. Also they admired the ease with which the airplanes could drop fire bombs and burn down villages. When I reached the Congo border I found many wounded people who spoke of these things. They had done nothing but carry on their work in the cotton and coffee plantations, and the soldiers had arrived, or the airplanes, and those who were not killed had left their villages forever. These people had no weapons and had done nothing.

"I spoke to others," affirmed Ahmad, "who had been frightened by noises and troops, but when they had complained to the chief, and he to the *administrador,* the *administrador* had said that this was a mock battle, that it was part of an exercise in which soldiers were taught to throw a cordon around a village.

"One expects," reasoned Ahmad with unconscious irony, "to be raided by policemen and asked about the work pass, but to practice a battle . . . Another thing was the dead. These could not be buried in cemeteries because they were said to be enemies of the Catholic state, and thus were put into a mass grave like carrion.

"I have since heard from Angolique," concluded Ahmad proudly, "from the Secretary General of the APP, and he tells me that in the countryside the *administradores* have taken away the lands of the *indigena* who had been frightened and had run away. When these returned they had to sell this land at a nothing price. They were given less fertile lands in replacement. Many were forced to become laborers or tenant farmers on plantations, and

36

many times they had to see these soldier-settlers or absentee plantation owners eat the fruit of their hard labor. Many of them have become victims of the *chef de posto* and the compulsory labor.

"The Secretary General wishes me to communicate the anxiety of the APP in these matters. He has no wish for violence, but points to the anger of the other African countries. He is in despair about the status of the parties in Angolique. The Portuguese deny we exist, and if we exist, they say, we are agitators and Communists and can be killed or thrown into the torture chambers."

The third man, Henri Arroio, was as young as José Ahmad, but rather more serious in demeanor, and his large brown eyes had the granular excrescences in the lids which indicate trachoma. He was the most upset of the four men here today, for he had left behind in Angolique a wife and four children, whom he would perhaps not see again. He had been in Vila Lobanda on the day of the disturbances. He had spent a short spell in a Portuguese prison for alleged subversive activities, but there had been a clerical error and he had been released. He had reached Tanzania by routes he refused to disclose and had been in touch, at Dar es Salaam, with the Organization of African Unity.

Arroio was more politically inclined than the previous petitioner. He was, in fact, a politician, although his party had never held office and perhaps never would.

"The progress that has been made is a mockery," he said. "The repeal of the Statute of 1954 in theory ends the distinction between the *indigena* and others as regards political rights, but in practice the *indigena,* to qualify as an elector or a candidate for political office, still has to meet the educational and financial requirements, and this cannot be done. New legislation was, as you know, promulgated on many matters, such as the option of using Portuguese law, a simplification concerning rights over land, protection for the land around any *regedoria,* which is a group of villages under a chief, and rights of possession and transfer of immovable property. But these things mean nothing if the bombs fall or the soldiers set fire to huts or the *indigena* is driven away in terror and returns to find others in lawful possession.

"In law, forced and compulsory labor is prohibited, but there are loopholes in the legislation and who but a lawyer could dispute

37

them? When people are rounded up in the night, with policemen or soldiers smashing their way into buildings, and the *indigena* is then asked to sign a contract, can the *angariadores,* who are the recruiting agents, claim that this is a request for our services? Of course, it is true that we are only black men and they cannot tell which of us is which, so we must have cards with thumbprints. It is true that we do not stumble about in chains as they do in the streets of Johannesburg. And when we go slaving away on the roads and airfields which are being built so that it will be easier for the *voluntarios* to come and kill us, we cannot go home even with our employer's pass, not even if there is a death in our family.

"Of course I received wages," acknowledged Arroio. "I was not paid in accordance with my contract, but no doubt much money— my money—was needed for bribes, such as the payoff to the *angariador* who obtained me in the first place. They overcharged me for food and clothing deductions, and naturally I was forced to buy many things from them at prices they fixed. But, after all, I am an African, not educated in these subtleties.

"In a newspaper the other day I read that while the Chinese regard the Americans and English as red-faced hairy barbarians they regard the black man as just an animal. It is interesting to learn that there are people in the world who despise us more than the Portuguese, who, within limits, do not despise us at all. They are prepared to make love to and sometimes even marry the *indigena* women. It is a very strange world we live in. Very strange.

"A cousin of mine—I have sixteen cousins, and all of them have problems—worked in the cotton region of Ambrizama. Before the *voluntarios* killed him he explained to me—seeing that by then I was a politician and interested in these matters—about the difficulties of being a cotton worker. He was required to grow cotton in a certain area. He received no wages, but at the end of the season he was paid by the Government for what he had grown at prices they fixed. He was not allowed to move from the area, of course, so he had no choice but to implement this splendid cotton program. But it was not so splendid after all, for after a while the soil was exhausted and so my cousin and others were moved to a new plot on a shifting-cultivation basis.

"After a few seasons my cousin was many miles from his home

38

—so far, in fact, that he could not walk home after his leisurely fourteen-hour day. So his family moved to the cotton plot. But they were not allowed to grow food on cotton land and were punished if they did. Some of the family had to be left in the original village to take care of the cattle and crops. It was very confusing, my cousin said, in terms of family life. When my cousin heard of the troubles in the north and in Vila Lobanda, he and the others got very excited and smashed a few windows and so on. Burned a few sheds. You know how excitable we Africans can get in our immaturity. It took the policemen and *voluntarios* hours to calm them down. They had to kill some of the women and children, too, there was such a commotion.

"I was unaware of these matters. I was a member of the ANP—indeed, I still am," claimed Arroio. "Perhaps I had an exaggerated sense of my importance. I took to assuming that, as a politician, I could negotiate on a basis of equality with the Portuguese authorities. Oh, goodness me! How quickly was I taken to prison. I was everything terrible. A saboteur, a Communist, a subversionist. While I waited in prison for the authorities to see if these charges were true, it was found that there had been an error by a typist! I was released!

"We had stressed our desire for a peaceful solution and cooperation among racial groups on a basis of equality. But, as you see, there were no channels for discussion with the Government of Portugal directly or via its apparatus in Vila Lobanda. I appreciated the loss of face, the embarrassment of the authorities at our impertinence and existence. But my friend Mr. Ernesto Gomais, who also was a founder of the ANP—and you must realize, gentlemen, that we are no students' organization; we have a membership of 70,000—well, Mr. Gomais said that a demonstration was necessary.

"It was the first of its kind and therefore was unsuccessful. We made the mistake of going into the hotel where important journalists stay and telling them the time and places of our demonstration. They were waiting on the boulevards outside the police station and the prison, and I think the rumor had gone through the town that we were coming. We wished to stress our desire for a peaceful solution to our problems. Therefore we carried banners and we intended to sing songs and hand in a petition. In the case of the prison, we were perhaps a little more ambitious and hoped to persuade the authorities to release political prisoners. But I accompanied the group that went to the police station. There was a possibility of dogs being set upon us, with all the consequent problems of diseases, and the doctors did not, of course, attend to us except at our places of work. So we took a few sticks and bars to discourage dogs.

"There was a lot of chanting outside the police station. No singing at all. But they refused our petitions. Indeed, they started to make arrests. Well, many of our people were bitterly disappointed, for they did not expect arrest. And some of the policemen were waving guns about and using their boots. And some of my people not unnaturally got excited and hit the policemen with their sticks and bars. And I am very much afraid," explained Arroio, "that a few were killed, for it was very difficult—in the lack of experience —to estimate how hard to hit a policeman to express an opinion, or to convince him, or to offer comment only. And then the shooting began and we had to overturn their jeep to stop it.

"We lost twenty-nine party members that morning," acknowledged Arroio. "But at the prison, where eighteen were killed, a number of prisoners were released. They were a little tired, with the excitement and the strain of the *Stehzelle* punishment, which is the standing-up treatment. A few had been punched and kicked, but there had been no torture, you may care to note.

"I had a wife and little children," said Henri Arroio. "Now I have no wife or children. Who knows what will happen to them, for they are known to belong to me, and I am a political criminal."

McQuade did not know what the other twenty-three delegates of the committee were thinking, but he saw how difficult it was for this man to speak at all. He was overcome by the place and the situation and the hopelessness of his cause and his distress, finally communicated to someone else. The committee looked at Mr. Arroio; they sipped water and adjusted their spectacles and waited in some embarrassment and pity while he wept and then wiped his nose with his hand.

The distinguished delegate from Argentina had his arms folded in a manner familiar to McQuade, a manner indicating absolute

40

attention, but rather startling nevertheless, for the delegate, Mr. de la Plaza, had the habit of resting his left elbow on his right palm so that he could, using this fulcrum, dig his left-hand thumbnail into his left nostril. Perhaps the other delegates thought of how hot the central heating was, or wished they'd been to the lavatory before sitting down, or wondered what the Asiatic lunch in the delegates' dining room would be, or planned to catch someone in the north lounge or on the hoof through the corridors where he might be intercepted and lobbied, or day-dreamed about their wives or other people's wives, or tried to picture Vila Lobanda in the hot subtropical sun with people overturning jeeps and running down police-station steps to be killed. It all had the very slight unreality of words.

It was impossible to read the delegates' minds. They tended to look alike—were of the same age group, wore similar suits, had bald patches beginning on their heads; at least half wore spectacles and (alarming notion!) despite their many nationalities looked rather like Americans. Some of them had been to foreign places and seen a great deal of distress. Perhaps they, like McQuade, could identify the symptoms of trachoma, yaws and yellow fever. Perhaps they thought about Africa, that one-sixth of the world that had been changing so rapidly since the United Nations had come into existence.

The fourth petitioner wishing to give evidence was Portuguese. He was a deserter from the Portuguese Army, Captain Luis Nogar. He had arrived in Angolique with the reinforcements who had come to deal with the "wave of terrorism." After a while he had deserted and escaped to Swaziland. Then, accompanied by a British citizen and wearing civilian clothes, he had traveled by air to Cairo. He was twenty-seven, unmarried, small and heavy, with a serious disposition.

"I was a soldier," he told the special committee, "and proud to serve Portugal actively. I fought in the normal way against attacks on villages and convoys in the north of Angolique. In some villages we found that there had been massacres with the *catana,* which you call the machete, and all had been slaughtered—children and girls, white, colored and *mulato.* It was sickening—heads stuck on poles and so on. It was said that these bands were commanded by

41

foreigners—presumably Communists—but I only saw Bakongo in the fighting. They were pretty rough, but so were we when we saw the massacres.

"Then, farther south, some villagers came into the town of Baixange to protest about the cotton program. I know this because after the fighting I picked up leaflets in the street and that's what they complained about—the hours of work, children being forced to work, the pay and so on. These people broke the windows of a warehouse, smashed some shops, and gave the local government officials a hell of a fright by breaking into their houses. A few people were killed, it's true, but there always are in a panic. Then they went back to their own villages, for they were not soldiers and had nowhere else to go. But the officials were very shaken and demanded soldiers. We were ordered to attack two villages.

"We killed the lot of the villagers. Some fled, of course. I walked around one village which we had mortared and then machine-gunned. And in the smoke and burning huts I could see and smell them. None of these people were soldiers. I saw a few *catanas* lying about, but they work with those. Many of the bodies were of women and kids anyway. I know it was a mistake—the authorities really thought they were terrorists—but I felt very sick and scared in the stomach because I had arranged a lot of this and God watches, you know, to see how a Catholic behaves.

"The Lisbon newspapers called this day's tragedy 'intertribal fighting.' The Governor General in Vila Lobanda, who was an honest man, and a few other officials said that the *indigena* were right to complain and the Army had been foolish to attack a village or two because some people were scared. The Governor General submitted a report to Lisbon recommending changes. I know this because his typist was my sweetheart and she wouldn't talk to me again after that day. A little later this man, the Governor General, Colonel Jorge Unguanda, was accused of corruption. It was probably true, for many are corrupt. It is the hot atmosphere. He fled by automobile in the night.

"There is no end or answer but death," concluded Captain Nogar pessimistically. "I am afraid for Portugal. I have the intention now of going to Brazil, where a man may speak Portuguese and still express an opinion."

42

These four men took the whole day to give their evidence and be questioned. Two more petitioners were heard the next day, and their evidence was similar. On the third day a white man, a South African journalist, gave his views. If he was a liar he had come a long way and at his own considerable expense to tell his lies. But he spoke like a man who at least is sure that he utters the truth. His view was that minor incidents had been magnified for the convenience of those who wished them to be magnified into major suppression. His point was that he had lived in Angolique for twelve years and had seen nothing except an easy-going, tolerant society of white and black men—not quite the multiracial paradise the Portuguese claimed, but not bad—and better, he felt, than any of the sixteen other African territories, independent and otherwise, which he had visited in a deliberate search for trouble. He pointed out that while the Portuguese authorities in Angolique had to have some trading relations with the Republic of South Africa next door, they, and Lisbon, condemned the racial policy of apartheid. There were, he suggested, plenty of people who thrived on chaos, and they were neither Portuguese nor African.

Portugal was under what seemed to be tremendous pressure. Every country in the world free to express an opinion or who found it convenient to do so and seemingly every journalist complained to her or about her. But this was on paper or in terms of resolutions separated by chunks of time. And almost nobody at all went to Angolique to find out if the shouting was justified. The painful truth was that the UN was capable only of moral persuasion, and this acceptable to only one kind of morality. There were some states which, while joining in the moral chorus, abstained from voting or, if they voted, were capable of far more powerful private actions which they simply did not undertake. All member nations of the UN were juridically equal, and this seemed to indicate political equality. But in fact this left out of account the relationship between power and influence. The many new countries, nonaligned and uncommitted, might condemn Portugal until they were exhausted, but as long as the Cold War endured (from which ideological struggle, surprisingly, most African states remained aloof), Europe was in agonies of embarrassment on the subject of Ango-

43

lique's independence, for a friendly Portugal was needed as a member of NATO.

As the months became years and the resolutions on many other matters besides Angolique were ignored the new African states found that, although they had not inherited a legacy of obligations, enmities and grievances of the sort which still bedeviled Europe, Portugal was able to claim (and frequently with justification) that never before had there been so much unmitigated oppression and repression in Africa as in these newly independent territories. Some ex-colonial powers were inclined to agree that perhaps they had been too hasty in being too democratic.

The political problems of the world had become like a thousand chess games, different from normal chess games in that each was played on a board with five different levels and all games were interrelated. If a good move was made on one board, it might have a disastrous effect on two hundred other games at one or more levels and on the original game at two of the other four closely related levels. Thus it had become too complicated and there was no one total ending possible, and truth had no bearing except on one game at one level at one time.

If there were a thousand chessboards, certainly two hundred of them formed the African-continent game.

The Africa game had many surprises and absurdities. Everybody cheated, and those who didn't were unaware of the nature of the game. There were thousands of meddlers who interfered in the games—senior clergy of the West who traveled extensively around the world in jet planes, assuaging their personal inadequacies and trying to save a defeated church by joining in this game and that, unaware that they were ruining God's purpose in many other games. There were committees, societies and politicians who cried, "Police state," and received immediate acknowledgment and supporting votes from representatives of states which had no use for the vote at all and which were the ultimate in police states.

An "expert" committee of the UN sent out a grim little questionnaire to ascertain how the "civilized" countries could defeat South Africa economically, by sanctions—all in the good, idealistic cause of justice, of course; and, curiously, the lineup on that particular chessboard turned out to be the not unusual one of the Cold War.

44

The countries of the West would have to sacrifice billions of dollars in exports and investments to make South Africa heed the moral views of the USSR, Czechoslovakia, Ivory Coast, Morocco, Mongolia, Nepal, Ethiopia, Haiti, Rwanda and other "idealistic" countries. There were professional petitioners going from one UN committee to another. There were organizations, societies and individuals in the free world devoted to the idealistic aspects of the Africa game, but they played around with espionage, sabotage and corruption on the basis that the moral end was what mattered. There was considerable confusion within UN and Commonwealth alignments caused by an average of one African revolution every two months. Who was one to negotiate with after each of these? Almost as soon as one had said, "This is the honest fellow," the man concerned started throwing people into prison, shooting the opposition and burning down houses.

When the *indigena* in Angolique had a few months earlier begun what are called "disturbances" by those not involved in them, the problem which had been facing the Security Council, General Assembly, Trusteeship Council and, more recently, the Committee of Twenty-four could no longer be shelved. It demanded at least a simulacrum of action. Britain in particular began to persuade not Portugal but the United States that a gesture was necessary or there might be a war in Africa, with many African nations eager to settle the problem of Angolique. If Angolique collapsed, Britain explained, Rhodesia and South Africa would be that much closer to chaos. And this would be embarrassing for all white nations except Russia, much as they despised apartheid. The entire structure of the financial world in the West would be involved because of South Africa's position regarding gold. It was absurd that a useless metal like gold should still hold a supreme position in a world financial mechanism that was otherwise regulated sympathetically by a system of credits from the IMF. But it did. And as if this did not make Britain in particular sensitive enough to any destiny that might overtake South Africa, there was the position of her investments of around £1,000,000,000 in South Africa and her annual exports of about £300,000,000 to that country. So Britain was torn between "idealism" and realism on the matter of South Africa, and the liberals, students and journalists who wanted South Africa

45

smashed politically were pleading powerfully for their own suicide. The Americans could ride through this sort of situation if it came, but the British might well not survive it as a world power.

The United States diplomats—who had an interest in Britain's survival—saw the point and joined the United Kingdom in private persuasion of Portugal. They pointed out that things would become very nasty—they were bad enough *now*—if a gesture was not made. Hundreds of UN resolutions ignored! The African nations had differences among themselves, but on anticolonialism they were united and angry and frustrated, although they had so far shown remarkable patience. A very awkward chain of circumstances might develop. The Portuguese Minister for Overseas Boundaries asked what sort of gesture could be made. Well, the Americans and British said, you could admit a committee of inquiry. We would do our best to see that such a concession did not do too much damage.

On the statute books of the United Nations, among all the ignored resolutions, was a request by the General Assembly to the Committee of Twenty-four. They had been requested (nobody gave orders in the UN) to give high priority to an examination of the territories under Portuguese administration. Like all other committees, they had not gone very far—in fact, hadn't gotten out of Manhattan on this project. The Portuguese Minister was very uneasy but agreed that some of this committee could visit Angolique, with the condition that no Communists be allowed to come. The United States, with its massive lobby and power, assured Portugal that it would do its not inconsiderable best to see that the people chosen—for what would probably be a subcommittee of six members—were both reasonable and responsible, although some of them—certainly one—unfortunately would have to be colored.

The United States delegation was in a strong position to keep its word: it had its slate of candidates for any committee, for which it lobbied energetically and usually successfully. It was no longer possible—as it had been in the 1950s—to elect an entire subcommittee of stooges. The trick was to produce a subcommittee which would look as representative as possible, but would in fact be responsive to United States policy and pressure within the factors of loans, aid, NATO and so on.

Now began a sequence of events which could not be forecast

46

even by the State Department. Those delegates on the Committee of Twenty-four who had ambitions for themselves or their nations and aspired to this kind of subcommittee let it be known that they were available.

Competition for nominations began and representatives sought the support of groups to which their countries belonged. It did not work out quite as the United States, United Kingdom or Portugal wished, but perhaps, in part, even better. There had been recent upheavals in Brazil and a new Brazilian Government was represented by a fresh Brazilian Mission to the United Nations. There was a new Brazilian delegate on the Committee of Twenty-four, a very likable, vigorous and persuasive man named da Cunha. Portuguese is the language of Brazil, and da Cunha had married a Portuguese girl whose parents and relations were in high places in Lisbon. Da Cunha made it clear that because he spoke Portuguese and knew the "right" people in Lisbon he would get the subcommittee into Angolique. (Permission to enter Angolique, although conceded to the United States and United Kingdom in private discussion, was not yet public property. The subcommittee was being formed because of the situation in Angolique, not as a result of the private discussions. It did not know how successful it was going to be in its application!)

From the points of view of Portugal, the United States and United Kingdom—indeed, from all points of view—it seemed that da Cunha was the perfect man to head the subcommittee. He would "get the subcommittee into Angolique," and his views were bound to be sympathetic to Portugal because of his wife and her family. A hurried check confirmed that his marriage was a happy one. The Communist member elected was a Pole, Franciszek Ribowski. The Dutch member was the popular Theobald Alferink. There were also a very serious and well-intended Swede, Hjalmar Ekelund; the younger Asare Johnson, a pleasant and idealistic delegate from Ghana; and the Canadian Shaun McQuade, who had been to other territories.

At its first meeting the subcommittee, as expected, elected da Cunha chairman, with McQuade as vice-chairman because he happened to be the only one of the six who had been abroad on similar missions and, by happy coincidence, he had served in the Canadian

47

Embassy in Brazil and had a working knowledge of Portuguese. Da Cunha at once approached the Government of Portugal through formal channels and through his relations in Lisbon. Despite his confidence he was not sure of being received in Angolique—for in more than ten years no one else from the UN had been—so he also approached other governments that had granted asylum to large numbers of refugees from Angolique or where persons had taken up some scholarships and training. He contacted the Red Cross and some specialized, nonpolitical United Nations agencies which had managed to get into or near Angolique, and he received some statements from Protestant organizations. In addition, he went on a hurried visit to Lisbon.

Permission for the subcommittee to visit Angolique was granted. Everyone—well, nearly everyone—was startled. The Afro-Asian delegates were exuberant. The press of the world, or such of it as took the slightest notice of either Angolique or UN affairs, was informed, and indeed the pundits at once began to tell the intellectual public what they thought the implications would be.

And then Mr. da Cunha was killed in a road accident.

The Portuguese, American and British politicians who had contrived the subcommittee's trip were very worried, for da Cunha had looked like God's gift to the problems of Portugal, Angolique and the United Nations. The Portuguese could not withdraw their permission for the visit.

It was inevitable that the unknown Canadian delegate Shaun McQuade—whose record was quite good and might just possibly give hopes for a reasonable view—should be appointed the new chairman. An Argentine delegate, Gregorio de la Plaza—the same gentleman who in nervous attention picked his nose—was brought in as the sixth member and was made *rapporteur*.

The man now by accident in charge of the contrived situation was not aware that it was contrived. He was assumed to be amenable to the situation, but it could hardly be pointed out to him. He was neither well known nor regarded particularly highly, although his record was good inasmuch as it was not bad. He belonged to a nation which was regarded as sympathetic to the United States and Great Britain, a member of NATO, and a country of the West, with all the involvements of industry, culture and power. Nothing startling was likely to happen.

48

But in fact this man had sympathies that were allied to nothing except the situation in Angolique and the people who were within that situation. And the situation was an unpleasant one from the inside. Further, he had in war seen the burning villages and the tanks passing through—had seen them from the view of the man in the tank—and he was, a quarter of a century later, ashamed of this by-product of war. He was an idealist who was also a realist. He was a man neither preconditioned nor afraid. He was interested in the truth of this matter and in acting upon it when he had found it.

God had given him something to do within a fortnight of his prayer, but had moved in His mysterious way so that it was a long time before McQuade sensed any purpose, and longer still before he guessed what that intent might be.

It was a hundred yards from the small conference room to the delegates' bar and dining room. McQuade, thirsty after his unfamiliar task of chairmanship talking, strolled along in the stifling central heating with the Dutch Minister Plenipotentiary to the UN, Theobald Alferink. Alferink was a tall, heavy man of forty, the youngest on the subcommittee with the exception of Ghanaian Counselor Asare Johnson. He had untidy fair hair in an organization where many members had no hair at all. He tended to be frivolous, but was intelligent and tough, and McQuade was glad of this because one or two of the other members were, he felt, decidedly anemic.

In the hundred-yard walk, McQuade noticed, Alferink addressed seven girls. Four of these smiled, one just stared at Alferink as if wondering who in hell he was and two looked decidedly sour—or at least uncomfortable. McQuade did not know any of these girls even on a "Hello" basis. Alferink addressed them all by Christian name.

McQuade could not resist the idle comment "You seem to be a success with the girls on the third floor."

Alferink answered, on a man-to-man basis, an assumption of properties in McQuade, "Suzé wouldn't like to hear about *all* my diplomatic passes. Do you think we'll see a few dollies on this mission?"

49

He spoke with expectation, like one going on a holiday who hopes a few girls will be there to brighten the beach.

"There'll be no time for that sort of thing."

"There's always time," Alferink said with a bellow of pleasure. "It's usually a question of place."

"I wouldn't know."

"What about our two girls from the Secretariat?"

"What about them?"

"They're probably good-looking."

"They'll be busy."

"What, all night as well?"

Alferink was evidently the sort of philanderer who could not imagine another man not seizing an opportunity—Lisbon, Vila Lobanda, Brazzaville. "There'll be some black girlies, too," he said now, "and those lovely mulattoes . . ."

"This deal has nothing to do with the Rockettes," said McQuade good humoredly. "They're just for stimulation!"

Alferink roared again with his gigantic laugh, and passing delegates, rather quiet and anxious, or perhaps hungry, turned to smile.

But for McQuade Alferink's attitude was a little worrying. This man was the only one of the other five members of the subcommittee whom he knew, who was in fact almost a good friend. Their two wives had met—very infrequently, it was true, but often enough to dine together and go to the theater even if they did not do shopping together. McQuade recalled that Suzé was unusual among Dutch women in being very slender and dark; she had a classical, rather beautiful, sad face. Why Theobald should deceive her or need any other woman's attention he did not know. He hoped the Dutch delegate's admiration of the female of the species was limited to words and would in no way interfere with the progress of the subcommittee's work, which would be difficult enough as it was.

"Ribowski says there's been logrolling and *he* ought to have become chairman. Still only the Western powers, he implies, never a Commie."

"There's nothing I can do about that," said McQuade. "Isn't he the one who's always got aches and pains anyway?"

"That's correct," Alferink agreed. "Personally I never ask my

50

doctor to come and see me. It's too expensive in this city, and anyway he's too busy playing the stock market!"

Sitting in an armchair surrounded by potted plants, apparently reading a copy of *Time*, was Portuguese delegate Gaspar Namora. "Ah, Mr. McQuade! How fortunate that you should be passing!"

"Allow me to take you to the bar—"

"No, Mr. McQuade, I am in something of a hurry." (That's why you're sitting there reading *Time*! McQuade thought, but naturally he did not say so.)

Alferink suggested, "I'll get you a Bloody Mary, Shaun?"

"Okay. Be with you in a minute." McQuade sat down near Namora among the potted plants and facing a tremendous view of the East River and the tissues of smoke rising from the industrial shambles of Queens. "I am glad to talk to you, Mr. Namora."

"As I say, a tremendous hurry," Mr. Namora said apprehensively, as if doing something he shouldn't. "It was just a thought. Perhaps I shouldn't. It might mislead . . . You'll be going quite soon?"

"As soon as possible."

"Before Christmas?"

"I'm afraid so."

"How unfortunate for your family. I expect you will see many people. Some you may not see. With respect, there may be problems."

"I'm sure there will be!"

"Then I suggest, if you get time, when you are in Lisbon, try and see Mr. Rossio. It just so happens—I do not *know* Mr. Rossio. You understand? It is nothing to do with *me*."

"I understand," said McQuade.

"I just happened to meet him once. I think he's not a bad sort," said Namora oddly. "I think he has an interesting perspective of the territory of Angolique. If he is a nationalist," reasoned Namora to himself, "he keeps quiet about it. So you'll find him in Lisbon. This is his telephone number."

"That's very helpful," said McQuade. "Have you ever been to Angolique yourself?"

"Once, when I was a boy. I remember it was very pleasant. The fishing and so on. Vila Lobanda has grown into a city since the

51

war. I would not know it. I must leave you now," said Mr. Namora, smacking his leg with the copy of *Time*. He resumed with a rush of words, "It would be nice to discuss this over the weekend. Suppose we have lunch in my apartment on Saturday?"

McQuade recalled that he had promised to do the Christmas shopping with Kristan on Saturday, but he knew that Namora was anxious to communicate but not be witnessed doing so. It might be important so he accepted at once. "That would be a great pleasure."

When he told Kristan about his appointment she did not take the same view.

"Saturday morning's off, honey."

"Oh, shoot," protested Kristan.

"I'm sorry. I can't go shopping because I have to lunch with the Portuguese delegate."

"Couldn't you lunch on Monday? You work in the same building."

"He suggested Saturday."

"And you didn't tell him you were taking me—"

"It's most important to see him."

"I'm not important?"

"When he's available—"

"I'm available any old time?"

"He doesn't want to be seen with me—"

"Neither do I," said Kristan, and rushed out of the room in tears.

But in fact McQuade did not lunch with Namora. The Portuguese delegate telephoned on Friday evening and with much apology for his discourtesy said it had become impossible for him to see McQuade. Nothing but death, Namora said, and death it was—the funeral was in Portugal and he must fly there at once.

"I understand," McQuade acknowledged, "and I regret it very much."

Whether Namora really went to Lisbon or not, or whether he had taken fright or had received instructions from his government not to be communicative to the subcommittee, McQuade never found out. "It couldn't have been a *very* important lunch," Kristan commented, "or he'd have stayed in Manhattan. Come on, big boy.

What do you want for Christmas? Some tropical clothes or a subscription to the *National Geographic?*"

Gregorio de la Plaza was singing—just a sad little cavatina brought on by wine and impulse. They all listened to the Spanish words about family and death, and a few knew what he meant. The waiters stood by the plates and empty bottles and eyed their watches surreptitiously; it was nearly the end of the party.

The delegates and their wives applauded and Asare Johnson said, a little unexpectedly, "I propose a toast of good wishes to our chairman."

"Hear, hear!"

McQuade looked around the hotel room, which was intended to be styled in the German manner—a peculiar choice of room, for this style was of the Wagner-Nietzsche Germany, and neither of the two later Germanies was a member of the United Nations; but it didn't matter a damn tonight. Then he rose to make a short speech, expressing regret and sadness that it should be him because of another man's death, a wish for good company in the coming weeks, the expectation of a fair amount of work and the hope that they'd find the truth and that the truth would be acted upon with something stronger than resolutions.

They applauded that—even the wives, to whom it meant nothing. Even Mrs. Ribowski, who spoke no English and had just smiled vaguely all evening, clapped.

Then, in the confusion of intended departures, Suzé Alferink pulled at McQuade, insisting on privacy, and pleaded, "I must talk to you." "I'm all attention," said McQuade agreeably, not drunk but contented.

She was an intense, serious, beautiful woman, and he saw distress in her face. "Not here," she urged.

There was nowhere to go.

They stood in a corridor with the consciousness of doors and laughter and music fading as an elevator went up—or was it down? "Aren't you cold?" McQuade asked.

"I wanted to talk to you." Suzé was in a hurry. She had something for his ears only, not to be overheard, not even to be witnessed.

53

"Listen, Shaun. You're such a good person."

"Oh, come now, Suzé—"

"You are. I trust you. Can I ask you a favor? It's a bit silly and I feel ashamed."

"I'm sure it's perfectly reasonable and if I can—"

"Look after Theo, won't you? For me."

"I'm sure we'll be in no danger, but I will, Suzé."

"I didn't mean that."

"No?"

"You know Theo. Oh, you *must* know. You've heard rumors. He likes to be admired. By girls. Such *silly* ones. That was what I meant."

"You should ignore rumors. Ask yourself, what kind of people spread them?"

"I'd be grateful," Suzé said, ignoring his comment. "I know I can trust you."

"We've got a ton of work to do. I can promise you that if Theo wastes time I'll be suitably angry."

"That's all I ask."

It was enough. McQuade had already noticed Theobald's accelerated buoyancy in the presence of the two stenographers who were to accompany the subcommittee to Lisbon and Angolique.

There had been, despite the death of da Cunha, the need of a party so that the members of the subcommittee could get to know each other informally, their wives could meet and all could become acquainted with the two Secretariat girls.

Now, as he unfastened sleeves and took off his tie in the vehicle going home and Kristan chattered, McQuade held the analysis.

"What did he say? What *about?*" he asked Kristan, referring to Ribowski, who had been talking to her earnestly but had been rather silent toward everyone else. Perhaps Kristan had gained some small insight into the Pole. For it was not only the Portuguese officials and unknown Africans McQuade had to understand, but the seven people coming with him from Turtle Bay. And so small at present was his knowledge of them that he hoped Kristan might help. But she answered, "Oh, he was talking about how lonely his wife would be, not being able to speak English. Even the food is a problem." And that this useless, sad little bit of information was true, McQuade did not doubt. For many were lonely in New York, and there was a tendency among foreign delegates to drift to their own restaurants and even to have their own small environments. All he himself had gotten out of Ribowski had been a gloomy refusal to drink alcohol. "Because I am ill and must not drink foolish liquids."

McQuade had even wondered if this had been an instruction from his government. He had inquired anxiously, "Are you fit enough to come to Africa? There will be strange foods and great heat." The Pole had answered, "It is my duty to come. I am not going to forgo my duty." It sounded a little too mechanical and was disquieting. Ribowski was a small, thin, gloomy-looking man of forty-seven. He had a face that surely could not register any further exhaustion: it was as creased as crushed tissue paper. Under his spectacles even his eyes looked tired. His wife, Basia, on the other hand, untroubled perhaps by politics, was small and fat, with a round face as innocent as pudding.

The only other guest to be serious throughout the evening was Hjalmar Ekelund. He had mentioned their work even at a party. "I have read the documents the Secretariat was able to supply concerning Angolique. It seems to be hopelessly developed economically . . ." He listed the minerals and forests and even fish in terms of world economics. "They have scarcely touched it. I am hopeful that it can become economically viable." Ekelund was like a detective who has found the first evidence and it is so impressive he is ready for the Assizes. McQuade qualified, "The population is small and in trouble. Let's see what we can find, eh?"

McQuade would remember this evening and these people with a false perspective, he knew, or at least an incomplete one which would alter as time passed. De la Plaza singing his sad Spanish song that few of them understood. The waiters standing by the bottles and silver dishes, watching these antics and cautious personal explorations, the warmth from wines breaking down hesitation. The fat little Mrs. Ribowski, with a creased round face smiling at nothing, understanding no one. The cool, inquisitive eyes of the other wives as he made his informal speech: not interested in the agonies of the *indigena* thousands of miles away, but scrutinizing this Canadian who would be responsible for their husbands in another land, as if by mere examination they could tell . . . a kind heart, he is honest, you can trust him, but does he *know* that my husband is different from all others: he belongs to *me* . . .

And the two Secretariat girls, unmarried, who looked at him, met his eye during his speech, smiled very faintly with a different warmth: I am female, beautiful, bound to no one. To them he was a man, partly an employer, the boss. They sensed the honesty, the purposefulness, the lack of pomposity and fuss, and a determination in terms of the project—a sexlessness in the friendship whose demands would be functional, related to their Secretariat capabilities. He was all right, they could almost see it—it would narrow down to how hard he worked them, how generous he would be about time, and the thoughtfulness and protection he could give them. He seemed to know what he was doing. At once they were prepared to lean on him, and for them the trip would be a sort of adventure, one without his responsibility of decision. The two girls were typical of a certain American type—droll, good-natured, intelligent, talkative and in no need of mother. They wanted a job with travel involved, something different, something worthy of their minds and education. They belonged to a restless generation, often absurd but frequently inspired—usually by honesty. Other girls did not have their particular qualifications or nerve and sought what they called "life" in sex or sport or horses. It was quite possible that these two were virgins. Although Miss Barney Widener was very handsome, she gave an impression of good-humored defensiveness. She was a tall girl with a magnificent body. Her face was not pretty—her jaw and mouth were too large for that—but was beautiful in a healthy, sporty way. She was good-natured and probably unflappable. She was twenty-four, and the other stenographer, Miss Marianne Saavedra, was thirty. Miss Saavedra was tall and slender, but looked puny by the side of Barney Widener. She also was droll, tending to be good-humoredly sarcastic and even sour, in an intelligent, interesting manner. Miss Saavedra spoke a little Portuguese, which might be useful. Both girls talked with the equality of opinion of the educated American girl and had plunged easily into the conversation of the delegates at the party.

Before surrendering to sleep, McQuade suggested to Kristan, "Go and see Suzé now and again, won't you?"

56

"What for? I don't know her all that well."

"She's going to be lonely."

"So am I."

"She's a very sensitive person," urged McQuade, dangerously near to pleading. "She might become depressed."

"I noticed you seemed very receptive to her kind of sensitivity."

Kristan said this without any particular emotion, but he flared in minor irritation, "I'm only asking you to be human."

"I have problems as well as Suzé Alferink."

"If you could find something to do—"

"I'm not bored."

"Some work. There are so many things."

"I'm no good at anything," she said with resignation.

They had fallen asleep when the phone rang. McQuade awoke, filmed with sweat. Heat emanated from Kristan, who cried "The phone." She did this indifferently, with curiosity only—the responsibility was always his.

A complaintive male voice told McQuade, "I've been ringing all evening."

What could be so important but war, death, disaster? Good news could wait until morning.

"We've been to a party."

"A party!"

It sounded like a protest.

"You said it was important."

"I said? No," disputed the voice, justifiably, and McQuade struggled with the mixture of improbability—how could this sort of dialogue be part of duty, the endless ideological struggle? "I understand that within the next thirty-six hours you will be going to Angolique?" the voice said.

McQuade was startled and protested, "You do business at strange hours of the night. It is two in the morning."

"I have to go to Chile. I did phone twice before," the voice protested. He gave the impression that, urgent though it was to deal with the problem of McQuade and Angolique, there were other and greater matters. "All sorts of prejudiced points of view will be put to you—"

"We deal in ideas and points of view."

57

"I am in a position to approach people in Vila Lobanda and, indeed, Lisbon, who will make your stay more comfortable."

"I do not anticipate a comfortable stay! Will you please tell me who you are and what it is you wish to say."

"My name does not matter. The important thing is that no mistakes are made because of a condition of ignorance."

"By whom, for heaven's sake?"

"Primarily yourself, but also, of course, your subcommittee."

"And what are we supposed to be in ignorance of?"

"I am sure that you are, above all things, a realist, Mr. Mc-Quade. The point is that it concerns you. You are a Canadian?"

"I am."

"On the territory of Angolique there are industrial investments of high value to Canadians, especially Canadians in the Toronto area. Thousands of shareholders are involved. Serious, intelligent people. Would we wish them to be placed in a position of discomfort, even of distress? Not Canadian companies, you understand, but associated. Equally, we would not wish you to suffer. What would you regard as a reasonable proposition?"

"I do not know what you are talking about," said McQuade angrily. "Put it in writing if it's an honest proposition, and if it isn't, go to hell."

He went back to bed, but was unable to sleep. After a while Kristan asked, "Who was it?"

McQuade said, "I think it was what is known as pressure, or perhaps bribery and corruption. What a pity I didn't listen to find out how much I'm worth!"

Nevertheless, he mentioned it to the ambassador when he said his farewells, and that ebullient gentleman counseled, "If you're going to take on big business as well as the Portuguese Government you'd better pack your Smith and Wesson!"

4 ▪ ▪

LISBON. McQuade stood by the marble landing stage of the Terreiro do Paço, observed its *cais das colunas* with something between respect and astonishment, and watched the ferry crossing the dull water of the River Tagus, which, at this part, had the curiously romantic name the Sea of Straw. On its other three sides the Terreiro do Paço was filled with arcades and tall towers of tender harmony of line, and cabbage-green roofs touched by dull light almost gave the effect of an opera set.

Lisbon was a beautiful city. He had walked miles on his own to see it—to see if in itself it conveyed something which would help to explain Portuguese attitudes. And, in a way, it did. It was a grandiose mixture of beauty, history, dignity, squalor, romance and tradition, with a touch of Manhattan thrown in. The traffic swept through the Praça de Dom Pedro IV in a lethal pack reminiscent of Paris. The Avenida da Liberdade was full of palms and trees which would be flowering soon. There was the dignity of the squares and the attractive terraces, the long flights of steps pausing at smaller terraces from which could be seen an ever-increasing view of the Tagus and the Castelo de São Jorge. He saw the old, gabled houses which had withstood the earthquake of 1755, and the winding alleyways slippery with cobbles, smelling of fish and oranges, where flowers trailed from iron-rail balconies and washing hung. It did not escape McQuade's notice that this impoverished quaintness and noisy humanity, reminiscent of Naples, was genuine, was not a contrivance for tourists. It was very near to squalor: one tap in the open supplied an entire row of houses with water. Did the women, who certainly smiled and greeted him, really wish to walk barefoot with heavy loads on their heads? Tall apartment blocks rose out of this area, proof of Portuguese acknowledgment that it was a problem. Out of this crumbling, colorful old quarter McQuade had come back into the city, with its yellow trams, huge cafes, shoeshine boys among the coffee tables, the long side streets full of shops, the car-and-passenger ferries crowding away from the river road near Black Horse Square, the chapels with their onion domes, the graceful terracing of the buildings crowding the seven hills.

The city was, even on a winter's day, at its most crowded in Rossio, and this reminded McQuade that he had been given the name of a man called Rossio. McQuade's hotel was high up, with a superb view from his bedroom—possibly the most attractive bedroom he had ever been given—furnished in period Portuguese style.

The hotel was perhaps too splendid for one on his way to examine tragedy. It had marble halls, tapestries, thick carpets and sound-proofing everywhere, as if it had been built for conspirators who couldn't do without luxury.

The restaurant was by a courtyard terrace which even today was full of flowers and greenery.

He was hungry and eager to eat. After a while he noticed that Barney and Asare Johnson weren't present at table.

"Where's Barney?" he asked.

"Gone to a bullfight," suggested Marianne.

"It is not the season."

"This bull does not know that."

Ekelund said as if a serious explanation was necessary, "I think she may have gone to a different restaurant with Mr. Johnson."

Marianne considered it whimsically. "I wonder why? To avoid *us*, to hear the fado, or to engage in the Portuguese taste for gossip and intrigue?"

McQuade smiled and said to her, "Not a taste limited to the Portuguese, I think?"

Marianne flushed a little and conceded, "Sorry I spoke, Mr. Chairman."

After the dinner, while they were having their first sample of the white port, McQuade suggested, "I was thinking we might try to get in touch with this Rossio man."

Ekelund questioned, "Does he have an official status?"

"No. Does that matter?"

Ekelund evidently thought it did, but did not argue about it. It proved unexpectedly easy to contact Rossio. McQuade rang the number he'd been given by the Portuguese delegate. It was a hotel's, and he was put through at once.

"United Nations? And you want to see *me*?"

The voice laughed enormously over the telephone.

"We understand you may have information about the territory of Angolique."

"I was born there, so I would have information."

"May we come to see you?"

"If you want to come you'd better come right now. We're off to Paris tomorrow. That's a civilized city."

Within a quarter of an hour McQuade, with Ribowski, was outside the hotel bedroom door.

Rossio had a large bedroom, which at this moment was very untidy. He sat on a double bed with his shoes off. He had no jacket on and his sleeves were rolled up, baring black, powerful arms. He was about thirty, McQuade estimated, large, drunk, good-humored, and with an intelligence gone sour. McQuade's knowledge of Angolique tribes was not yet extensive but he guessed that Rossio was of the Kuvale.

There was a young woman with him. She was in her bra and pants only and was not bothered about the visitors noticing it. She was the most pulchritudinous female McQuade had ever seen. At first McQuade, before looking away quickly, thought she had stockings on, but then realized that she had not. She had superb coffee skin. When he looked again he saw that she had one of those international, sophisticated faces that are seen where there is money. But the face was that of a *mestiça*—a mulatto—the fierce, beautiful, defiant, promiscuous face of one interested in nothing but love, money, restaurants, automobiles. She had her counterparts in Rome, Paris, New York and London. Politics were not likely to interest her.

Rossio said with huge enjoyment—as if he was showing her off deliberately, "Glória. *Não-civilizado,* as the Portuguese would say. A beautiful bitch, you say in New York." He was speaking English. "European father, African mother. I'm all for that kind of united nations!"

"I am McQuade. This is Mr. Ribowski."

"Have a whisky?"

"Sure."

Ribowski said, "I think not, but thank you. My stomach is a little upset." He was looking out of the corner of his eye at the girl with disapproval, and she, not liking it, stared back with contempt. She then put on stockings, marring the beauty. Clearly, McQuade decided, politics takes me into strange places.

"We are going to Angolique, you see," he told Rossio. "Six of us. Your name was given to me in New York as one likely to return to the territory to organize things."

Rossio roared with amusement. He even slapped McQuade on

61

the shoulder. "Me?" he said, changing to Portuguese so that the girl could understand. "Me go back to take up the fight for those black bastards? You're *crazy!*"

The girl shrieked in high-pitched laughter and rolled over on the bed. Rossio, still shaking with uncontrollable mirth, dug his fingers into the fat of her buttocks. "They'll love her in Paris," he commented.

When he had recovered himself he said, "If there's a war in Angolique I can tell you who will win it. The Portuguese. And why not? They're *soldiers*. These others—they're down from the trees. It's ridiculous. These freedom fighters don't know what in hell they're fighting *for*. They sit around in comfort in Tanzania and Malawi and the Congo and shout about *Independência ou morte,* and then they go on sick leave or hold a press conference. And talk about Portuguese atrocities. The young ones with any brains, having got out of Angolique, find someone with sympathy to give them education. Then they get the hell out of Africa to New York or Paris or somewhere. Like me," he admitted. "It's true the Bakongo had a high old time slaughtering girls and farmers up in the north, and some of the Bamakonde in the east want to fight but are not organized. It's ridiculous. Get a few hundred together and a few Chinese or Soviet advisers and after a while they have a party or sail up river in a yacht. But *fight?* Your problem, I think, is that they make such a mess of it that their Chinese or Russian friends may have to do the fighting themselves. And that is the kind of trouble, I presume, with respect, you do not wish to have."

Ribowski suddenly spoke up in French in a bitter voice, "I can see that the indigenous persons of Angolique are better at bed than battle."

The girl said at a furious pace, "What do you do, sick belly? Talk? Stare at girls? You think he is going to get himself cut to pieces in your stupid little plans? Hypocritical Americans, killing and talking about God and spreading your stupid culture and venereal disease all over the world! He is a *good* man."

Ribowski shouted her down, "I am a Pole, not a damn American," which, unexpectedly, caused the girl to fall over again and go into the hysterical tiny laughter.

Rossio put his hand between her legs and tipped her off the bed. All seemed back to normal. He said with seriousness and some embarrassment, "Don't think I don't care. But I have the misfortune to have been educated—Protestant mission and a French school," he explained quickly. "An interesting mixture. But it means I am, like yourselves, a talker, not a warrior. And maybe words will win this battle in the end. So I go to Paris. Write a book. The situation in Angolique," he said, after a swallow of whisky, "is not normal. There have been some reforms. But the refugees go out and the soldier-settlers come in. The *regedors* still hold their areas and do what they like. The civilian white population is armed and trained and the law is not bothered if someone gets shot. The Portuguese say all the trouble is organized from outside and is perhaps Communistic. And it does not help to remove this charge when your own United Nations, along with foreign powers, pledges support to the people against the Portuguese Government. It is surprising that you have permission to visit the territory."

"These were mere expressions of sympathy or the granting of asylum to Angolique groups which had had to flee—"

"Nevertheless, it shows the Portuguese where your heart is. Preconditioned, prejudiced, they could say. Never mind. You are going," acknowledged Rossio. "It's great fun there. You'll get a good impression. Dancing and drinking and hunting and good food and courtesy. And no color bar except in terms of miserable power. It is not like England, where all are equal so long as they remember their position in society! Nor like South Africa, with the opposite logical conception, the racial segregation in elevators and public lavatories and even racial separation of clothes in laundries! Although, oddly enough, you will find that many South African men like to go to Angolique for a daring holiday and try a black girl in a brothel in Vila Lobanda or Porto Girassol. Oh, there's some strange indication in that, eh? But in Angolique the Portuguese have no record of any color bar in sex. I'll say that for them! No taboos. Mongrelization is, or was before everyone took fright, encouraged. The Portuguese are not like you Anglo-Saxons," Rossio said frankly. "That goes for efficiency, too. They are obsessed with order and dignity. So you fill in forms and wait—forever. This is one of the abuses, of course. Passes and bribery to obtain them and arrests whether you've got them or not. And there's only one black lawyer in the whole of Angolique. I'm an *assimilado,* you under-

63

stand, but I had to have my pass to get into a restaurant. The education's improving, but how slowly! And not enough! My God, not enough. Just enough to make us realize how bad it is. I wish you luck," Rossio concluded, standing up in a polite gesture of dismissal, and putting one hand tenderly on Glória's shoulder.

The girl crossed her legs as she sat on the bed, and said to Ribowski—whom she seemed to have disliked from the moment of his arrival—"Take your toothpick, Mister Pole. And stick to hippo steak sauté! It is like pork, but not so greasy."

Rossio laughed, then questioned, "You know about the students, of course?"

McQuade answered doubtfully, "Not if this is recent information."

"Twenty of them arrested here in Lisbon. Some from the Azevedo Machato Lyceum. The usual stuff about 'Communist infiltration which may threaten the cohesion of society and particularly the armed forces.' "

Glória commented excitedly, "And girls, too. One of them swallowed the crushed lenses of her spectacles while in custody."

"It is nothing to do with Angolique," Rossio pointed out. "But it indicates that they have minds, too."

As they went down in the elevator Ribowski sneered to McQuade, "What a garrulous fool. No dignity at all, sitting there with his fleshy tart."

But McQuade, smiling to himself in the privacy of the darkness of the street, thought it more than possible that Rossio would turn up in the political history of Angolique.

On the following morning McQuade went with Hjalmar Ekelund to an interview with Dr. Ferreira Pessanha, who was the Minister for Overseas Boundaries.

He was a small, heavy man, neatly dressed, with a fine head and an acute sense of humor. He was even recklessly cynical about his own regime in Portugal. "You must not hurry us. Give us time to die decently!" This rather disconcerted Ekelund, who had come to the graceful old office to prove things like a statistician. They sat in comfortable chairs among bookcases, busts and cupboards of beautiful wood; portraits from the dynasties of Burgundy, Aviz and Braganza; with a superb oil of a sailing ship by the door. Even the lampshades were works of art and the view out of the window was like a landscape by Domingos António de Sequeira. Nevertheless, McQuade was positioned so that the light was in his eyes, and he was the observed, not Dr. Pessanha, who remained in shadow.

The doctor spoke of the Lusitanians, who a thousand years before Christ built the fortified *citânias* on the tops of hills, of the Phoenicians sailing along the Portuguese coast, of the Carthaginians and of Viriathus, the Lusitanian who outfought the Romans. He talked of five centuries under Rome, of barbarian invasions, the Visigoth kingdom that followed and the landings of the Muslims in Spain in 711. He described how Portugal seized independence from Spain and the Moors and became a kingdom in 1143, with a border hardly altered since. One of a long line of kings and queens, John I, had married Philippa of Lancaster, thus securing the long alliance with England. He spoke of maritime exploration and the fights with Turks and Barbary pirates, of Henry the Navigator exploring the routes to Ceuta, Lagos, Cape St. Vincent, Madeira and the Azores, and other Portuguese blazing the way to Alcacer, Arzila, Tangier, the islands of Fernando Po, São Tomé and Principe. He reminded them of Bartolomeu Dias rounding the Cape of Good Hope, of the discovery in 1492 of Labrador and of how two years later the Borgia Pope Alexander VI had found it necessary to divide all future discoveries between the two Iberian kingdoms, allotting Portugual all lands east of a line joining the Poles and running 370 miles west of Cape Verde Isles and thus retaining Brazil.

Dr. Pessanha was in no hurry, for he was defending Portugal from people who he knew were in complete ignorance of her. That these were just samples was his implication. Vasco da Gama rounding South Africa in 1497 and in 1512 Afonso de Albuquerque capturing Goa, Malabar, Malacca and the Moluccas; in 1514 an expedition reaching China and in 1520 Magellan setting out on the first voyage around the world . . .

He conveyed a romantic picture of wooden ships with billowing sails and bright flags anchoring in hot, unknown harbors; of knights in armor and plumes wading ashore to defeat the savage, the infidel, the Dutch, the Spanish, the French, or the unknown . . .

McQuade had the feeling that the Minister for Overseas Boundaries was overdoing it a little. Perhaps he considered McQuade a bum Canadian, one of a nation of pulp manufacturers and wheat

65

and oil men, ignorant of history and culture. He had lived with this curious European fixation about their own particular dignity in United Nations and in embassies elsewhere long enough to be undisturbed. Canadians worked every bit as hard and skillfully as anyone else, and a good deal more successfully.

The Minister for Overseas Boundaries was approaching what was, for him, the point.

"Portugal is an old country. We have matured by experience. We have seen young nations and political ideas come and go in a froth of idealism. It *may* be that in scarcely twenty years the UN has achieved what Europe failed to do in two thousand. We belong to this new organization ourselves, as you know, and are glad to see it acknowledges its own faults now and again. Now, tell me, Mr. Minister," he requested suddenly, "what are you going to do? Do tell me"—Dr. Pessanha was almost laughing—"in confidence. We have no secret microphones or infrared cameras here. The room is not bugged. This is Portugal, not North America or Russia. How can six people go to a territory of three-quarters of a million square miles, full of people whose languages they do not speak, and understand its problems in five or six weeks? Be frank. Admit it. Your Secretariat has prepared your report. You will fill in the details of conversations."

Ekelund said solemnly, "I really must protest, Excellency, at this frivolous attitude of yours. You are suggesting we are puppets—"

Dr. Pessanha waved a hand. He was still in a good humor. "No, no, Counselor. Do not be cross with me. That would spoil our intended lunch! I am being frank with you. I want you to be frank with me. You will still go to the territory. But I would like to have the dignity, the friendship even and the comfort of the truth. Is not the truth that none of your commissions has ever found out anything which was not known before they left New York? Is it not a fact that American pressure is still a major factor in the selection of your committees and subcommittees? Is there any reason why I should not believe what I am told? Can you tell me of a single commission whose conclusions haven't been exactly as the United Nations desired and this in turn the wishes of the great power which is running the circus, consciously or not, that is, the United States?"

The minister was concluding. "All we in Portugal and our Overseas Territories wish to do is continue to exist and grow, commercially, socially, in culture, in education. Your Cold War is of no interest to us except inasmuch as it attacks Catholicism and affects Europe. But UNO? Who is she working for? One has the unpleasant feeling of being betrayed by one's friends rather than defeated by one's foes. This is confusing, it is ridiculous and absurdly unnecessary."

McQuade said, "You speak with great conviction, Excellency."

Dr. Pessanha bowed from his seat. "I am surely right."

"If you are right and I find it so, I shall say so."

"We have always supplied information," said the minister, "despite the hostility of the United Nations and others and the misuse of the information. Now we invite you to look around our territory. Is there, I wonder, anything else I can do for you?"

McQuade said, blasting the blarney apart, "Yes, Excellency. There are two people I'd like to interview who are believed to be in prison. Their names are—"

The humor faded from the minister's eyes.

"There was an amnesty," he claimed. "It is true we had to arrest many people for the safety of others when foreign-inspired trouble occurred in Vila Lobanda. But most have been released now. If not, an interview can be arranged on the territory by the Minister of the Interior, whom you will no doubt talk to. Naturally I do not know of individual cases."

"We have," said McQuade woodenly, "received in New York information concerning measures going beyond the requirements necessary for the reestablishment of law and order."

Dr. Pessanha waved his short arms in a gesture that conveyed impatience. He commented, "Naturally you get that kind of information—in New York."

"The same groups," McQuade told him, "stress their desire for a peaceful solution and cooperation among racial groups within Angolique on a basis of equality. They say they found no channel for discussion with the Government of Portugal."

"Naturally we do not hold discussions with bandits who shoot policemen!"

"We were told that the demonstration outside the police station

67

of Vila Lobanda was the result of frustration and the firmly negative attitude of the Government of Portugal. Some newspapermen were there and this was a means of drawing attention to the problems of the ANP group."

"You sound as if you listened to this nonsense, Mr. Minister. Of course killing is good newspaper material—especially if no libel suits or other action is possible against the newspaper. And if policemen fire back, this is repression, abuse and so on. I see, alas, that you did indeed come with prejudice. The disturbances in Angolique—and I acknowledge that they existed recently—were almost entirely the result of foreign intervention. We have hostile borders, Mr. Minister, and very strange people come across them— from the Congo, Tanzania and Zambia we find Chinese soldiers, Frenchmen, colored men who've been trained in Cuba, Ghana, Tanzania, Soviet Russia and even Peking. What for? one wonders. Justice? Truth? Love for Angolique? Is it likely, Mr. Minister? This constitutes a menace to the security of Portugal."

"Excellency," said McQuade. "I did not come here for an argument. If I admit to any prejudice it would be on the lines that Portugal is spending 3.5 billion escudos annually in defending her moral and territorial integrity in Africa—"

"I see that I must ask to be allowed to explain *why* that is so," said the Minister for Overseas Boundaries, neither angrily nor sadly. He lifted a telephone and said in Portuguese, "Bring the albums of photographs the Army took in Angolique . . . You *know* . . . Luvo, Carmiza, Quixuma . . . "

Dr. Pessanha addressed McQuade and Ekelund seriously:

"When the trouble began a few months ago in Angolique there were two thousand white troops in a territory of 750,000 square miles and about seven *hundred* policemen, half of them African. Then why did the terrorism not drive us into the sea? Because, Mr. Minister, it was an attack from the north, planned in Leopoldville, and it was contained in the north, or, more horribly accurately, it ran out of impetus and victims. There has been no trouble at all in the center or the south. But in the far north fifty places of the plantation or very-small-town type were attacked on that first terrible day. Five hundred Europeans were slaughtered. In the next three weeks seven thousand were killed, over half of them innocent

68

or loyal Africans, in the conditions of butchery you will see shortly. It was the biggest slaughter of Europeans in Africa this century, and it was ignored by the world press, who did not want to hear about it and preferred to remain prejudiced. They call these terrorists—drugged on the wild hemp that grows all over northern Angolique and the Lower Congo—'gallant freedom fighters.' You will see how gallant when the photographs are brought; and you will see who was fought."

McQuade interrupted, "Excellency, are you disputing what Danton said?"

Dr. Pessanha was cautious. "And what would that be?"

"He said that revolutions are not made on tea."

"That is amusing but pointless. This is not a revolution."

"You are saying these people were crazy on drugs?"

"It is very probable."

"Then without the drugs they would be normal? There would have been no fighting? Are they murderers on drugs or irrespective of drugs? You can't have it both ways."

The Minister for Overseas Boundaries countered, "You are playing with words, Mr. Minister. I do not know. You must judge for yourselves from the photographs and the statements which are available. If you wish to score in a debate, you have just done so. Ah! Here they are."

There were at least ten albums of photographs. Dr. Pessanha passed one each to McQuade and Ekelund.

The pictures were appalling.

McQuade had never believed such things could happen to the human body. He had seen corpses in Italy, but not like *this*. Whoever had done these things was beyond reasoning with, was not worthy of any kind of freedom, belonged in the strait jackets of the raving mad, had passed beyond the human and animal urge to fight. It was slaughter for enjoyment—crucifixions and decapitations; sexual bestialities and cut-off organs; hands and legs and heads lying in grass or on patios or stuck on poles; people still alive but who had had both eyes gouged out; human beings in postures of death by vile, unbelievable humiliation; limbs dangling from trees; women's bodies without breasts and with hacked stomachs; children severed almost in half. Close-ups taken inside a saw-

69

mill showed great mounds of shredded torsos, a litter of chunks of human meat which had been through the rotary saw. On the back of each hinged photograph was the official stamp and signature of the Army photographer, the date when it had been taken and the place. There were many places.

After a while Ekelund couldn't bear to look at any more. "Excellency, these are the most horrible things I have seen in my life."

McQuade admitted, "I had not heard of these things."

Dr. Pessanha said, "All you have heard of is a campaign of atrocities by Portuguese civilians and the Army. These horrible events of a few months ago were followed by a campaign of lies and half-truths about us—for it is true that some civilians in Vila Lobanda were terrified and shot a lot of Africans, but they did not do *this* sort of thing. And there was the prejudice which already existed and merely needed inflammation from Leopoldville and elsewhere, and the other prejudices based on religions which had nothing to do with the issue. But here and there the truth asserted itself. A British fact-finding team was allowed in—would we do that if we were indulging in genocide?—consisting of the Consul General in Vila Lobanda and two Air Force attachés from Lisbon, and they found no evidence of slaughter by Portuguese troops, nor did some experienced journalists we allowed in. The others—perhaps fearing for their skins—preferred to collect 'evidence' over the border.

"We have the evidence of the dead, but also of those who came back or sought our protection. And there were the prisoners who talked. And all these say that the attack was planned in Leopoldville. The agitators were sent to make contact with the witch doctors and chiefs who might be disloyal. They promised the usual nonsense—independence at once, white women to rape, the banks emptied and the money shared, all white men to be killed on the first day so there would be no interference. These agitators were followed by the professionals—the toughs from the former Belgian Congo and French Congo, from Algeria, Cuba and so on. It was easy enough to get over the border. It is 1300 miles of mountains, swamp, *capim* grass and jungle. Even the rivers are full of wooded islands. You could hide millions. The border and the arrangements were no problem. Practically no white men live up there on the

border. They recruited five thousand and in Angolique many joined
—the Bakongo, of course, overflow the border anyway—joined
from fear of the consequences if they did not. They received radio
instructions from Leopoldville and used, to begin with, shotguns,
canhangulos and *catanas*. You see the effects in the photographs—
the hacking off of limbs in one blow, the decapitations and so on.

"Now they fight the Army with automatic rifles, grenades, booby
traps and even the *plastique*. The professionals are quite well paid,
as they were in the Congo—checks made out from Leopoldville
banks have been taken from prisoners and dead bodies. Who sends
money in to Leopoldville we do not know, but we think sources in
Ghana, Moscow and, I fear, various organizations in the United
States and Great Britain. There is evidence of professional gunrunners in the business who've found the UN embargo on arms to
South Africa a little heavy going at times. Leopoldville is God or
the Devil's gift to the people who want to profit by war.

"You have to remember that the Africans in the northern areas
of Angolique are very primitive indeed. Also, they overflow each
way over the border with the Congo, being of those tribes. You
must bear in mind too that the average African there—and possibly elsewhere—is not politically conscious, but likes, as we all do,
more money for less work. Indeed, he does not have the European
compulsion for work. He does not regard it as ennobling and if
possible leaves it to the women. There is a further point of confusion and it is emotional. The Bakongo people, as I've said, overflow the border each way. When self-government came to the
Congo, north of the river, it became an exciting possibility south of
it; and the chaos and atrocities in the north might well be regarded
as what you would call the political norm.

"Oh, certainly reforms are due and will take place. But there is
danger in haste. Too rapid detribalization is one. The older generations resent the education of children who grow up cleverer than
their elders. Then there is the problem of schools in remote areas
and for nomadic tribes.

"There exists a blasphemous atavistic technique which you may
see or hear of in Angolique. This is to confuse fetishism and Christianity symbols and service. You may recall that similar things
happened at the time of the excesses of the Mau Mau. Terrorists

71

have shown a predilection for crucifixion, you may have noticed in the photographs, and crosses have been traced on the foreheads of *indigena* during initiations. Aroused by witch doctors and hemp and a bellyful of *aguardente,* the homemade brandy, or the *pombe,* they chant a parody of Christian hymns and are told that if they die fighting they will rise again in three days. What do we do, gentlemen? How nice it would be to hand over the problem to the arrogant and the intellectual who talk so endlessly about it in the safety of the armchair. There is a report, common in their newspapers, that two thousand Africans were massacred in the village of Quilhoxu. Why don't you go to that village, gentlemen, when you are in Angolique? I see by your faces that you have read this newspaper lie. Go there then. Look, here it is on the map. Ask the villagers and the German mineralogists and the Danish agronomists if anything *at all* happened.

"It passed unnoticed by the press four months ago, when there took place in Angolique this massacre of Europeans and Africans, but when Portuguese civilians fought back in panic and the Army came and justifiably restored order, a howl of indignation went up, especially from the society of intellectuals and angry young men who do everything on paper, who think it broadminded to despise the Army, the police, the church, morality, and indeed anything to do with law and order, which they call 'restraint.' How safe they are in that law and order of London and New York to make these absurd parodies of protests for justice! They were completely silent when one million Moslems and Hindus were slaughtered in the intercommunal riots which followed the transfer of power in India. How they sided with the Mau Mau rather than their own soldiers and settlers! And how they sneered in disbelief at atrocities in the Congo! But what did they do about Budapest or the killing of thousands of Tibetans? You know what they did. They wrote their weekly articles and watched the TV! How their minds followed the fashionable trend of immorality when Goa was seized! For these sick people with no principles, atrocities, by definition, are the property of the gutter press. They do not wish to hear about them. Fighting is something they do with policemen, not with people who might kill them. I wish they had been *there,* in Angolique, that is all. They have talkative mouths, but their guts are untried by slaughter,

72

castration, rape, terror, decapitation. They expect calm, intellectual debate about these Bakongo, a delicate discussion about the whys and wherefores of *our* behavior!"

There was truth in what Dr. Pessanha said, justification in his anger with the press. If these things in the photographs had happened to United States, Canadian, British, French or Belgian citizens, the paratroops and jets and armored cars would have been over the Atlantic in hours and there would have been a kingsize hullaballoo in the White House and elsewhere. But the massacre of the Portuguese hadn't even been reported at first and, when it had, Portugal had had to forgo sympathy and suffer disbelief. It was McQuade's job, however, to calm down bias, to avoid hatreds, to ignore them and to report impartially on the total truth. His approach had to be in terms of economic viability and the wishes of the people of Angolique and with the question of whether they—or an educated part of them—were able to cope with independence if it was granted. And the largest problem in Angolique would evidently be a familiar one: that once thousands of persons have been killed, calm is difficult, hatreds linger and a return to the *status quo* proves impossible. Dr. Pessanha was making an emotional plea for the restoration of Angolique to what it had been. That was impossible. Even if McQuade and the subcommittee were or became prejudiced in favor of the Portuguese and were, by some miracle, backed by the world press, it would still be impossible. There was going to be change. How much and of what kind might well depend on McQuade and his companions.

On a mild rainy afternoon the subcommittee boarded the weekly airplane to Angolique to find the truth.

5 ▪ ▪

THE BOEING CREPT IN over the trees and depressing earth. As the engines shook it to a standstill in a great roar of engine braking, McQuade, looking out of a window, saw a few old jet fighters, British Javelins with the romantic Portuguese markings.

73

"Christ," commented a South African who had been to Zambia, "this looks a dump. How long do we stay?"

Outside, the heat did not strike noticeably at first, for the air felt fresh briefly after the heat of bodies and the stink of cigarette smoke in the Boeing. There were precisely nine passengers for Vila Lobanda—the UN group and one Portuguese businessman from Lisbon. The South Africa-bound passengers were confined to promenading around a small balcony and the restaurant and using the airport's one lavatory.

The *cassimbo* caused a misty dullness that made everything look cracked and shabby. "What's the smell?" Marianne asked. "They having trouble with the loo?" It was in fact the smell of this part of Africa—a fascinating odor of almonds, acacia pods, sewage and the interesting smell of one's own armpits on a summer day. Two days were to pass before McQuade no longer noticed it.

Contrary to expectation, the PIDE—the secret police (who were about as inconspicuous as Woolworth's and had offices with splendid mosaics over the doorways)—and the customs officers weren't bothered by the arrival of foreigners. They handed out forms to the UN group, but filled in the necessary data themselves—incorrectly, McQuade noticed.

The Portuguese businessman had greeted a man waiting outside the customs hall, had embraced him with his right arm in the Portuguese manner. Now this second man was waving away the porters and taxi drivers who wished to claim McQuade and party.

He was a man of about forty-five, of medium height, with a narrow, indeed, a kind face if one could estimate Portuguese faces. His hair was cut short, American style, and he wore a dark-gray lightweight suit.

"I am Hermano Costa," he said. He shook hands with McQuade and was on the point of embracing him. "You are Mr. McQuade. I recognize it from the photographs."

"The photographs?"

"Ah, yes. The secret police have photographs. They show them to me. Does this not seem logical? You were checked by Interpol, all of you! They found nothing! So here you are! This is Mr. Tiago, an old friend of mine. He sells coffee in New York and Baltimore. Once he got on the wrong plane and went to Brazil. Business was terrible that trip!"

74

Mr. Tiago said, "Welcome to my country. I hope you have a nice holiday."

Mr. Costa smiled. "They are not here on holiday. They have come about the war."

"Ah!" said Mr. Tiago sadly. "In Lisbon I saw Ana Lameiras and her boy has had his ankle blown off by a grenade."

"Ah, that is tragedy," agreed Costa. He explained to McQuade, "He loved football, you see. Are you tired? Did you have a good trip?"

"Not at all bad," said McQuade, a little overcome by the acceptance and friendliness.

"Let me get you a taxi," urged Tiago. *"Two* taxis!"

"It is not necessary," said Costa. "I have two vehicles waiting." He had been speaking in English, but now he offered affectionate farewells to Tiago and concluded in Portuguese, "I think they come in a spirit of criticism, but they will see and learn."

Then Costa indicated the first thing wrong—perhaps a portent. "I am sorry but your own vehicle has not come," he told McQuade in English. "But no doubt it will. Perhaps the English are on strike!"

The UN party had ordered a Land Rover. Without it they might be limited to taxis or what the Portuguese supplied and perhaps restricted to where the Portuguese wished them to go.

Outside the small airport building, in an avenue of mosaic pavements and acacia trees, were two vehicles, a Fiat estate car and a Mercedes taxi. A group of black porters brought the suitcases and smiled with great satisfaction as the UN party, not yet familiar with Angolique currency, tipped them with Manhattan carelessness.

Riding in the Fiat station wagon, Costa pointed out things and talked as if they were on holiday. The suburbs of Vila Lobanda were a curious mixture of villas and bungalows painted in pastel shades, an occasional tall new block of apartments with shops on the ground floor, churches and hospitals of modern design, and slums of grass and corrugated-iron huts packed together in hundreds on the stale grass and red soil. The suburbs were separated by large areas of sandstone. The main roads weren't very good and the side roads were simply ribbons of the same depressing red earth.

"It is very sad," said Costa. "Two years ago the soil subsided and a whole suburb collapsed. A terrible mess. But we shall put it right. You know, when I was a boy this was bush. All of it. A thousand meters from the harbor the bush started. Now look at it! Parks and skyscrapers! Cafes and museums!" He was really proud of this city, which looked like an estate being constructed in a provincial Canadian city around the basis of a few historical buildings. He was proud, because he had never been anywhere else. McQuade felt a little pity and the shame of the richer, more sophisticated visitor who comes and complains.

Of the grass huts and corrugated-iron lavatories—McQuade noticed that someone's front porch was a large Canada Dry advertisement and someone else lived part of his life in an aged Chevrolet automobile—of this Costa said sadly, "We are ashamed of this. It will go. Two years, three perhaps."

Barney asked, a little too obviously, "Is that where the Africans live?" and McQuade was embarrassed, not wishing to offend Costa, who had been born here. But there was no need for Costa to answer, for the truth was self-evident: both Portuguese and Africans lived here together.

"It is a fine country," Costa insisted. "There is some foolishness up in the north, but that is not a pleasant area anyway. South and east, the territory is good for visitors. Animals, sport, scenery, fishing. Do you like fishing? None of your little trout here! Giant dolphin, which weigh two tons," he explained in genuine pleasure, leaning over the front seat to address a startled Barney, who did look like a girl on holiday.

Barney responded, "I didn't bring my glass jar!"

Costa laughed and went on to tell her about the black whales and cachalots and immense octopods, but McQuade was watching, identifying streets and major buildings so that if he had the chance to meet people the Portuguese did not wish him to talk to he could find them in a hurry.

"There are special reserves," Costa was telling Barney, "for the bustard, black antelope and the hippopotamus. Why not visit them? Take pictures. There is no need to go to South Africa."

"We're not on holiday," Barney disputed, a little confused.

Costa smiled and shrugged while still driving.

"What do you do? Stop our little war? A nice girl like you?"

"Is there a war?"

76

"It is more or less over. Nothing to worry about. The Bakongo cut a few heads off and left them on doorsteps, but that is all under control now. You must realize that they are very primitive people. I have been there," claimed Costa. "Two years ago. I attended a trial. It was very funny. This fellow had bought a wife, you see. He'd given four cows for her. A fortune! And she proved to be a very bad wife, so he cut off her head and took it back to her father and said, 'Look, old man, this is a very bad woman you sold to me. I want my cattle back.' Well, the old man wasn't so much worried by his daughter's decapitation but he wanted to hang on to those four cows. So there was an argument and then what we would call litigation. And I went to the trial. It went on for hours. It worried the chief very much. In the end he and his counselors decided that the woman had been bad and the husband must have his cows back. It was a very complicated trial, for the woman had had two daughters by other men before marriage, and this had value—for a girl child is not valueless, as some white people suppose, but has value in terms of an eventual purchase price. Ah, now you see the harbor. Isn't it splendid?"

It seemed to McQuade that Costa was either supremely innocent or far more subtle than he at first appeared. The propaganda effect of his primitive and no doubt true story was effective as far as Barney was concerned.

They were above the crescent of Vila Lobanda harbor. Just below were villas of some size and elegance, with pale blue walls, iron balconies and heavy red pannen tiles. There were thousands of small trees and here and there the brilliance of bougainvillaea and scarlet hibiscus. One could see a few old churches and a new white stone one, and above the south end of the harbor a fort which might have been taken from a child's box at Christmas. A few domed towers appeared.

"That is the Observatory," Costa pointed out, "and that long building, the Saint Alves of Luso College. I have found you a villa halfway down the slope. It is near the consulates and by a convent: convenient and quiet for you. It is called the Villa Amélia, but do not," he added with a laugh, "confuse it with the Lycée Amélia on the other side of the convent. That is an international school for girls. World famous. The girls are very pretty," Costa said with the same deadpan innocence. "From Belgium and France as well as

77

Portugal. It will be someone for you to talk to," he suggested to Barney. "The night life here is rather poor. Two cinemas and the dancing. But there are parties."

"Who lives in these large houses?" Barney asked.

"Some are foreign consulates," Costa answered. "Some belong to rich old men! Coffee and diamonds and oil make a few men rich! We have the occasional bullfight," he went on, like a tourist-agency representative who sees doubt. "No killing. It is as good as in Portugal. In fact, they bring the bulls by boat. You know that our young men have a sport in which they throw themselves on the horns of the bull and drag him down. It is proof of manhood."

"We do it in Texas," Barney countered tactlessly.

"Did you get to the Algarve while you were in Portugal?"

"Only to Lisbon," replied Barney, in this dialogue which was becoming individual.

"A pity. On the way back you must try. Hot empty sands which come up to the houses, and there are pine woods along the shore. Little lime-washed houses in the villages. You understand? The girls dance to the *corridinho*. You must persuade one of your friends to row a boat from Praia da Rocha to the caves called the Two Brothers. It will explain to you why the spirit of the *Discobradores* still exists in Portugal."

"It sounds marvelous," agreed Barney. "I envy you."

"Envy me?" questioned Costa.

"Going to such places."

"I have not been," said Costa. "My brother has and he told me about it."

He could not understand why Barney laughed. Eventually he asked, perplexed, "Am I not to believe my brother?"

"I guess so," acknowledged Barney, but she still shook in subdued amusement.

"Here is your villa, Mr. McQuade," announced Costa, turning into a short semicircular drive. "How do you like it? You see that it was once part of the convent. *That* is the Lycée. And the skyscraper across and down the road is, as you see, the Hotel Marromeu. This is our best hotel and all the Europeans go there. The food and wines are excellent. If you do not wish to cook for yourselves, what could be better?"

"Has a program been arranged?" McQuade asked.

78

"Certainly," acknowledged Costa. "That is my job. I have left it fluid and arranged nothing at all today, believing that you would not wish to do anything strenuous. You have a look around the town? Go to the island for a swim? But certainly, if you are insistent on this terrible American habit of working at once, I have arranged a meeting for you tomorrow morning with Mr. Tamagnini de Oliveira. He is the Minister of the Interior and the very *last* person I would wish to see!" Costa laughed frankly. "But the signal from Lisbon was that you wished to see him at once."

"There are two people in prison—"

Costa grimaced. "I doubt if you will see them," he said. "How can I explain it to you? The Portuguese attitude to political crimes is that they are much more serious than the ordinary because they are thought out in cold blood. A lover is rejected for another man and he is insane with grief and kills a girl. It could happen to any of us. But to sit and plan a bomb outrage days in advance—this is bad, it merits punishment. And there are some very funny fellows up north, you know, Mr. McQuade. We cannot operate the same open-air discussion about it as you can in America. They would laugh at our weakness. We are as fair as possible, but now and again it is necessary to frighten, to cool down the noisy fellow, the bombast. And what happens? He does not go to prison. He is not tortured. He is not hung. He just disappears off the face of the earth. Even I cannot tell you what happens. So there is much alarm and discussion. He has been buried alive, these Bakongo say, and they tremble. He has been imprisoned. He is being tortured. It worries them."

"And what do you think happens?" McQuade asked.

"Oh, I think he has been dropped to the sharks at Ponta das Uamba. But these things I tell you in confidence. Mr. de Oliveira is not a nice man. He has no happiness within him. I do not think you will like him. You must not talk in a casual friendly manner as I do now. All the consulates know of your arrival and no doubt will be in touch."

It was quite a small villa, seventeenth or eighteenth century, of ornate baroque stonework, and, as Costa had said, had been part of the convent immediately below. When Costa left them for the day, they inspected the building and chose their rooms. From the room on the first floor he selected as an office, McQuade looked out over

79

trees and shrubbery upon the worn domes, cupolas and lanterns of the *capilla real* of the convent. There were at least sixteen cupolas. It must, he considered, be a fantastic building inside. As he watched lizards creeping up the stone and a Christmas butterfly making its weightless way in the torrid heat of noon, a bell began to toll. It had a deep and beautiful note, but it was not a bell of the convent. A hundred yards away the excited voices of schoolgirls disturbed the sluggish air. The animated chatter was in French and very distantly McQuade heard that it concerned the prospects of food.

Ribowski, inevitably, was complaining. "There is no air conditioning." The temperature was over 90° Fahrenheit, but McQuade suspected that the absence of air conditioning was not a Portuguese irritant but simple lack of this particular comfort. Nothing could quite take away the pleasure of arrival and Barney's delighted cry, "I've got a balcony. Look at the *view!*" It was a view, McQuade guessed, which they would in time learn to hate, but not now.

They strolled to the Hotel Marromeu for lunch. Here there was air conditioning, as the sign told them: "Hotel Marromeu: Hygh Note of International Society. Bar, Restaurant, Air Conditioning, Dancing and Nyght Clube." They were to learn that "nyght clube" simply meant that the restaurant stayed open late and sometimes someone from Lisbon sang the *fado*.

The hotel was quite large, but gave the impression of being empty as a huge staff rushed around attending to the needs of two or three people. The bar and restaurant were on the second floor. It was noticeable that the staff were Portuguese. Boys, clerks, maids seen in empty bedrooms, all were Portuguese; there was one African sweeping a corridor. It indicated something, but McQuade did not know what.

In the small bar were four French or Belgians with three young women. They stared at the newcomers with a peculiar arrogance as if they were well established here. They were a little noisy and the women were tarted up out of all proportion to the place. Did they never look out of the window and observe the poverty, the Africans in rags lying on benches, the cripples too tired to beg, or breathe the smell of sewers and misery? It was obvious that they did not.

They were inclined to paw the men—three of whom were under forty, the other was perhaps forty-five or more—and the whole group viewed Marianne and Barney with amusement. None of them budged a hip to make room for the arrivals to order drinks, and the older man was talking to the barman in French and continued to do so in an effort to make these newcomers feel unwelcome —or so the irritated McQuade felt. Ribowski looked with his usual disapproval at the three noisy young women. Alferink stared with frank sensuality. The three younger men were in shirt sleeves. Faint smiles of superiority spread across their pale square Gallic faces under their sparse black hair, and they looked at their tarts with a kind of snobbery, as if to say, "*We* belong to Africa. My God, look at what the airplane has brought today!"

They were not diplomats and did not have to disguise their contempt when they learned that this group was from the United Nations.

The older Belgian ran out of conversation with the barman, who attended McQuade and asked him, "Are you staying in the hotel, *monsieur?*"

McQuade answered in Portuguese, "I am not staying and I am not a Frenchman." He ordered the drinks.

The older Belgian had evidently understood McQuade's Portuguese. "One wonders what business you are in, *monsieur,* if you are not staying here and have no wish to speak French, which is the language one has to use here if one is to do business."

"We are from New York."

"*That* is obvious, *monsieur!* Only an American would bring a nigger into this hotel."

"I shall speak Portuguese to do business in a Portuguese territory," said McQuade. "I presume you are Belgian?"

"Why do you presume so? You are, I may say, correct."

The others were listening intently, the women staring with that sophisticated indifference which recognizes the bumpkins of the world and wonders how they got in here—how tedious it is to be involved in argument with them!

McQuade said evenly, "Only a Belgian would talk with such gross ill manners on racial issues."

"I am a realist, *monsieur,* not a lout. Your black friend can in

81

theory enter here, but in terms of realism he will be uncomfortable. I presume you are an idealist?"

"We are members of an idealistic organization."

"The Salvation Army perhaps?"

"No. The United Nations."

"That is terrible, *monsieur*. I say so with honesty. Have you not done enough damage farther north?"

He referred to the Belgian Congo, and there was some justification in his misgivings.

But McQuade countered, "I think there are two sides to that long story."

The Belgian shrugged. "I only heard the one. But I happened to be living there. Of course that is of small interest to an idealist."

"It must have been very unpleasant," said McQuade in an effort to be reasonable.

"No. Not unpleasant. Merely stupid," the Belgian declared. "People interfering who did not know what they were doing and had not the power to do it anyway."

McQuade said calmly—he was not going to be ruffled by this fat Belgian businessman, with his entourage of tarts—"In a situation of immorality the moralist is naturally not welcome."

"I am sure you know all about it," the Belgian said. "On paper . . ." He turned his back on McQuade and said in French, "I hate these idealists."

The girls sniggered obediently and looked with cold, blank eyes at McQuade.

McQuade was angry, and he, too, spoke in French, addressing a bewildered Asare Johnson. "It is a pity we have to eat with provincial Belgians and their trollops, but it will be useful in terms of disagreeable experience."

Very faintly one girl smiled.

Marianne asked in her deafening American accent, "What do you think they do? Sell beads to the natives?"

"I think they make money out of other people's misery," said McQuade.

He was being as rude as he could be—in fact, childishly rude—but the Belgians did not take up his challenge. Their party went to the dining room and were still in a far corner of it when McQuade and the others entered.

82

There were only twelve diners in the dining room and seven waiters, but a quarter of an hour passed before any waiter came to their table. When one did, he looked very uncomfortable and said, "I regret we cannot serve colored persons."

Asare Johnson said wretchedly, "I will go back to the villa."

"Like hell you will!" protested McQuade. He said to the waiter, changing from French to Portuguese, "You know the law?"

"Yes, *monsieur.*"

"Don't call me *monsieur!*"

"No, *monsieur.*"

"The law says that *all* are equal. Serve us at once or I shall fetch the police."

"Yes, *monsieur.* It was only that the other guests said it would be disagreeable."

From sixty feet away the Belgians smiled.

McQuade counseled earnestly to Johnson: "Don't hold this against the Portuguese. It is a discomfort contrived by the Belgians. As far as the Portuguese are concerned there's no color bar except money. It's probably an effective color bar, but it's the only one."

Asare struggled out of a mood of depression in which his appetite had suffered and acknowledged, "I understand all the implications, Mr. McQuade. I was brought up on them. The English were a little more good-humored, that's all. There is a lot to be said for their hypocrisy."

Lunch took an hour and a half in an empty dining room.

Later in the afternoon they had a walk around Vila Lobanda. The *cassimbo* had long since lifted and the town was less depressing in the sun. The thermometer still stood at about 90°, but it was, on this first day, pleasant after the winter temperature of New York.

In a ninety-minute stroll along the crescent of the harbor and back among the main streets behind it, it was possible to play a grim guessing game. It was surprising how many of the small things of interest observed were relevant to a UN inquiry on racial status, work conditions, health of the people and so on.

From a distance the bay of Vila Lobanda was beautiful, the Avenue Manuel de Arriaga a fine crescent of traditional seventeenth-century Portuguese buildings mixed with colorful, tall semisky-scrapers of imaginative design. But at closer range the city was dirty. There were the scents of old walls, dust and urine. Rats ran along the sand where Barney proposed swimming sometime. On dusty red laterite plots between buildings, Africans in rags slept in the full sun, a few with cloths over their faces. The colorful but shabby cafes everywhere had their quota of Portuguese, but no African sat down. Nor did any African serve coffee or beer. This was a sign, not precisely of racial discrimination but of poverty: whatever the jobs were that had a status lower than waiter, *those* were for the Africans. They removed the garbage at four o'clock each morning and worked in gangs on the railways and roads.

Among both Africans and Portuguese there was a great deal of hawking, spitting and coughing. It was neither dirtiness nor contempt, but the symptoms of tuberculosis. Other diseases were there to see. There was an alarming number of cripples. A girl in a pink dress, with a beautiful black face but legs useless from the knees down, crawled about the pavements, talking to herself, but did not beg. A boy leaned against a wall. His right leg was withered into a grotesque mess. Others were acutely bandy, the sign of childhood rickets neglected. In the three miles that they walked they encountered two midgets and a madman. The madman stood on the pavement by a cafe, a black man in filthy rags, who marched up and down, parodying soldiers. The waiters stood and smiled and the clients ignored him. After a while he grew angry and began to throw things at the tables. McQuade waited in apprehension for violence or arrest, but still no one took any notice. Someone finally threw a coin and he went away.

As the afternoon faltered the shoeshine boys and vendors of lottery tickets ran about the pavements. It was a sure sign of poverty when a town was full of shoeshine boys—and a grim irony that poor Portuguese, wearing cracked black shoes that were very little better than rubbish, should sit down and have the creased black leather polished. It was the blind giving pittance to the blind.

The flamingos stood on the anchored police speedboats and waited perhaps for the next rush of sewage into the harbor. Three soldiers, one with a leg missing and another without an arm, sat looking at the sea, the vehicles and the girls. On the sea a few small, very old fishing boats were moving off, the African crews roaring with laughter. As in all hot countries the cars were driven

84

to the limit of tires and gears. The traffic density was negligible compared with Manhattan, but whenever McQuade remembered Vila Lobanda his acoustic memory was to be of the howling shriek of tires in the day, and cocks that didn't sleep and the melancholy note of ships' sirens in the night. Little did the drivers of the Italian, Japanese and German sedans know how limited was the safety factor of adhesion—if they ever tried the same manner of driving on a wet road they would soon be in disaster.

As for the girls, they came out of offices at half past five and hurried along the avenue. The soldiers stared, but the girls ignored them. They were attractive, many of them, and, as in Lisbon, gave an impression of old-fashioned dignity that was a change from the brash, sexy self-assurance found in New York. Among them walked the clerks, and some of these, McQuade noted, were black. On the other side of the road, by the sea and the rats, as if in some class arrangement, the long-legged African girls moved with their high-hipped stride, in colorful shabby dresses, their bare feet in the dust, baskets on their heads. It was curious that in Africa the female human had so small a status, for she was the most gracious thing that moved.

Trucks loaded with salt raced along the harbor, the black workers cheering themselves, hanging on recklessly as if they knew life was cheap. Sitting at a cafe near a crossroads, McQuade saw a policeman halt the traffic on one road so that a convoy of jeeps could cross. He counted the number of these Portuguese Army vehicles. One hundred and twenty-three jeeps and two heavy trucks crossed the junction. All were full of soldiers armed with machine guns. The soldiers laughed and cheered. A few people waved from the pavement, but the Africans meandering about just stopped and stared.

In a small park the butterflies fluttered like paper darts and a hornet as big as a sore thumb buzzed around. On palm leaves that bent to the ground were scratched hearts and initials. Love existed here somewhere—tenderness in the heat and stink of sewage, the muzzled dogs that ran about, the kids (black, white and brown) who played on a dusty plot, and the shabby shops that had nothing in them but pornography and cheap watches and the labels of phonograph records.

85

Down by the docks the African and Portuguese women haggled over fish and fresh fruit and vegetables in a two-story modern market. There were notices on a wall about a motor race: the International Grand Prix of Angolique, to be held in three weeks. Traffic would be diverted. Opposite the harbor was Lobanda Island, palm fringed, with white sands, like a poster in Cook's, with restaurants and weekend bungalows among eucalyptus groves. On the shore a few naked African children shrieked and played and older Africans mended fishing nets. A convoy of Army trucks crossed the causeway to the island, and after a while scores of soldiers began to bathe.

The descending sun gleamed violently on the misty waters of the harbor. The *cassimbo* rolled in like a sour mood. In a while dusk came and the blue crescent of streetlamps came on; by the cranes the few merchant ships were illuminated. Hot air blew the smells of pepper and fats and sewage out of the jigsaw of streets and bent the tall romantic coconut trees. The palm leaves rustled against each other in this evening breeze like newspaper scratching its way along a suburban pavement, and, as if reminded, the small boys came around like ants with evening papers for the people, half of whom were illiterate.

After the unpleasantness at lunchtime, none of McQuade's group were anxious to eat at the Hotel Marromeu, even though it was clean and the food good. Ribowski did not wish to eat at all, and Asare Johnson and Barney had their separate plan, but the remainder decided to eat in a restaurant run by a Greek.

It was on the causeway to the island. McQuade strolled in the hot night air with Ekelund, de la Plaza and Alferink. Plenty of people were about and it was noticeable that, despite the hundreds of deaths in this town sixteen weeks earlier, there was no atmosphere of tension at all. There was obviously very little to do in the place at night, but the people strolling about—Portuguese and African—were as full of laughter and excitement as people going to a party.

There were twelve tables in the restaurant, five of them occupied. It was pleasant and clean and there was a great hoo-ha of welcome by the proprietor. The waiters here were all Africans and they rushed about in attendance, bringing bread, wine, napkins,

86

whatever was needed. Inevitably, the Greek proprietor spoke English and had been to Chicago. "I had three places there. Big restaurants. Did you ever get to Chicago?"

De la Plaza had been there and now became involved in a polite series of lies in which he assured the Greek that he had indeed been to one of his restaurants. It became a little comic since the Greek had left Chicago in 1957 and de la Plaza had spent precisely two days in the city in 1962.

They were stared at by the Portuguese at the other tables and received smiles and nods. They were eating the sweet pastries when two African girls entered the restaurant. They were dressed in European style and were obviously clerks in Government House. They looked very anxious and sat near to the door.

The Greek was derisive.

"See how brave they are!"

He was assuming that these visitors from America would hold black people in contempt.

"Ready to bolt! What are they trying to prove? I did not stand for it in Chicago. Look at the one fool. She wears glasses. Have you noticed the way these stupid Africans will wear glasses if it blinds them. Or carry a briefcase—look, she has one!—or a walking stick. It makes them look like intellectuals!"

The Greek roared with laughter.

"I can't throw them out," he said. "It is the Portuguese law that they are equal." He winked. "Nor can my waiters. But you watch! In forty seconds they will be gone. My boys do not want them here."

They looked like nice quiet girls, and McQuade worried as to what would happen in the next few seconds. He loathed the Greek for his assumptions. It was another restaurant they wouldn't wish to return to!

The Greek walked over to a waiter and this African disappeared for a few minutes. The African girl with glasses on had lit a cigarette. The other one's fingers played around a wineglass nervously. They waited for trouble, too frightened now to get up and leave.

Four waiters advanced on the girls, who positively shrank into their chairs with fear. The waiters tipped the girls' chairs backwards and began to fondle their legs. Then as they shrieked the

87

waiters put hands into their blouses and handled their breasts. The girls knocked over a table in an effort to scramble out of the place. In seconds they had gone. The waiters turned to smile, almost as if they expected applause.

This had been done by black men to black women in front of white people. Why? Why? How did one put *that* into a UN report. McQuade was shaken and disgusted.

The Greek, on the other hand, was pleased. He had proved his point. "You see? They leave!"

McQuade asked, "Why did the waiters want them out?"

The Greek was a little puzzled, because surely if it was obvious to himself and the Portuguese who had resumed eating with unimpaired appetite, why was it not self-evident to this American?

"My boys know that you do not want them in here. The girls will not leave tips. You will."

There was only one way to show displeasure and this was the one the UN group used—they left no tips at all. The waiters were obviously astonished; they couldn't believe it; it would be quite ten minutes before they were sure it was so and became angry.

It was only eight o'clock, but there was nothing to do but return to the Villa Amélia. The strain of the long journey still left them slightly dazed. After a while McQuade went to his bedroom and began a letter to Kristan: "Dearest Other Half of Me, I am a long way from you now, but my heart is near . . ." His feet were tired and there was a stone in his left shoe. He kicked the shoes off and was startled to find that it was not a stone but a piece of paper. It seemed completely unreal. But there it was, and he knew it had been pushed into the shoe by the one very persistent shoeshine boy to whom he had surrendered in the afternoon. The handwritten message was, incredibly, in English: "2 km. past Fort Eduardo, road to Zeira, LHS, track to cashew plantation. ½ km. down, 11 P.M. tomorrow. One plenty. You are followed."

An hour later, in bed but still awake and listening to the sea, he was startled by the telephone ringing in his office. He had to answer —it could be anyone in the world. In the long first-floor corridor he encountered Mr. de la Plaza. "I'll see to it," McQuade said. The caller asked for Mr. Regio. Ten minutes later someone else rang, also asking for Mr. Regio. McQuade was a little suspicious. Was this a Portuguese irritant to keep them awake all night?

He was returning to his bedroom when Barney and Asare Johnson came into the villa and up the stairs.

Asare said, as if an explanation had been requested, "There was some trouble in the ballroom. It was all right in the restaurant, but not the ballroom. No blacks."

"I keep telling you," Barney said, obviously picking up an argument that had been going on all night, "that it was a private party."

"Oh, yes, indeed. Exclusive."

"He doesn't believe me, so what the hell?" Barney said to Mc-Quade in exasperation. "He thinks I'm being polite. *Me!* And so we went to an open-air movie," she followed up, as if she, too, had to justify something. She giggled about this other half of the evening and told McQuade, "And that was just *crazy* because it was an Indian film with long significant silences and there were bats flying all over the place. These two lovers were in a clinch and a bat flew into the projector. I spent half the time hiding behind the seat in front!"

The telephone rang again at one o'clock and again at two, the plea for Mr. Regio, the most popular man in Vila Lobanda. It was intended as an irritant all right. In the very early morning road drills began work right outside the villa, and this must have been intentional, too, although no one would ever admit it. It was absurd, childish, but effective, for they all slept badly.

In the morning McQuade told the others about the note. As to be expected, Ekelund considered it an improper approach which should be ignored. But McQuade had every intention of going to that track by a cashew farm. "While we see the Minister this morning," he instructed Barney, "go and buy a bicycle. And a street map of the town." A bicycle would be a silent form of transport in the dark—and one easily hidden from Mr. Costa.

The uneasy secret of the note touched him with anxiety now and again during the day—starting with breakfast, when the Belgian women stared across the dining room of the Hotel Marromeu almost as if they'd heard his unkind thoughts of the night before. He was restless knowing that somewhere, only a few miles away, someone wanted to talk to him so badly that he was prepared to risk his life. The responsibility for that other unknown life caused the omelet and coffee to lie uneasily on McQuade's queasy stomach.

They had a working lunch with Mr. Tamagnini de Oliveira and some of his officers in Government House. It was as near to refusing to see them at all as Mr. de Oliveira could get. Throughout the meal the atmosphere was that of an important man with many things to do who has surrendered two hours to accommodate people who were by definition liars, criminals, anxious only to harm Portugal.

Government House was a very small building from which to control not only Vila Lobanda but the entire territory of Angolique. It was in fact merely a handsome large villa set in four or five acres of luxurious gardens and surrounded by a stone wall along which creepers grew. African paratroopers with fixed bayonets guarded the wrought-iron gate, but they did so in a fairly leisurely attitude, as if nothing serious was going to happen again here. There was a private house across the road which had been turned into a police station for the particular district, which was just behind the hill on which stood the fort.

Tamagnini de Oliveira was very small except for a large head and an unpleasantly big nose. His hair was thinning and gray, and his pink complexion, heavily lined, could have been that of any European nationality. He could have been German, Czech, or even English, for he had blue eyes and wore a gray pinstriped suit. He looked like a man with a heart of stone. There was obviously no love or humor in him, only efficiency. His officers—who were not introduced, a calculated rudeness, and who may have been advisers but were more likely secret police—were large, easy-going men with human frailties written upon their faces. All four of them paid breathless, serious attention to every word the Minister of the Interior uttered and examined the members of the subcommittee with deliberate care and no embarrassment, as if it was part of their job to remember these faces.

It was heavy going and not likely to be successful, for if anyone was put into prison, or was shot, or "disappeared" or was arrested for political reasons, the responsibility was Oliveira's, and he clearly did not have the resilience of American or Canadian police chiefs; no half admissions of anything were likely. He examined his wristwatch as if his time had an exact value. Out of a window McQuade saw the two sentries in their hot camouflage uniforms checking an occasional car. Oliveira was the first Portuguese whom McQuade actively disliked. Whether he was subtle or not was impossible to tell through the syrup of translations in both directions —for McQuade was not admitting yet to a knowledge of Portuguese.

The minister finally approached relevant matters:

"The stated objective of the Portuguese has always been to create a multiracial society here as the only lasting solution to the human and economic problems. As the Prime Minister said some time ago, those who intend to dedicate themselves to the job of emancipating Portuguese Africa come too late, for the task has already been done. That unity, already achieved, does not allow transfers, cession or abandonment. The juridical figures of the plebiscite, the referendum and autodetermination do not fit into its structure either."

McQuade could not allow this to pass unchallenged.

"Am I to understand that you consider the emancipation satisfactory and complete?"

Mr. Costa translated—accurately, McQuade was pleased to note. And the Minister of the Interior answered, "Some expression of African aspirations was allowed as far back as the 1920s and a number of indigenous associations were recognized by Portugal here."

"Would you say, Mr. Minister, that nationalist activity is allowed currently?"

"Indigenous persons occupy posts in the Government, Mr. Chairman. Career officials have for long been recruited from the overseas territories as well as from Portugal herself—providing they are either Portuguese by birth or have attained the status of *assimilado*. Entry locally is by qualifying examination."

"Would you say that it is easy for a person to become an *assimilado*, Mr. Minister?"

"It is not difficult, providing they are not in conflict with the law or their employers."

"And is it possible for such *assimilados* to rise to or beyond, say,

91

the rank of *chef de posto?* We were informed that by custom and practice senior posts are held by Portuguese."

"I think you are misinformed, Mr. Chairman."

"Perhaps, Mr. Minister, you could give me the names of some persons of *assimilado* status who hold senior posts. We would like to talk to them. It would prevent prejudice."

"I find your request offensive," said the minister.

"Come, Mr. Minister, remove my prejudices. Let me talk to the Army. Is there, perhaps, an *assimilado* of rank higher than lance corporal?"

"You will find, Mr. Chairman, in spite of your obvious briefing from prejudiced parties, that 40 per cent of administration officials are nonwhites. Lack of education holds them back a little, but there is no racial discrimination as in Harlem."

Gregorio de la Plaza now changed the subject—although not much.

"Mr. Minister, since we are being frank, let me ask you about the disturbances in Vila Lobanda some months ago. We were informed —whether with prejudice or not is what we are here to find out— that preemptive actions were applied to areas where there had been no threat to the European population. 'Plots' would be discovered, in panic perhaps, and protection requested, and Army patrols would give the examples of summary executions. Many abuses were committed, it is said, by functionaries no longer subject to criminal trial."

Oliveira said in irritation to the interpreter, "Tell him that such few abuses as existed were dealt with and this was acknowledged publicly. Perhaps the gentleman has been working backward from those acknowledgments of the truth to a position in which his organization and himself feel morally superior. The Minister for Overseas Boundaries has made it clear that the local authorities must commit no injustices and that the just must not suffer."

This was duly translated.

De la Plaza countered in equal temper, "Representations were, we understand, made by many Portuguese civilians and even some administrators—one of rather high rank—who did not subscribe to terror to end abuses. These pleas were ignored."

"I know of no such pleas," said the Minister of the Interior. "And I would be the first to know of them."

"If we hear of any we will draw them to your attention," said de la Plaza, red in the face.

The Minister shrugged and looked at his wristwatch. His officials stared like stone statues.

Theo Alferink continued the discussion: "This would be, I presume, why the plea of the United Nations to the Portuguese authorities to stop repression was regarded as 'theatrical' and 'offensive to a sovereign state'?"

The Minister presumed the question to be without sarcasm and answered literally, "Yes, that is so."

McQuade moved the dialogue on to the subject of prisons.

"Were many persons arrested during the disturbances, Mr. Minister?"

"A few hundred," acknowledged de Oliveira. "And a few perhaps in error, who have since been released."

"Do you still hold Mr. Andrade and Mr. Maúa?"

The minister looked at one of the officers, who nodded.

"Can I ask why?"

The official told his minister what the crimes were alleged to be, and the minister said to McQuade via Costa, "Sabotage, corruption, confidence trickery and incitement to violence."

"Would it be coincidental that these two men are leaders of a political party?"

The minister said after thinking about it, "A leader naturally leads, whether in opposition or not. These two were anxious to lead masses of fools to destruction."

"Are they likely to be released soon?"

Again the conference of faces, and a head shake by the policeman or whatever he was. The Minister of the Interior shook his head. He also reexamined his wristwatch.

"Dr. Pessanha in Lisbon said I might talk to them in prison."

"That is impossible."

"You cannot give authority?"

"Permission has to come from Lisbon."

"Dr. Pessanha said he did not know of or deal with individuals, but in principle I could see them. I have, however, to have your sanction."

"With such persons I have to have Lisbon's authority," said Oliveira with finality.

93

"At least I know they *are* prisoners," McQuade pointed out sourly, and the minister flushed when this was translated.

"I will seek permission on your behalf," he said, but McQuade knew that he would hear no more of the matter.

He decided to finish the conversations unpleasantly, since no one was fooling anyone and Oliveira was going to concede nothing.

"Is it possible for us to travel beyond the area of the city?" he asked, for that at present was their limitation, as Costa had explained earlier in the morning.

"It is not necessary," said the minister. "All the facts can be given to you here in Vila Lobanda."

"I take it, Mr. Minister, that the area—a very large area—of Angolique is unsafe except Vila Lobanda and that you are concerned for our welfare?"

The Minister repeated, "All the information is here in the capital, Vila Lobanda."

"And suppose I ask you to give us permission to tour the other parts of Angolique? Are you going to refuse us? Are you so ashamed of Portugal's achievements in Angolique that you wish only to prove them on paper?"

This was brutally rude, but effective.

Oliveira couldn't think of a thing to say, but after a while he answered, "If it contributes to the pleasures of your stay I am, of course, the authority who can grant you the necessary licenses to visit certain reserves for hunting."

"I have not come to hunt crocodiles, Mr. Minister."

"What, then, do you hunt?"

"The truth."

"The truth, Mr. Chairman, is that I limit you to the city because of the prejudices with which you arrive. Only the Governor General can change my mind. It is true also that on our borders there are many Frenchmen, Belgians, Rhodesians and others who have gotten into the habit of shooting these black people for whom you are so concerned. It is a sport for them, begun in Algeria and the Congo. They are ready with the kind of gossip you evidently wish to hear. There are others—Chinese, Russians, Cubans, Ghanaians and adventurers who thrive on arms and death—who retire to safety over indifferently guarded borders on the other side. It is Portugal's problem to deal with them and it is *we* who have the

94

right—which in pride and dignity we do not use—to claim your sympathy, not bank robbers and schoolteachers with a grievance and a sense of power. Have you yet seen these absurd little politicians? They eat with their great big mouths hanging open so that you can see what and how much they eat at one time! Have you seen them playing politics? They run like rabbits and then complain about Portuguese atrocities. An American television team was allowed in some months back to film these atrocities. *We* allowed them in. After a while they grew tired of not finding any and hired a few boats and Africans from a trader to row about in miserable disarray. I'm sure it looked fine on the TV screen. But dignity and truth? I hardly think so, Mr. Chairman."

McQuade said as calmly as he could, "I am not disputing that there are fools in a free society, Mr. Minister. They have the freedom to be foolish. And since the African does not have the opportunity of sitting in restaurants to observe his betters using their toothpicks, we cannot expect him to eat in the style of an epicure. I am sure, of course, that Portuguese atrocities—if they exist—are carried out in a gentlemanly manner."

The minister stood up. His hard eyes looked at McQuade and despite his tiny stature he was formidable. "I have work to do," he claimed. "You must excuse me from this dialogue."

Mr. Costa took the party back to the Villa Amélia. It was a hot afternoon and the interior of the Fiat estate car was like an oven.

"As I told you," Costa said, "the minister is not a nice man to talk to. But he is strong."

"I'm sure he's efficient," McQuade agreed.

"Did you sleep well? How do you like the food at the Marromeu? Have you been to the island for a swim yet? You must do these things before you become too involved in work."

McQuade was not sure he even wanted to swim or sail a hired boat. He was aware of a different atmosphere, the beginnings of isolation from the sea, the small groups down by the Naval Club, sitting on the lawn drinking fruit juice, or driving sports cars, knowing where they were going and wanting to go there. Somewhere in this attractive, dirty old city were the prisons and beatings and the injustices, the "masses of fools anxious to be led to destruction."

On the lawn of the Hotel Marromeu someone waved as the Fiat

went by to the villa. It was a girl in a swimsuit. When they had parked the car they strolled across to her, conscious of failure in themselves, nothing to do with the rest of the day except surrender to the atmosphere of pleasure which they did not seek.

Barney looked superb in her swimsuit—large, shapely and very alive. Asare Johnson was with her—he had not been to see de Oliveira—and was upset. The young Belgians talked and laughed and dived into the water of the pool, a hundred feet away, but not before they'd taken a final look, their minds scratching and fondling vicariously. Two of the young Belgian women sat under a striped shade, hot with hatred behind sunglasses.

"It is not nice, the way these men stare and snigger," Asare complained. "It is as if I am not here and they can insult safely. For I am a black man and I can't start trouble, only receive it. And I do not wish to get this subcommittee into disgrace."

Costa looked anxious. Barney, however, objected, "Don't fuss. I haven't said anything, have I? And it is I who am supposed to have been insulted."

They sat in the sun and had cold drinks. Costa suggested, "You must become a member of the Naval Club. That is your answer. There you can swim and play tennis without this indignity."

"Sounds like a good idea," Barney agreed.

They were in effect waiting again for Costa to leave. He was a pleasant man and eager for them to like Vila Lobanda. McQuade felt he ought to ask him to dinner—his wife, too, if he had one—and it was difficult to harden the heart and not do so. But in his mind was the anxiety of tonight's probable encounter. And he had an idea—clumsy, obvious, but perhaps effective—as to how to get rid of Mr. Costa altogether for long periods of the day. Meanwhile he talked sympathetically to Johnson.

"Why aren't you married, Asare?"

"What's that got to do with anything?"

"You're in your thirties, educated, tall, and so on."

"You know why, Mr. McQuade. Because I had a long fight to get into politics and become such as I am."

"You must be strong willed to work that hard and long without noticing that girls existed!"

Johnson laughed. "Well, I have not been quite so monastic as all *that!*"

96

After half an hour Costa suggested items for future examination and left them for the day.

Ekelund asked in his serious way, "What are we going to *do?* We can't just have a holiday. If we can't interview Andrade or Maúa or see the Governor General or move more than five miles. . . ."

"Costa has arranged a tour of some local industry, including the docks in Porto Girassol fifty miles down the coast. That will be a start."

"This is doing what the Portuguese suggest," Ekelund objected. "We are not here on a guided tour. We represent a hundred and seventeen nations who want to know—"

"Yes, we are aware of that," McQuade agreed. "But for the moment we have to play it by ear. And you forget that I am meeting someone tonight. Did you buy that bicycle, Barney, and the map?"

"Yes, Mr. McQuade. It's a woman's bicycle but a big one."

"What is the use of it?" de la Plaza argued. "We cannot ever be rid of Costa."

"What do you think, Barney?"

"About what, Mr. McQuade?"

"About joining the Naval Club, suggesting to Mr. Costa how nice it would be to sail in a little boat if you knew how! And how dull these members of the subcommittee are! And how you long for a game of tennis and dinner on the island."

"I get the picture, Mr. McQuade! I hope UNO does not expect me to suffer a fate more pleasant than death!"

"I think," said McQuade, "that you will find Mr. Costa an agreeable and honorable companion. You, too, must play it by ear. A dinner that takes two hours of an evening, or an afternoon's tennis or sailing might keep Mr. Costa out of the way while we meet people the minister would like to hear about."

Johnson objected, "It would subject her to possible indignity."

De la Plaza, too, argued against it: "It's ridiculous that a subcommittee of the United Nations—"

"Of course!" agreed McQuade. "It is not constitutional politics. And that is why it might be successful for a time. But it is for Barney to decide."

"I will do what I can," Barney said. "He seemed to like me," she added self-consciously.

Alferink said thoughtfully, "Mr. Costa does not, presumably,

97

work a twenty-four-hour day. I wonder if we are watched or followed when he is not on duty?"

McQuade looked around at the lawns and tables under sunshades of the Hotel Marromeu and saw people in groups, the Belgian girls on the edge of the swimming pool, two waiters with trays, no one alone.

He studied the map that evening and saw where he had to go. It was not far on a bicycle. At ten-thirty he climbed over the wall into the grounds of the convent and others handed the bicycle to him. McQuade carried the machine to an opposite wall beyond which was a minor street.

There was little traffic. He had not ridden a bicycle for many years and it felt strange and rather pleasant. Barney hadn't thought of a lamp, but in the strong light of the stars and the streetlamps it only mattered in terms of policemen.

Reaching more crowded streets he felt conspicuous, and certainly an explanation would be difficult to offer. He had a bad moment passing a group of soldiers, but they laughed in the indifference of alcohol and didn't stop him. The town was on a slope, with the villa about halfway up. Experience didn't quite work out in terms of the map and he felt a nibble of panic at the considerable distance he was covering. Now he came into a slum area. A bony dog snapped at him and he kicked at it in alarm. He was conscious of a change of road surface and dust rising in his face. He heard a train shunting and a phonograph wailing sadness. It was an area of slum dwellings—some built of mud, others of packing cases from the docks, parts of old automobiles, slats of wood, old pipes found or stolen, all covered with the mud of the street dried in the African sun. It was not an area for black people. The poor of the world clung together and many of the people were from the slums of Lisbon and Oporto. This was their bright new world—a mud shack, the dust and the sunshine to insult them. The richer expatriates had gone to Brazil and Venezuela. These people were a long way from the hard mind of the Minister of the Interior. McQuade acknowledged that he must pity and work for them, too, and if there was violence, they must not become victims.

It was a long ride to the Fort Eduardo. McQuade's legs were shaky from the unaccustomed exercise. But now he was out of the town, and the main road was empty and the lights of Vila Lobanda became a mere glow in the sky. The dust was in his teeth. It was already after eleven o'clock. He would be tired tomorrow.

He found the track to the cashew farm and walked down it, stumbling a few times. When he stopped, the silence was tremendous. In front of him Africa stretched for two thousand miles. There wasn't a town for seven hundred.

McQuade was hot from cycling and moved uncomfortably to adjust the stickiness of clothes. The air was damp and hot with the smell of decay. His ears seemed to throb in the huge spatial quiet. Above, the stars shone with startling size. Were these the stars of the Southern Hemisphere? He wasn't sure. His breathing was somewhat poor and he realized that he had a cold. It was ridiculous, having a cold in the middle of Africa, but he had noticed that Marianne and, inevitably, Ribowski, also had heavy head colds earlier in the day.

His watch could be heard ticking and some way off frogs began to croak, startling him. In the silence a noise concussed the air miles away so that his ears again pulsed under unknown pressures. The noise was mechanical and not one he understood. It came from nowhere, and his heart thumped, ready with terror. He remembered a night in Italy, exhausted (how one recalled war in terms of exhaustion), the third night of a flap, and in this darkness came the squeaks of enemy armor and a mental, unwelcome deduction that they were surrounded. Quiet movements in the dark with fuel cans. In vain. As they'd roared their tanks into life just before dawn, there, confronting them, had been a line of Tigers. Flames and noise and the thick smoke of flaming fuel and the smell of burned humans . . . The sound in Africa twenty-two years later rumbled the earth so that McQuade flinched with the expectation of gunfire.

And then the train went by toward Vila Lobanda. Half a mile away McQuade saw the lit-up dining car and people's faces, and a voice said, causing him to go cold in shock, "Who are you?"—a voice speaking English two yards away—and he heard a click of a rifle bolt and the movement of feet, and, when the train had gone in a long wail of siren, became conscious of several people, a faint smell of humans, indeed, the sweet smell of the colored man.

He said, "You know who I am."

"The American?"

"Canadian."

"Is there anyone else?"

"No. I came on a bicycle."

Another voice spoke in a language McQuade did not know.

The first voice continued in English.

"I am glad you came. I am Manuel Bajune. I was a school-teacher in Porto Girassol. A long time ago I was in London. If you go there you must give my warm regards to Mr. Swinnerton at the LSE."

"What is the LSE?"

"The London School of Economics," said Bajune, evidently surprised that McQuade didn't know. "I have reason to be grateful to the LSE. Many people in Africa have, for we were taught how to think politically. We acquired the jargon of the political battlefield."

"My name is McQuade. I have come to Angolique with others to collect evidence for the United Nations."

"And what will the United Nations do with this evidence?" asked Bajune. "Will there be a boycott of Portugal?"

"It depends on the evidence," McQuade said. "You will understand that most of our pressures are moral and reflect world opinion."

"I know this, but it is hard to bear," acknowledged Bajune. "Others do not understand it and want some killing. As a school-teacher I know, I *know* what this continent needs." He sniffed in the darkness. Perhaps he, too, had a cold. "It needs education."

The other voice interrupted in excitement.

Bajune said, "He talks about a column we ambushed forty miles north. We have more control in the north, Mr. McQuade. Camps and even hopes one day of an airfield. We ambushed this column of trucks full of soldiers on the way to kill us. Then, hours later, they came back for their dead—for the Portuguese don't leave them, being good Catholics—and we killed many more."

You can play that trick once too often, McQuade thought.

"The priests have friendly faces and say they love us," Bajune said now with anger. "But someone betrayed part of our organiza-

100

tion three months ago and I wonder if they love fellow Catholics and white men more than the oppressed."

"Would you say the disturbances in Vila Lobanda were the work of foreigners? This is what the Portuguese officials say."

"No. I think these were a spontaneous explosion, although there are foreigners in the north and east. We have many grievances," said Bajune. "Some have even been admitted by the Portuguese. Does not that indicate the validity of the others?"

"What are the aims of the Tando Party?"

"Simple," replied Bajune. "The total independence of Angolique from Portuguese control. We wish for an autonomous state which fulfills the needs of the people."

"This is representative of violence, inevitably," argued Mc-Quade.

"What do you want us to do? Wait?"

"Violence becomes a habit when it has been seen to obtain results."

"You are posing the problems of a situation which does not and may not exist."

"You realize that in Vila Lobanda there are many Portuguese who are as poor as any African citizen? I have seen many today. I trust they will not become the victims of vengeance? Are there no Portuguese you can appeal to? I have heard there are many liberals. I have even heard that the former Governor General was sympathetic to your plight and this was why he was transferred."

"He was not transferred, Mr. McQuade. He was accused of corruption because he admitted sympathies with the *indigena*. He has disappeared. What does that mean? You and I know it may mean anything. It is rumored that he is in Lisbon, in Brazzaville, in Madrid, dead, in prison. Colonel Unguanda is, I believe, in Africa. I have hopes that he is alive. He made the authorities very angry when he said that no acknowledgment is made of our language in an effort to pretend either that we don't exist or that we are Portuguese. Bantu is taught at the colonial school in Lisbon, but soon forgotten by the officials once they receive their appointments, for they see that no negotiations with the Africans are likely or intended. Then Colonel Unguanda protested on our behalf about the new settlers' indifference to our needs, especially in the coffee-growing regions in the north. For they seize the land near the road, depriving the *indigena* of his traditional holdings and obliging him to move into the bush. And bribery takes care of the law."

Afar, headlights shone on the main road and passed across the faces of Bajune and the two men who were with him. He was, unexpectedly and in contradiction to his voice, small and slight, and he wore the large round spectacles popular in Africa among colored people.

"Time passes," commented Bajune. "You must depart, Mr. McQuade. You mentioned friends. I was a schoolteacher. Have you met the Minister of Education? He is a liberal with a warm heart. Talk to him, but with care if others are near."

McQuade cycled back. He was confused as he reentered the city despite reference to the map, and it was one o'clock when he climbed over the convent wall. Some lights were still on in the villa and he presumed that the others had stayed up in anxiety for his return.

He was quite near the villa, approaching in silence, when he saw that Barney and Asare were standing on the terrace. Their voices had the urgency of a quarrel or a plea rejected, and McQuade made a noise deliberately to break their privacy.

Inside the villa Alferink and de la Plaza were still up and stared at McQuade in astonishment. He and the bicycle were covered with red dust. His face was bitten by insects.

He brushed the dust off and washed, and realized how tired he was. He told his companions what had happened and afterward, too tired to move, sat in a chair drinking some coffee which Barney made.

Asare said, "Goodnight, Barney; goodnight, Mr. McQuade," and went slowly upstairs like someone who wanted to stay but couldn't find the excuse.

Barney was inclined to linger. She leaned on a desk as if waiting for comment or criticism, or as one who had to explain something.

"Nice coffee, Barney."

"I'm glad I can do something."

"What does that mean?"

"I haven't typed a letter since we left Lisbon."

"What brought you to the Secretariat, Barney? It's a long way from Texas."

102

"I came with a group to the World's Fair," Barney explained, "and decided to stay around."

"We're glad to have you."

"I don't want to upset anyone."

"You've upset Asare?"

"He says he's in love with me. He's terribly serious. What can I do? I don't want to hurt him, but he means nothing. Well, not nothing, but you know."

"I know, Barney."

"So what do I do?"

"You ask *me?*"

"Sure. Impartial opinion!"

"Asare has an illness," said McQuade. "You are that illness. Nothing that you can do will be quite right. I can only say to you, be gentle, because he will see suffering here—suffering of colored people, I mean—and this will hurt him, too."

The telephone rang.

"I'll see to it," McQuade said.

Last night's voice asked for Mr. Regio.

Two hours later the road drilling recommenced.

If there was a battle, its pattern was emerging. Nobody would win it, but it had to be fought.

6 ▪ ▪

"THERE IS A POSSIBILITY," Mr. Costa had announced in the morning, like a theatrical impressario who has at last engaged the supreme act—it had cost money and sweat and many hours of humiliation on the telephone and in strange bedrooms, but was finally accomplished—"there is a possibility that the Governor General will return on the airplane today. I am trying to fit him into your program. Would it be suitable if you met at the party of the British Consul General this evening? I presume you have been invited?"

Since it was a party for the UN subcommittee they had indeed been invited. The British Consul had done more than send a printed card. He had telephoned and explained, "It will be just our-

103

selves, you know. No emotionalism," which McQuade had not understood.

And here, ten hours after Costa's announcement, here they were, outside the attractive British Consulate, having driven the whole three hundred yards in a Mercedes sedan they had hired, rather to Costa's disconcertment. Here they were, still hot despite the changes of clothes and the showers and on the edges of exhaustion, for they had had a hot and tiring day in motor vehicles. They had been fifty miles down the coast to Porto Girassol with Costa and three members of the Legislative Council—all of them polite, good-humored and reasonably frank. "Is any of the labor still forced?" McQuade had asked as they drove through a village of thatched houses of baked mud, dust rising into their eyes and teeth. The contiguous Portuguese had answered, "It is a fundamental concept of labor that the native must be educated, instructed and made moral and taught to work. I would not say," the Portuguese official had said amiably, "that the African is educated. He still builds his round huts so that there are no corners for devils to lurk in. The roof has to be on before sundown or the devils will get in and nothing throws them out. I would not say he is moral," the Portuguese had continued with laughter. "I would say that he fornicates like a young goat. I would not say either that he would do a stroke of work if he can boot the girl friend into doing it! You see the difference between theory and practice, Mr. McQuade? How cruel it sounds when I tell you that idleness has to be punished! But he only has to work six months in the year. Ah, that that was all I had to do! I work thirteen! But he is so idle that we have to have proof in a workbook that he has done his quota. When he gets money he spends it on beer and shiny trash, gives some to the chief and some to a political party perhaps. Some of them are so dumb they can be persuaded to join two or three parties!"

It had all seemed a little remote in the dust and squawk of chickens and the women walking with heavily laden baskets on their heads through the burned grass.

And how strange was the African's ignorance, and how peculiar those aspects of European civilization thrust upon him! Above the straw and dust and long-horned, bony cattle of one village was a church like an Italian cathedral, with white marble that stung the

104

eye of the beholder. The Africans spent fourteen hours a day bending their backs in 90° weather on some plantation, and then, in the middle of the squalor in which they lived, *this* giant building rose. What did they conclude? A god who was infinitely more terrible than these petty fools of theirs? A god who liked splendor for himself and work, who loved the poor so long as they stayed poor and ill and ignorant? A god who loved pain?

It had been an inconclusive day otherwise. No points were made either for or against the Portuguese. Endless facts were recited about zinc, cobalt, iron ore, coffee, sugar, exports, investments in petroleum, oil mills, boot and shoe factories, tobacco, cement, sisal stripping, soap and canned fish . . . "Diamonds?" McQuade had questioned. "Ah, yes, we employ 25,000 *indigena* in that industry." In the north, McQuade well knew. It was hard to get information about the north, impossible to go there. The war was in the north. Whether for diamonds or politics or self-defense or the protection of coffee plantations or part of the strategic defense of South Africa McQuade wasn't going to be told.

The sun had glared over salt pans and on the red pannen tiles of Porto Girassol, which was not greatly different from Vila Lobanda —the same semicircle of colonial seventeenth-century pastel-colored buildings, the semiskyscrapers, the miles of red roads, dust and tin huts. Flamingos flew in perfect unison across the harbor to sandy beaches and palm groves. But these were empty. No one swam. Patients smiled in Porto Girassol Hospital—smiled at the nurses, the visitors; their illnesses were the normal ones, and the staff seemed adequate and kind. They drove back to Vila Lobanda a different way, through miles and miles of brilliant green fields of sugar cane, a phony green like a small child's painting book. People working in the fields waved. Trucks loaded too heavily creaked on the dusty roads. Africans sat dangerously insecure on the high loads. Recklessness, youth or a knowledge that life was cheap?

"It was a desert," Costa had proclaimed proudly. "Now, with irrigation, it is productive. Thousands work here."

Far off, across this lurid green landscape with smoke rising leisurely miles away and variously colored barns and old houses, were the humpbacks of a dolomitic mountain range. Clouds stood still in the flare of day. It was beautiful. To look at.

105

What to think? What to conclude as they were, in the haste of time, thrust upon the doorsteps of the British Consulate and the outstretched hands and the smiles and the voices and the heads turning to see them, the enemy. They were red-eyed from the dust of the potholed roads, drunk with tiredness for their first cocktail party.

Now McQuade knew what the British Consul meant when he'd explained—it had sounded like an explanation, although not one McQuade had understood—"It will be just ourselves, you know." For there was not a colored person in sight. There wasn't even a *mestiço*. English, Portuguese, French, Belgians, Rhodesian and some Germans, but no indigenous or colored persons from the consulates of other African territories were there. The British Consul had meant just ourselves, the white rulers of Africa. Asare Johnson stuck out like a sore thumb and knew it.

If the party was meant to achieve anything more than the introduction of the UN group to those who thought they were the ones in Vila Lobanda (and, by implication, the rest of Angolique) who mattered, it was, as such, a failure. There were the consuls and their wives, drab mostly, and bored, but a few were very forthright. There were a few doctors, engineers, a number of senior Portuguese Army officers, the Minister of the Interior, some teachers, including some attractive and intelligent ones from the Lycée Amélia, and some German businessmen with a bulk of tired skin and expressions of being involved elsewhere.

They were all anxious to express their points of view, their wisdom and superior knowledge of Africa and "the natives." McQuade knew from experience that it meant nothing. Neither side— presuming there were "sides"—hoped to persuade the other to its view. As in the UN General Assembly they were, in effect, claiming a platform from which to express their positions. A little ground would be conceded, McQuade knew, by those who liked your face, *you* as a human being; but this was unlikely at a first meeting and improbable in Vila Lobanda since the UN subcommittee was known to be there only for a few weeks. The others were here for years; they *had* to learn to endure and like some of each other.

The British Consul, Mr. Duffin, tall and thin and baked dry after years in Africa, was at least frank. McQuade stood talking to him and a small group, including some rather beautiful French and Belgian women who stood with whimsical smiles of superiority on their faces. The conversation soon got around to the purpose of the subcommittee's visit and the characteristics of the indigenous population—not a phrase Mr. Duffin used. It was in fact a phrase brought into common use by the United Nations itself. In the General Assembly it was not "just ourselves" but *them,* too . . .

"They're not *bad,* you know," Mr. Duffin said, "but are just like kids. They don't understand our way of thinking. And, of course, the ones who've got the power now hate *us,* the old ones. We know too much. I was in Nigeria for twenty years. I know a whole group of politicians who were in prison for theft and corruption when *we* were there." He laughed. "All the Prime Ministers of ex-British territories have been to prison, of course. It's practically a qualification!"

His wife, a small waspish woman, tired, perhaps, by the preparations for this party, was more acid.

"Have you been long in Africa, Mr. McQuade?"

"Only a few days."

"Days! Well, my dear man, I've been here twenty years and I wouldn't presume to teach you . . ." But she did presume. "But you must realize one fundamental point, and that is: if you persuade the Portuguese to leave Angolique you'd be left with fifteen or so tribes who would bring the territory to a standstill or make a bloody battlefield of it. One thing you Americans just don't understand. It may be right in *theory* to do all sorts of things, but in practice the European—"

"I'm a Canadian, not an American, Mrs. Duffin," McQuade pointed out a bit brusquely, unwilling to stand and be lectured like a child.

"Oh, well," said Mrs. Duffin, as if that explained it all. Americans, her old face and eyes implied, are bad enough—brash and noisy and so clumsy at table and like a steamroller in politics, but at least they had money and technical know-how. But Canadians. They were *nothing!*

The French Consul's wife, who had been in the Congo, said, excitable after one martini, "You have not seen a city in the chaos of riot? No?" McQuade qualified, "Yes," but the lady wanted to make her point anyway. "There has to be law and order. It has to be *ours* because these people have none of their own. So I do not feel anything should be surrendered by the Portuguese."

Mrs. Duffin added another irrelevant contribution before moving on to her party's needs. "Do you think such primitive people can be sincere? Time and time again I have found it not to be so. Just when one grew quite fond of them . . . They become drunk and bombastic on the tiniest bit of learning. Isn't it your experience even in New York, Mr. McQuade, that most Africans are liars? Simple liars, like children who lie without concern for tomorrow when the truth, they know, will out?"

"You may be right, Mrs. Duffin," McQuade countered pleasantly. "The difference is that it sometimes takes *years* to find out the white man's lies!"

The French and Belgian ladies laughed, but Mrs. Duffin moved on. "You've upset Doris," said Mr. Duffin. "You won that round! Have another drink, old man?"

McQuade talked to a Portuguese colonel whose attitude was that the United Nations was all right but powerless. Idealism and hot air. Useless without armies to back them up. Doing a lot of harm *here,* inflaming the workers and half-educated schoolteachers and priests in Protestant missions.

"Clobbered a lot of them the other day," said the colonel. "Not much idea of fighting either." He shrugged, two hands indicating What can we do but kill them if they play soldiers? We are the civilized, was a second implication. Out there is the non-European, the savage. Nothing will alter him. Pretend, of course, Your job, of course. Pretend that it will. Give him a little schooling to tone down the cannibalism and intertribal fighting. Teach him about coffee and cattle. But power? He abuses that like a kid with a temper.

Across the room McQuade saw Asare Johnson, an intelligent, sensitive, good black man, ignored by the entire room except the UN group. He was included in conversations because he happened to move a few paces with Barney or de la Plaza. As he listened to the colonel, McQuade heard a woman say in English, "Who on earth is that black person?" and another woman's plea, "Why doesn't that American girl move away. People will think she's his mistress."

108

"The Americans," the colonel was saying without much tact, "do not understand Africa."

"How about the Russians?" McQuade asked. "And the Australians?"

But the colonel missed the last few words and was amused. "Oh, the Russians! Hopeless! One of these groups we're fighting had a planeload of Soviet Red Cross come in from Tanzania or somewhere. They didn't speak Portuguese or French. Nothing. One day, in a bit of a scuffle, the whole lot got beaten to death by error. So they've got no Red Cross, which is pretty tough on them! The Chinese in Africa are even more stupid," continued the colonel. McQuade wondered how he could know these things. "One thinks of the Chinese as extremely subtle. But in Africa they're just plain stupid. No subtlety at all. They make it obvious even to these birdbrains that they're in it for power politics, so even a little country like Rwanda kicks the whole embassy out . . ."

The threat of the Chinese in Africa was touched upon in conversation by the two bulky Germans when McQuade drifted over to them.

They did not take McQuade or the United Nations as a serious threat to German or any other interests in Angolique. They made heavy jokes about it.

"You belong to the United Nations? Do they pay you? Have they recovered from their last bankruptcy?"

The second one sneered and said, "Mr. McQuade, in this territory of Angolique we do more business in one day than the UN does in a year."

"The UN is not in that kind of business," interrupted McQuade.

"That is why it is so unsuccessful," said the first German, whose name was Frischauer. "Mettallic Angolique does a million dollars a day here."

"A million dollars!" commented McQuade. "That's a lot of money! That's *respectable!*"

The sarcasm was wasted.

Mr. Frischauer inquired, in what he evidently considered a purely theoretical possibility, "What do you want to drive us out for? Who is going to follow us in? Soviet women's conferences? A flood of cheap Chinese literature, cultural personalities and propagandist broadcasts? Do you want the spread of Dr. Potekhin's edu-

109

cated 'scientific socialists'? The guerrillas from Ghana and the Czech and Chinese troops? Or the World Federation of 'Free' Trade Unions spreading the gospel from Moscow? Or the young men here with any brains at all to go for a spell—like others before them—of training at the Friendship University in Moscow? Although I have heard," qualified Mr. Frischauer, "that this sickens them rapidly of communism! Someone would have to follow us in, Mr. McQuade, if this country is not to revert to jungle. For the *indigena* couldn't manage. We in investment and industry give this territory life and economic survival. The alternative is for Warsaw and Moscow and Israel to buy coffee and nuts in bulk until they tire of the game and move in. Or, if they don't move in, the economy here then collapses. Is the United Nations so stupid that she urges chaos and invites her own enemies to step in afterward to make what they like of it while she raises her impotent hands and says, 'We deplore this'?"

He had a point, but McQuade answered, "If the country is not economically viable and the people are neither ready nor capable of self-government I and my subcommittee will say so."

"All this in five weeks?"

"We have long since received extensive reports from the Portuguese themselves on many aspects of the economy."

"And how will you throw us out if we refuse to go?"

"Negotiation," suggested McQuade.

"I am not impressed by such politics."

"You are interested in staying here?"

"Oh, I shall stay here. Mettallic Angolique is bigger than your Turtle Bay edifice."

"To stay here you, too, must negotiate sooner or later."

Mr. Frischauer was amused.

"With you, Mr. McQuade?"

The two Germans laughed.

"No. I am merely here to observe."

"You talk as if you have *very* great powers of negotiation," the second German, Mr. Unger, observed sourly.

Theo Alferink was enjoying the party at any rate. He was talking animatedly to a mistress of the Lycée Amélia. McQuade joined them.

110

"We were just saying how it widens the girls' minds, experiencing Africa during childhood," said Alferink, with a wink at McQuade that suggested other prospects in mind.

The teacher, Miss Montguerre, already being addressed as Donine by Alferink, explained to McQuade in a delightful Continental accent, "It is so tiring, the heat, at times. But the girls stand it. While we're miserable and changing our clothes they run about with the energy of children in Paris in midwinter. There's not much illness," she went on, seeing McQuade's attention and believing he was concerned. In fact he was thinking what a beautiful, innocent, heart-shaped face she had with half his mind, and with the other half he was conquering the dullness of alcohol with the question How *can* they make a million a day since the whole economy . . . ? A million dollars, he had said, almost as if he dealt in them. "With the drugs, you see, there is no risk of malaria and yellow fever or dysentery," Miss Montguerre said, blushing a little at the word "dysentery" as if it were one of many words just not mentioned in the Lycée.

"What," McQuade asked, "is your experience of the problems here?"

The beautiful face was startled. "What problems?"

"There are political problems."

"Oh, I don't think so," Miss Montguerre said. "The Portuguese have it all under control."

"Do you teach history?" asked McQuade bitterly.

"No," said the young lady, taken aback. "I teach deportment and social grace, physical studies and dancing. It is a beautiful place," she added, "for the girls to swim. For many kilometers there are splendid beaches."

Such innocence of heart was painful to encounter. It was a godlike, creative view of Vila Lobanda and upset McQuade to the point of despair. For she had a point of view—Africa as it should be, a beautiful series of natural features to enjoy—and she was going to be disenchanted violently because of the theories of men about each other.

"Are there any colored girls?" he inquired. He had to ask the question, to put the Lycée and its charming teacher back into the perspective in which it ought to be.

111

"Yes," Donine Montguerre said. "Not many, of course, because they are girls from Europe really, not local girls. Some of them were at Belgian schools in the Congo when . . . We have seven hundred girls. There are about twenty African girls among them. They are all very happy, I think," said Miss Montguerre, with the purity of one who, feeling happy herself, was not given to violent self-analysis and the conceits of misery. "They love the African animals."

Across the room McQuade had several times noticed a Portuguese man in a gray suit looking at him. Now he was standing near, in the next group, and McQuade moved on to join it. He was a young man with the face of an idealist in a rotten world, one who was working against odds and not acclimatizing himself to a situation willingly.

Someone introduced McQuade, "Mr. Minister, this is Mr. Brandão."

"Are you having an uncomfortable party, Mr. McQuade?" the young man asked, and when McQuade was obviously startled he commented, "They know everything, don't they? I know nothing. I am merely the Minister of Education! You'll be all right with me!"

He saw something in McQuade's face and inquired, "You have heard of me?"—an odd question if McQuade did not know of his implications.

McQuade moved to one side, forced a little privacy, and answered, "Yes, I met a friend. A Mr. Bajune."

It was Mr. Brandão's turn to be shaken. He said quickly, "I see you are a man with more heart than discretion. It is as well others are shouting and did not hear you. Even this room has its quota of PIDE. What did our mutual friend have to say?"

"Not a lot. It was late and we both had long journeys to make. A little about politics and armies."

"I am hopeful of our friend, but he needs assistance. He leads an adventurous life, one not likely to attract the insurance brokers. I am worried for him. You see, Mr. McQuade," Brandão said, leaning forward so that no one else heard—the gesture was irresistible even though no one could possibly overhear in the total noise—"we have an opposition here, but it is its own worst enemy because of its ignorance. Thus the Portuguese have the advantages of edu-

112

cation and communication as well as aircraft and an apparently unlimited supply of *voluntarios* in Portugal. The sophisticated young *indigena,* half educated, up against nearly hopeless odds in their political struggle, get over the border all right to, let's say, Tanzania. And there they get a hero's welcome and the chance of education by means of scholarships and so on offered by the Organization of African Unity. And the temptation to leave the very difficult liberation of their homeland in its nastier aspects to the Bakongo and Bamakonde and such tribes and to get to some part of Africa where education equates with a good job must be very great."

"What *about* education, Mr. Brandão?"

"What, indeed? Evidently I must talk to you at length and show you some of its aspects. Of course *these* people," observed Mr. Brandão sourly, with a sweep of one hand to indicate the entire room, "will tell you to leave him alone. The African in his traditional, primitive world, untouched by the intricacies of civilization. Why not leave him alone? How convenient that would be! Mr. Mc-Quade," he asked, "why are you here?"

"To collect facts, to observe, to see what the country is ready for."

"If you happened to express an interest as to whether the Protestant missions are harmful to Portuguese interests—they claim they are not, but Mr. de Oliveira with the sour face over there doesn't believe them—and wished to see also the Catholic missions outside the city and the *liceu* within it, they might well allow you a little farther than the Fort Eduardo or escorted tours of Porto Girassol. I would of course have authority to take you to a number of schools myself. If you happened to see things on the way, I could not help that. And if you stopped to mend a puncture somewhere and we met people who are not schoolteachers, that would be the accident of motoring, agreed? How many schools would you like to see?"

"A great many on that basis," said McQuade. "And I shall speak highly of them to the Minister of the Interior and the Governor General, who has not, I see, turned up for this party."

"Since he is in Rhodesia for ten days that would be difficult," commented Brandão. "I fear they are giving you the diplomatic runaround, Mr. McQuade."

113

"I'm afraid so," agreed McQuade. "And the road is drilled every morning from three o'clock and there is a phone call at midnight and one o'clock exactly for a Mr. Regio."

"How tiresome! Which is exactly what is intended—to exhaust you. But to return to schools, Mr. McQuade. You will have to get rid of that man Costa somehow. I cannot do it."

"Barney will have a day off and play tennis?"

"Mr. Costa is married and a good Catholic."

"Nevertheless, Barney could be persuasive."

"Then let us see what we can arrange for the day after tomorrow. Do not underestimate Mr. de Oliveira or his minions. You are probably watched and perhaps followed in the street, but whether they do so when Mr. Costa is with you is doubtful and it is unlikely in a vehicle, for that would be too conspicuous on an empty road upcountry. It would be difficult to do it discreetly on the roads to Catholic missions and, after all, Mr. Costa and I will be assumed to be with you. And they do not know how liberal I am. I do not shout it around," acknowledged Brandão sadly, "for I, too, have a wife and children and I have no wish to go to prison or disappear or to be beaten to death."

"This happens?"

"One must assume so. But I am talking too eagerly. It is likely to be noticed. I suggest you leave me and some time tomorrow propose to Mr. Costa how desirable it would be to visit the missions—the Catholic for proof of Portugal's historic purpose and the Protestant to see what mischief they're up to."

The guests were beginning to depart. Mrs. Duffin was hemmed in by handshakes and smiles. Her husband caught hold of McQuade on his way out, literally, and, being equally tall, put an arm around his shoulder. "A word in your Canadian ear! Don't take your colored friend into the bush. He'd be killed by someone and that would be most embarrassing, eh?" He laughed hugely. "A good party, eh? You enjoyed it? We shall see each other again, I know."

"A very good party," agreed McQuade. "A little rough here and there, but enjoyable."

"Ah, and watch that damn toad of a man de Oliveira. He is very unpleasant, but shrewd. I expect he has you followed and your phone tapped. Might be useful in terms of confusing him, y'know. A nice girl, that Miss Widener. Very handsome, eh?" Duffin smiled

114

at the Minister of the Interior, twenty feet away. "Nasty things go on in the north, Mr. McQuade. Logical, but not cricket. But no doubt you'll learn about them."

On the way back to the villa McQuade explained what had been suggested.

Theo Alferink was slightly drunk and exuberantly noisy.

"I'm glad your Education friend said the day after tomorrow, for tomorrow—no," Alferink qualified. "Today! In a mere thirteen hours I shall be lunching with the delightful Miss Montguerre. We'll both pop over the road to the Hotel Marromeu. She is going to teach me social grace and sport. No, she will show me around the Lycée. And any of you gentlemen who are interested in the education of *nice* girls . . ."

"Include me out," said McQuade. "It is irrelevant and will merely be Paris and Brussels. I wish you wouldn't, Theo. It is a little humiliating to have to mention it."

"Wouldn't *what?*"

"Waste time on pretty faces."

Alferink was a little cross at his weakness being mentioned in front of the subcommittee. "Mr. Chairman," he disputed, "I am in search of information like yourself. One never knows what the pretty Miss Montguerre and her more formidable associates might know of the conditions here. If I wanted to pursue a pretty face," Alferink ventured, "I would unhesitatingly choose Barney's."

Barney said nothing.

Asare Johnson spoke in an angry voice, the bitterness of what had been for him a humiliating evening. "You talk too much. You are making a mockery of our serious purpose here."

Nobody in the Mercedes spoke for the remainder of the short journey.

Just after they'd gone to bed the telephone rang. They ignored it, but it went on and on.

And just after he'd fallen asleep McQuade stirred to curse the road drills. He was hot and tired and slightly the worse for alcohol.

In the morning Ribowski was ill. He had a high temperature and rolled about in his bed. McQuade was anxious and went to the Hotel Marromeu and asked the receptionist for the name of a doctor. One came in twenty minutes.

The doctor's name was Pais. He was a man of about fifty, small

115

and fat, rather dirty and very anxious. He kept looking around as if expecting to find something remarkable. McQuade took him into Ribowski's bedroom and left him there. It must have been an odd consultation, for Ribowski had no knowledge of Portuguese.

When he heard the doctor leaving the room, McQuade went to meet him and invited him to have a glass of port. When the doctor hesitated, McQuade led the way into his office, asking, "How is the patient?"

Dr. Pais smiled.

"He has encountered a well-known insect. He will feel an ache in every bone for a few days, perhaps ten. There is no cure," said the doctor, "although I shall claim my fee for the diagnosis! Equally, there is no medicine. He has to wait, that's all. Where does he come from?"

"Poland."

"Ah, Poland. He has some very strange scars."

"I did not know that."

"Many people in the world have inexplicable scars. Your friend had a bad war. He is not strong."

"I did not know that either."

"Yes, many people. I have seen scars like those," said the doctor. "And not in Poland." He was on the point, McQuade could see, of confidences. "If this town could talk—"

"All towns have suffering."

"I could tell you things," the doctor said. He seemed quite nervous, as if he regretted venturing this far even in words. "I am a patriot, a loyal Portuguese."

"Of course. But truth claims allegiance, too, does it not?"

"You must not mention my name," Dr. Pais urged. "As a doctor I have seen some things. Not in the war. Machinery. Accidents. But this . . . There was a demonstration. Cotton workers. Nothing serious. Broken windows, smashed cars. Noisy. But the reprisals . . . I attended many people in the Baixange Hospital, and they had wounds indicating bayonets and severe beatings with instruments, bars, that sort of thing. Panic, of course. There were bodies lying in these streets, sir, only sixteen weeks ago. All calm now. That's Africa. Except the prisons. Plenty there. No one knows who has been arrested and no one wants to know since they are *indig-*

ena. There are no trials in these situations. They offer an excuse. Educated people who were not involved disappear, educated *indigena* and *assimilado,* I mean. Not many Portuguese. Not yet. There were women and children among those cotton workers who got excited, because they, too, are part of cotton labor. It is not as bad as it sounds," Dr. Pais said oddly. "It isn't as if they had anything else to do but work. Some of our own women and children in the outlying districts have been brought into town. This I know because I have new patients, I see new faces. Many farms, I hear, have had to be abandoned. These people will have to be taken seriously sooner or later. I suppose, since you are here, they *are* being regarded seriously. There is no trouble in Vila Lobanda now," concluded the doctor, "but there are still raids on the native quarters here and in other places—the search for guns and machetes."

"What is the health structure in Angolique, Doctor?"

Dr. Pais made a movement now with his mouth as if to say, Not bad in the circumstances. "You could say that the only thing wrong with it is that there is not enough of it," he said. "It keeps its eye on endemic diseases, particularly leprosy, malaria and tuberculosis. It controls trypanosomiasis, maternity service and sanitation and the health of those Africans who work. There are several hundred nongovernmental institutions. The Church, of course, is very realistic in the territory. Employers have their obligations . . . But it is the shortage—three hundred doctors in three-quarters of a million square miles. Much of the care of the *indigena* outside the towns is by mission doctor, private leprosia or dispensary. Only a small proportion of the people have good water. There has been a good program against sleeping sickness, tuberculosis and malaria. Most of the Portuguese doctors hereabouts, I am ashamed to say, have come to Vila Lobanda for the sunshine, not the treatment of Africans. Perhaps I do them an injustice and it is the accident of their living in urban areas. Certainly some work for particular companies who employ *indigena.*"

The doctor sighed with the hopelessness of a failure beyond him. "The situation in the country will be aggravated because of the fear now of going beyond the safety of the towns. There are only seventeen hospitals in the country," acknowledged Dr. Pais. "It is true

117

that the population is far less than that of New York, but still . . . It is pitiful. The infant mortality rate in the towns is about 200 per 1000 live births. I fear that in the bush a half of them must die. And now, with armies moving about and napalm bombs burning villages and refugees fleeing and some starving, I am afraid for Portugal," confessed Dr. Pais. "She did not want this ugliness. She is on the verge of panic, and panic, as you know, brings brutality. But I am talking far too long. I have patients waiting."

"One thing, Doctor, before you leave. Tell me, was there any rioting in Porto Girassol?"

"No," Dr. Pais told McQuade. "It would be suicidal to have any uprising there because the main Army depot is just outside the town."

"They took me around the hospital yesterday."

"And you saw no injured?"

"No. It was all very domestic."

"It would be, in view of that. Why not ask to visit the Hospital Baixange here? I doubt if they'll let you, but you'll collect some startling evidence if they do."

Costa arrived as the doctor departed, and McQuade did ask him. But Costa was evasive. McQuade feigned irritation. "Then what may we see, Mr. Costa? The Portuguese Army on leave? The Angolique Museum of African Folklore? I am interested as a Protestant in seeing what effect their missions have in the territory, and indeed what the Catholics do. I would like to visit the *liceu* and the adaptation schools and the technical-training schools. May we visit such places or are we confined to the open-air cinema?"

Something like relief came into Costa's eyes. This man is a fool, his eyes said, who wants to see schoolchildren when there are many worse things he should not see. Let me not concede too quickly or he will, even though he is a Canadian, become suspicious. "I will speak to the Minister of Education himself."

He took the subcommittee on a tour of the public-authority buildings in Vila Lobanda that morning. Some time after lunch Theo Alferink rejoined the party, which was inclined to sag in the afternoon's heat. Alferink was exuberant, like a man on holiday who has found a mistress.

"She was very gay. Giggled like mad on half a bottle. A bit scared when she found I was married, but is ready to see me this

118

afternoon on the basis that it's all for the great cause of enlightenment. Who is going to be enlightened and about what we shall decide later."

"It is so undignified," said Asare Johnson.

"Don't be sour," said Alferink. "I appreciate that you're not making progress yourself—"

"I am working and that is what I am here for," said Johnson loudly. "I do not regard such matters as a joke."

Barney looked uncomfortable and stood up. "I'm going for a swim," she told them.

Gregorio de la Plaza walked away with her. Johnson was disconcerted by what looked like an arrangement for the afternoon.

"It's all so romantic," said Marianne with sweet acid. "I wish I could join in. But who's going to do the laundry?"

"I will help you," said Asare, with the face of one who is black and must therefore expect to be lumbered with the least dignified chores of the subcommittee.

McQuade sat by Ribowski's bedside and looked over Vila Lobanda. In the convent grounds the nuns were gardening. They moved slowly in the hot afternoon among the plants. Beyond them the faint noises of the town filled the afternoon air.

"How are you now?"

"Very nearly useless. This is a great embarrassment to me, Mr. McQuade. I want to do something useful."

"You will. When you are up and about in a few days. What I can't understand is why it is not me. I was bitten to pieces by insects that night I went out on the bicycle."

"I am not strong," claimed Ribowski. "This is a source of amusement to others because sometimes it is hard to bear and I complain. Miss Widener was very kind."

"Barney was?"

"She came back and made me something to eat, talked to me, radiated the room with that big personality of hers."

McQuade blushed. They'd forgotten all about Ribowski's lunch! He said, "Barney's a pretty solid character."

"I am serious, you see. Alferink acts like a clown. I am a Catholic. You saw Basia. And people think that in Poland there is no religion. This is wrong. Only the young are confused."

"Where do you come from?"

119

"Cracow. It is a beautiful town although it has a history of hell."

McQuade said nothing. He was utterly ignorant on the subject of Poland, although he had joined the Canadian Army to save her.

"There are many buildings as old as Europe," Ribowski told him. "The Collegium Maius dates back to 1400. Floriańska Street and the Market Square, the Drapers Hall and Cathedral—they are like bastions of God. Only the smell clings."

"The smell?"

"Governor General Hans Frank selected Wawel as his residence and the camp at Oświeçim as his investment in Poland. You would call it Auschwitz."

"And now?"

"Now Cracow is an industrial giant with a medieval heart."

It seemed remote and unreal. McQuade had seen the huge smelter and reduction works at Copper Cliff, Ontario, the grain elevators and the piggy-back trains, the Peace River Project in British Columbia and the giant cities on the edges of the Great Lakes and he did not really believe Ribowski. Poland was never mentioned in the industrial reports he read. But it was real enough to Ribowski: it was what he worked for.

In the evening a letter came to him from Kristan. In it was enclosed one from Peter. Peter was now in Europe with the RCAF's No. 1 Air Division. He was flying that CF-104 Starfighter as a part of the Cold War. It worried McQuade a little although he was proud, too, as he told the others about it over dinner.

He could not sleep and lay in his room listening to the town quieting and insects croaking. The night and the big sky and the events of the week, not exciting perhaps but all strange and full of responsibility and with possibilities of tragedy and the misery of others . . . He got out of bed and began to write to Kristan, easing the loneliness and longing for her that were heavy in the belly so that he felt afraid as the pen moved across the airmail stationery. . . .

"Dearest Other Half of Me, In the heat of the bright sun I miss you and now in the ticking silence of the African night so that it hurts. There are many terrible things happening here, I feel it in the atmosphere as part of the heat, although we have scarcely touched the edges of it. And it makes me aware of how real and beautiful—"

120

Outside, the night air was concussed by the road drills. Mc-Quade could not believe that so many hours had passed, and his sweat-moistened hands reached for his watch, which he'd put on a dresser. The watch said midnight only, and McQuade's scalp crawled with sensation as if a frost had settled on his hair—for it was, three-quarters of a mile or so away, the brisk businesslike noise of machine guns—not road drills—and, far away, he could hear the shouting.

Someone out there was being killed. Or was it maneuvers and not the real thing?

Gregorio de la Plaza and Ekelund were at his door and asking, "Did you hear that?" and he felt the weight of their reliance on him. They were his responsibility. He had not realized it so fully before.

7 ▪ ▪

THEY WERE GIVEN permission to drive north a little way to see schools and Catholic and Protestant missions.

Ekelund was driving today. He delighted in the Mercedes and compared it with his native Volvo. The car had a sliding roof, which was now open, and a blast of hot air blew on the faces of McQuade, de la Plaza and Marianne. The feeling of escape was very satisfactory, and everything was of interest despite the tremendous heat. Barney was playing tennis with Mr. Costa. It would soon be too hot for that and they would go to some cool terrace at the Naval Club and drink fruit juice. Later they would lunch together. Time would be used up, and meanwhile the rest of them—except poor Ribowski, who was still in bed—were losing Mr. Costa in terms of distance.

"Do you think he will come?" McQuade asked the Minister of Education.

"I sent the message. If he received it and it is possible . . . He is anxious to meet you," Mr. Brandão assured them, "and if he is prepared to come all the way from his headquarters in Tanzania I do not think a few more kilometers will deter him."

121

"How did he get to Tanzania?" asked de la Plaza.

"Ah, that was something you did," Brandão explained. "He has had a curious education, has Mr. Gomais. Catholic mission. Then he was able to take advantage of your Resolution 1808 and accept a Swedish secondary-education scholarship. This can be used in any territory, as you know, and Gomais chose Tanzania. He has recently been to Europe, I think. He was very lucky to have such an all-expenses scholarship. I was able to help there. Very few *indigena* have the necessary qualifications, you see. It is a vicious circle—no education means no qualifications. And no qualifications means no vocational or further education. I have to tell lies quite often on behalf of such people."

"You are taking big risks," said de la Plaza.

"It is morally necessary," said Brandão. "There is a policy of assimilation, but it means little if the majority are denied even the opportunity of education and are the subjects of so much discriminatory legislation. Even the *assimilado* is losing ground because of the influx of Portuguese immigrants. The poor of Portugal and the soldier-settlers still want to come. It is a proof that Portugal has its own problems, too."

"Surely the *indigena* are not denied education?" questioned McQuade.

"In theory, no. They start at what are called rudimentary schools—"

"Primary schools?"

"No. The children of *indigena* or *mestiços* have to go first to rudimentary schools. School, even being in a room, is very strange to them. When they have reached a stipulated level of mental and social development—in other words, adapted—they go to primary schools, where they mix with white children and those of *assimilados*. If they are able to speak Portuguese it hastens things. They have four years in primary school. It is not unfair, Mr. McQuade. If they can adapt they can go all the way to the *liceu* or technical professional schools. The emphasis in such teacher training as exists in Angolique is upon primary education. The same goes for Catholic and Protestant schools. The Catholic missions in overseas territories are regarded by the State as instruments of civilization."

"And the Protestant?"

Brandão smiled. "The State is a little anxious about those!" His smile faded and he reasoned with Portuguese sadness: "One worries about all of them in times like these. And there are other difficulties. One is the requirement of a birth certificate and a retroactive tax if the child was not registered at birth. These civilized requirements are madness in the bush, where many women have children before and after marriage. These requirements drive the child, perhaps, to a private school—one of your Protestant missions which use approved curricula but whose very existence worries both the authorities and the Catholic Church. It is all so enormously frustrating," concluded Brandão. "And now with a war . . ."

"Is there a war?"

As if to prove there was, a Portuguese spotter plane passed hardly a hundred feet above the open roof of the Mercedes.

"We are too late," conceded Brandão. "We could have made this country into a Brazil, but we've started too late and too small. Others will, I hope, give the *indigena* his freedom and his education."

McQuade asked, "What is the answer, then, to Angolique?"

Brandão answered, "To understand Angolique you have to understand Portugal. Despite his present faults, Salazar did a lot for Portugal. It was not easy to derive a viable economy from a country whose main assets are sardines, cork, pineapples, olives and wines; or from an agriculture where, for instance, in the Alentejo, crops were only produced once in four years because there was no water and irrigation was costly; or in which 40 per cent of the population is still illiterate; or in which much of the Army is also illiterate and has to be taught by its officers. And it is still bitterly true that what wealth there is is channeled into a few pockets, what we call 'the eleven families,' who can, you may be sure, breed relations! Did you know that in Portugal the vote is still denied to one-third of the population?

"You must realize that in Portugal herself there is a qualification for the electoral roll—proof of educational attainment or a certain minimum paid in taxes. Since Portugal has the lowest annual income per person in Europe and nearly 40 per cent of the people are illiterate many Portuguese don't get on the electoral roll. The peas-

123

ants look significant under the summer sun and there are many festivals to alleviate distress and all seems beautiful to the cultural visitors from England and America. When the fairs are over and the decorations and paper lanterns have been taken down and put away for the next summer and the bullfighters have gone to Brazil or even Angolique, the families in the small towns and half of Lisbon seal their windows, for they cannot afford fuel, and they go to bed early and sleep in their clothes. We are plentifully supplied with pawnbrokers' shops!" said Brandão. "I suppose Portugal is rather like England was in 1850. And we are not going to be richer while this war goes on in Angolique. Already our gold currency reserves have dropped by many millions.

"But do not imagine that revolution is around the corner in Portugal. True, there is this absurd, very rich and uncompromising top class—again, I feel, an echo of England before 1914. There is a frustrated, indistinct and embarrassed middle class; and then there is the great mass of hard-working, poorly paid peasants, apparently apathetic about it all. But the strongest opponents of the regime in Lisbon are restrained by the unfairness, the lack of foreign sympathy or understanding, the feeling that a sophisticated world not interested in honor or dignity—and therefore suspect—is ganging up on Portugal. You see, we have the absurd situation in which harsh criticism is hurled at Portugal as a colonial nation, and it angers and bewilders the Portuguese who live under a similar state of affairs!"

There was a long silence.

Brandão smiled and commented, "I have given you much to think about?"

"Indeed you have!"

Ekelund said, "This is a fine road."

"Ah, you are going to leave it in a few kilometers!" Brandão told him. "But, as you say, it is good although not wide enough. In the rainy season the roads are very unpleasant. Many of them are deep in mud, and one has to stop and fill up the quagmire with branches before proceeding sometimes. You see the ant hills, Mr. Ekelund?"

They had passed many that were twenty feet high.

"These little termites produce a hard, water-repellent mixture to live in. Excellent for the manufacture of roads and airfields in a

124

hurry. Good for the palate, too, I'm told. Turn here, Mr. Ekelund. No! Wait! The plane is returning. Wait for it to go."

The spotter plane flew over the road so low its crew could have read the Mercedes' license plate. It made a great clatter of noise but was soon gone.

"Are they looking for us?" de la Plaza asked.

"It is unlikely," Brandão considered aloud. "They are in search of trucks or the movements of men. But I do not wish him to notice us turning from this main road."

The side road was only a track, and although the Mercedes took the ruts carved by heavy rain and the potholes that couldn't be avoided, Ekelund had to slow down to a crawl. They closed the windows and the sliding roof as dust billowed around the car.

"I am hoping to show you something wonderful," said Brandão. "Something that will make you weep for this fool man in Africa."

After two miles the track ended in a clearing. There were a number of wooden buildings with verandas, which had an air of neglect as if they'd been left alone for years, but Brandão's observation was: "A mere six months and the forest has taken over. But there are no longer tourists in these reserves in the north."

They now walked along a path. This, too, was being retaken rapidly by the forest. It was impressive and a little overwhelming. After the tropical sun the shade seemed like darkness, but there was no cool relief. If anything, it seemed hotter, and the sweat rolled from their faces and their shirts stuck to their backs.

McQuade still had the remnants of his cold, but could smell the powerful fetid odor of damp and rotting plants. Man was dwarfed in the thick lush vegetation of herbaceous plants, shrubs and creepers, and the ground was covered by thick layers of moss on which grew many sorts of ferns. And out of this rich chaos grew the trees—some as high as two hundred feet. Their branches were festooned with creepers and their fallen leaves covered the ground like a wet pile carpet.

Brandão, leading the way, observed, "No spotter plane can find us here. It can only fly up and down the road—for the canopy of trees is a complete screen. It even covers the smaller rivers that move in the forest. You can imagine the Army's difficulties farther north."

It was dark and hot and wet in the forest, and full of the noises

125

of things that crawled, leaped, ran and climbed, chattered and shrieked. There was no season and there were all seasons. Leaves fell from some trees; on others the blossoms were surrounded by bees and brilliant, blood-red, floating nymphalid butterflies; and on others fruit was eaten by vivid birds and monkeys during the endless summer, with rain and night the only varying themes. The foliage of the forest canopy maintained an everlasting shade from the tropical sun, which would otherwise have killed the humus or allowed the torrential rain to wash away the fertile elements of the soil.

The great crowns of many trees had broken into bloom. And the woody stems of the lianas crept five or six hundred feet, supporting themselves on such trees, meandering up and down. In the armpits of many trees, lodged in crevices and branches and rooted in dust and crumbling fragments, were orchids and other voluptuous flowers, ferns and mosses of the epiphytes. Some hung roots in the humid air to suck its moisture. It was a greenhouse of a world, savage with life, useless, quick, violent, with death there organized as well as any big undertaker's business. The worms and insects and their larvae and particularly the white termites ate the fallen trees, and the fungi on the sweaty floor of the forest extended their thread-thin hyphae to penetrate the rotting vegetation, dissolving and feeding on it.

In the dense shade and the chaos of vegetation alive and dead, things falling and growing, there was a great tumult of noise. There were innumerable varieties of birds—hornbills and parrots shrieked recognizably close at hand. Hyenas and chimpanzees would be moving about, and perhaps leopards. It was a little daunting as well as impressive, these few days beyond Lisbon and New York. Marianne voiced some of their apprehension, commenting laconically, "I hope I don't tread on a snake. It'd *ruin* these shoes!"

Brandão smiled and said, "It is true that there are a thousand species of serpents, but I am more anxious on your behalf about the million different types of insects—all of them prolific! But, if I am right, you will find the journey rewarding. Slowly and quietly now as we come to the river."

It was unexpected and enormous. "It is the Katuala," said Brandão, and they scarcely had time to absorb the huge width of it,

126

the thousands of fish jumping for insects, when they saw the herd of hippopotami.

Only a little way out in the slow-moving water was a sandbank a few hundred yards long, and there the great beasts were standing or lying about on the sand or in shallow water like overweight aunts on holiday at some respectable seaside resort. It was possible to see the way they had come, the enormous footprints and the tunnels they'd made through the long grass at the river's edge. They had shiny brown skin and pink feet and faces. They looked absurdly self-conscious and couldn't be bothered to move. One bit at another, but it was merely affection. There were a few of the splendid animals in the water, only eyes and noses visible. On the other side of the sandy island the current of the Katuala moved faster and carried a sea of hyacinths. It was one of the most beautiful sights McQuade had ever beheld, but even this was attended by tragedy, for the hyacinth was choking up the rivers of the whole of Africa. The truth of this was evident when he looked down to the next bend of the river, nearly a mile away, and saw that the whole elbow was clogged with these flowers, so heavy that it was surprising that they floated at all.

"Don't move or the tick birds will sound the alarm," cautioned Brandão. "Aren't they immensely splendid? All night they have eaten grass or sugar cane—two hundredweight of it each if they could—and since dawn they've been here digesting it."

"They're bleeding," said Marianne in fascinated shock.

"Ah, no," corrected Brandão. "They are not sweating blood either. It is merely a gland liquid which shows itself when the hippo is on land."

In the river one of the great animals yawned, and McQuade could see that its lower curved tusks were at least three feet long. As it walked ashore, he could see that its body must have had a circumference around the hind quarters of about fifteen feet. It must weigh tons, he thought, impressed. Marianne was making sentimental "Ah!" sounds because one beast had some babies.

The tick birds had been strutting about on the sand and on the heads and backs of the hippopotami. Now they flew up from the sandbank piping shrilly. A hundred yards away McQuade saw three men walking along the river bank toward them. The hippos

127

got to their feet ponderously and walked heavily to the water's edge. McQuade could see that each had four toes with large nails and their feet were webbed. One or two went straight under the water and seemed to stay there. "They don't swim under the water, they *walk*," Brandão told him. The whole herd was in the water now, some submerged completely except for their eyes, noses and ears. "That is how they keep cool," said Brandão. "Yes, it is Gomais." Marianne hadn't noticed the approaching trio and was cooing over the spectacle of the mother hippos swimming with their babies on their backs.

Now McQuade saw pelicans, but the business of the day was here as the three Africans greeted the UN party and Brandão cautiously.

Gomais and his two companions were dressed in khaki drill and heavy shoes. They carried nothing, not even food. Only Gomais was talkative. He was tall and tough and looked into one's eye searchingly, as if he were suspicious of all white men. He was a little startled when Marianne produced a notebook and started to take down in shorthand what was said. A smile altered his face from something not far from dislike to humor.

"I will speak in English," he said, "and declare the meeting begun. I have been to many places since we last talked," he told Brandão. "I have been in London, where I studied for two years at the London School of Economics. Why is this man smiling? Is it foolish to be instructed in London?"

McQuade had been smiling, and he explained why. "You've *all* been to the LSE! I recently met Mr. Bajune."

"He is a fool," said Gomais, "and not worth grinning about. Many things have happened and many will happen. It is thus commanded by the Lord."

"Ernesto studied for the priesthood," explained Brandão. He could see that an explanation was necessary.

"I have a new problem to explain to you," Gomais said importantly. He addressed Brandão, giving the impression that if McQuade smiled and talked to people like Bajune, clearly he, too, was in the great army of fools. Gomais obviously belonged to the category of those who did not tolerate them gladly. "You know that under certain conventions Angolique labor is recruited for work in

128

Rhodesia and South Africa. The Portuguese receive about two hundred escudos for each man recruited. All this is done with the relevant papers. You know also that we who are fighting the Portuguese slip over many borders. I am informed that the Rhodesian and South African authorities now have regular roundups to see if all Africans have papers. Those who do not are passed back to the Portuguese. In this way the Portuguese have had a bonus of political agitators taken prisoner."

Brandão thought for a moment then said, "I must do something about that. Perhaps if I can obtain a few hundred of these documents?"

"It can be done. I know it," said Gomais. "Prayer is successful. For I prayed earnestly. I am a serious Catholic. In London I saw many disgraceful things. There is much decadence and idle talk and corruption. Many girls offered themselves to me, wishing to sample an important black man. They talked on the one hand of freedoms and intellectual rights, but that is all it was. Talk and the playing with bodies. There are a hundred and fifty million Negroid people in Africa and they are not to be denied. You smile, Mr. American, thinking you are a white man and therefore superior, with your television and cocktails and fancy clothes and houses?"

"I am here to help you," objected McQuade.

"That is doubtful," said Gomais frankly. "When have resolutions made in New York, Geneva, Moscow or anywhere else made any difference to the African? He is patronized as a fool who can sing or run races or operate an elevator. The girls in London go to parties with him because it is daring, it irritates their parents and makes men angry, and they copulate to see if he is bigger. Africans must join together and get rid of the white man—Portuguese, English, Rhodesian, South African, French, Spanish, Belgian—all must go. I shall join the African Congress of Unity. God has decided I shall be the first President of Angolique."

This bombast was uttered cheerfully and inoffensively and apparently in experiment to see the reaction. Only the words about white girls in London had a sting of real personal anger.

Asare Johnson said quietly, "You are talking faster than any girl. There is an airplane out in the sky now looking for you. If you do not trust white men at least trust our organization, which, as

129

you know, gives a platform to all nations. If you do not trust us, why do you come? Why do you shout? Do you wish to impress these Tiki-tiki men you have brought along?"

Gomais was startled, penitent, and moved his feet in embarrassment. Then he grinned self-consciously and disputed, "You speak as if the problem had just been found. We have communicated to the United Nations for years. Nothing has been given us except sympathy and resolutions."

Asare told him, "I am an African and a black man. We, the rest of Africa, support you in your struggle. If you are a man of God and if you have been to Europe you will know that violence is not an answer. Violence creates a desert. The white man knows this and is afraid of it. Words have to be used, tiresome and slow though they be. But do not think that freedom from the Portuguese is the answer to your every problem. The arrival of independence in Ghana was easier, for the British were willing to grant it. But there have been many troubles since independence. You, too, must not expect a paradise when the new flag is raised on public buildings. You will have huge problems of education and economics. It may be that God intends you to be the first President of Angolique when the Portuguese have gone, but I think it would be safer to assume that others—whether intended by God or not—may covet that position and these may think you are unimportant. They may have grown into the habit of shooting to solve problems."

McQuade lowered his head to smile. Raising it, he saw de la Plaza listening intently, his left elbow, characteristically, resting on his right palm so that he might comfortably dig his left thumb nail into his nostrils. McQuade saw that one of Gomais' companions was staring at this distasteful spectacle, and he wanted to advise de la Plaza of how odd it looked.

Asare was still talking seriously to Gomais.

"Since you have been in London and such places," he said, "you know the nature of the Cold War. It would be very easy for Britain, for instance, to give you moral support and to damn Portugal in her Parliament and the United Nations, suggesting that Portugal be boycotted. But your small war is within a larger and more terrible one and in this larger one Portugal is a member of NATO and England's oldest ally. You must bear these things in mind, Mr. Gomais, and show great patience."

130

"You speak eloquently and indeed there have even been minor improvements," said Gomais. "Many of the legislative and administrative practices discriminate against us. The Portuguese have recognized the courts of first instance, it is true. In theory it is no longer possible for administrators to exercise what are in fact legal functions. But these things in practice mean nothing. It is a little exhausting to bear things in mind and show patience. We have been doing it for hundreds of years. For the *indigena* the employer and the *chef de posto* and their liverishness are still the bosses. The body is still scarred with the whip and the *palmatória,* and the *indigena* cannot move without his workbook. It must carry the print of his left thumb as if he was a criminal. Imagine how much 'great patience' the London worker would show for those trifling conditions as he went on his daily monkey ride in the subway! The *indigena* can be imprisoned if he does not work hard enough—cannot you imagine the world of spite and meanness and victimization possible in just that?—or if he leaves work. He might try to obtain exemption from labor if he can qualify as a private farmer. But he needs permissions and qualifications, and the *administrador* who wants him as part of a labor force is not likely to give them to him. He, too, has a book and it is stamped and receives entries from the authorities, and it is the *administrador* who is believed, never the *indigena.* Can you not imagine the frustrations? And the hopelessness? To be an illiterate laborer for*ever.* No Shakespeare or television drama or five-course restaurant meals or automatic cars for *you.*

"I have heard of many people in the so-called cotton program who have received inadequate prices for their labor or their crops. Imagine working like a dog in this heat for months in expectation of a medium-size pittance, only to be told that you can have half of that promised. A kick if you argue, and worse if you become angry. What happens to the other half? Oh, well . . . Bribery and force are used to recruit contract labor for the plantations. Public officials are not allowed—on those statute books which the Portuguese never read!—to recruit labor for private employers, but their mere presence at the place of recruitment, talking to tribal chiefs, is interpreted as coercion, and the *indigena* is persuaded by this pressure to accept contracts he does not like. There is much bribery, of course, at all levels of officialdom, and how could the *indigena* dis-

131

pute even this, if he was allowed to try, for he is invariably illiterate?"

"You must give us examples and figures if you can," Asare suggested.

"Tomorrow or the next day if you can come to another place I will bring men—and women, too—with grievances and the marks of the *chicote*," Gomais assured him earnestly. "But let me begin now with the events regarding my brothers and cousins . . ."

They all stood languidly in the heavy shade and looked at the brown water of the River Katuala flowing sluggishly, at the leaping fish, and they listened to the shriek of birds. Gomais talked quietly, but very fast, for there was a lot to tell. Now and then his companions prompted him. Marianne's left hand brushed back hair wet with sweat that kept falling over her nose, but her right hand propelled a ball-point pen rapidly down page after page in the strange configurations of shorthand.

Twenty miles farther south they crossed the river on a ferry. It was a ramshackle raft made from trees and oil drums lashed together, and it sank several inches under the weight of the Mercedes. Ekelund was no longer enjoying handling the car. He was sweating and straining to maneuver it onto the ferry while Kimbundu tribesmen grinned and shouted encouragement. They were cheerful boys dressed in very patchy shorts and vivid shirts. They worked with their hands tirelessly and the raft, spinning a bit, was nevertheless across the quarter-mile-wide river in ten minutes. "The rains wash the bridges away," commented Brandão, "so this kind of thing is not so primitive as you might think."

Having been driven off the ferry, the car moved along a dusty track in countryside of a tamer nature: small trees and bushes that seemed withered by the heat of the sun, dried-out pools caked with cracked mud, a smaller, sluggish river full of water the color and scent of urine. A long way off, among yellow grass and trees, half a dozen giant sable antelope ate *kundo* with their necks arched, but at the noise of the vehicle they cantered off.

There was a little excitement as Ekelund accelerated and ran over a snake zigzagging across the track. A few minutes later the party reached a village. It centered, unbelievably, around the ruins of an old seventeenth-century fort. There were some wooden huts and circular thatched mud dwellings. Chickens and goats moved in agitation out of the way, and with a violent flutter of wings some doves flew up to settle suspiciously on the corners of a wood and cement church. This building was not old, like the fort. It was hideously ugly and weatherbeaten by the sun, and yet, from a distance, it looked blue and beautiful, there in the trees and defeated grass.

As if the doves had been a signal, a priest came out of the church to greet them. He was very fat indeed and walked slowly in the heat. He had the round face of one who is cheerful, but his flesh was sagging and he looked ill. Brandão made apologies for their late arrival and introduced the UN subcommittee. The priest's name was Father da Silva.

Children had begun to gather excitedly around the Mercedes. A dog barked, but without determination—it was too hot—and soon returned to lie in the shade. Somewhere children were chanting the alphabet. The sound of a ringing alarm clock came through the open window of a large hut and a man's voice protested and demanded silence as the children stopped chanting and chattered. About twenty children now came out of the hut. They were all about ten years old and stared with the outright interest of the innocent. A few were acutely shy when approached; others giggled.

Their teacher followed them out.

He was a young man of the Kongo tribe, dressed in European-style clothes. "This is Cristovão," said Father da Silva. "Cristovão Faure. He is a good teacher and a fair Catholic." He talked rather as if Faure wasn't there. "Take them to the schoolroom, Cristovão, while I see if the lunch is ready. It will be bean soup, sardines and tomatoes. Then the chicken with hot peppers. I have a refrigerator of sorts for these things, and the wine."

Father da Silva walked away heavily toward a wooden building.

Faure said, "He is angry because I read poetry."

This defied comment.

McQuade asked, "How many pupils have you?"

"Twenty-five in this school."

They were entering the school hut. It had an old stale smell. On a wall was a poster of the *Divisão dos Transportes Aéros* showing white women on a scorching beach in bikinis, under sunshades, with a palm grove to prove that it was an African beach—that this leisure was possible in Africa. What did it mean here? And on a second wall a longer poster, beginning to curl: two children drinking Cokes, with a Chevrolet station wagon as backdrop. "They walk three miles or so to school," said Faure. He had a thin little cane, which he'd taken off his own desk, and he flicked it now against his trousers—an endless self-chastisement or an urge to thrash these other selfish bodies on the beach?

There were chalk drawings of trees and animals done by the children. The group admired them.

"Have you been to Portugal?" de la Plaza asked.

"No," said Faure in the tone of one who has no expectation of going anywhere.

"You went to a *liceu?*" persisted de la Plaza.

"No. Father da Silva educated me. He saved my soul," said Faure conversationally, then he added, "I must set the alarm. Your food will be ready."

Outside, in the stunning sun, Father da Silva hurried. It was the briefest school inspection McQuade had ever made.

"It is not bad?" Father da Silva suggested. "Good enough for these people. Cristovão could not, of course, pass any examination in Lisbon or Paris, but he's suitable for bringing education to these little savages."

Again he talked as if Faure wasn't there—or his pupils, who in fact hung about, fascinated. "Well, Mr. Minister, if you will come . . . " The priest was breathing heavily. "How do you like my bougainvillaea and moonflowers? I will show you my beans later. I put in sticks to prop them," claimed Father da Silva, "and so rich is the soil that the dead sticks root and sprout. God provides, Mr. Minister, in His fashion." He shouted to Faure, who was standing about in some embarrassment, "Have you set the clock?"

"Yes, Father da Silva."

"Is not Mr. Faure having lunch with us?" McQuade asked.

Father da Silva was shocked.

"To see the priest eating? Of course not! This is a visit by distinguished persons! We do not want the interruptions of ineradicable superstition. He will look after the children."

Asare Johnson did not understand this conversation, which was

134

in Portuguese, but he, too, hesitated, seeing Faure's discomfort. And Father da Silva, noticing it, asked, "Is this fellow sitting with us?"

"Yes, if you will," McQuade said stonily. "He is the delegate from Ghana."

"Well, I have not been there," conceded Father da Silva. "But I have been to Brazzaville, to Bechuanaland and to Goa in India, and I find the smell of them offensive—at mealtime anyway. They are like children who sweat at play and then forget to wash. He who teaches and loves must be respected," affirmed Father da Silva. "How am I to talk of the Holy Spirit if I do not myself remain aloof? Must I not chastise promptly and severely to maintain respect? This is most necessary for the African, do you not agree, Mr. Minister?"

McQuade was uneasy at such unrealism and unable to answer, but it was Brandão whom the priest addressed, and that minister answered rather doubtfully, "There must always be respect, of course."

In the priest's hut they were refreshed by a wash and glasses of wine. The hut was small—a bedroom, an untidy kitchen and the dining room where they stood sipping wine. McQuade and Brandão translated now and then for the others. On a wall was a portrait of the President of Portugal, and farther along, a print of the Resurrection, with faded colors. There were books and faded old air-mail letters on a mantel. From a candlestick a colorful little saint hung frivolously, like a memory of some Christmas cake in Portugal. But "I bought that in Orvieto," Father da Silva told McQuade. "It was on my only trip to Rome." He spoke like a man who had long since forgotten the Holy City: it was theory, too complicated for real use; out here was practice—the miracle of the beansticks and the necessary aloofness; one conceded a little of the mystery and ignored some of it.

McQuade thought that the priest was remote from the realities of what was happening in Africa, but in the middle of the meal Father da Silva said, "I have been here thirty years and I wonder now if it was a waste of time. The churches of Africa are emptying because they are of the white man; they belong to colonialism. They came with the white man and they will, perhaps, go with him.

135

I have said this in letters to Lisbon—for it is a matter of fact, not opinion—and the Order is making my life uncomfortable because of it. They want to hear that God is winning out here. The Order has tried to rationalize the empty churches of Africa, but they are still emptying. Who am I to ram religion down the throats of these people, a quarter of whom are educated and whose lives are miserable in disease and discomfort?"

McQuade, although a religious man, was inclined to agree with the priest. He recalled one of the most embarrassing moments of his life, when he had been talking to educated people in Tunisia about his God with the superiority of the North American. They had listened in amusement and mild anger, but had later explained to him in great detail what the Christians had done in the Crusades. They had recalled, with a sourness that might have referred to yesterday's events, the attacks on Carthage and Tunis many centuries before. They had explained their position with sincerity and McQuade had felt humbled. After that experience, he'd regarded Arabs as sincere and pious people who had a religious formula of their own—observed rather more strictly than sophisticated Canadians and Americans observed theirs—and, like Father da Silva, he had given up ramming Christianity down their throats.

"I have heard of fighting farther north," observed Father da Silva—again speaking with remoteness, implying that these things had nothing to do with him. "And of killing by soldiers and airplanes. This, too, is not likely to help the priests or the missionaries in the bush. For what will happen is that the *indigena* in the forest and savanna will associate the white man—*any* white man—with the gun. They will flee before the legionnaires, but if they have the opportunity they will kill him with the same emotions as when they fight a battle with the soldiers. Thus the priest will have to take a gun for his own protection or will have to travel with soldiers. This is what happened in the Congo and it is a negation of religion. All the good work of at least a century has been undone in months."

After lunch they looked at the church and the ruins of the fort. Neither was impressive. Then they went back to see the school again.

The children sat in rows, their small, cheerful Bantu faces singing, smiling and full of friendliness. Father da Silva whispered to

McQuade, "Cristovão is a good teacher, although he wastes time with poetry. These little ones do not need to learn Longfellow— they *are* poetry." He went on talking and explaining, and what he said was true in theory and love. Long before these little ones were grown up their elders would settle the problem of whether they were to be, at an improbable best, *assimilados* or part of a free if penniless national race or, more bitterly probable, refugees with starving bellies and terror in their minds, fleeing uselessly in a hateful war.

The alarm clock rattled and they kicked their feet about, eager to be free, although they waited, hopeful that today might be unusual.

Alferink said, "I will take some photographs?" which McQuade translated into a request. Alferink had a Polaroid camera which meant that he could show them the results right away.

The children assembled outside, very enthusiastic, and Father da Silva and Cristovão Faure stood like people at a ceremony. "Let me see," requested Father da Silva, when he saw that the photograph of himself was ready within seconds. "Oh, no, not like me at all."

"Vain old sacristan!" murmured Alferink.

The children in their cotton frocks and T shirts and shorts squealed with shyness and wanted to see. Alferink gave them one or two. Perhaps they would be pinned on the schoolroom wall in memory of a great occasion. Some of their mothers had arrived, equally giggly in shyness. "Take one of my dog, Alfonso," pleaded Father da Silva. But Alferink had noticed other girls on the edges of the small excited group and he whispered hotly, "Take a look at *these* beauties!" He had noticed older girls. Some had shaven foreheads and mud-and-dung coiffures, but others wore simpler, more Western styles, and most of these girls had bare breasts. They had shy, attractive round faces and wore bangles around their wrists and strings of small beads across their heads and around their necks. One stood there balancing a gourd on her head, steadying it in the jostling group with both hands, and this action lifted fine breasts and arms into a beautiful posture. Alferink took a photograph of this girl.

They drove away before the sun set and the ferry ceased to operate. Alferink delighted in the picture he had taken. "What a dish!"

137

he said in admiration. "What a pity they turn into old crows so early. How old d'you think this one is? Do you reckon she's a virgin?"

He looked at the girl as a vehicle of pleasure for his own satisfaction, not realizing the implications of his words in terms of education and life expectancy and diet deficiency.

No one answered him.

Only McQuade analyzed why they felt disgust.

The girls at the Lycée Amélia walked past the villa with straight, properly fed backs and bones, physical and mental pride, unconscious superiority, wearing straw hats and carrying hockey sticks. Where would their advantages of education and status take them? Lisbon, Rome, Paris, Madrid, Oporto, Athens? Would they use the advantages constructively? Perhaps not. Perhaps all they had obtained would be withered away in the usual absurd snobbery, a parody of culture, useful in restaurants but wasted in the metropolitan values of the glossy magazines. Or they'd become bored with themselves and burn themselves out in a frenzy of what they thought was "life"—the same pitiless glossy journalism, the arrogances of fashion, or the promiscuity around the edges of stage, screen, TV and journalism. They would not come back *here*. Man was fundamentally a self-destructive fool. Surely God had not created him? A sort of capricious, crazy, sadistic God without visible justice must have made man. Or the first God had tired of insult and man's conceit and sin and had left him to wallow in his own foulings like a monkey posturing in the bush.

The girl's eyes stared from the photograph in innocent perplexity, unaware of motives. McQuade felt how close and easy was despair. *You* would never have their Lycée status. Already it was too late. Perhaps your children's children . . . Nothing could be done. She was doomed to carry a calabash on her head to get water. The risks of death for her were high in this area. And there was a war not far away. Her children's chances of being born were not the lowest in the world, but were near enough for it not to be perceptibly different. Love. One could hope she would find it, for there was nothing else in the world for her. Sunshine, of course, and impure water. When she was in the school had she stared at the poster? What had she thought? There, but for the capricious grace

138

of this curious, indifferent God they want me to believe made me with infinite love would I be, lying on the beach, protected from the insects by strange sweet-smelling creams, my breasts covered with silk. A man brings me a drink in a glass. It has a lump of ice in it to keep it very cool, like Father da Silva sometimes drops into his. I drink this delicious white people's *pombe* and it turns me from an introvert who stares in the mirror all day and thinks of herself to a foolish extrovert and I go in search of a man to be humiliated by or drive a vehicle very fast to be rid of this terrible *ennui* . . .

Seven hundred million adults in the world were illiterate in Asian, African and Latin American countries alone (and the implication was not that these people were simply unable to read *Lolita* but had empty bellies, too). In eighty-five countries on these continents only 110 million schoolchildren out of 206 million had, in the statistics of one year McQuade recalled, attended primary school at all. That some twenty to twenty-five million illiterates would be added to the adult population of the world each year had terrifying implications. A program of two thousand million dollars over ten years was being attempted to give literacy to 330 million people of the ages fifteen to fifty. The estimate was a low one, for it did not take account of the cost of *keeping* literate . . . The existence of so much illiteracy was the biggest of the many problems in raising the standard of living throughout those parts that were below the breadline of mere existence. Meanwhile, in a world crying out for mere literacy, ignored except by a relative handful, and breeding so that the new and vaster problem waited for the next generation of UN and similar workers, in a world always so near disaster, there was the terrible backwash within the educated, the rejection of God and morality and truth and justice . . . Even among the educators themselves there was a high percentage of corruption, failure, greed, vanity, arrogance, foolishness and lack of belief in what they were doing. What an impossible problem for himself was man . . .

In the light of the descending sun, vivid colors reflected in the dirty river, a flock of parrots flew toward the forest and the Kimbundu boys, pulling the ferry rope, were still singing. There was still innocence, McQuade thought, and there was always hope. Each man was his own battlefield on which were many defeats and victories. This man that is me must do what he can in the light of what he believes. God is His own computor.

They waited in the stifling heat for Gomais to come at the time and place arranged, a junction of tracks related to distances and horizons. Perhaps they were in the wrong place. It was not fair to pin Gomais down in terms of time, but they had no option. Their program for the day was a visit to a Protestant mission sixty miles north of Vila Lobanda. This allowed some meddling with time, but the arranged hour passed and much of the next hour, and the spotter plane seemed to do nothing but circle in the far but visible distance. McQuade tried hard to turn away the depression that filled him with anxiety, with the certainty that something had gone wrong.

They had to leave if they were to reach the mission at all that morning, so they hastened back to the Mercedes, which was as hot as a pressure cooker despite being parked in the shade. The car bounced half a mile over rough grass.

"Stop!" shouted McQuade.

Ekelund stopped the Mercedes.

"What's the matter?"

"Look!"

They got out to stare.

Miles away black smoke billowed into the still hot air. This meant nothing. Pretty, but too far away for color photographs. Crops being burned. And then, very faintly, they heard the rifle fire. The spotter plane circled around and around. More smoke billowed up in thick, belching mushrooms. And then in the air at hand was a strange sound—the beating of thousands of wings—and whole clouds of birds passed over the car in the straight line of panic.

They drove uneasily north. Five miles along the dusty red potholed main road was the source of the disturbance. It was visible a long way from the main road through thornbushes and yellow trees. A village was going up in flames. It was not an accident. For a mile around there were Portuguese Army vehicles and soldiers. They stood in that grim casual attitude of people who are at war, not on the parade ground. Arms pointing and waving, a man running, an officer standing in a jeep, and all the time the spotter

140

plane clattering around and around in a two- or three-mile sweep at scarcely two hundred feet.

It was not a situation McQuade could ignore or watch from a distance. He made a motion with one hand and Ekelund swung the Mercedes off the road, following a sweeping pattern of scores of tire treads.

Distances were deceptive. It had looked like a village not far off the road, but they had covered a mile before they came anywhere near the Portuguese vehicles.

Nobody took the slightest notice of their arrival.

When the engine was switched off the noise was heard to be considerable and, outside the steel and glass of the Mercedes, the heat hit them. It was not the heat of day but of burning fuel. The Army had surrounded this village and the flame-throwers had approached it from at least four directions—this was obvious from the nature and pattern of inferno and the long tongues of flame that crackled through trees and bushes and grass effortlessly and licked at huts.

As the huts burned the people and animals ran out. This was what the *voluntarios* standing and kneeling around were waiting for. They shot them as they came. The soldiers were a good thousand yards from the village—the heat kept them there—and there was a litter of bodies from the first rush to get away. Men, women, children—they lay about in the grass, the tongues of flame went over them to burn the next, inner circle of huts. But now there was so much smoke and flame the Army could not see what it was doing. The soldiers stood around waiting.

Bits of straw and cloth and burning leaves floated about, and hot ash dropped everywhere. Sweat poured from faces a thousand yards away from the inferno.

Animals screamed and brayed and ran out, skin and hair burning. Trees collapsed. Above the noise of fire and rifles, McQuade heard the screaming. It caused him to pale. In war he had heard a tank crew trapped by fire and too badly wounded to move; he had heard them scream just before their ammunition exploded. But this . . . It was far away, but he could hear it all right, could hear the men, women, children. Now and again they could be seen rushing out of huts, their hair and clothes on fire, running in absolute terror and agony hither and thither—running around in an inferno

141

from which they couldn't find the way out. The convulsions of burning flesh and melting sinews carried a few beyond the flames, where they collapsed and writhed at an intensely animated pace in the grass. But that, too, burned . . .

There was nothing to say. Not yet.

McQuade was conscious only distantly of Marianne vomiting and turning away to weep in shock.

There was a sudden violent series of explosions on the far side of the village. An officer standing in a staff car turned to a group with him and laughed as he said something. In the distance rifle and machine-gun fire began. There was, then, some opposition, some reason for this slaughter.

The officer had seen the UN group as he'd turned his head, and he pointed them out to someone. One could almost hear him say, "Who are they? Bring them here!"

Rather than be fetched, which would put him into a position in which explanation was required, McQuade strolled, with a casualness he did not feel, to the staff car and the group of officers. His companions followed slowly, dazed and not knowing what to do.

The officer was a major, and he wasn't particularly bothered. McQuade had taken color photographs—indeed, he'd taken sixteen out of the twenty on the roll in his camera, but this did not seem odd to the major. He was looking through binoculars to one side of the inferno where fighting was going on, although it was nothing much and would obviously soon be over.

"They are running," the major said to McQuade in Portuguese. "That was their ammunition that went up. You are South African?"

McQuade did not dispute it.

It wasn't that he didn't have the courage to tell the major who and what he was. It was just that he knew the truth would come more readily this way.

"The lady has been sick!"

"We didn't expect this."

"Neither did we," the major told him. "We only heard about these jokers two hours ago. They've come for a fight! So we fix 'em, eh?"

"The village, too?"

The major shrugged.

142

"Inevitably. Do you think they spare anyone when they attack a plantation? It is a grim little war because no one admits it exists. So no one takes prisoners, or rarely we do, when we are able. And in the jungle and mountain farther north the Bakongo are very primitive indeed. To have a little talk here and ask these fellows to come out of the village and surrender or have a fight down the road—would that be logical? I would prefer it, yes. But all that would happen is that I'd lose a lot of my boys. To hell with that. I lose enough as it is. Here, have a look! You can see the jokers running. They are running the wrong way! They're heading toward the Duque de Machaze waterfalls. They'll get wet! It is not often that we are so beautifully positioned."

McQuade looked through the binoculars. A mile and a half away he could see the Portuguese *voluntarios* here and there among bushes and hot yellow grass. He could not see any waterfall, only trees in the distance, trees that were green and lush, suggesting water, and many bushes. He could not see the bodies, but above the crackle of burning huts he could hear the distant machine-gun and rifle fire.

He handed the binoculars back to the major.

"I can't see any waterfall."

"You would hear the water if it were not for . . . this."

"We'll go and have a look."

The major laughed.

"You South African tourists are real devils. Speedboats, safaris, fighting sharks, drinking, chasing women! Wait ten minutes or you might get shot! Then go around the proper road and you will come to the falls. You know Victoria Falls?"

"Yes."

"Well, this is better."

Brandão asked, "Is it safe to continue to the mission at Macqueca?"

"What in hell do you want to go there for?"

Brandão shrugged. He commented, "They have come far south?"

"Yes," agreed the major. "This is as far south as we've found them. Not many though. And not much good now, eh? I should think the road is safe for many kilometers."

They walked back to the Mercedes. No one said a word. They

143

were soaked in sweat. The fires in the village were still burning but most of the huts had collapsed now. The spotter plane had gone. The smell of burned flesh wafted across the thousand yards and Asare Johnson leaned against the vehicle to vomit. The tears rolled down his face. Marianne looked very pale and tired.

It was brutally hot in the car. No one complained, but Ribowski was with them today—a little shaky and gray and very quiet—and this extra passenger had the effect of squashing them even in such a large automobile. The discomfort had been hard to bear before they had seen the smoke, but was now a mere nothing . . .

On the road they encountered part of the Portuguese column—a dozen jeeps, a few trucks, some ambulances and two staff cars. The *voluntarios* stared and a few half-waved or saluted. They smoked and talked, presumably waiting for the skirmish to finish so that they could go somewhere for food and drink. They had pointed noses and sad, romantic, striking faces, many of them, under their long, soft, peaked tropical hats. But it was difficult to like them.

They sat in the Mercedes silent in shock. Only Ribowski had any comment, a bitter growl: "They are as efficient as the Germans were." They had all read the words and heard the petitioners but each time starvation, disease, misery and violent death in actuality startled and appalled them, for they were inevitably of their own comfortable environment, no matter how concerned they were on behalf of the less fortunate of the world.

Five kilometers farther was the track—as a faded notice board told them—to the Duque de Machaze falls. It was not possible to drive the Mercedes more than a few kilometers, and when Ekelund stopped it they were all aware at once of the gigantic noise of water. Then, as they stood indecisively, a shot startled them. Marianne jumped and flinched and made a little moaning sound of fright and protest.

A few Portuguese soldiers appeared, tense with the attitude of those who kill or are killed. One shouted as he saw the Mercedes.

"What does he say?"

"He says to keep away."

McQuade instructed Asare Johnson, "Stay in the car and look after Marianne."

"Why, Mr. McQuade? What is happening?"

"They are shooting black faces."

Asare said, "I must not be confined to the car. I must see." He looked very upset and was trembling as he got out of the car.

McQuade said to Alferink, "I have used all my film. Do you have your camera with you?" When Alferink said, "Yes," he urged grimly, "Bring it."

There were many small trees and much dust and the grass was tall but seemed sucked dry in the heat. Even the trees did not have the stamina to produce more than the tiniest leaves. In the thorny and shoulder-high bush the *voluntarios* searched, a hundred feet apart, over the visible area of a square mile. The noise of the waterfall increased so that it stunned the senses, and as the UN group walked apprehensively nearer, there was a mist from its spray and the vegetation glistened wet and thrived. And there, hemmed in against small cool trees and shade and lumps of rock, under a slow array of tiny clouds in an intense blue sky, the remnants of the nationalists had been trapped, for there was a three-hundred-foot waterfall behind them. The noise of the water was deafening. It overwhelmed the emotions and shook the ground. Words were nearly impossible. Half or three-quarters of a mile across rocks and bushes and a torrent of clear water was one of the most impressive waterfalls in Africa. The water thundered down from a broad semicircular cliff which it was eroding and crashed over small islands of rock and lush vegetation and came around very fast and white over minor drops and went down, clean and cool now, but gathering dirt and twigs and the litter of villages until it became dull brown and calm when it reached Vila Lobanda, fifty miles south. It was intensely beautiful and not at all commercialized, and it was a grim parody of tourism that they had to see it, the spray and the two or three rainbows, in such circumstances. For here, in this spectacular view of Angolique, were the dead and the dying. A few dozen of them. Young, it would seem, some so small and thin they must be children who'd wanted to play war as the grownups did. Some were burned, their cotton shirts brown or black or in shreds, and their shoulders and hips burned raw. God only knew what momentum had brought them this far. A few had leaped into the water and had been carried to where their bodies had jammed in rocks and trees,

145

and here they would wait the flies and corruption or the river to rise and wash them away.

Alferink had taken two or three photographs.

Still the isolated shots.

Johnson said, or, rather, shouted in a tumult of emotion, "They are killing the prisoners."

McQuade answered, "No. There are no prisoners. The wounded." It was very much a relative qualification and not likely to persuade Asare of the civilized nature of the Portuguese. Actually, the *voluntarios* were hounding down rebels—wounded or otherwise. A few would presumably get away, but not many, for most had been caught in that terrible onslaught of petroleum.

Alferink said, "If I could get just one photograph."

"No. They would shoot you," insisted McQuade.

"That would be very good evidence indeed. And you said—"

"I know," said McQuade. "But don't. They would *have* to shoot you. It would be the usual claim of accident—'This man foolishly wandered onto a battlefield.' "

Asare cried in despair, "They are killing my kind of people."

"I suggested that you stay in the car."

"So I should not see?"

"So they would not shoot you."

Asare pleaded, "For the love of God, let us do something."

There was a *voluntario* a hundred feet off and he had found something. Asare ran toward him, with Alferink following. The *voluntario* hesitated, shouted and then pointed his submachine gun at Asare. When he saw Alferink behind, he was bewildered. There was a single shot. After a while Asare and Alferink came back. Asare was weeping with his head down. Alferink said nothing, but looked badly shaken. He worked on his Polaroid camera then passed over the photograph. It was a bit blurred, but showed with sickening truth the already lacerated body twitching on the ground and the agony in the face, the terrified arms pleading, and the *voluntario* firing from the hip in haste. There was nothing to be said, although Ekelund made the calmest possible comment: "That will be indisputable evidence."

They walked away numbly from the grisly spot, the sound of the huge waterfall dying with distance. In the car the waiting

Marianne, about to jest bravely, saw their faces and said nothing.

The rest of the day was hard to live through. They had to go through the motions of people who had seen nothing . . . At the Protestant mission an American lady welcomed the party from New York and tried to talk to them, feed them, show them what she was doing—her small contribution to Africa. Her classroom was better than Father da Silva's, her energy more robust, and children sang with innocent open mouths and staring shy eyes.

They were late getting back to the Villa Amélia. It was dark and they were hot and on edge. Ribowski was exhausted and went to his room, but the others were obliged to go to a party. A party was the last thing McQuade wanted to attend this evening, but Brandão had said that the Governor General would be there. There was little time to cool down after the heat and distress of the day. McQuade longed for a shower, but there wasn't even time for that. He was hot and uncomfortable in the lightweight suit. Only Barney was relatively unruffled. She had no comment to make about Mr. Costa beyond, "He's a very nice person and it makes me feel mean doing this. He wants me to meet his daughter tomorrow."

McQuade could feel the sweat rolling down his neck. His shirt stuck to his back.

It was a party for a cultural group from Oregon and, not unnaturally, was held in the American Consulate.

They were half an hour late despite hurrying.

"How do you do?" Mrs. Fairjon greeted McQuade. She was heavy, all teeth and arrogance, and as she raised a hand to him she boasted, "This hand has grasped the hands of your Bishop of Montreal."

McQuade stared stonily. He was hot and tired and in no mood for snobs. His clothes were not quite suitable, a little too heavy for the tropical evenings; McQuade damned the salesman in New York. His hands were a bit sweaty. He saw the distaste of the physical contact of flesh reflected in the eyes of the American Consul's wife. The urge to wipe her hand was irresistible and she did so, in front of him, on her buttocks. McQuade could have struck her.

Faces at parties in Vila Lobanda were beginning to become familiar. Mr. Duffin waved a hand from the middle of a group. The French and Belgian ladies, whose names McQuade hadn't caught,

147

were standing around delicately; it was, presumably, their profession, their place in politics. Miss Montguerre was there with another teacher and blushed uneasily and stared through Theo Alferink. Thank God *that's* over, McQuade thought.

The excuse for the party was the group from Oregon. They were folk artists bringing culture to Africa, but McQuade noticed that it was "just ourselves"—the sallow drained skin of the white man in the tropics and the attractive, painted faces of the young women who'd only come to this continent after new drugs had made it safe for their delicate skins.

"Intellectually, that is, we feel it will bring stimulation," a young woman in the Oregon group was saying without a qualm, and the French and Belgian women smiled with secret superiority at these fools who had to gush, while McQuade thought bitterly of Portugal's cultural mission here and the ghastly burned things in the village and the blood trickling from broken bodies into the hot earth while the senses were stunned by the roar of thousands of tons of water.

"United Nations?" echoed a bearded young man from Oregon when introduced, and he said it as if it implied Hello, fellow American. Perhaps he was one of those who believed it was an American institution; after all, he'd paid a dollar to go around the place with an American guide . . . "You've come a long way. What are you doing here?"—a naïve question that meant he was merely nervous and brittle in conversation. He could scarcely be that ignorant of both the UN and Africa. In normal circumstances McQuade would have been courteous if not interested. After all, the whole group were only in their twenties; coming to Africa at all was pretty important in their lives. They wanted to go home with a happy impression, success, mission accomplished. But tonight any perspective but shame and horror was merely a posture to get McQuade through the evening. To go through the motions of a party as if nothing had been seen or heard that day except colored children in print dresses singing "Soldiers of the Lord" was a strain alcohol didn't anesthetize, but Brandão had been quite correct in supposing that the Governor General would be here. He had arrived and was talking now to Mr. Fairjon, but his eyes looked around the room, examining and identifying carefully. He was a man of medium height and strong appearance, with a distinguished sunburned face, silver hair and mustache. His eyes met McQuade's unflinchingly but with the care of one who thinks, That is the man of whom I must beware in this room.

McQuade was in no hurry for the introduction. He was still cooling down while others were warming up. The beautiful Miss Montguerre said with concern, "You look hot and angry." She was disconcerted when McQuade answered, "I am. How about you? Has my friend Alferink been a nuisance?" This was too frank for her and she moved on with her female companion, looking with shock at McQuade, as if he'd said a rude word in the assembly hall of the Lycée.

Theo Alferink was in fact surrounded by young ladies, including Barney, who was four inches taller than any of the Portuguese, American or European women present and strikingly more voluptuous. She moved with a kind of untouched health while others, although beautiful, had the marks in their faces of Africa, age, hatreds and vanities.

De la Plaza, standing for a moment near McQuade, and looking at this group, said with fury into McQuade's ear, "Look at her! What superb arrogance masquerading as a kind of big-hearted Texan innocent! What an evaluation of the world! Everything in it related to herself! What preoccupation with self!"

He spoke with the bitterness of the disappointed or the rejected. There was some truth in what he said, for Barney did give the impression of being lightly unconcerned by what was happening around her. She still bubbled with good humor as if she were in New York's sophisticated atmosphere. But McQuade surmised that she had no option but to think in the limited terms of what was happening to herself, for she had to be on guard all the time against the assaults and maneuvers of an older battle.

"She has not seen what we have seen today, Gregorio."

"She is suffocated with vanity," said de la Plaza unhappily, giving himself away completely.

"What does it matter to you, Gregorio?"

"Oh, it does not matter to me," asserted de la Plaza hastily.

"Be glad of that," counseled McQuade, "for otherwise it might interrupt your work here."

149

"Alferink is squeezing her hand," de la Plaza said in shock. "And last night he was talking for hours past midnight. I heard them—"

McQuade looked, but merely saw Barney laughing—although the joke was Alferink's. Asare Johnson stared down into his wineglass, hiding his face. De la Plaza protested hotly, "Does that man have a complex? Why does he not leave women alone? Is not his wife beautiful? Why does Barney take so much notice?"

"She's a good stenographer," said McQuade, "and that's all that really matters to us."

But he was uneasy about Alferink for all that. If he chose to make himself agreeable to Barney it would create tension within the subcommittee.

Brandão said from somewhere, "Excellency, this is Mr. Mc-Quade, who is chairman of the United Nations subcommittee . . . Colonel Domingues."

McQuade shook hands with the Governor General. Mr. Costa hovered anxiously around. McQuade wondered what the Governor General would say if he told him that Mr. Costa had been swimming with Miss Barney Widener while he, McQuade, and others, including the Minister of Education, had been witnessing the last stages of a successful massacre . . .

The Governor General spoke of his visit to Salisbury. He talked of the many things Angolique had in common with Rhodesia—thousands of miles of border for a start; railways and ports shared; the improvement of communications within Angolique which were relative. He talked of the benefits of Portugal's latest development plan and what it meant to Angolique in terms of hydroelectric schemes, industry and the building of new ports and towns, with increasing development of railways and roads and the handling of cargoes; he forecast highways and the irrigation of vast areas for Portuguese settlers and oil pipelines that would have their outlet in Porto Girassol. These things were in progress, he told McQuade, not ideas on paper.

"Where have you been so far?" the Governor General inquired, implying How many of these great things have you seen?

McQuade told him.

"That's a lot of schools," protested the colonel. "Who wants to

150

see so many? The statistics are available. Have you seen the dam of the Lower Bompopo?" And when McQuade said they had not (with the useless implication Who wants to see *water* when we've come to see politicians?), the Governor General flicked a finger and Costa began to talk of possible arrangements. McQuade had no wish to argue in case any emphasis on schools and missions aroused suspicions.

Instead, he pressed the limited opportunity the Governor General had given him. "Excellency, I am interested and grateful. If it is not trespassing on your generosity perhaps we could venture farther afield than the Bompopo River. Angolique is, after all, a territory of three-quarters of a million square miles. We have so far been limited to forty or fifty."

"I cannot allow you to go far north," the Governor General asserted. "There has been some fighting on the border. I must be responsible for your safety. But south . . . Why not? In ten days perhaps?"

"That would be most acceptable," McQuade acknowledged. "I wonder, Excellency, if, to fulfill my purpose here, I may interview some of those who are in opposition."

The Governor General stiffened in shock.

"I do not know of such people. Only foreigners who invade us."

"The two I'd like to talk to are politicians, I'm told, who are in prison. Their names are Mr. Maúa and Mr. Andrade."

"These men are criminals."

"That is possible," agreed McQuade. "But is it not true that they are the leaders of the APP?"

"That is an illegal organization," said Colonel Domingues. "The so-called evidence they would give you would be untruths and I consider that enough people are spreading malicious untruths about Portugal's mission in Africa without your typist taking down the statements of bandits so that the world can read them. I regret, Mr. McQuade, that on that particular request I have to disappoint you."

Asare Johnson stood by himself, neglected long moment after moment, for Barney was fully occupied by masculine attention a mere three yards away. If it had been a bad day for McQuade, how much worse must it have been for Asare? McQuade moved

151

across to give him the comfort of his presence in a hostile room.

He reasoned uselessly, "Try to look cheerful, Asare. It goes with the job."

Asare confessed what was on his mind.

"It is all so humiliating. It is because I am colored, of course. I offered myself with great devotion and respect, but she is perplexed. She claims she saw no sign of this previously. We were just *friends* working together. And now every day I have to meet her and watch her flaunting her good looks before these others who are married. That fool Alferink talks and she laughs as she never laughed for me. She seemed so beautiful and wise. Perhaps she is a fool, too? With the terrible things we have seen today it is unbearable. To have to chatter with these criminals and, as well, to see *her* laugh because she likes them more than she likes me."

McQuade thought, What a day! I'm not just a chairman but psychiatrist and father-confessor as well! But he was fond of Asare and tried to console him.

"She likes you too much to be frivolous."

"She has said this?"

"Something like it. She cannot be frivolous and it is hard for her to smile easily when she senses your seriousness."

"So she hurts me by chattering to fools?"

"Don't be too harsh. She is bothered by men who see her pretty face and wish to be amusing to attract her. They are like children showing off."

"It has serious implications, Mr. McQuade."

"Only if she allows them."

"Alferink held her hand here in this crowded place."

"What could she do?"

"Tell him to desist."

"She did that by withdrawing her hand."

"But still she stands there, talking to him."

"And others, Asare. It is a cocktail party. Listen, man. You are not here to fall in love. You saw those terrible things today. *That* is what you and I are here to fight against. We have to find out if this country is ready for the *indigena* to take it over and whether he is being exploited. Do not be diverted by infatuation."

"You speak wisely, Mr. McQuade," said Asare, smiling wistfully, "but a pain in the heart is hard to ignore."

152

The party finally ended. The UN subcommittee, shaken by the day, did not linger.

McQuade was tired, almost exhausted, but he still had work to do. Tonight he had his next appointment with Bajune, and he wished to keep it.

The telephone made its first nightly claim for Mr. Regio and McQuade hurried to answer it. Theo Alferink and Barney were alone in the office; it was significant that they'd ignored the call. Barney hesitated and then went off to bed. McQuade took the opportunity of talking to Alferink. It was a disagreeable experience.

"Theo, why don't you leave Barney and Miss Montguerre alone? Buy yourself a girlie magazine or go into the town and see if there's a cathouse if you're feeling randy."

Alferink was startled by the frankness and was quick to become offended. "Hell, I was only talking to her. Are you afraid I might make too much progress with our stenographer?"

"It's so damn *silly*. It's embarrassing. And Suzé is a very fine woman and a nice person. I'm sure she's not doing anything foolish while you're out here."

"She'll be drinking," said Alferink, red in the face. "Listen, Shaun. I like people, not just erotic experience. And Barney likes me. She finds me amusing." But he looked uncomfortable despite this innocent defense.

"You might drive me into a position in which I'd have to send her home and get someone else sent out. We're here to *work*."

"Okay, Mr. Chairman."

McQuade said in a flash of irritation, "Taking photographs of colored girls who don't know your motives was pretty cheap. It was like a pimply youth who's eaten too much starch and isn't getting enough exercise."

"Now we're really in the open! A typical Canadian reaction! Protestant at that!" sneered Alferink. "In fact a typical North American piece of hypocrisy. Christ, how I hate these Jesus-loving, shaven-headed tycoons and the crew-cut boys with their Bible and Declaration in one hand and napalm bomb in the other. Extroverts with the longings of introverts. And loved. They all want to be loved. Barney and I happen to be over twenty-one. What in hell's it got to *do* with our work?"

"You're out of breath!" said McQuade. "Save it, Theo, for the

153

liberal journals. I just happen to be fond of Suzé, who happens to be your wife."

"And I happen to be fond of Barney, who's the one human being around here . . . Are you going somewhere?"

"To see Bajune."

"At this hour? You're working awfully hard for that Nobel Prize, aren't you?"

"I am working on the problem given to me," said McQuade calmly. "Mr. Bajune doesn't have the conveniences of an office or telephone or, for that matter, a stenographer. Not on this territory anyway."

Alferink saw the point.

"I'm sorry, Shaun. That was silly of me. Shall I come with you?"

"Better not," counseled McQuade, pleased to smile again. "The bicycle wouldn't carry your 180 pounds as well as mine."

"Do you really think it matters if I take Barney out to a restaurant or somewhere?"

"In theory, no. But in practice it's going to upset Asare, who seems to be in love with her, and Gregorio, who thinks he is. It also humiliates Marianne, who gets ignored socially but is expected to work as hard as Barney for us."

"You've made your point," admitted Alferink.

McQuade carried the bicycle across the convent grounds, as before, in case the front of the villa was watched. He was late and a little alarmed at the silence in the town; it made him conspicuous. He made the journey in half an hour and arrived hot and uncomfortable in sweat-soaked clothes, and cycled past the Fort Eduardo to the entrance of the cashew plantation.

Nothing happened.

Nobody came and all he could hear was his own breath and the croaking of frogs and the senseless chirping of cicadas and the wind stirring in the vast hot night. He pulled up a shirt sleeve over a wet wrist to examine his watch. He was scarcely ten minutes late for the appointment.

Bajune did not come. It filled McQuade with foreboding and fright on behalf of the little man with the deep, honest voice. He hoped that nothing had happened to Bajune and tried to convince himself that the ex-schoolteacher had become nervous because he,

154

McQuade, was ten minutes late. But he knew by the physical feeling of despair that this was not so and the little teacher who had been to the LSE in London and was still in awe of a Mr. Swinnerton had had his life altered, perhaps ended, by today's battle with petroleum and bullets.

It was real at last.

They'd moved out of the arena of words—the petitioners with sad faces in the Trusteeship Council, the caller on the telephone, the whispers in corridors and what the journalists had to say, and Dr. Pessanha justifying Portugal with good-humored reasonableness—out of the unreality of words into the flesh and blood, the tears and pain, the poverty, disease and death . . .

Notes with the gravest concern and regret that Portuguese soldiers, volunteers, young men of Catholic faith, with reasonable IQs whether literate or not, certainly with a knowledge of right and wrong, did nevertheless direct jets of flaming petroleum approximately one hundred yards long onto the grass and mud huts of African villagers irrespective of participation in anti-Portuguese activities and without any option of surrender, and did burn alive men, women, children, babies and animals; *notes also with despair* that equally civilized and morally conscious men did apply rifle muzzles to the bases of the skulls of African persons politically critical of the regime in Angolique (but not allowed free expression of that criticism), these persons already gravely burned or wounded. *Bears in consideration* that the morality of the people of civilized Western society is such that they are in little position to condemn these actions, their own honesty, morality, humility and dignity and concern for anything but selfish ends being of a standard greatly lower than for some centuries . . .

He was just one man in the world. What could he do about it? One man and a subcommittee, already divided among themselves. Ekelund, a good and serious member like so many Scandinavians in the UN. Asare Johnson, sincere and earnest but emotionally upset and involved. Ribowski, an unknown quality, critical already of his fellow members, already ill and not likely to be very active physically for weeks. De la Plaza and Alferink, already on terms of dislike, although both good workers and Alferink physically brave today obtaining that photograph. Marianne ready with the sour, humorous remark that was easy to ride through now, but the barbs of which might lacerate and cause pain and anger more easily as the days go by. They weren't two weeks out and the symptoms of living too close together were beginning to reveal themselves already. In the villa they each had the privacy of a bedroom, but there was nowhere for any two to stand and talk about a third without deliberately leaving the villa and seeming unnecessarily secretive and conspiratorial in doing so. The good-natured, attractive Barney was a problem. It was bad enough when she, quite reasonably, accepted invitations to restaurants or tennis or the swimming pool of the Hotel Marromeu and Naval Club, sharing her company with apparent impartiality. Once let her go off at night with someone and outright hatreds might begin . . .

It was one o'clock in the morning when he returned to the villa. As he came inside, weak on his legs after the unfamiliar exercise on the bicycle, the telephone rang.

He had to answer it.

It could be anyone in the world.

He expected the usual nonsense about Mr. Regio, but Brandão's voice said quickly, "They've arrested Dr. Pais," and hung up instantly.

Useless to try to sleep, although exhausted. Hours went by and finally anxiety couldn't keep him awake any longer. The road drills began at four in the morning. "An urgent program," Costa had explained—so urgent that it never moved more than a few yards. McQuade stirred uneasily in his sleep. In his dreams the tanks fought point blank and the Italian peasants fled from their hovels screaming. Somewhere, always out of sight, Kristan wept for him. He awoke, drained, to the problems of the day and the memories of yesterday. Across the balcony and beyond the convent and the acacia trees and the glass skyscrapers of the airlines buildings—and ignoring for a sour moment the sweet voices in the Lycée grounds —he saw the crescent of Vila Lobanda and the sea, bright under a morning sky without the *cassimbo*. McQuade already hated them . . .

156

8 ■ ■

IN NEW YORK IT WAS snowing. Kristan saw it out of the window as she conceded into the telephone, "Sure I understand, Della. Maybe I'll go along and see it this evening on my own."

It was impossible not to be angry, or frustrated, or whatever it was. In ten days she'd found out—for the third time in three years —how life altered and humiliated her when there was no man around. All of a sudden she couldn't go to the theater because Shaun wasn't here to take her. Abruptly, eating out was impossible and at home dull. She was a Canadian in an American city. Every mail delivery brought invitations to functions, but she couldn't accept any of them because they were part of an institution: politics. It wasn't even Shaun and his wife they were inviting, but Canada, with a view to—well—whatever it might be.

She had precisely three close American friends and she'd just telephoned one. It would be embarrassing to phone a second one, because if the first—or, for that matter, the third—found out that she'd phoned the second they'd know she was pleading. Kristan felt frustration—which had lumps of fright in it—for it was impossible to "go along and see it this evening on my own," for a woman of her kind could not go alone to a movie in the evening. New York might be the most impressive and interesting city in the world, but it was a tough one, full of people who noticed loneliness and took advantage of it in the dark.

It was, nevertheless, ridiculous that a woman of forty-three could not see a film which interested her. The snow fell steadily outside, but Kristan thought, To hell with that, I must do *something* and I'd like to see it. She flicked through the paper to find out what time the feature began. Theaters in Manhattan were pretty empty in the early afternoon. This one was downtown, she noticed, slightly alarmed, but decided to take a taxi. And she hurried an early lunch and ate it with enjoyment.

The taxi skidded here and there. "Y'know what I wanna do be-

157

fore they take me to the boneyard?" the driver confided. "I wanna go to one of them islands in the sun." Kristan laughed for the first time in three days.

She paid her two dollars and went into the small, clean theater and up the escalator, and sat in the sweetened gloom and relaxed, feeling safe from scrutiny. The theater was indeed nearly empty. Farther down sat three solitaries, widely separated, for some absurd reason reading newspapers in the negligible illumination. Gradually it subsided—the shame of being there, alone, at two in the afternoon, because she did want to see this picture and Shaun was away and she couldn't *plead* with people to fill her hours for six weeks, or ten, or more likely twelve. Her heart froze when she thought that what she had endured for ten days might go on for months. She had heard of UN wives who'd had nervous breakdowns, even of broken marriages. Perhaps a job might help, but a job for eight, ten or twelve weeks at most, and for a Canadian diplomat's wife in Manhattan? No, it was impossible. It was humiliating that a politician's wife should in loneliness have to resort to this sort of thing—coming to a theater at two in the afternoon— but she was bored. No. It was worse than boredom. It was like being bereaved and silent and close to despair. She was frightened —that was the truth of it—so full of fear at times that she couldn't eat. The big block of flats was new, and only five out of twenty-eight apartments were yet occupied, and of the people she knew the occupants of only two apartments and of these only liked those of one. And they were away for a fortnight.

There was nothing, then, to stop anyone who'd gotten into the vestibule—and the doorman couldn't hang around *all* the time— from coming along the balcony of number 17 (which was empty) to *her* balcony, and there was nothing difficult about the lock on her door. Anybody could break that. The prime safety was that she was high up, but once past the doorman any person would soon be wandering along hundreds of feet of empty corridors and steps. Not to ravish *her*—Kristan knew her position in the hierarchy of desirability: it was down from its maximum of 78 per cent in 1947 to around 45 per cent now—but to steal, or murder senselessly for trinkets, a few dollars, a wristwatch, and she'd have to die because, alive, she would be a witness . . . Even in the light of day she

158

saw the eyes staring at her in the street—hostile, hating her clothes and manner of walking, and wanting to humiliate them by violence —the eyes of men who were dangerous, had no normal work, Puerto Ricans and Negroes and tough-looking young whites . . . And people like Della O'Dowd didn't *see* how terrified she was. They assumed she went on as before, with good humor, and just had to do without a sex life. Instead, it was living a nightmare that drained away appetite and energy and even intelligence. She couldn't keep phoning. They were seeing too much of her, these few friends, but wasn't that reasonable if your husband was away and your son was in Canada still and likely to go to France?

The man sat by her in the darkness. He'd been waiting. He said in quite a pleasant voice, "I like British films, don't you? Sensitive. Bryan Forbes wrote the script. Did you see that other one a few months ago?"

Real terror made Kristan so weak she was bathed in sweat instantly and her legs fluttered, too weak to move. Logic made no contribution. She was in a theater: no rape or theft was possible— safe in theory and, surely, in practice. But panic poured over her like a hot exhausting mist. She moved ten seats away. He didn't follow, but he was there. The afternoon's escape was shattered. It had materialized into the horror for which she'd waited in trepidation these ten days. Ten *weeks,* the useless logic told her, and black despair weakened her. She tried to go on watching the film—after all, he hadn't been vulgar, which was, fundamentally, what was feared, nor did he persist by following. But the film became a parody of her own terror. And it would end at four-thirty and they'd all go out and he could follow or even seize her in the winter's darkness and snow in this rather drab downtown area of warehouses and shoddy little restaurants and people who didn't feature in the brochures or the travel magazines.

When the film did finish and the place was illuminated and the twenty or thirty solitaries moved out self-consciously in the sudden, almost embarrassing silence, the man had gone. At least Kristan thought he must have gone. She didn't quite look to see, believing that if she didn't see him she wouldn't know which one was *him* and he wouldn't exist. A surviving flippant part of her analyzed: maybe he's looked and doesn't fancy me in the light! But the fear ignored this as a forest fire will sweep past a tiny stream and jump across highways.

Outside, the snow was quite heavy. Soon it would bring automobiles to a standstill. No sign of taxis. Kristan rarely used the subway. She normally moved in an orbit that was Shaun and United Nations and was surprisingly separate from the rest of Manhattan.

In the subway the rush hour had begun—sweat and fumes and tremendous noise and blasts of hot air on her legs and an atmosphere rich with the parallels of panic. People of another world. Advertisements. Dirt and litter. And faces staring. Tired, dirty faces, some of them, that hated or scrutinized frankly this female who had an indefinable "I don't belong" look. Not far. Downtown 23rd to the stop at 96th. But packed and hostile. Was *he* among these? Faces and bodies all around. She, too, had to stand; she wasn't beautiful enough for courtesy. Indeed, courtesy was impossible; it was a desperate fight to get in or out. A man's face a mere ten inches away, every sallow pore sweating and shining, and his big, sad bloodshot eyes looking too often, becoming hot, and certain of reciprocation, and behind, a body, seizing opportunity, squashed inevitably, but prodding with more than permissible suggestiveness into her buttocks. A face never to be seen. Was it *his?* And nothing to be done but accept this parody of rape and scream silently in the mind until he'd finished, was ashamed, or the ride ended for one of them. She moved inches hopelessly, in vain. And then a stop, thirty people went out, forty came in, and a new face, replacing the bloodshot-eyed one, surprised to find a woman's face so near, pleasured, anxious to stare, but more easily avoided, a conscience perhaps, and the probing had ended. What strange satisfactions the peculiar ones of this city must obtain for the price of a ticket, although the statistics of the other things they did disputed that.

She hurried along 96th Street, forgot to buy food, greeted the doorman and the central heating and the safety of the vestibule with hysterical relief. "What an afternoon!" The doorman, six feet tall, anonymous but never doubted in blue coat, gold buttons, peaked hat, acknowledged, "Yes, it's coming down nicely now," and then, as Kristan stood by the elevator's bronze door, he cried, anonymity lost, human, he cared, he'd thought of her, a lonely human, "There were some letters for you," and joy weakened her as much as terror had. In the ascending elevator she flicked through them. The Military Staff Committee invites Mr. and Mrs. Shaun McQuade. The Japanese Delegation, the Cultural Attaché of the Ivory Coast, the Permanent Mission of Panama to the United Nations, the Air Attaché of the Italian Embassy in Washington, the Mid-Canadian Bank . . . *Please* God, one from him. I can't bear it if there isn't. But there was nothing for her, Mrs. McQuade, the individual, only for the wife of the Canadian Minister to be escorted by her husband.

In the apartment the telephone was ringing. It was like someone answering a cry for pity. But she was too late. If she'd stayed home . . . She had no idea who it might be and felt like weeping in frustration at the ridiculous afternoon.

After a while she couldn't keep it up. The mind relaxed, believing that Shaun was there, or coming soon, and Kristan ate a meal. Not enough. Soup and a drink of coffee, but it was adequate. The rest of the evening stared her in the face. She began her daily letter, but found that she was admitting her frightened loneliness. This wouldn't help Shaun out there with his problems. She tore that one up and began again, but lightly: "Dearest One, I'm missing you. I didn't think I would, you know! I thought I could use a rest! But it's part of the fun, cooking for you and emptying the ashtrays . . . It's snowing hard here, but I went out this afternoon to see a movie . . ."

The snow silenced the city. It really had brought traffic almost to a standstill. Nor were there the usual noises outside—bells, sirens, feet, voices laughing and the great roar of rubber tires on highway which you could hear as one everlasting sound even if you went up to the 102nd floor of the Empire State Building.

The book didn't hold her. It was too dull for a mind that had fear creeping around in it. Kristan knew from experience that the visual could claim her attention—whether movie or TV—by the sheer process of bludgeoning the senses. She turned on the TV. Any nonsense would do if it helped her to overcome loneliness and resist using the telephone. She'd been making too many calls and knew it.

On the little screen the girl was undressing. Sweet music came

161

from her transistor set. It was quite a glamorous bedroom. The girl sort of unfastened her hair and shook it free. Her undies and stockings were black. She was beautiful, but pretending tonight to be just an ordinary girl, stenographer, nurse, or whatever it was. Long shots of her moving about slowly in the undies. This was to rivet the male audience presumably. The girl looked in the mirror at herself, sat on a bed, picked up a magazine, yawned. Curtains fluttered and the maniac stared in. In a moment the girl would look in the mirror and see him. He was tough, ragged, unshaven.

Kristan stared, paralyzed with fear. It was *her* situation. It was nonsense, quite ridiculous, even the mirror business had been done thousands of times before. Pure corn. But she was numb with horror. The girl had seen the maniac now. She didn't scream. Kristan's brain knew it was the beginning of one of those two-hours-alone-with-a-madman stories, with suspense and tiny hints of sexual possibilities one after the other. Instead of screaming the girl breathed heavily, pumping her full breasts in and out in the closeup and asking (as they all asked—it was the formula in this story), "What do you want?" And then began the terrifying dialogue, a parody of all previous dialogues in a thousand films and plays: "My husband will be back in a minute" . . . "What's his name?" . . . "Ed" . . . "The woman in the post office said he'd gone for two days" . . . "He phoned just now" . . . "How long ago?" . . . "Oh, only about two minutes" . . . and the grim, humorless first crisis: "I hate liars. You're a liar. Why do you lie to me? I cut the telephone wires ten minutes ago."

The situation faded out to give way to the commercials. Now was the time for Kristan to rush across the room and turn off the TV. There would still be a residue of fright. But it had gripped her too hard. She had neither the will nor the physical strength to get up and cross the room. She had to see what happened to the girl. She must know. So she sat watching the play, horror and fright in such a quantity that the script writer would have been astonished at his own success, and in the end, when the husband *did* come home and batter at the door as the maniac's hands tore at the girl's lingerie, with the visual, morally permissible intention of strangling her, not ravishing, by then Kristan was so scared she could scarcely breathe.

162

She had to go to bed eventually, and the fear was a hard heavy lump in her that made even walking a problem. She went around locking doors, opening and closing cupboards and feeling all the time that someone was behind her, just in the next room, standing laughing, waiting until terror had reached a maximum, whereupon he'd step in from the little balcony that was eighty feet above 96th Street. She even opened the glass doors and went onto this snow-covered balcony. There was nobody there, but it was no consolation. He'd come. He'd be here. He was even now walking up Third Avenue or West 155th by Trinity Cemetery. He'd been offended by a woman and had a deep, foul grievance. The knife was in his pocket. His hands were dirty. He was partially drugged so there was no hope of reasoning with him . . .

Kristan undressed slowly, full of fear, hiding behind the screen of doors as if he really was watching from the balcony. She went around the apartment again, checking on doors and keys. She locked herself in, but it was useless and merely filled her with the certainty of having locked everyone else *out*. Except him. He'd materialize from somewhere. The wardrobe! She hadn't checked that. She got out of bed, looked fearfully in the wardrobe. Nothing.

The telephone rang and she ran out of the bedroom hysterically to it, a friend calling in the night. She'd surrender, admit terror, and whoever it was would take pity, come and fetch her. Logic knew in the thirty footsteps that this was not so. Nothing would be admitted. Friends didn't stir themselves: they'd advise you to take a drink. No. Nobody really *cared*. They'd merely be fascinated. And, aware of this, she knew even as she ran and fought with the locked door like an enemy in the way that you had to die before acknowledging that you were a fool . . .

Wrong number anyway.

Kristan put down the receiver. It was midnight. The human contact had helped a little. A woman's voice, too, not some man testing to see if you were at home waiting to be terrified by him . . . What's a'matter with me? she cried to herself. Maybe I'd better get some tablets. No. That's dangerous.

After another hour and a half, tension relaxing slowly, she fell asleep and when she awoke it was half past eight in the morning and there was the sour tiring taste of terror in her mouth. She was

163

ashamed, felt like a fool, but it had been real enough and would happen again. She felt no joy in the day and thought, I can't be bothered to eat, with a qualifying voice of normality and sanity insisting, You must, you must, you can't go on like this day after day.

She had to *make* herself go outside and do something. Buy food, see faces, look in shops, select some magazines, walk around in the hope of meeting someone she knew, talking to them. She fled out of the apartment, careless now of locks and doors. And in the vestibule the same tall doorman in his blue coat with the gold buttons asked, "Shall I get you a taxi, Mrs. McQuade?" and she said meaninglessly, "Yes," because she didn't know where she was going. Now she felt a panic about where to tell the taxi driver to go to, in six inches of snow at that.

Kristan realized with shock that she hadn't thought of today's mail. It was always like that. If you longed for a letter, prayed for one, asked if it had come, it never came. But here now, thought about casually, almost ignored, was a letter from Shaun. It had been mailed in Lisbon. She knew that he was now beyond Europe, had been in Africa for days, but still her heart cried with love.

She sat in the taxi, going nowhere, near to tears as she read his calm words "Dearest Other Half of Me . . ." —a diplomat's wife who was lost in this city of millions, as lonely as if it was on another continent and had a language she didn't know.

Thirty-six hours later she went to a New Year's party given by Irene Hayott and her husband, Julius. Irene was the second American friend. Julius was in the UN, but very few of the other people who turned up at the party had anything to do with the organization. Strictly, Julius was third rank, while Shaun was a minister, far higher in the gradation, but Kristan hadn't been able to resist the last-minute telephone call. And Irene seemed to understand loneliness all right. She greeted Kristan, "Hello. How goes it without Shaun? What on earth did you do at Christmas?" "Oh, I spent that at Della's. We had a fine time." It wasn't true exactly.

Della was there tonight, standing with her husband, Goodwin, in a group. They all had their husbands there. It was impossible not to feel out of things accordingly. Kristan took a long drink of punch

164

to get rid of the terror and loneliness, the exhaustion of a private battle. How foolish she'd feel if any of these people knew the distresses of that battle. But they didn't. It was her only advantage, although it was hard to be sure that her fears did not show on her face like other weaknesses, drink or debauchery.

"How's the world using you?" Goodwin asked.

There was nothing to say in answer except, "Oh, not bad. Life chugs on."

Della thought of something and apologized: "Sorry I couldn't come the other day to that movie," and Kristan stiffened in anxiety, felt the beginnings of a flush, wanted the subject dropped. The other few people standing there, meaningless, strangers to Kristan, holding glasses half empty, examining her. Kristan McQuade—the name and the person had just been given to them, had entered their lives, and they wanted to see what they should do about it, if anything. Only her brain assured Kristan that they couldn't at once identify all her foolish terrors. Her instincts shouted that they could and did.

She therefore anticipated their condemnation by an explanation. She giggled, mildly hysterical, too funny. "You know what happened there? A man tried to pick me up. An intellectual at that."

"Jesus," Della said excitedly, two or three drinks ahead. "That's *living!* Nobody ever tries with me," she complained with a laugh. "Not even the Marines. Did he take you off in his Cadillac? What did he *say?*"

Not for a moment did any of them see the terror.

"Oh, something about the script."

"Maybe he wrote it," a woman said. "Some people live life like a script. I have a theory about that."

"You shouldn't go to the theater alone," Della chided. "Kristan's husband's gone to Africa," she explained to the group, and they all stared at her as if they knew how it was when your husband went to Africa. She had to say something, talk, not just stand there being scrutinized and feeling all her nerve ends were exposed for their interest. But what was there to talk about except what you lived?

Thus she found herself saying, "Did you see that play on TV the other night, Della, about a girl and a maniac?"

165

Della laughed. "No. It just feels like that all the time. Trouble with real-estate men is they have to live it, all day and night so their wives don't see anything except clients . . ."

"It was so *funny*," Kristan explained. "And so quiet outside with all the snow. And this crazy play got me more and more scared. It was ridiculous. I even looked under the bed . . ."

She'd told them, confessed, unburdened herself. And it didn't mean a thing to them because they didn't believe it. Someone said, "I *always* look under my bed, but there's never anybody I know there. Just the FBI, the CIA and all those characters!" This got a laugh and then the girl took up *her* theme, half serious: "Exactly, Kristan. It fits my theory. People *live* the scripts they see. So your intellectual, for instance, gets more and more like someone in a play no one can understand—"

Irene said from behind, "This is Bill . . ." And Kristan half turned to see who Bill was. He meant nothing and neither her mind nor her heart were touched. She was still deep in self-consciousness and the aftermath of fear. Later she liked to pretend that his name and arrival had an immediate impact, but it was not so. He came as just a name at a party. She was at the party because she was involved in a long struggle against loneliness. If Shaun had been in New York they would have been at another, more important party.

Irene went along the group, introducing in haste, "Well, if you must turn up late. You'll never remember anyway. Della and Goodwin, Saul and Audrey, Ralph and Susan . . . Kristan . . . Bill's just home from—"

"Don't tell 'em," pleaded Bill. "Let's have a guessing game."

"Give us a clue," suggested Audrey, who was the girl with the script-life theory.

"I've been traveling a lot. Very hot countries."

He was a tall man with a pleasant, perhaps reckless face. Hot countries. The Middle East. Ah, oil!

Others were casting about wildly: "You're in the refrigerator business?" "You're in a circus?" "You're a spy?" "A journalist?"

Kristan said, like an announcement, "You're in oil."

He had to admit he was. "You're a clever girl. How did you know? Is my coat stained with the lousy stuff?"

Kristan had had two drinks now and was warming to the eve-

166

ning. She answered impertinently, "I knew you were in oil or deep water," which obtained a roar of laughter. "And I guess you must be from Oklahoma or somewhere, 'cause no one's called me a girl since they dropped the first A-bomb."

This, too, raised a mild flurry of amusement. Bill, whose other name they still didn't know (but it didn't matter: time passed, the year was ending, the tiredness of fear was forgotten), said now, "It's a great place, the Middle East. But I'd forgotten all about this white stuff. What d'you call it? Snow? It's beautiful. Don't disenchant me and say it's lousy to drive in. I've been dreaming of rain and snow for eighteen months."

There were other groups to talk to. Kristan wandered about, a lot lighter in the mind, and when there were things to eat she ate with appetite. Once or twice she thought about what time of day it was for Shaun, what he'd be doing, and when midnight and the New Year came realized he was already several hours into it. People kissed those standing near. This Bill was quite an amusing character. If he was shy, he had a likable way of covering it. He was only a few paces away and affected to growl at her, "Come over here so's I can bite you!"

Kristan was too much of an introvert to accept such a challenge, even at a party, and stared dumbly. Then she responded, scarcely hearing her own voice in the noise of the party, "You come over here if you want to take a bite." And he came, said, still in the spirit of the party, "I can't stand these girls who think you want to kiss them on the cheek!" He kissed her on the mouth. There was no particular sensation, and she merely commented frivolously, "You woman-starved out there in the oil country?" He answered, "You could say that, but the money's good."

"How long are you home for?"

"Four months. And New York's not home. You weren't quite right. Home was Kansas, not Oklahoma."

"*Was?*"

"Was," he said with finality. "So here I am in the big city for four months."

Very faintly Kristan sensed that he was suggesting, perhaps pleading as she wanted to do to drown fear, saying to her, If you're lonely too, let's do something about it.

167

She said, refusing automatically by implication, "My husband's in Africa with the UN."

People were leaving.

Irene suggested, "Bill, why don't you drive Kristan home?"

"You wanna get rid of me or something?"

"Kristan came in a cab."

Bill said, "Don't you drive?"

Kristan couldn't think of what to say except the truth. "I didn't bother in the snow. Skids scare me," which she knew was the way into his inevitable courteous response, "Then you must allow me to drive you home."

She made a suggestion of hopelessness, a movement with her hands that conveyed All right, but don't think you've talked me into any obligation. But aloud she merely uttered a clumsy, "Okay."

"Be seeing you," Irene said—to Bill, not Kristan. "Phone me one morning."

"I will. And thanks. It was fun."

Irene smiled. "Looks like it still is."

Kristan didn't smile.

She sat in Bill's wide automobile. "I hired it," he told her, "so I hope the thing starts. Do you mind if I swear? That helps."

But the engine turned over at once. Now Bill found that the windshield was coated with ice. After a while he cleared it and came and sat in the driver's seat. "Sorry about that. Where d'you live?"

She told him and returned the question. "How about you?"

"In a hotel on 42nd Street," Bill told her. "It's pretty lousy, but where else could I go but a hotel?"

"Expensive," Kristan suggested.

The problems of oil men on leave from the Middle East hadn't come to her attention before. Presumably the anxieties of UN wives whose husbands were away on dangerous territories were equally unknown to the average newspaper reader. Life was full of things people didn't know even if they kept up their subscriptions to the magazines. What else didn't she know?

"Aren't you lonely out there in the desert?"

"For women, you mean?"

168

"I suppose I do."

"It was my wife who couldn't stand it and she was *here*—well, in Kansas."

"I'm sorry," Kristan said. "Although I can understand a problem arising." She couldn't resist confessing to him, a near-stranger in the dark of an automobile at one in the morning. "I get so scared. Can you understand that? I know it's ridiculous with the phone handy and so on."

"I can understand now. I didn't then," Bill admitted. "So Viola went off and that was that. After fifteen years."

"That was rough . . . What do you do out there?"

Bill took it to be a continuation of the subject of the problem of women. "The workers go into the town and drink and find some floozie. You'd be surprised how many white girls'll travel to find that kind of 'adventure.' But I haven't the stomach for those kind of places. I just grin and bear it."

"I really meant the work."

"It's so hot the touch of metal will burn your skin off. I'm an engineer, of course. The money's good, that's one thing."

They were moving in the white slush in 96th Street. Kristan said, "If you just stop at the next block," and she sensed the reluctance as he did so. Bill said in a complaint that was meant as flattery, "That didn't take long," meaning it was too short a journey.

"Well, thanks," said Kristan, opening a door, aware again of her own ungraciousness. She was conscious of the difference of behavior in reality and in the magazine stories: in *them* women knew exactly what to say long before they were forty-three; their timing was right with words, car doors and New Year escorts. "Thanks for the buggy ride."

"Will I see you again?" Bill asked, and the simplicity and lack of subtlety in his phraseology suggested that he, too, wasn't very capable in sophistication. The wrong magazine subscription perhaps?

"I don't know," she countered clumsily, but she'd shut the car door far enough for it to click and she was still inside the vehicle.

"Why don't we meet for lunch some time?" he suggested. "It seems logical if we've both got time on our hands," he persisted, all too aware of her hesitation that bordered on panic and flight.

"I'd like that some time."

169

"Don't go away like that or I'll never hear from you again. Give it to me straight—you don't want to?"

"I didn't say that."

"You're nervous or something?"

"I just happen to have a husband."

"Would he mind if I took you to lunch?"

"I don't suppose so."

"One thing I like about women. They're so logical!"

"And practical," she chided. "He'd like me to at least know your name."

"Didn't Irene tell you? Dardick, that's me. Bill Dardick."

"All right! You've talked me into a lunch."

"When? Tomorrow?"

"Well . . . Okay. Which tomorrow did you mean? It's rolling on for two o'clock now."

"We could go and have a look at the Guggenheim," he claimed. "It's not that far from here."

"We could but we are not going to," Kristan said coolly.

"Okay. Lunch it is," he agreed. "Today."

Kristan didn't ask him in for coffee or anything, it was so late. This, too, seemed ungracious, but she was already regretting her acquiescence and was becoming scared. She wondered in amusement if he'd regret being so persistent when alcohol and the party had worn off and he saw her in the cold light of day.

When she left him she strode indoors and around the apartment without fear. She had something to think about, to overlay terror, and, more than that, she had something to *do* when the morning was older, a human contact, even a responsibility to deal with.

She slept for nine hours uninterrupted, not bothered about locks or doors, and awoke refreshed, despite the drinks and the party, feeling like one who has been critically ill for ten days, but is now out of danger and looking around at the world anew.

She found that she was selecting what to wear with too much care and was staring at her reflection in the mirror anxiously. Shoot, I'm as vain as the rest of them, she thought. It's ridiculous, a women of forty-three tarting herself up and feeling nervous just because she's going to have lunch with a man. I'm just a hick Canadian, that's been my trouble all along. But at least this kind of

170

apprehension was tolerable, even pleasurable (although Bill meant nothing, was just a cure for today's loneliness), and it was worlds apart from the nightmare of absurd fear in the night, so suffocating she'd felt faint.

He was outside the rendezvous just off Fifth Avenue as the taxi approached it. For a second she hesitated, wondering whether to tell the driver to go on; it was perfectly in order for a woman to do this. But standing there he looked human and scared and that was what decided her. And he was humble enough to admit, "I'd just gotten to the moment when I *knew* you wouldn't come." "Well, here I am in the light of day," Kristan said, and waited to see the disappointment in his face, the acknowledgment that no man could hide, that he wasn't interested, he'd made a mistake, she was older, fatter, or whatever it was. But he said in outright praise, "Jesus, it suits you! I didn't realize last night—" and this clumsiness was fervent, it was honest, and Kristan felt the slight shock and responsibility of something she'd long since forgotten—being beautiful in another person's estimation.

In Rockefeller Plaza on the ice of the open-air rink girls were skating, beautiful in a brittle sun, watched by the midday crowds in fur coats. Kristan, watching, was conscious of Bill Dardick just behind her, silent, not watching *them* but examining *her,* her coat, her hair, her height, her manner of standing. Hell, she thought in indulgence, he must have been right in the *middle* of the Middle East! An icy wind stalked between buildings and caused them to walk on, but inside the restaurant it was pleasantly hot.

They had looked at each other in the light of day a little too quickly. Now, across a table, she had no option but to stare. And she was surprised to find that he was a thin man in his middle or late forties. He was dressed very respectably and she hid a smile, aware that the care had been for her. His clothes looked slightly incongruous with his leathery, outdoor face. She noted his continued interest in her clothes and was warmed by his obvious belief in her good looks.

There were, nevertheless, long silences.

They weren't at a party now. She was conscious of failure in herself and after a while admitted across the table, "I'm not very good company."

Women in the magazine stories never admitted a thing like this,

171

but Kristan knew that she had nothing in common with Bill Dardick except a party and loneliness in the city of New York. The loneliness didn't really bother him, she could see; at least it didn't exhaust and frighten him. But here and now conversation was limited to oil territories, the party and minor apologies for being in each other's company at all.

He challenged her remark vigorously. "You're great. Do you think I want an extrovert, chattering her head off? What I like about you is that you talk sense. Where do we go this afternoon?"

Kristan was startled. "Hey, wait a minute! You asked me to lunch."

"I don't know this town," Bill told her. "I'm just a bum from Kansas and the Persian Gulf."

"Then I'm no use to you. I'm a Canadian and I don't know it either."

Bill smiled and said, "I've never taken a Canadian lady out before! Why don't we look at this big city together? Do the night spots, the museums, the whole business?"

"You know why not."

"Because your friends might talk scandal?"

"They'd be right to, wouldn't they?"

"No harm in going to museums, surely to God!"

By now Kristan had had a martini that made her lightheaded and ravenously hungry. They were waiting for Philadelphia Pepper Pot soup, whatever that was. She was so hungry that each time the girl came past with a basket of popovers she took two.

Bill commented, "Say, you can *eat!*"

"All women can if they still have their teeth."

"I mean you look like you mean business!"

"Aren't you hungry?"

"It must have been the booze at the party, but I feel as if I've been kicked in the stomach," Bill admitted. "Still, it's great to watch you."

"Do I rate as cabaret?"

"Sorry. I'm rude. I haven't seen civilized people for eighteen months."

"I might, just for the hell of it, and because it's on the way home, have a look at the Guggenheim with you."

172

"You'll never make it with all that soup and beef inside you."

"Statistics prove that women have better digestions than men. Men have three-quarters of the ulcers."

An hour and a half later they walked up Third Avenue looking at antique shops.

"I think it's a lot of snobbery," was Bill's view.

"I don't. I think that old French furniture is beautiful," Kristan disputed.

There was a diver's helmet on sale. Solid brass. Kristan was slightly lightheaded still. "Now *that's* what I'd really like for my sitting room! For watching television under water!"

"Where do you suppose it came from?"

"I think it got here on its own!"

"They want a hundred dollars for it."

"Well, it's brass. It'd be cute to put flowers in. Come on, let's move. I'm beginning to freeze."

Outside the Guggenheim Museum there were, despite winter, planted flowerbeds. Inside, the huge spiral ramp inspired a frivolous "Oh, goodness, now I'm really dizzy!" from Kristan.

"The correct procedure," explained Bill, "would seem to be to get an elevator up and then walk down. Otherwise you'll never make it to the top."

"Let me tell you, I was in the Girl Guides. Do you want a bet about it? Statistics prove—"

People were looking at them.

"Come on!" he urged.

They came down the spiral gallery, looking at the rich colors, the paintings that staggered the senses. But they were still two people more conscious of the human contact of the day and weren't really paying attention.

"Tomorrow," Bill whispered, "we'll stay sober and stare at the Hayden Planetarium."

But Kristan felt a slight headache coming on and with it returned normality and the problems of convention and the very real absence of Shaun. Loneliness ought to be endured as if it was her part of the mission. He'd laugh at her right now, but he wouldn't if she went around with Bill Dardick tomorrow and tomorrow and tomorrow. Or would he mind?

173

She counseled earnestly, "Tomorrow I think you must make other plans."

He recognized her determination. "Don't be like that," he said meaninglessly.

They walked in the snow, almost conversationless. The least she could do was offer him coffee; he looked a little tired. The same doorman was in the vestibule and responded politely to Kristan's "Good afternoon" with a remark about the snow and the afternoon mail. But she felt his stare on her back like public opinion as she stood with Bill waiting for the elevator.

"Thank God for central heating," Bill said in the apartment. He was enthusiastic about the place. "This is great. Yes, I can see why you like old French furniture. It fits in here."

After a while, sipping coffee, Bill came to the point reluctantly, aware of impending failure.

"What about tomorrow?" he asked, and his voice had the anticipation of rejection.

Kristan said nervously, "I don't think so, Bill."

"Another time? There's a lot of theaters and places. It seems a pity to go alone."

She might have said, "You could find someone else," but was confident enough to feel that was not what he wanted. He wanted *her* company. They had something in common. Nevertheless, the letter in her hand was from Shaun and there was one from Peter, too. It was her duty to be scared in the night and to endure the long days that sapped away strength. So she said seriously, "I don't think we ought to see each other often. I know," she acknowledged, "it's dreary and conventional."

"You're afraid of other people's opinions? I understand that."

"You do?" she asked doubtfully.

"Of course. You're the wife of a diplomat, among other reasons. But I'd be happy to go around with you whenever you felt free to do so. If we're both—"

"I don't care about other people exactly," said Kristan. "And there's nothing wrong with— Nor are there any United Nations' rules for wives. There might be a few Canadian Embassy expectations of behavior, but not what I'm likely to offend. It's just that Shaun's in Africa and it would feel wrong. I mean it'd feel wrong even to enjoy myself."

174

Again Bill agreed with her so that now she felt ridiculous in her position. "Anyway, Bill, that was fun today."

"I'm glad you feel it was. I'll leave my phone number and if you ever get hungry or scared again . . ."

He had scarcely gone when Della rang. After a while Kristan experimented with words, attempted to sound out whether her own instincts were right or whether she was just being old-fashioned.

"Guess who I went to lunch with today?"

Della said, "Tell me! I have to pay for the call!"

"Bill Dardick."

"I don't know him."

"That funny man at Irene's party."

"Oh, *Bill*. I didn't know his other name."

"He's a bit of a rough diamond, isn't he?"

"What does that mean?"

"He says what he thinks."

"Does he have interesting thoughts?"

"Not bad. I meant he's so honest."

"Are you seeing him again?"

"Not as far as I know."

"How disappointing! No scandal for me to enjoy!"

This, expressed humorously, gave the answer to Kristan's problem, or at the minimum confirmed its existence. And the sad letter from Shaun, telling her about the *indigena* of Angolique and their woes, was the reality she must abide by.

The other letter, from Peter, told Kristan that he'd arrived in France, near the Moselle town of Metz. He had met an exceptionally nice French girl, Peter wrote. He didn't know if it was serious, but certainly he'd never before seen anyone like Yvette. She was fair and gentle and very dignified. He was already very fond of her. The news about Starfighter airplanes and operational flights meant little to Kristan, although the very technicality worried her. She had a mental picture of the French girl—vaguely collected from photographs in *Harper's Bazaar* and a memory of Paris restaurants—as being a tall, slender girl, with small bones, elegant hands, wearing superb clothes which were simplicity itself, but perfect. She imagined an unusual, heart-shaped face; piquant, sad, serious eyes; hair the color of corn, absolutely straight, untouched (or apparently) by any stylist. Very faintly, at the back of her mind, hopes crawled

175

about, even plans. Peter spoke French. When he'd finished with the RCAF they could go to Quebec, where the girl would feel at home and have no language problem . . .

She spent half the evening writing to Shaun. She didn't mention Bill Dardick, not out of purposes of deceit but to prevent even the slightest unnecessary anxiety. She did describe Irene's party and her feelings at the moment of the New Year. This day with Bill Dardick was nothing, she decided, not worth mentioning. If it hung around in her conscience she'd tell Shaun about it when he came home . . .

But in the morning she received a shock. For there on a shelf was the pencil Bill had used to write down the name of his hotel and its telephone number. It wasn't an ordinary pencil she could ignore. It was made of gold and could operate in five colors.

Kristan didn't know what to do. She had to do something. She couldn't keep a valuable pencil; that would be tantamount to stealing. She would have to telephone him. Things got lost in the mail. She was sure it was an accident and he had not left the thing there intentionally.

She stood by the telephone and her hands refused to lift it. She knew she must not touch it. Her hands began to sweat and tremble. It didn't matter, surely, if she lifted the phone. He had to have his pencil back. It seemed reasonable and logical, but she was shaking and tense with nervousness. She felt in her trembling flesh that it might matter. He wasn't anyone special, but he found her attractive. Well, she could handle that if it became a problem. She'd done so today. Oh, this is ridiculous, she thought. Give the man his pencil back. She lifted the instrument and with shaking fingers dialed the number.

Sunday evening in Metz.

It was an important occasion.

Peter wore his RCAF uniform not in conceit or arrogance but in an attempt to persuade Yvette's parents that he was no callow youth who'd tried to pick up a girl in a drugstore. It would be the first time he had met them and only the fourth time he had seen her.

He was scared. It was ridiculous and he knew it. The bells of the

176

cathedral of St. Étienne boomed solemnly in the wet evening. It was the first time Peter had heard *them*. The cathedral had hitherto been a piece of architecture which had a place in his life in terms of navigation. It was part of a pattern. Metz, first seen as the eyesore on a green and brown horizon known from 30,000 feet as an urban area, became identifiable as he flew lower by a particular pattern of fields, loops of the River Moselle, ugly coal mines, then the new buildings of a city shattered in wars many times and rebuilt. Prominent within this city was the thirteenth-century cathedral which had survived all of the violence.

Yvette lived with her parents in an old house, neglected but impressive. The rain dripped from a broken pipe by the front door, so that dirty water ran across his arm when he rang the bell.

Yvette answered.

He had not seen her before without the cover of her street coat or the white uniform she wore in the dispensary. She wore absolutely no makeup. Presumably her parents did not approve of the green eye shadow she used at work. Or did Sunday have something to do with it? He wasn't a Catholic and was ignorant of France and, indeed, Europe except as seen six miles below the Starfighter. She wore a wool dress which, while plain in design and sober in fashion, tended to outline her roundedness. She wasn't tall, not next to him, but was slightly plump, the remnants of a schoolgirl's healthy beauty. It was impossible to imagine her being anything but innocent.

"Hi!" Peter greeted, and was conscious that it sounded terrible.

"It's raining," Yvette commented, equally irrelevantly.

That was all they said to each other directly for another two hours.

It was a peculiar evening.

They sat in a room and drank wine and at times Peter's French was not good enough and he had to repeat in English a trivial remark about the weather or a complicated explanation of the RCAF's mission in Europe so that Yvette could translate it into French for her parents. When she spoke to them, she did so at a pace that was twice as fast as when she spoke to Peter. He recognized uneasily that she had a slightly greater reality speaking with breathless intensity to them, a personality not known to him. He

177

lived in a world that was acutely masculine and tremendously technical and in which only someone very fit in body and devoted in mind could survive. It was quite difficult to slow down, to translate himself into this other world of normality—the wine, the silence, the smells of books and wood, the orientation around property, food, prayer, health, television and work.

"Your father is a politician?"

Her parents were young enough to be almost of his type if not of his generation. Her mother was attractive; she could be compared with her daughter feature by feature because she had some youth left. The comparison was, of course, unfavorable, but she was young enough for it to be made.

"Yes," Peter said, "in the United Nations."

"It is, I suppose, important work," Yvette's father acknowledged.

He did not approve, Peter sensed.

"I don't know," he said lightly. "Perhaps it is a load of nonsense."

They were completely baffled. They could disapprove of an organization but were unable to be frivolous about it.

"Will you stay in the Canadian Air Force all your life?" the mother asked.

"I haven't decided."

He did not tell them that the decision depended on their daughter. That was something he was a long way yet from discussing with Yvette. While he talked to her parents and they frowned intently in concentration—trying to understand not only his French but also his unfamiliar point of view—Peter knew in pleasure that Yvette was using the permissible opportunity to stare at him, to examine him inch by inch, expression by expression. And when, not very often, she talked directly to them, grasping their attention, taking their faces away from *him,* he used the opportunity to satisfy his hunger for the very spectacle of her. His eyes delighted in her fair hair, soft rounded face, the agitation of her hands, her moving mouth that he had kissed precisely twice—a soft warm mouth. She had ears that stuck out rather noticeably and she tended to loop her hair behind them, but even these delighted him, for they made her fallible and human.

178

"It must be dangerous," the mother was saying. "Are you never frightened?"

She was surely at least forty-five. Had she forgotten so completely the greater dangers she must have lived through at his age?

"Not really," said Peter. He grinned. "Not often."

Nothing that he said could convey it to them. It was a technical situation. Everything that could be done to ensure his comfort, mental ease, his physical survival in a permutation of possibilities —from navigational discomposure to a flamed-out engine which could still windmill and be restarted in the air to actual ejection even at low altitude—all these things had been prepared for in advance of any other problems that he might have to face. He had a mental picture which, to them, would seem terrifying, but which was in fact safe within a Cold War pattern. Typical was yesterday's luck. He flew over East Germany at 500 m.p.h. at tree height, to a series of positions which were checked now and again. He'd done them all in oblique or trimegroton photography as he flew toward or over them. Then he saw a road accident involving a huge, articulated truck and something else. There was a small crowd, who stared at his Starfighter approaching half a mile away. The shape of the articulated truck was suspicious. He'd lifted the port wing and a preset Vinten camera—one of a bank of four—had taken a "squirt" of photographs. They had blown up well so that the stenciled paint on the object could be read. Translated, it gave a message about pressures and dangers of explosion and source of manufacture. At the time, he'd shot up to 35,000 feet and rammed the throttle through and done a long burst at Mach 2.2 to get the hell out of there and over the border . . .

In answer after answer he told Yvette's parents about Canada, the Starfighter, his food, work, feelings, even a hint of his pay check and religious faith. He asked nothing in return—he had made his estimate and was prepared to accept Yvette, if it ever came to that good fortune, on any terms she and they might regard as necessary.

They drank wine, ate a little, put on three very tedious phonograph records, told him a little about their miseries in the war and rewarded him with a contrived ten-minute absence, which—they made so painfully intentional that all four of them blushed outright

—was for him to hold hands, kiss, talk or whatever it was he expected and wished to do.

Peter wasted half of that time getting around to it, sitting in another chair, knee to knee with Yvette, shaken by the evening, sipping the last of his third glass of wine. When he finally dared to
touch her, Yvette did nothing, neither rejected nor encouraged, just
dipped her head in shyness, being wooed. He touched the wheat-
colored fine hair delicately, kissed the top of her head, breathing
the faint smell of soaps and scents. After a while she lifted her head
and looked him in the eye. He kissed the warm generous mouth so
hard his own mouth felt bruised, but the posture was difficult to
continue. Yvette smiled and stood up, pretended to put her glass on
the mantelpiece, turned her back on him. Peter was hurt, slightly
frustrated. Time was valuable. He turned her around bodily. Her
body dragged slightly in resistance, but she met him, was willing to
be crushed hard in eagerness. "They liked you," she said, and he
was glad, but it had small meaning within the certainty of her own
affection. He was aware in warm tenderness of the firm stomach
and breasts pressing against him, and, as well, something metallic
that dug into him. It was the small gold cross that always dangled
from her throat . . .

9 ▪ ▪

THEY HAD A FINE position from which to watch the
race. It had been impossible to refuse the invitation. What could
they claim to be doing? Their host was inclined to make a party of
it, and, from his point of view, why not? His apartment was on the
third floor of a modern building with an interesting marble façade,
positioned perfectly in the crescent of the Avenue Manuel de Arriaga near the park and the Radio Club and thus was very fashionable—as far as anything was in Angolique. The apartment opened
onto a balcony with room for twenty people to stand or sit without
overcrowding. From here McQuade had an impressive view of the
whole arc of the sixty-foot-wide avenue with its outer arc of red
locust trees and its dusty promenade.

There were a few merchant ships at anchor and over by the island two small sailing vessels bobbed. The flag at the fort hung limp, and streamers and other flags dangled from poles and lampposts along the whole two-mile parabola. The crowd was six deep on both sides of the avenue. On other balconies other people watched and waved in an atmosphere of pleasurable anticipation. White people, of course; the *indigena* stood below, in the sun. The more lively of them hung on the lampposts or sat precariously on the crumbling old walls of disused warehouses and the railway station.

It was very hot, too hot, perhaps over 100°, a day for long cold drinks, and Dr. Araujo, the host, was energetic in handing out iced beer and fruit juices.

McQuade stared down almost vertically to where thirty cars in six rows of five waited for the beginning of the race. His spirits did not have the brightness of the day, although the atmosphere was not entirely of gloom, for both Gomais and Bajune still survived. He had seen them again, although it was becoming increasingly difficult to move outside the suggested program. Once, Costa had joined the party unexpectedly and on that day they had had to forgo gathering any evidence other than that intended. Both Bajune and Gomais had brought men and women who had given evidence of abuses and punishments, imprisonments and beatings, disappearances and arrests. It had a terrible remoteness even now: like a dream it was never seen in daylight. The Portuguese, who were, were cheerful and talkative, apparently frank, but had shown him nothing on the lines complained about by those in opposition. He had looked at factories and plantations, the massive dam at the Lower Bompopo, sugar and coffee estates . . . It was done so well that it was almost possible to believe they were in genuine ignorance of what went on in their own territory. It made the petitioners seem like liars, or people interfering with grand schemes because they had chips on their shoulders, grievances against individuals. But McQuade had seen too many people by now to doubt that there was cause for complaint . . .

The same party faces were here. They would still be here, smiling, when the UN subcommittee returned to New York, when its report was published, when it was ignored. One of the two obese

181

Germans was laughing—the beer was good and effective in the high temperature—and it was the laugh of supreme confidence, or, in terms of McQuade's evidence, complete indifference. Mettallic Angolique would still be in business with the Portuguese here when McQuade had been returned to the Canadian diplomatic service at the end of his UN duties. "We would be reassured if we could inspect the prisons at São Damba and Bahia dos Alexandre," McQuade had said to the Minister of the Interior ten minutes before. Oliveira's cold eyes had looked into McQuade's face emotionlessly but as if he had seen and heard Gomais telling McQuade of these grim places two days before, almost as if he was at last smiling and McQuade and his group were a bait being used successfully to find and trap the political enemies of Portugal. There was that anxiety, too, for McQuade, that concern for others' safety. "There are no prisons at São Damba or Bahia dos Alexandre," Oliveira had said with finality. "Only mental hospitals. You wouldn't like to see these *não-civilizado* when they go mad, would you?" And when McQuade had countered "Yes, we would," the minister had ignored the request.

The two French or Belgian ladies—McQuade still didn't know their names although he greeted them like old friends at party after party—smiled, as ever, as if they constituted a political diversion or were a slave available when the men became hot tempered with irreconcilable difficulties. Costa was here, but was not his cheerful self today. McQuade wondered if he was at last suspicious, or, worse, some of his own people had found him out in his enjoyable neglect of duty. He kept away from Barney and McQuade was anxious to know if they had quarreled, but Barney said that they had not. She did say, which was just as worrying, that Costa (and, more cautiously, his daughter) were beginning to ask questions: Where did they go? Whom did they see? Gregorio de la Plaza stood looking at Barney with secret hatreds. Most difficult of all was Theobald Alferink. He was certainly leaving Barney alone, but he had boasted an hour earlier of the girl he would be bringing to this very gathering.

"I've found a really hot little number from the Lycée. Eighteen, and quite the little snob about the wine list. Very anxious to prove how capable she is at life. They all do it, she says—meaning herself and two others who sneak out to the hotels and restaurants to pick up someone on holiday or an aircrew member here for a day or two. She's had four men make love to her, she claims—rather modestly, I thought; perhaps she didn't wish to shock me too much —and one committed suicide. Takes antidepression pills in the morning and peppermint at night so matron won't sniff the whisky." McQuade had urged hopelessly, "Take it easy. This is a political mission, not an adventure."

Here now this young tart came, stared at in shock and fascination. She was rather a beautiful girl, tall and dark-haired, with a face that could have been dignified, but had touches of slyness and eager sophistication. McQuade sensed her electricity. She was nothing special, but emanated a delicate sexiness, and despite her neat, quiet but fashionable dress nothing much of her was disguised. She was all body and legs and the dangerous face that knew it. And her greatest danger was that to enmesh a married man with responsibilities in degraded, private madness would give her pleasure. All these qualities were recognizable. She was nicely dressed and behaved with a conscious propriety, but no one was under any illusions. Some of the men smiled—they *all* stared—and thought Alferink a bit of a dog. Of course it might get back to the Lycée— the Belgian lady might see to that, or even a minion of Oliveira, anxious to discredit the UN group. And, most exasperating of all, didn't Alferink know—even though he did not *see*—that the PIDE kept an eye on them all the time?

Dr. Araujo was the Minister of Health, and within the limits of the party atmosphere and his duties as host he talked about the health situation in Angolique. He was inclined to be sympathetic to the health problems of the *indigena*.

"The north is the difficult area," he told McQuade. "And it is in precisely that area that the military have lost some control. This aggravates things. Bilharzia exists, and schistosome infestation causes morbidity and often death, although we could deal with these if we were allowed to. We did some aerial antimalarial spraying of residual insecticides, again in the north, and would have augmented this with gametocidal drugs if the troubles had not arisen."

"The World Health Organization exists precisely—"

"I know, I know," said Dr. Araujo. "But we are at the whims

183

of the Bakongo and the Army. They'll get around to it. Those who survive. Then there's fairly heavy tuberculosis and a shortage of beds. We've given many thousands of children BCG vaccine, but we're short of specific antituberculosis drugs. Plenty of eye diseases, I need hardly add—trachoma in particular. You've probably seen frambesia on Negro faces in the street. Not pretty. Trypanosomiasis exists, of course—and I'd say especially in Lisbon!"

This was frank enough criticism, but they were, after all, at a party, and someone had to blunder in while the doctor was so talkative. In this case it was Alferink and his girl friend. Alferink was acting like a man who'd escaped from the rigors of office routine in New York and was here on one of those business trips that were sexually rather than mentally exhausting. More disturbing was his ridiculous attitude that everyone else should be pleased about it.

The girl, whose name was Lilli, was enjoying being the shock of the afternoon.

On one beer she was talkative. "Do you know, they make us go to bed at eight-thirty. In this heat! We just lie there feeling sexy. And all of us in my class are over eighteen. But it's so easy to get away. And the place is like a rabbit warren. There are places they *daren't* look in after dark! We're awful snobs, of course. The latest is lavatories. If your parents have a big house you must prove it by the number of lavatories! I've claimed eight. It isn't true, of course. Two of them are for the gardeners and don't have water at all!"

She laughed with the rest of the attentive group. McQuade saw Alferink stare down the neck of her dress to where her breasts, unsupported, shook with amusement. "We lived in Charleroi. An awful dump. I shan't go back there! We were in Elisabethville when all that started. I was only a child," she claimed like a middle-aged woman. "It grew so boring, all the shooting. Sex is so much more stimulating, don't you think?"

She delighted in the shocked inhalations. McQuade presumed that her parents were dead. The Lycée couldn't expel her and perhaps wouldn't; she was a problem of the time and needed pity. She'd hate it, of course.

He heard Duffin say in admiration from a distance, "What a jolly girl. Where does she come from?" and his wife's dampening comment, "She's Belgian. Trade, I should think."

184

"Lilli, you are a shocker," protested Alferink in pleasure.

Down below, the drivers were strolling out to their Saabs, Peugeots, Mustangs, Fiats and Toyopets.

Frischauer whispered in contempt, "How's the United Nations going on?"

"Where's your friend?" McQuade asked for no reason.

"He is in hospital. An electric shock. He'll be all right. Some burns . . . Look at those cars down there, Mr. McQuade. They're all European or American. A Japanese! Even the Portuguese can't make automobiles. Very good with little things like sardines! And your African with his shouting for freedom! Can he produce a car? Not one nation in Africa produces vehicles, let alone jet aircraft."

"Does it matter?"

"The distances, Mr. McQuade. It is symptomatic. I am explaining Africa's need for the European. Without him here in Angolique, without his finance and guidance and tools, the vast resources here would be limited to the black man's capabilities—to secondary processing industries based on agriculture, sisal decortication, processing of coffee and sugar, at best canned beer and insecticides and coir matting! Who would do the geological mapping if the European went? Do you know how long such a survey takes to reach the minimum reconnaissance standard? And only with foreign capital can the indications of the mapping become mineral surveys. This sort of thing costs millions of dollars and is the mere beginning. Who, if the Portuguese leave, is going to finance and build the dams and boreholes and organize irrigation and flood control?"

"The FAO would guide on these sort of matters—"

"But who will *pay?*"

"There is no objection to foreign investment."

"Who will guarantee law and order? *You* at UNO?"

There was logic in what Frischauer said—as there had been in what he'd said at that earlier party. But it was the logic of the computer and statistics and board rooms. It ignored the unwillingness of the African to remain at a lower intellectual or political level; it dismissed the aspirations of the African mind altogether. Indeed, Frischauer had talked as if the African and European had

185

been in competition on equal terms and the European had, by greater virtue and intelligence, won. Certainly Angolique should be developed, but with the *indigena* who lived there and for them.

"You assume the black man has no qualities or capabilities. Why not give him a chance? He lives here."

"You have a soft heart," Frischauer said, as if he were complaining. "You are an idealist." No use to Africa, was his implication.

Down below, the sidewalk cafes had been barricaded with bales of cotton. The band stopped playing. The voice over the loudspeaker had tired of talking about the timing and personalities and was growing excited about the actual beginning of the race. For the Grand Prix d'Angolique, cars had been brought from Portugal, Rhodesia, Belgium, England, Italy, South Africa, Senegal, Finland and Sweden, although the race did not have championship status. Engines were now roaring below and conversation ceased on the balcony. In the press of bodies leaning over the parapet Alferink had a hand on Lilli's buttocks . . .

The sedans shot off in a crescendo of noise and the smell of the blue smoke drifted upward. They raced along the avenue toward the observatory, the fort and the Palácio do Governo Geral, where they would turn up the slight incline by the Hospital Militar and then reach the main road parallel to the sea, the Avenida dos Combatantes do Grande Guerra, into which they would turn and race around both sides of the colossal marble statue which acknowledged the dead of that war. They'd roar along roads by the various consulates and near the Villa Amélia and the Lycée, come around to the railway station near the cathedral and reappear at the starting point below, by the Restaurante Marialvas, which was the strolling center of the town. The cars were expected to do this five-mile lap for four hours, at the end of which the sun would have dropped below the horizon. Above the noise of engines the voices of the crowd filled the hot, smelly air, and if there were three hundred thousand people in Vila Lobanda then half of them must be here.

And then, as the first car, rocking dangerously and with tires squealing, came around onto the Avenue Manuel de Arriaga by the railway station and the neat buildings of the harbor authority, about a hundred people walked onto the road and lay down. This took place quite near Dr. Araujo's apartment and close to the start-

186

ing line, foreign newspaper photographers, race officials and, indeed, the bulk of the police. The people lying down mostly were colored; some were young women and a few, children. A small dog ran absurdly among them and licked a man's face. Some white people joined the group hesitantly—students, by the look of them.

They'd positioned themselves well politically but badly in other terms—they evidently had no knowledge of either vehicle acceleration or braking ability. Already policemen were dragging at some and flailing others with clubs, but it was the cars that broke the demonstrators' nerve. Many scattered and ran as cars bumped into each other or swerved violently and in one case ran full speed into an acacia tree. The bang of steel and shattering of glass and shriek of tires and panic of humans caused people at the back of the crowd to move restlessly, crane heads, anxious to know what was going on. A great confused shouting and various aspects of hysteria spread; it was possible from the balcony to see a physical effect, chaos spreading outward in a ripple.

On the balcony the effect was that of shocked fascination. Oliveira rushed away to the telephone. Mrs. Duffin commented, as acid as ever, "I can't think what's come over these people. Don't they know their place?" The only thing one could say in favor of Mrs. Duffin was that she had guts. In everyone else McQuade sensed a perturbation bordering on fright, anticipation of a riot with harm to themselves possible, but Mrs. Duffin was simply outraged by what she considered to be lack of good manners!

Two shots came from somewhere. McQuade flinched and instinctively, with the others, stepped backward into the protection of stone. Then, cautiously looking over the balcony again, he saw the two spots of smoke at the edges of the boulevard. Some policemen must have panicked. Like a television play that hasn't been switched off during a quarrel, the surviving cars came around again. Only two had crashed with any damage.

Then an ugly aspect revealed itself as part of the crowd took this opportunity and began to smash things and hit policemen. They shouted in a terrifying roar and the nearest restaurants suffered damage. Already, McQuade could see, one wave of people moved in fright while another ran into it and across it in rage. People were getting trampled. The actual fighting, between ten or so policemen

187

and an array of workers and shrieking young women, had drifted out of his view. It was his job to see what happened, not seek his own safety. McQuade made no apologies for an abrupt departure but rushed out of the apartment and saw too many people waiting by the elevator—and they, presumably having seen nothing yet and therefore being calm, stared at McQuade, who carried the symptoms of haste and shock. He ran down wide marble steps, out through an impressive porch full of tropical flowers, saw a girl in a telephone booth who also looked at him in astonishment and went out into the street. There the heat struck him like a blow and he hesitated.

It was very frightening. An enraged crowd was loose, and although they had his pity and he had some knowledge of their reasons, they wouldn't know that and might kill him in the momentum of their hysteria. He stood in the vestibule, just outside swinging doors at the junction of two roads with the avenue, and saw a police van stop at the next street junction down one of those roads. There was a wild group trotting on the opposite pavement toward that very corner, smashing through pedestrians and a crowd that had been pressed down. All were shouting. Out of the police van jumped five or six dogs, and the whole street seemed to turn in panic from them, fleeing and crushing into doorways and up steps. The police did nothing to stop the dogs, but followed with clubs. McQuade was horrified to see dogs tearing at people knocked to the ground. In twenty or thirty seconds there were more than a dozen people dazed and bleeding, with split heads or torn hands and feet; one lay unconscious or even dead in the street among parked cars and small bright trees.

It was surprising how much debris soon accumulated, like the chaos of a battlefield. Restaurant chairs had been thrown about, bottles rolled along pavements, there was a great litter of trash and papers, as if some newspaper shop had been ransacked . . . hats and sticks and a shoe. It was astonishing that there could be such a mess in such a short time. A group of *indigena* stood across the street from McQuade, and while some wept or cried with pain and fright, others disputed at a distance with policemen. But the disturbance was over. All were arrested. In a limited silence that followed, McQuade was astonished to hear the noises of the race

188

continuing. It had all been so quick that three-quarters of the crowd along the harbor were unaware that anything had happened.

McQuade became aware of the girl Lilli standing just outside the swinging doors with Alferink. She was fascinated and said with complete indifference, "How madly exciting! Was anyone killed, do you think?"

"I wish I'd had my camera with me," Alferink said to McQuade.

"Well, you had your eyes," McQuade told him.

It was difficult to keep up the party spirit in Dr. Araujo's apartment. They watched the cars tearing about, but the greater excitement of the disturbance made the mere racing of vehicles absurdly tame. Nevertheless, they went through the motions. An air of anticipation hung around for the next two hours but was resolved when a curfew was announced and the party had to end. "Dreary little people," complained Lilli bitterly. "Scared by a bit of excitement. Oh, well, back to the Lycée. Can I have a cigarette?"

Night came while they waited in the Villa Amélia for they knew not what.

It was a confusing situation, for a curfew was now imposed from dusk to dawn. Yet the sedans were still racing around an empty town in their final laps, headlights on at a corner not far away.

Alferink had his own problem within this other madness.

"I'll meet her anyway," he said, half thinking aloud, half boasting. "She's in a very excitable condition. And it's only across the road."

"You're not thinking of going out, are you?" McQuade asked, and they all stared at Alferink as if he'd gone mad.

He colored and countered, "I'm dining with her at the Hotel Marromeu. If she goes and I'm not there—"

"Are you crazy?" protested McQuade. "And schoolkids—isn't that a bit sordid?"

"Here we go again with the Canadian lectures," sneered Alferink, with shaky defiance. "I took your previous message, but don't limit me to golf and the museums."

McQuade said loudly, not far from shouting, "Can't you at least pick a student with brains? One who'll give you some idea of *their* views on the problems of this territory? Why choose a slut? Have

189

you gone mad? Can't you think of anything but your own pleasure? Anything might happen in this town tonight and especially to people walking the streets. You saw what happened this afternoon."

"If it happens, being in a villa won't save you."

Ribowski, pale and tired, said from a chair into which he'd collapsed exhausted, "You bring humiliation and indignity not just to this subcommittee but to the entire organization for which we work."

"How morally upright you make that organization sound!" protested Alferink with anger. "Are you all so sure of it or yourselves? Are your wives behaving their little selves back in New York?"

He was facing McQuade and apparently addressing him. McQuade, startled, said, "I am more sure of Kristan than myself."

Alferink shut up rather disconcertingly and merely said, "Don't wait up for me."

As he went out of the room in which they were gathered, Marianne said for his benefit, "It's the heat, you know. As for me, it makes me completely sexless."

Some of them—particularly Marianne and de la Plaza—evidently wanted to talk about the problem of Alferink since it had come into open conflict, and these two were more full of evidence on this small matter than they were on the territory of Angolique. But McQuade saw that this kind of gossiping would cause a complete loss of dignity and purpose.

In his room he surrendered to his depression and anxiety.

How frail was the human heart. What a curse were the longings of the body. McQuade felt gloom in his belly, for he had lost a friend on this journey to Africa. There would be no reconciliation now: he didn't even want one: his authority in the subcommittee had been flouted. There were disciplinary problems ahead with Alferink and they would be immensely difficult. The absurd Lilli, whose existence wasn't known a mere few days before, had engendered an infatuation so powerful and humiliating that it had smashed through all Alferink's common sense and knowledge of himself and the human pattern, and caused him to respond as a cat does to a particular smell. In a room which his brain surely had acknowledged was full of persons anxious for him to be discredited and the whole subcommittee to fail, he nevertheless couldn't stop

190

his mouth being foolish and his itching hands had to fondle the ridiculous girl's buttocks through her dress.

He hid this distress as he wrote a letter to Kristan and meant it fervently when he wrote, Thank God for you and your devotion . . .

It was impossible to sleep until Alferink returned. The whole town was ominously silent. Hours later McQuade heard him moving about and it was he who answered the telephone—even within a curfew the call for Mr. Regio hadn't been neglected. He wanted to go to him, to plead and argue and cry out. Remember the good times? The parties and the theaters and a mutual love of books? And the affection for dear, kind Suzé, calm but brittle, anxious and devoted, in love? *Love,* not this mad parody with a sexy child who wanted crudity for the hell of it, to boast to the senior girls or write in hot phrases in some secret diary. But he knew that nothing could cure this tropical fever except the child herself, whether by her presence or her absence. He couldn't, or wouldn't, protest to the Lycée himself, not even drop a hint to Miss Montguerre who would certainly act upon it. He could only hope that the outrageous behavior of Alferink and Lilli's obvious misbehavior in terms of the Lycée discipline would cause an abrupt but discreet ending to the embarrassing affair before it got out of control and sent the cables flying over the Atlantic to involve Suzé who had pleaded so eloquently for McQuade's protection.

10 ▪ ▪

Now McQuade traveled in an arc of two thousand miles south and east, from the forests of the tropics to the savanna and desert of the subtropics.

The Land Rover had arrived. He suspected it had been down by the docks all the time and now appeared because the Portuguese were anxious to be rid of them.

There was not sufficient room for them all to go, and in any case McQuade did not wish to leave the Villa Amélia empty or depart without knowing of the further developments in Vila Lobanda. The girls were surprisingly nervous, not at all eager to visit strange areas. They'd gotten into the pleasure and safety of a routine already in Vila Lobanda. He had to take one and chose Barney on the basis that she had had her fair share of tennis and swimming, while Marianne, a little under the weather anyway, had had hers of hot vehicles and violent scenes. He could not take Ribowski, who might be very ill, and did not wish to take Alferink if Barney was coming. In the end he took Asare Johnson and Hjalmar Ekelund, both serious and in good shape, and left de la Plaza in charge. Costa, who seemed agreeably surprised to be still on duty, brought a man "for tribal translations." This was Captain Duartes, who just smiled as if perfectly aware that nobody was fooled. Whether PIDE or Portuguese Army, as claimed, McQuade did not know. Captain Duartes certainly brought a splendid rifle "in case we see any sable . . ."

They traveled with much equipment in two vehicles—the Land Rover and the Fiat station wagon, which had been fitted for the journey with heavier tires. The first day they made a mere comfortable seventy miles and stopped at a fishing village. Here they picnicked while watching fishermen mend nets outside picturesque pastel-shade houses. They spent their first night comfortably indoors in one of them. After that the feeling of towns and villages dropped away. They were loaded with tubes of ointment, mosquito nets, bottles of mineral water and such things, but nothing could really protect them from the strength of Africa.

McQuade took his turn driving the Land Rover, sitting for hours by Costa. In the mirror he saw Captain Duartes driving through his dust, a dark man who'd been out in some fierce sun lately, a man who was worn down to leather, but who was perhaps enjoying this "easy" mission, talking in a Fiat station wagon to a pretty American girl. No doubt he'd had his verbal inoculations against her. The sweat poured out of McQuade as he drove, as if he were in a Turkish bath. Insects beat on the windshield. It was too hot even to talk and certainly to translate or think in Portuguese.

Now and again they stopped to drink beer or mineral water or Portuguese rosé, and the alcohol scarcely stirred the blood in his brick-red face. Barney's brown hair, too long for this climate, lay about in sweaty ropes. The motors of the standing vehicles throbbed heat visibly. But very faintly a camaraderie grew between these men who weren't enemies but were too cautious to be friends. Costa grew more human and likable as the distance from authority and Vila Lobanda increased; he was a man who genuinely loved the grim hot landscape through which they were moving. He had something on his mind that he wanted to be rid of, and he was too good-natured a man to conceal it for long.

After a silence that seemed to distress him he complained sadly, "You did not tell me that you spoke Portuguese, Mr. McQuade."

"I speak it so badly."

"It was a little discourteous."

"I'm sorry I seemed discourteous."

"And it got me into trouble."

"You got yourself into trouble, Mr. Costa."

"You have been seeing people you should not see—"

"What does that mean, Mr. Costa? People you did not wish me to see?"

"You do not deny it?"

"How did you learn that I speak Portuguese?" countered McQuade.

Silence, for the truth must be that Dr. Pais had told the authorities, and why should he do that unless he had been asked? And that almost certainly under stress.

McQuade concluded, "I would have liked to have visited the hospital at Baixange."

"You want to see that which is bad only?"

"I heard that people were bayoneted and so on."

"There was certainly something of a panic. We accept that. Instructions were broadcast in a plea for fairness. Did you know that?"

"No," admitted McQuade.

Costa relaxed, something achieved. But McQuade persisted, "Why are we driving south, Mr. Costa?"

Costa was startled.

"Did you not wish to?"

"Suppose I had said north?"

"I do not understand."

"Are you not taking me to areas of safety where all looks beautiful under a Portuguese sun?"

"Certainly we want you to see things that are worthwhile,"

193

agreed Costa. "The north is jungle and not developed much. If you see thousands of square miles—*colonatos* and good cattle, fishing and electric power and railways and coffee-producing areas—is not this a proof of good administration?"

"Where all men are equal?"

"Not equal, but happy. Are all men equal in Moscow or Montreal? They are not in Lisbon. It is a question of degree and common sense, yes?"

That afternoon the road ended and they boarded the two vehicles on a small, shallow-draft ship, scarcely a steamer but more than a ferry. It was one of those craft built half a century ago for the back end of the world, and somehow transported from Scotland to a river in Angolique. The paint had long since been burned off by a murderous sun, and the very iron looked old and tired. The boat moved off down a tributary of the Katuala, and the stench of engine oil and cattle throbbed with the engine, itself pulsating an oven heat within half an hour.

There were two priests and a farmer and some *indigena,* these latter clearly not of the towns, as passengers.

McQuade stood on deck with the heat of the Land Rover trickling up his sleeves like hot gas. He and Ekelund stared around and were pleased to stretch their legs and obtain the benefit of a faint miasmal breeze. Butterflies followed the ship like spots before the eyes. Crocodiles slid off tree roots and mudbanks as the small motor pulsed the sluggish, rancid water and warned them. A sour dank smell came from the mud where the reedy green papyrus grew. In the shallow backwaters of this tributary McQuade could see storks and spoonbills feeding. And in the low branches which now and again reached far enough to clout the little ship, weaverbirds' nests hung only inches above the water. Barney had not been with them when they'd seen hippopotami before, and now she looked, expectantly but in vain, at their tunnels through the thick reeds and bamboo.

As the day tired and faltered, thousands, perhaps millions, of insects, mostly large ants, dropped on board the small ship, in the vehicles, in clothes and hair.

The *indigena* who were on board held out their hands to catch these insects and, having caught them, stuffed them into their mouths to eat; but not those that dropped on the deck . . .

194

"The rains are coming," explained Costa. He pleaded suddenly, in genuine emotion, "It is absurd. You cannot do it. Look at them! You must not even recommend it. You know the pattern. You've seen it elsewhere. Violence. Chaos. Public buildings used for pigs and horses. All over this continent are superb French and British and other buildings. Empty. Used for lavatories. They need education. Bring them that, not independence."

"It is true," acknowledged McQuade. "It is also true of San Francisco and Marseilles and Ankara and Southampton. The whole world needs education, if by that you mean understanding. But more than that it needs peace and dignity."

"Many nations on this continent," said Costa fervently, "are so ignorant they have no written language to be translated into your UNO documents. You have been in too much of a hurry."

McQuade didn't answer.

Perhaps there was no answer.

He took Costa's argument in the spirit in which it was made and did not offer the pedantic reply—which was the partial and tedious truth—that some of these African languages had once been written in the Arabic script before Europeans came to Africa, or that missionaries and colonial officials had sometimes brought conflicting orthographies to one territory . . . He knew what Costa meant and it had its content of truth.

He stared a few hundred feet, as Barney was doing, at the towering forest, sweating and rioting and dying in a luxuriance that had gone on since God made it. Something of a wind was driving the hot smell of fertility and decay before it. In there, contributing to the stench of tropical Africa, were life and death, a vast debris rotting away—rhino and elephant and monkey droppings, piled high in the case of the larger animals, as if the dark sunless hot world in there did not have enough in its own endless compost heap of dead ferns and leaves, old rotten trees, fungus, butterflies, moths, cockroaches and the corpses of violent carnage. And in there were the very last of the real primitives, little people dying of disease and malnutrition and misery.

Some monkeys with white-banded coats began to scream and laugh at him and went on their way swinging through trees on the river's edge and looking at the small ship.

Half a mile away tremendous lightning forked sideways, so that

195

not only Barney jumped, and then came a great crack of thunder and the same million trees began to sway and all life went silent, about its secret business in the storm. The rain came as if God had lifted an almighty colander and out poured old vegetable water. It hissed on metal and boiled in the river and within seconds seemed to fill it half again. Steam rose from the hot grass, and red mud at once trickled like blood in a road accident. In seconds McQuade's shirt was wet and he hastened into the old cabin. The river seemed now to hurry with its bits of grass and branches and had turned as brown as coffee.

It rained for an hour and a half with thunder as hard as artillery. And then gold beams came through the dull gray clouds and suddenly the sodden world was steaming and noisy again.

The two priests stared with interest at the foreigners and sometimes smiled. They were young bearded men. After a while they comprehended that McQuade could speak their language and they asked him, "Where are you going?"

"We're driving southeast."

"Very far?"

"Cuando-Zambeze."

"That is a very long way indeed."

The vessel's regular engine pulse stopped and McQuade was conscious of the increased speed of the river, something of a push that nudged the boat about as if it was yet another piece of flotsam. Ahead was a wooden jetty, broken in many places. Some nuns stood with bicycles and a small crowd of colored children and other people. It did not look like an easy jetty to drive onto and McQuade was perturbed as to whether he could manage even the tractable Land Rover. However, he was fortunately positioned and drove it straight off board and up a slight incline, where he paused for Captain Duartes in the Fiat. The nuns cycled past with muddy-edged habits and went straight into the forest. The two priests walked by and McQuade asked, "Want a ride?"

"I think," said one priest with a laugh, "that it is you who will need the help, not us!"

"There will be mud for some distance," explained the other.

They nevertheless accepted a ride and told McQuade, "We are from the leprosia mission. It is only a few kilometers."

196

The forest was dark and cool, with the smell of ferns among the trees. The arrowlike tsetse flies darted at their faces. The rain began again and the fierce lightning, and the Fiat bogged down completely. The rain came through the canvas of the Land Rover, and after a while they gave up and all sat in the Fiat waiting for the storm to end. The heavy rain fell onto the metal roof of the Fiat with the noise of steel balls. Torrents of water poured and there was the feeling of complete defeat at the hands of the elements. This storm did not end until after sunset, when they all—priests included—got into a saturated, muddy, exhausted conditon trying to move the Fiat. McQuade now had a sore throat and hoped he was not in for some illness.

After a while the Land Rover was able to haul the Fiat out and they moved the few filthy kilometers to the mission. An invitation to stay the night was accepted with alacrity and gratitude.

The priests—there was a third one inside, full of laughter at their sorry state, "And you unable to swear a solitary oath!"—were shy but with the flushed mild friendly excitement of people cut off from the world who are happy to see visitors, *any* visitors, and eager, like young men at college, for news or intellectual talk. And, faintly, McQuade also sensed the wish to show broad-mindedness, an understanding of situation, in the way Catholics do, as if to say, Look, we are very serious in our religion, but not so very different from other people . . .

The sisters, on the other hand, much older, with skin sucked dry like medieval parchment, seemed drained of sociability, but were extremely practical. They had problems with sewage and food and the injections and now the behavior of the river.

The priests shared the beer willingly and, over food brought in—something of a shock, this—by a patient with mutilated hands and no nose, put in their plea for equality, too, of a sort, and independence, for a reason. "Freedom from their own chiefs and the absurdities of the customs," said Father Jorge, the most talkative. "And independence of us because they imitate us at our worst."

Mr. Costa and Captain Duartes looked uneasy, as if the PIDE might expect them to report this opinion.

"Here there is suffering," went on Father Jorge. "As they grow wiser they will realize how much they are suffering. At present they

197

do not. And we give them God, who finds their suffering acceptable. But not desirable. I feel, myself, that man would be lost without problems and one of these is suffering. It is in overcoming problems that man distinguishes himself. But I dispute that it was intended for the *indigena* here to have yaws or tuberloid leprosy or flukes that eat out their livers."

He looked around as if expecting argument, whether from his fellow priests or the visitors.

McQuade sat in a basket chair in a room hard with use; the only new thing in it was a photograph of a bishop recently arrived. He was dead-tired and struggled to be courteous and at least stay awake.

Another visitor gave answer to Father Jorge. He came in out of the rain with an air of authority, the *chef de posto,* a small, very fat, good-humored but callous and determinedly outrageous Portuguese who had the look of one who has been in trouble all over the earth and has finally found somewhere where it is impossible for himself to be in trouble, only others. The news of visitors on the miniature steamer and now at the leprosia had reached him somehow through the storm and (again, in spite of the rain and muddy tracks) he had come several kilometers in a Volkswagen to see these strangers a long way from Vila Lobanda. He was not impressed by Mr. Costa or Captain Duartes, who were taking the evening cautiously themselves, but hearty and anxious to be liked by the fathers and their guests, with the possible exception of Asare Johnson whom he ignored.

"I am Carlos de Faria," he announced. "Do not take any notice of these idealists! I heard them talking their treasonable nonsense about suffering. I am a man of facts. A good Catholic, but a realist. The African is a dying race owing to the sterility of the women, which is due to the gonorrhea and syphilis. This is not seriously disputed from east to west of this continent. I do not think the white man gave *that* problem to Africa."

He noticed Barney and positively sparkled with admiration and the wish to be noticed. "Am I not to be introduced? May not a ruffian express his pleasure?"

The tediousness of translation slowed him down a little, although he was encouraged by Barney's frequent plea for the first

198

half hour: "What does he say?" After that no one showed off for her benefit—it was too exhausting to go through the pantomime of joke, translation and then the response, a blank stare or a difficult smile. Occasionally McQuade translated for Ekelund, who sat very upright, his pale hair and face the cleanest things in the room.

"I am prejudiced," boasted Mr. de Faria. "I do not deny it. We shall talk all night. You must attempt to break my prejudices."

It was like a holiday taken in the wrong place and with the weather—which had been fine when others at the office had taken their time off—breaking up when you went away, and the company at the hotel not that you'd ever seek again, but adequate at the moment; and around the room old magazines and curtains and other people's kids and dogs . . . You were drinking too much to combat tiredness, but in the alcohol finding a camaraderie which would be paler at the breakfast table, but forming a bond for a little while . . .

The conversation was fast and pleasant, but naturally began to exclude Barney and Asare Johnson, who, in shadow, began a separate, private, fierce but good-natured argument. They, too, drank, and Asare's clear eyes became a little streaked with blood. The sweat trickled down his face. Barney's saturated long brown hair and the faint smell—defeated in the other smells of tobacco and fetid Africa drifting in the room and the inevitable sweating—the smell of her special soaps and perfumes was the last olfactory presence and admission of cities. McQuade heard Asare arguing love with logic, which is useless but is nevertheless used by the wounded: "But you talked to all those people . . ." And Barney's defense, not as arrogant as the words indicated, "Yes, but I don't have to ask you, do I?" Both laughed, quiet private laughter that took hold of them and made them shake to the point of pain and complete physical weakness. Hands touched and moistened each other, and happiness, whether qualified or not, leaped into Asare's face.

A silence when all talking stopped and out in the forest could be heard the violent squabble of monkeys. The rain had died down, and, if anything, it was cooler, and a damp air now blew the smell of pigs and decay into the crowded room. Moths fluttered in through the open window and now and again McQuade felt the

199

light touch of insects falling on his neck or hands, cockchafers and beetles.

These interrupted Mr. de Faria, or perhaps bothered him, for he insisted on slaughter and in tireless hygiene kept stamping on beetles and smashing his hand on insects—an endless mess of smears on tables, shelves, pages, clothes and windows . . . It kept him on the move endlessly, so that he was a particularly tedious person to listen to, for the eyes were wearied as well as the ears if attention was to be paid. After a while McQuade realized that he was going to learn nothing, or so little that the rigid posture of Ekelund, like someone alert in the first hour of a day of conference, was too demanding. And when he'd tried to puncture the man's admitted prejudices, it had been all too easy and Mr. de Faria had resented it. He had to win—perhaps it was a habit due to ordering *indigena* about, stamping documents, telling minor chiefs what had to be done. But now he startled McQuade with a cry of excitement: "I almost forgot. There was news on the radio—there have been disturbances in Vila Lobanda." As with Father da Silva there was no association between the news of events a hundred and sixty miles off with the area of *his* control.

It filled the tired McQuade with the energy of a new horror, that of failure. He felt the uncomfortable possibility that he had made an error and the balance of his subcommittee back there in Vila Lobanda was in trouble. And, under that obvious anxiety, was a more personal and humiliating possibility—that of himself and these others being lost or cut off and having to plead with someone to get out of Africa at all, complete fools and laughable failures. There had been one or two disastrous missions by UN subcommittees. They were quoted regularly as part of the organization's history, no doubt to the distress of the extant participants.

"How bad were these disturbances?"

Mr. de Faria was full of it, sensing the anxiety.

"There was a motor race," he began to tell them, and the alarm died down in McQuade at this late arrival of old news.

McQuade tried to question Mr. de Faria about local conditions, but that gentleman was not as garrulous as he seemed. He was in fact curious and had come to find out, not inform. Perhaps he was conscious of Mr. Costa and the silent but formidable Captain

200

Duartes. But de Faria's last observation was an acute one: "It is not diseases they are dying of here," he said. "It is inanition, a staleness of purpose in the heart."

His departure was the signal for sleep. The fathers had not really had the intellectual or spiritual stimulus they had stayed up for and now they looked tired. Nevertheless, to McQuade's embarrassment, they surrendered the sleeping quarters.

McQuade was too tired and hot to sleep well. As he tossed about restlessly he heard the idiot gurgling of the hyena as it moved along the riverbank. The smells drifted into the bedroom, decay and the half-imagined sweetened odor of disease. Somewhere in a tree near the building a little, ratlike hyrax screamed like a madman in agony.

Before dawn he couldn't bear it and went outside in the hope of air. Even so, he was not the first up and about. The early scratchings of light revealed the silhouettes of long wooden huts. One, more solid than most, was a church and from inside it came the sentimental notes of prayer. The sun climbed like a fiery rocket into the sky, and before it burned away all moisture McQuade saw glistening spiders' webs and ferns outlined carefully in water. Ferns even grew out of the palm trees, like feathers from a pineapple. The river was moving faster than it had yesterday and had swollen feet higher. It carried bits of grass and fallen branches, and the white nenuphus lilies bobbed up and down like uncomfortable swans.

On his return to the mission McQuade found prayer ended and the priests at work. Morning was for practicality. The idealism and words were kept, like good wine, for visitors and evening talk; the day was for hard usage, practical goodness. Father Jorge was scrubbing wooden benches which he'd dragged out of what was presumably the surgery. He greeted McQuade with a laugh and said, "You should wash your vehicles!" When McQuade looked at them he was startled at their condition. He felt the city dweller's urge to wash down the painted steel in the certainty that otherwise it wouldn't move.

Already patients were gathering—mutilated and anxious Africans who had to drag themselves in some cases. "They have an innocence that is like the beginning of the world," said Father Jorge. "That is why I am glad I came to Africa. I can *touch* their innocence and their sins. I cannot hope to begin with the civilized of our cities, for they are stupefied by the wisdom of superficiality, the dross of culture. They look at me with pity, for they have lost innocence and really believe they are wiser than God . . . All miracles are science and all human behavior can be predicted in the lecture rooms. Here they are on the other side of innocence and I have to think hard and work in terms of electrical gear and plants and cleanliness and injections so that they may be well enough to have functioning minds. I am too busy worrying about their survival to be too concerned with their motives. They are, of course, animists, believing that the spirits of the dead return and cause disasters. This makes them fatalistic when there is no need and thus, as de Faria said, if they do not die of tuberculosis or yellow fever they do so of hopelessness. But you must see what the sisters do in their school with the young ones. They use a system intended for illiterate adults and it works. These little ones grasp knowledge with both hands. They find history hardest, but that's obviously to be expected, for they have no history. They are the new Africa. We must stay to help them. The old—if anyone did grow old—with their sores and goiters and diseases of the liver and their belief in the brews of witch doctors, their malaria and parasitic intestinal diseases and their yaws, the old are being changed for the new African who needs guidance but must not be exploited."

After breakfast they inspected the dispensary, the small hospital and the school, with its hundred and forty small children who had come a long way, through mud and the risks of snakes and insects, for their education. It seemed only right that they should have it and the freedoms that an educated person finds necessary. The Chokwe with his teeth filed to points, lying on a dispensary bed with the eyes of a terrified animal—even he sensed that here in this small compound was some kind of justice, while an Ovimbundu medical orderly smiled at his terrors as he prepared prescriptions. McQuade knew that the World Health Organization could multiply this sort of good work by a hundred if Portugal or Africa, or both, would allow it.

They drove twelve hours or more a day, stopping to eat under trees or by streams. Twice they were lucky enough to sleep in set-

202

tlements, and, once, in what was still a National Park, with its quota of round thatched huts. The rough road wound through ravines bordered by thick jungle, and when they stopped there was often the sound of roaring water somewhere among the immense trees and a smell of sap filling the nostrils in the motionless atmosphere.

After a while the nature of this equatorial landscape altered and the vehicles bumped over shale and rock, and the track wandered apparently without meaning through high yellow grass. Clouds of dust rose behind the two vehicles, and they kept at a distance of several hundred feet apart. The sun stood over this subdued stony landscape with stupefying power. It was a physical presence, flaring like an immense lamp so that McQuade felt he could hear the explosions of gas and the crisp crackling of neutrons. They were now beyond the patches of countryside blackened by the Africans who by fire cleared the land for their crops of manioc, beans and pumpkins. They were very near to the semidesert. Yellow dust rose in the day in clouds caused by herds of game—zebras, in thousands, like a children's shop at Christmas, other immense herds of brindled gnus, roan, antelopes and oribi. In the flood of hot yellow light these scenes were enormously impressive and man was the intruder in Africa. At six o'clock—if one paid attention to clocks in these endless distances—beyond the landscape of grass galloped to powder or eaten voraciously to the same point of erosion by the useless zebra, shedding its ticks as it went and spreading disease, at six the sun went down in a dead and silent world. The animals seemed to pause. On two nights McQuade stood in such a landscape and watched the bronze dust of the day turn the fierce sun into a feebler red disc, and before night came the entire sky in the west was filled with red dust and just beneath it, in a final show of strength, was a slice of gold sun that the eye couldn't bear to look at. And then for ten seconds after the sun had gone there were violent beams of green and blue, after which nothing . . . But although the wind whistled through the grass and thornbushes in the cooler air the rocks and soil still ached and throbbed with an oven heat. During the night things panicked from the smells of creeping carnivores and there was again the drum of panicking hoofbeats. And, alarmingly close at hand, the killers roared and screamed—the lions and leopards, the hyenas and jackals. In the morning the Fiat and the Land Rover might pass the corpse of a zebra, its yellow fats giving off a powerful, sour smell.

And then they came to the last administrative post—a mere cluster of white buildings—and the two vehicles were ferried across a river on a board platform floating on empty oil drums. Beyond was the desert.

It was really semidesert, and out of it, on the horizon twenty miles ahead, rose jagged mountains like ramparts. On that first morning there was a very slight fog drifting in from the ocean. This limited moisture fed a strange, rare plant, the *Welwitschia*. From each ugly, foot-high stem grew two wide, dry leaves which twisted along the ground for twenty feet. These unusual plants were perhaps a hundred years old.

Halfway to the mountains one of the Fiat's tires burst. While it was being repaired a band of Bushmen came from nowhere and stared from a distance. They had probably never seen automobiles before. They spoke a peculiar, clicking tongue which even Captain Duartes could not translate. The women carried their babies wrapped in antelope skins and picked vermin out of each other's peppercorn hair. They were extremely shy, and when the cars' engines were restarted the Bushmen were too terrified to move.

At the foot of the mountains, in the sweltering heat of noon, Captain Duartes stopped and pointed to a cave. They ate lunch in its shade. On the way across this arid stretch of land they had seen bleached animal bones, but here in the cave were old human remains. On the ceiling of the cave were umber and ocher drawings of birds, fish and scorpions. Outside, on an immense granite slope, were engraved hundreds of petroglyphs—one was of a giraffe, an animal which had long since ceased to live in the area, Duartes told them.

For two days they drove eastward across the trackless desert. The two major problems of these days were the heat and Barney. Barney took a good-humored and realistic view of herself among these five men and simply stated, "I am going to walk into the distance," and the men smiled and turned their backs. In the Fiat Duartes was carrying a tent which, unbelievably, had refrigeration —it was the sort of tent used on very expensive safaris. Barney took her turn in this on the first night and slept in the oven heat of the Fiat the second.

Then, on the third day, the thorn turned to grass, there were hills in the distance and beyond these were fields, crops in regulated lines and a neat small town. "A *colonato*," Mr. Costa explained. It was quite a pretty town, and tolerably cool, up on a plateau. Some of the town, part of the experimental *colonato,* was new; the remainder was old in the picturesque Portuguese manner. Oxcarts and jeeps moved in the streets. The strangers were conspicuous and interesting, and children gathered around the two vehicles from the desert.

There was no hotel in the town—it was entirely related to agriculture—and McQuade wondered where they would sleep. It was four o'clock in the warm afternoon and they moved with a kind of inevitability to the square in the center of the tiny town. There was a fountain here, and the whole sidewalk was a beautiful mosaic. A few people sat in wicker chairs outside a cafe, and one of them, startled, said, "That is the United Nations' flag."

The man was blond, sunburned and not Portuguese. He stared at the two vehicles, which had stopped as if of their own volition. The six occupants stepped out, sick of travel, and their heat, and that in the two vehicles, billowed out with the smells of clothes, oil and sweat over the colorful boulevard.

"I am the agronomist here. My name is Herluf Bloend," said the blond man in English. "It is fine to see you. I am a great believer in the UN. You have my support. I am glad that Portugal has come to realize this is the eventual solution . . . "

This surprise was followed after introductions—Mr. Bloend becoming more and more excited and others joining in or watching with pleasure—by a greater one, for the good-natured, earnest Mr. Bloend continued, "I presume you have come to see Colonel Unguanda? He will be glad to meet you. He has been very worried. It is so silly. He thinks the secret police will come to kill him or take him away. I mean, what has he done? Merely resigned because he wanted reforms hurried.

"Where are you staying?" he asked before they could dispute this. Sensing their bewilderment, he pressed the invitation: "You must stay with me. By all means telephone the colonel first. No. I

205

will phone. We will all be invited to dinner. You will see. He is very sensitive, but a good host. He has a fine house. Beautiful. Too large for the two of them, but after all there is dignity to be considered. He is not a *colono*. He was the Governor General . . ."

It was grimly humorous.

All of Portugal and Angolique was looking for this man.

McQuade remembered his name, Colonel Jorge Unguanda, from Bajune and newspaper reports that said he had resigned, and others that accused him of corruption, and later ones that said he had disappeared, and from the petitioner Captain Nogar. He had assumed that the colonel had been murdered. Now all that remained was for Captain Duartes to arrest him—if the captain was, as McQuade had assumed, of the PIDE. Certainly the captain, soaked in sweat and tired though he was, looked inquisitive.

But there were some further few ironic hours to be played out. The impulsive Mr. Bloend, a Danish expert advising the *colonato,* said that he was on his way to the railway station. Would they follow him and then all drive back to his dairy farm? It was irresistible. There was the agonized possibility of a bottle of cold beer, even a shower bath. No one knew quite what to say about Colonel Unguanda, and when Ekelund tried, speaking in Swedish, the Dane protested in English. "We must not talk in these barbaric Scandinavian languages!" and laughed hugely.

At the small railway station others were waiting for the train. Its arrival once a week was an event. But Bloend soon found out that it was running four hours late, which was not bad, for it came through tortuous countryside and took three days to travel from Porto Girassol.

They drove three miles to Bloend's farm. There was great excitement, and a visit by this United Nations party had clearly made Bloend's day and month and year . . . He was talkative, presumably, because it had been a long time since he had conversed with a European or American. He seemed to have no political anxiety or premonitions of trouble at all, and McQuade took this to be an indication that things were calmer here, farther south. His wife was a tall, equally blonde Dane—she spoke English well enough to make a pun about being a blonde Bloend—and she saw more readily than her husband how travel-stained the UN group were. What

206

did they require? A lager? A shower? She laughed at their obvious pleasure. And, sure enough, when her husband telephoned Colonel Unguanda, all of the party, including their Danish hosts, were invited to dinner. "He is a fine old man," Mrs. Bloend said. "I cannot understand why he hides in the house and looks thinner every day."

When the visitors had had their showers and their beer and had recovered a little from their tremendous fatigue, Bloend could not resist showing them around his farm before the sun went down. The dairy was beautifully clean, with tiled floors throughout. It had giant stainless-steel vats, sterilizing equipment and temperature-controlled rooms in which cheese was ripened and butter processed and stored until it could be transported to Porto Girassol in refrigerated railway vans.

Bloend was operating on quite a scale. He had three hundred Danish cattle here on the farm within twelve degrees of the equator. They were thriving and having calves. Bloend was tireless and did not notice if his guests dragged themselves somewhat. He assumed that this was why they had come. "From the bedrooms you can see three villages," he said. "That is what a *colonato* is," he explained. "A collection of villages, each with church, school, community barn and so on. And this allows good agricultural planning. Come and see. Tomorrow . . ." He was full of plans for the morrow. From an upstairs room of his house they did indeed see thousands of acres under cultivation. Corn, wheat, soya—even potatoes—stretched in mathematical array for kilometers . . . It was impressive. This, McQuade knew sadly, was the way things ought to be, and to a large extent were, on this cooler plateau five hundred miles south of Vila Lobanda and a thousand from the Congo. But in his mind was the inevitable anxiety about tonight's encounter.

"And there is fishing and the salt industry on the coast," Bloend enthused, justifiably proud of what he had helped to reclaim from swampland. "Several *colonatos* are settled entirely by Africans. And when the new settlers come from Portugal they are not allowed much African help because they are expected to work for themselves. They are loaned money for about 150 acres and a house. And my God, how keen they are! How hard they do work!"

McQuade looked out of a different window onto a citrus orchard

207

which stretched to another horizon. In the late afternoon workers were picking oranges.

There was a full moon that evening and under its pale illumination they arrived at the residence of Colonel Unguanda. It was a house to be seen in moonlight and was part of the original village. A fairly large, white stone house, nineteenth-century colonial and provincial Portuguese, with a wide stone staircase from the neglected garden to a veranda on the second floor. A tired but beautiful place with an air of dignity and decay. There was the smell of cabbages in the night air and on the veranda a dog tore at a chain and gasped with hatred and the frustration of not being able to tear at the visitors. New barbed wire glistened in the moonlight at one side and the rear of the house. Somewhere in the pannen tiles baby birds squeaked in anxiety.

The massive front door was opened by a Ganguela servant dressed in white, even wearing white gloves. It was as if they'd arrived at an expensive Harlem brothel. But inside a hall of considerable dimensions hung game trophies: old heads and horns from, McQuade sensed, another decade. There were lion and antelope skins over a flagstone floor. The door handles were ivory. But these were, it seemed, other people's possessions—some plantation owner long since dead or a great hunter now appearing on TV or writing a book, for there were heavy leather cases lying about which gave the place an air of temporary visitors and early departure . . .

The colonel came out of a drawing room. He unlocked a door to do so and another to obtain drinks and a third to enter a bedroom to get photographs. He was a large man, but his clothes hung slack —he had presumably been larger. An old woman moved about, shifting vases of sweet basil from place to place, and after a while McQuade realized that she was terrified. She tried very hard not to show it for her husband's sake, but she shook like someone anticipating disaster.

Neither spoke English and the evening was a mixture of Portuguese and French, with tedious translations. The colonel was shaky, not with alarm, but with the lack of people to talk to, for he never went far outside. But after a while he grew talkative and authoritative, for he was a kindly and wise old man and he had been in Angolique for twenty years.

208

Three servants in the same white suits and gloves served dinner, one of them carving the meat—it was excellent beef—on a carving table. "This is good cattle country despite the latitude," said the colonel. "Mr. Bloend brought excellent beasts from Denmark. It could have been a great experiment, but the world does not want it."

He seemed to be torn between deep depression verging on outright despair and occasional lapses when he talked as if there was no political upheaval and he had taken no stand in it. His conversation was interspersed with remarks about his personal situation. These references, too, were divided between the gleeful story of his escape in a car and the fearful possibility that they (whoever "they" were) would find him. His wife sat between Barney and Asare and said nothing. They, too, could only listen and eat.

The colonel asked, "Were the roads bad?" and then, almost to himself, with a laugh that was bitterly useless, "It's a long way to come to kill an old man. Do you think they will?"

He addressed this question to Captain Duartes in grim ironic ignorance of the captain's position. He was seeking advice about avoiding the PIDE from one of its members!

And then he continued, "The train has broken down, I hear."

"That is not so," countered Costa. "It is merely four hours late."

"Four hours? That is all?" The colonel was alarmed. "Then it is due now." He spoke as if without the train to defeat distance "they" might not stir out of their torpor in Vila Lobanda or Porto Girassol to come and kill, arrest, or whatever was intended . . .

McQuade could not get him around to the reasons for his resignation. He seemed in his anxiety to have forgotten that these visitors, or some of them, were of the United Nations and were collecting evidence. But the colonel was relevant in a more general way.

"For a long time Angolique handled the traffic of slaves and all dignity was lost for centuries. Then it became a prison colony, which caused lack of prestige in Portugal. It was a backwater, even in Africa, until ten years ago. Now they want to make it into a nation in a hurry. The need," he said, switching oddly from the general to the particular, "is to end forced labor and the price fixing of the Africans' cash crop below world levels. And an end in the same manner to the danger of a color bar, which, ironically, has come with the many peasant-immigrants who've been crowding out

209

the *indigena*. And an end to fear and imprisonments. Provincial autonomy, I think, is the satisfactory answer, with independence, if that is what the world insists upon, a long way off when education is better. In other words, a multiracial state—we almost had it when the fighting began—within a Portuguese Commonwealth. This would spare we Portuguese humiliation . . ."

Captain Duartes disputed this somewhat.

"First of all we must have order. An end to killing. Do you know that in the last lot we captured many of these black fools were expecting automobiles, United Nations and Cabinet posts, diplomas and medals?"

"I do not believe that," said Colonel Unguanda simply. "You must not believe what you read in the newspapers," he explained as to a student.

"I speak their languages," claimed Duartes, restraining irritation. It didn't matter much. This old man was finished, he shook with fright like a girl. Let him have a last pitiful insult or two.

Another servant entered and, with permission, told the colonel, "The train has come, but there was no stranger on it."

They drank green port in another room until they were almost asleep, and McQuade's memory before he did rest in one of the Bloends' comfortable bedrooms was of the old man, still anxious, asking again, now that he was satisfied about the train for a week, "Were the roads bad?" It seemed almost unfair that he and his wife should be kept waiting in such suspense. In the morning McQuade caught Captain Duartes as he came away from the telephone in the dairy, and he knew that the old people would have their verdict settled soon and their curious attitude of being guilty would be assuaged. He could still be wrong and Captain Duartes could be a mere clerk good at translation, but the truth asserted itself in his stomach, and McQuade had to struggle with the soup, eggs and sausages which the others ate with enormous appetite.

They had come through the hundreds of miles of savanna land, followed tracks around the spur of a group of *serras* and now were at or even beyond the end of the two-thousand-mile arc. The rain fell and it was dismal and wet and cold. They were only two hundred miles from Vila Lobanda, but night was coming and those two hundred miles would take many hours.

Ahead were two sheds of corrugated iron, the first "buildings" seen in twelve hours today and eleven hours of driving yesterday. There were stacks of logs in a clearing and this was, presumably, the periphery of a timber mill. Here, far north of Vila Lobanda, the major industry was, or had been until the fighting, the felling of trees.

Captain Duartes admitted, "I think we took the wrong track thirty kilometers back. Let us stay here for the night."

They were all very tired, an accumulated weariness of days of heat and little sleep. The vehicles were parked by the corrugated-iron huts and the party strolled about stretching their legs. The sun went down very abruptly in the gloomy day and left them in absolute darkness under the rain. They sat in a hut in the fetid smells of dampness and bugs and talked listlessly while the rain dropped, reminding them of home, for it was not heavy tropical rain but the low cloud that hung over the mountain. They were four thousand feet up now, although not conscious of having climbed.

Again there was the minor problem of Barney, but it was easily settled. She slept in the Fiat while the others dispersed themselves in the Land Rover and the huts. It was becoming difficult to keep clean, and McQuade, lying on a rug in a hut, was conscious of being dirty and tired beyond belief and of a two-days' stubble. He was far beyond caring about insects or even snakes and slept at once.

He awoke in darkness with fear in his bowels. He was aware of having slept for some hours, perhaps many, but it was still black outside. The fear was so fierce and inexplicable and apparently needless that he was weak with it, a conscious weakness in the stomach and shoulders. It went through him in waves meaninglessly. He hadn't felt this before in the whole journey. It was the sort of fear a child has in the night: when the owl cries out again you will die: the wind taps a branch against a window and it is God, angry about the lies . . .

Then he heard the drums.

They were monotonous, as if there was a shortage of them and with the shortage a limited range of music or messages or whatever it was. Cigarette smoke drifted from somewhere and a foot squelched in mud outside. McQuade had been sleeping fully dressed and he was up at once and went out.

211

"Who is that?"

"Duartes," said the captain, and in the black world the pinprick of light was taken out of his mouth and moved half a yard to one side so that he could speak.

The fungoid smell of the jungle and elephant grass, saturated and warm—for heat and humidity had come from somewhere—added to the terrible sensation of being lost: a deep sensation, known right in the bowels, the knowledge that, only two hundred miles from Vila Lobanda, they could not be found; if the whole party had food poisoning they would have to lie groaning and, if necessary, die. And there was the additional primitive certainty that whoever were banging drums would know these thousands of square miles of forest as McQuade knew the concrete pattern of Manhattan.

"What is the time?" he asked.

"Five o'clock."

"What do the drums mean?"

Captain Duartes said briefly, "Trouble, Mr. McQuade." He, too, was frightened. "No lights, Mr. McQuade, and we'd better have my rifle handy."

"How far away are they?"

"Hard to say. Sound carries under the *cassimbo*."

"Where are they?"

"In the hills. In the grass. Bakongo having their bodies rubbed with *milongo* for immunity and getting coked up on something, excitement and perhaps *aguardente*. They don't know about your concern and resolutions, Mr. McQuade. They haven't seen your flag. They've had great fun ever since that business started in the Congo. And they are encouraged and supplied from Leopoldville, of course, and possibly Brazzaville, by people who 'love' Angolique, but have never lived here or studied our problems. So these Bakongo are encouraged to kill the *Wazungu,* which means you and I. Can you blame us for despising the United Nations? These people do not talk. They just slaughter and then go back into the forests."

"There are others?"

"That is true. I do not deny it. With the others there will eventually be a solution, although it will not be imposed on us. But with these . . ."

212

Barney came from somewhere and said cheerfully, "Say, listen. Drums. Monotonous, but pretty impressive."

"We'll move as soon as it's light," suggested Captain Duartes.

The humidity of the night was as unbearable as the fear. After a while McQuade said, "I think the drums are moving away," and he was ashamed of his relief.

Daylight came at six o'clock through the trees and elephant grass as if God had an alarm clock. The *cassimbo* hung so low that the trees seemed to grow downward out of it. They stood around eating cold meat and sausages and drank the last of the coffee. In a few hours they could be in Vila Lobanda, and McQuade thought of that attractive dirty city now with positive affection. To see old Theo Alferink again, drink a cool beer and laugh with Marianne and the others in the elegant modern bar of the Hotel Marromeu. Letters from Kristan to read. But the uneasy feeling persisted that these things were half a continent away and there were things to live through and take note of.

It was certainly the wrong track.

They had continued a few miles along it when they came across the ambush.

It was an old one. There was nothing they could do about it. The whole countryside reeked of fear: it belched out of the ground. Birds shrieked like police whistles and animals laughed hysterically. The humans stood and walked about, overcome by the morning spectacle.

It was obvious what had happened. There had been two vehicles and the leading one had dropped into the hole prepared for it: canvas camouflage covered with dust. The vehicle behind, a jeep, had swerved and hit a tree. The first vehicle had a hard top and its dimensions fitted the hole in the track so tightly that the occupants hadn't been able to open the doors. The roof of this vehicle was peppered with little holes from the shot of *canhangulos*. The fetid smell of the corrupting corpses stayed among the trees. The Portuguese soldiers in the jeep had put up a good fight, but they had all been overcome. It was difficult to say how long ago these Portuguese and Africans had died. They were decomposed already and rats ran away from the putrescence and the whole fifty square yards of mud was alive with armies of insects.

213

Walking in the *capim* grass McQuade stumbled on a soldier's head, which still had a cap on the face hacked from its body yards away and now a vile mess of collapse, the diet of insects. McQuade said nothing about this decapitation, not wishing to upset Barney, who was white enough.

Perhaps the Portuguese soldiers, like Captain Duartes, had taken the wrong track.

There was nothing to do. There were perhaps twenty-five bodies, too many to bury and in any case too decomposed to carry or move. Costa stood in silence and was evidently praying for these fellow Catholics, but it was a hurried prayer and soon over. The vehicles were maneuvered among the trees and the reverse direction taken, Captain Duartes now most concerned about the inaccuracy of maps . . . He was also worried about the fuel. They had carried many cans, but these were all empty now. If they did not find the correct track soon, they would be humiliated and even lost. It would be a ridiculous situation for six educated people, but the forest was not interested, it seemed, in education, only in life and death, its own great compost heap.

The heat of the day had now broken up the mist and clouds, but it was humid under the fierce sun. The view was at times gigantic and overwhelming—dolomitic mountains like broken teeth and forests that stretched forever, undulating with this daunting topography.

They picked up the track where Duartes thought he might have made an error on the previous day. At once they encountered two jeeps and a semiarmored car of the Portuguese Army. This was a detachment of the *Caçadores Especiais* (Special Hunters), who were as startled as they were. Later McQuade learned that only astonishment and Ekelund's fair hair had prevented the officer in charge from giving the signal to fire. There were machine guns and a bazooka on the jeeps. The detachment consisted of a lieutenant and a dozen soldiers, some of them Bailundo who served in the Portuguese Army.

The young lieutenant was businesslike and in a hurry. He asked Captain Duartes in something near to irritation, "Who are these people?"

"A subcommittee of the United Nations."

"Those pious liars," said the lieutenant with loathing. "Do they know what they are doing and where they are?"

Duartes said nothing.

The lieutenant thought about it and then said authoritatively, no argument expected, "You will have to come with us. I must give you our protection. We received a wireless signal from a plantation up here that there were drums—"

"We heard them."

"—and nothing since," concluded the lieutenant ominously. "The weather stopped the spotter planes and we ourselves have been traveling two hours."

"You think there has been trouble?" McQuade asked.

The lieutenant was startled by his knowledge of Portuguese, but was in no mood for analyses or conversation. He seemed to know his business. "Do you know what trouble is?" he asked bitterly. "You may see what Portuguese people have to endure because of the idealists' gossip. Bring the woman, too. What in the name of God is she doing here?"

He was not interested in Barney's beauty. Perhaps he had knowledge and anxieties that put it into a new perspective. But he said, "I am sorry about it. If there is fighting you had better stay in your vehicles and lie down."

It was a coffee plantation. They reached it in fifty minutes. McQuade saw that the war was gradually defeating it. Presumably the workers fled in fear from the area. Even so, there were still acres and acres of coffee trees laid out in quadrangles according to age. The soil was perfectly tended and no weeds grew among the rows and rows of pyramidal trees, all in the nearest quadrangle being about eight feet high. The leathery leaves and scarlet berries shone in the sun, and, closer, McQuade thought he could distinguish the white delicate starlike flowers in the axils of the leaves. A very slow hot wind carried the sweet smell of the plants through the open car windows . . . But farther away the trees grew tall and thin and wild, and here the elephant grass was having its way and weeds grew so vigorously they took on the proportions of bushes.

Half a mile away were the administration buildings, a row of white cube houses, a dining hall, a small school, warehouses, a church and a dispensary, and scattered about neatly were various

215

sheds and garages and workshops. It was a big plantation, but, McQuade suspected, had been busier. And there was no one at all working in the quadrangles this dry morning.

Over the area of the administration buildings birds sailed sluggishly.

"Oh, my God," whispered Ekelund.

A horse was the first thing they saw. At first they thought it was lying down. Then they saw the torn-open belly.

The military vehicles in front stopped and the soldiers jumped out and began spreading about, one man remaining in each jeep revolving his machine gun.

McQuade stepped out of the Land Rover. He knew they—whoever "they" were—were all dead. It was curious how he knew. The fields were empty. The horse. The buildings were dead. It wasn't that they'd been set on fire. They hadn't. It was just an absence of movement inside, not a sound of feet or dogs or radio or whistling kettles or typewriter . . . And the way in which doors and windows clattered in the gentle humid wind. And the birds. He knew they were vultures. They sat on tin and wooden roofs nuzzling under their wings. And then they sailed down to things out of Mc-Quade's view; it was not quite flight, but as they went down or moved to another perch to await opportunity and position they flap-flapped their dusty wings with a minimum of effort, and then indulged in this curiously bestial nuzzling under their wings with their small knobby heads.

He had to see. It was part of duty. He knew it would be terrible, but walked beyond the vehicles and the soldiers stared but did not stop him. Around the corner of the office was the most ghastly spectacle he had ever seen.

On lawns and a patio and near and in an orchard and among the huts and outbuildings the dead lay in groups. This was not the worst of it. Nor the pools of blood. Nor the squeak of rats running out of huts. Nor the clatter of birds on corrugated iron. Nor the smells of blood and (somewhere near) slaughtered pigs in the heat of day. Nor the hens, unaware of this day's difference, still idiotically banging beaks into the soil and gravel and wandering about with jerking necks. Even a snake lying in the sun did not touch McQuade.

216

He did not see the full horror at first, only the ghastly mutilations—the area strewn with scores of heads and cut-off arms and corpses with heavy stains of blood on the clothes and especially between the legs. He swallowed and swallowed and prayed, trembling, oh God, oh, God.

The birds could not differentiate between the manner of death, nor between those who had been white and those who had been black or brown, nor make the further distinctions such as who had been shot or who had been hacked to bits with the *catanas*, which had been women and which had been men. It was indeed a problem to distinguish, for many men had had their genitals cut off and their heads were far away. So it was a problem, but clearly not one that worried the vultures. They sidled about the dead in an agitated flurry of soft bloody brown feathers. They strutted about on the corpses, digging with their beaks and staring around with vicious, small, indifferent eyes for a moment or two before resuming. Sometimes they had a look to see if others were faring better or stared around at the hurrying soldiers and this Canadian, who were not far away. It was very disturbing for them to be interrupted at table. They craned their obscene scalded necks this way and that and hopped about, and looked at the sky, which was clouding over.

The lieutenant came out of a building and leaned against a wall to vomit. Then he came across to McQuade and said, "Don't let the woman anywhere near. But the others had better look. It's quite safe. Everyone is dead."

"In that building?"

"I shouldn't," the lieutenant advised. "I have seen things like this before, but the Bakongo always have a new idea, and this is what upsets my stomach."

Asare Johnson and Hjalmar Ekelund came around into this courtyard. They stared with sick eyes.

The lieutenant said, "I cannot bear those things and what they do. I am a Catholic and these people . . ."

He took a submachine gun off a soldier and advised, "Put your fingers in your ears," and fired. The vultures scattered, but did not depart, still hopeful, for there was a lot to attend to. The lieutenant walked around hopelessly with McQuade. In the distance Mr. Costa was being sick.

217

Now, venturing nearer, they saw the full horror: the cut-out eyes, the opened stomachs and the claw and beak marks. Some of the women had been stripped and their breasts cut off. Sticks and bars and things lying about had been pushed up their vaginas. Similar things had been done to the men's anuses. In the orchard decapitated bodies hung from trees, and among the branches, or hanging from them, were limbs. Farther along, among parked jeeps and trucks, a few bodies had been burned in gasoline. The violent postures suggested that they'd been burned alive. The stench in the heat of day was vile. Ekelund threw up and in doing so his glasses fell off. Ekelund just couldn't bend down and pick them up, unbroken but lying in blood and vomit. He would have to buy another pair.

In the offices were the frightened ones, the ones unable even to attempt to fight back. Two large dogs had fought on their behalf, but had been cut to bits with the *catanas,* which were normally used for cutting the branches of trees or clearing a way through the forest. A good detective could have perhaps worked out the timing and manner of these other deaths. The dogs first, then some ten or twelve children to hack through—difficult to say exactly, for some had been cut in half and here and there along corridors was the odd hand or arm or head—and then the women.

What had happened to the women might have interested the professional masturbators, the "with it" bishops smiling on TV and advocating fornication for the "right" kind of student, or the staff of the girlie magazines so piously reasoning their broadmindedness. Certainly it could have been of interest for an intellectual piece of reasoning of some kind. For rape was of interest. Invariably the mind assumed that the victim was beautiful, and a little envy crept in. If only one could get hold of one of those superb girls—an Italian one, or perhaps a Scandinavian—and, with a little extension of clerical authority (and one or two to hold her down), indulge, carry the wishful thinking of the girlie pictures to a physical end. But the girl had to be beautiful, a soft, long-legged cushiony body, well fed, with wild eyes that rather enjoyed it all. But here the Portuguese and *mestiço* women were not of that kind. They had fat bodies and short legs, and their hands, cut off and lying about for examination, had the toughened texture of hard work. They clutched rosaries and evidently had no wish for violation or death.

218

Shoes and frocks and rather old-fashioned underwear were scattered about. The quantity of blood was considerable. It was very hard to believe that these bloody trunks and buttocks and old legs with the varicose veins and the tired old feet with hardened toenails had been of sexual interest. But the evidence was there. Kitchen instruments shoved up the vagina. And so on. The pools of blood were unnerving and overwhelming. Blood was on everything—door handles, food, furniture, even the windows. Asare Johnson, who was very emotional about these things, had been weeping but now rushed outside in an absurd politeness to vomit.

Only McQuade and a few of the Bailundo soldiers hadn't been sick. Foolishly, perhaps, McQuade went into the huts and outbuildings of stone, and in due course reached the one which had so upset the lieutenant. And the young officer was quite right; he shouldn't have entered. For he would have bad dreams for the rest of his life. It had, in bitter parody of what it was now, been the place where meat was hung. And hanging now and besieged by flies were the bodies of ten or so young women and girls. The spectacle was so appalling that McQuade's mind couldn't take it in—the curse of memory gave him little details for hours afterward . . . After some fine sport the Bakongo had hung them up—the white ones who had long hair had been hung the "right" way around by that hair, or, where there was difficulty with the hair, by large meat hooks levered into the head or throat . . . The black females, who had rather short hair, had been hung by the feet; in one case they'd run out of hooks and the girl dangled from one hook which was inserted through the soft part of her right foot; the long bare blood-spotted left leg hung crazily downward . . . There had been resistance, of course—it was all too easy to imagine the screams and struggles in the hot foul air, the assaults and then, finally, still alive, screaming and weeping at mere rape and cuts and blows with *catanas, this*. And this was not mere hanging or the pain of hooks driven into flesh. For the Bakongo had skinned them alive. Strictly, McQuade didn't know if they'd been alive, but it seemed fairly evident, for the blood had still been circulating hard . . . And that, for a few instants, was why it had been difficult for him to tell which girls had been black and which white . . .

The smells of these various indignities and the reek of greasy blood was foul in the heat, and McQuade vomited instantly and

219

went outside before he should faint. There he stood and leaned against a wall gasping, trembling and with eyes watering . . .

Always in these things there is someone who survives. The lieutenant had been hoping for this and now he had found one. He had heard the whimpering in the grass and now carried a boy of about ten who, at his touch, screamed and screamed. The lieutenant put him on the ground where the boy sat and shivered and began to beat his head on the floor. He had done this before, as severe bruises indicated, and it was not surprising, for he had had his eyes gouged out . . .

However, the departure of the Bakongo was fairly well indicated in a trail of broken branches, things dropped, and the lieutenant sent half of his men to see where they had gone. There was practically nothing to say and certainly no one wanted to eat. The rain came like tremendous pity and drummed on the dead flesh and the vultures and the corrugated iron and the pannen tiles of the graceful house that would fall into ruin.

After an hour the patrol called on the walkie-talkie. "They are all heading toward the Moxama Mountains," the lieutenant explained. "But a little celebration is being held by a dozen or so who are lingering in a *sanzala* in the trees. They're tired and are smoking their pipes and having a bit of a feast. We may get some of them. There were about a hundred who came here. These jokers have shirts and bodies which are bloodstained. They're Muchicongos. I hope my boys can cope," the young Portuguese officer said anxiously.

The patrol came back an hour and a half later with two prisoners. They had killed another ten and one of their own men had *canhangulos* shots in his stomach.

The two prisoners were in dirty shorts and one had made the fatal error—perhaps he didn't realize what he'd taken—of wearing a woman's bright dressing gown. This one shook and giggled with laughter so uncontrollable that his eyes were bloodshot. The other one seemed scared, although not seriously frightened. Both were drunk on something and both had bloodstains here and there; the giggly one even had blood in his hair.

"I'd like to know where they're all going," the lieutenant said, while the Bailundo soldiers stood staring with obvious hatred at the prisoners.

220

"I speak Kikongo," claimed Captain Duartes.

"Try," suggested the lieutenant, "but I am in a hurry. Then they can dig the graves."

Captain Duartes addressed the two Muchicongos, but the one couldn't stop giggling and the other answered with obvious defiance.

"He is pleased with himself," said Captain Duartes.

A Bailundo soldier jabbed his rifle butt into the giggly one's mouth, breaking his teeth. Blood poured. The lieutenant was angry with the soldier. "Do you think pain will frighten him?" he asked sarcastically. "He is proud to bear pain. He thinks we are weaklings not to kill him at once. Fetch the field battery."

The two prisoners did not know what this thing was and the giggly one was now very alarmed and the urine ran down his leg, staining his shorts. "Try him first," the lieutenant ordered. "I am in a hurry, Mr. McQuade," he said with anger. "I realize this is not according to your charter, but I am at war and have to hurry if those others are to be dealt with before they attack another plantation."

McQuade said nothing.

He was thinking of those bodies hanging in the buildings and the hacked children, and he considered that the lieutenant was showing some restraint.

They attached the positive pole to the prisoner's nostrils and the negative to his left ear and turned the handle. The prisoner squeaked. He began to shake and plead and justify himself. The defiant one also began to have visible anxieties. He, too, became talkative, but, owing to the nature of his way of life, and that of his fellow, could hardly talk in terms of map references or latitudes. But after a while the lieutenant was satisfied that he knew where to direct the aircraft, and he said simply, "Get them to carry out the bodies. Then shoot them."

He sat on a wall with his hands on his knees, trying not to weep, a young man of twenty-two who had seen too much but still tried to put order into chaos.

They reached Vila Lobanda long after dark—tired, stunned, sickened and relieved to be back in this civilized African city which eleven days before they had despised. The air had the taste of the sea in it and soon they would be able to walk on the white sand under the palm groves, take a cool drink in the bar of the Hotel Marromeu and be glad to hear again the string of quaintly old-fashioned sweet music taped for use in that hotel. In the morning the bell would ring in the convent and soon afterward, far away, like something in a dream remembered with pain, the gentle voices of the girls in the Lycée would be heard singing. It no longer mattered about the curfew or the road drills. They were leaving Angolique in three days, heading north to hear petitioners in another country.

They would have a final party for the odd people whom they had grown to know at other parties in Vila Lobanda. At last McQuade would learn the names of the Belgian and French ladies. It would be possible to be quite frank with Mr. Costa and the Governor General and would be downright pleasant to see the earnest young Mr. Brandão again. It would even be possible to feel a little pity for Mrs. Duffin, staying in this territory, strutting about with curious snobbery and the bravery of ignorance . . .

The eleven days had been full of events and places. They had forgotten that the same days could carry a weight of problems here in Vila Lobanda, too.

McQuade had not realized how deadly tired and shaken he was until he found how little he even wished to talk to the balance of his subcommittee. And how irritatingly themselves they were! He could scarcely bear it, seeing them there standing around having drinks in an atmosphere of relaxation . . . Marianne's prompt little sour self-pitying joke about "Oh, my God, you look like you've been testing your clothes to destruction. Ah, well, a day on the laundry drill for Miss Saavedra tomorrow . . ." Only *then* did she comment, "You look sick or something," and, to Barney, "What's been happening?"

And Gregorio de la Plaza, anxious to justify himself, expressing *his* perspective of these eleven days: "As there was not a great deal to do I have made a draft report insofar as Vila Lobanda is concerned—you know, the schools and the tour of Porto Girassol and, I think, a fairly detached view of the motor race. Are things better in the south?"

Worst of all was the problem thrust upon him at once by an angry Ribowski. "It is ridiculous. We have done nothing. Only

222

that fool Alferink. *He* has been out all the time with this stupid schoolgirl, Lilli. He is out now. There is a curfew still, but oh, no, Alferink, he says, 'That is for the Africans. If you are in a car it does not really matter.' So he is out in the Mercedes. What time will he come back? Two o'clock maybe."

"Is there any mail?"

"Oh, yes, a little."

There was a letter from Peter. One from England. Nothing from Kristan. *Nothing.* McQuade was caught off guard. Eleven days of slaughter and heat and all the rest of it. He'd been sure there would be two or three letters. It was the reward he had been looking forward to—the atmosphere of love, and a distant smell, in the ink, of martinis and wallpaper and restaurants and cold air (he'd forgotten cold air) and her day-to-day small program, which was empty because it waited for him. He said in anger, "Is this *all?*" It was. It was hard to calm down and acknowledge that the eleven days for Kristan had been emptier than they had for him, or to admit the vagaries of jet planes, trains, weather or even censorship somewhere in Angolique.

As he went to wash he heard Marianne ask lightly, with indifference, "What's the matter with the chairman? Is he sore about something?"

Ekelund's voice answered, "He is upset. We have seen some terrible things."

"You mean worse than TV?"

McQuade could have kicked Marianne. She had to be droll, funnier than anyone else, even her own previous remark.

The telephone rang while McQuade was in the bath. It was midnight. He heard Marianne answering distantly. Presumably she had had to do all the Portuguese translations for the past eleven days and was cross about it.

Then de la Plaza knocked on the bathroom door and pleaded, "Hurry, Shaun. It is Theo. He has been shot."

"The stupid bastard! Why the hell— Who's on the phone?"

"The police, I think."

"You *think?* Find out."

"I said Theo—"

"I heard you, you old woman. I'm coming."

223

He was furious with all of them. Dull, dim, stupid people. Couldn't do a damn thing without a bloody charter to guide them and a chairman to hold their silly hands. He dried himself hurriedly, still stupefied with the day. This morning's slaughter had presumably given him a temporary callousness about idiots like Theo getting shot at—presumably by someone's husband! Alarm penetrated his tiredness and his heart thumped in his hot naked body. Suppose Theo was dead?

He almost smiled grimly at the way the whole lot of them stood about, shocked, but waiting for *him* to do something. "Well, where is he?" he growled at them.

"A car is coming."

It had in fact arrived.

Two uniformed policemen in their white tropical uniforms and a man in plain clothes. McQuade went out with them without a word. He was furious with his subcommittee. Unreasonable rage was burning him. He would tell Theo what he thought of him. The stupid fool, messing about with a schoolgirl while a curfew was on, not a fortnight after that motor race . . .

One of the policemen said to the others, "It was a good way to die though, eh?" and the others laughed.

McQuade told them coldly, "I speak Portuguese and I do not find it funny."

They were startled. The first one said, "I beg your pardon. It was unforgivable of me, but your friend—if it is he—was very foolish."

"What did he do?"

"He drove outside the city limits and parked without lights. A patrol shot him."

"Just my friend?"

"And a girl. You see—"

"Yes, I see," said McQuade.

And it was as humiliating as his mind had presumed. A group of soldiers and police stood by the Mercedes. The doors of the car had been opened and there were Theo Alferink and the girl Lilli, in the posture of love, white and undignified and bloodstained and just as uselessly and completely dead as the decapitated, raped peasant women around the patio of the coffee plantation.

McQuade was tired and angry, but thrashed his mind to think of

224

what the implications were. Not Suzé or the funeral arrangements, but the humiliations for this subcommittee before it left Angolique . . .

"Yes, that is my friend," he admitted, and he suddenly wanted to weep. "And that is a Belgian girl from the Lycée Amélia, I think."

The soldier who had shot them said, "So sorry," but couldn't resist smiling very slightly, for he had no problems; he had done his duty, and McQuade had to bear it whether he liked it or not.

"We had better separate them," he said woodenly, and the police and soldiers were startled to see how he handled the dead bodies without emotion—so that the press should not photograph them thus. Nobody stopped him. "I will tell you who is the next-of-kin." What time was it in New York? "The less said about this the better, gentlemen."

"We shall say nothing," said the senior policeman. "If you are satisfied that the circumstances—"

"I am sure it was the accidents of foolishness on his part and duty on yours—"

"Exactly," agreed the policeman.

This would not stop his gossiping, but it might prevent a too detailed report from appearing in the press.

It was now long after midnight. McQuade did not tell his fellow members of the subcommittee of the exact way in which Alferink had died, only that he had been shot and that the girl with him had been shot too. That was bad enough, and they were discussing it inevitably, but much to McQuade's irritation, when the press came.

The members of the press—who hadn't taken much notice of the subcommittee's presence in Vila Lobanda and Angolique—now crowded around like hounds for the kill. McQuade—it still had to be him, for he spoke Portuguese, he was the chairman and he had seen the bodies—had to restrain his anger and forgo his exhaustion and play the good-natured, calm, reasonable United Nations chairman, the unruffled Canadian delegate . . . As soon as the UN was in trouble there was a certain species of journalist who caught the smell of it and hurried thither with ballpoint pen at the ready. McQuade could not be sure whether or not in this strange corner of Africa these half dozen men here at one o'clock in the morning did include journalists of that category. Four of them were

225

Portuguese, one was Rhodesian and the sixth, French. The dull language of UNO was useful in this kind of situation, fending off the implications.

"What was Mr. Alferink doing out at night during a curfew anyway?"

"Like yourselves we are on duty twenty-four hours a day."

"Who was the girl?"

"A child from the Lycée here."

"What was *she* doing out?"

"I've no idea. You must inquire at the school."

"Was she a friend of Mr. Alferink's?"

"That's not likely."

"Who's his next-of-kin?"

"His wife. And, gentlemen, I don't suppose she knows of his death yet, so take it easy."

"Do you think this is a useful mission?"

"Very useful. I have just completed a long tour of half the country."

"You think the country's ready for independence?"

"We have to make a combined assessment on that. We still have more evidence to hear—"

"About Mr. Alferink—"

"He was a good delegate and a very brave man. He risked his life to take some photographs and these form evidence . . ."

The Frenchman asked, "Do you think he died on duty, sir?" and the Rhodesian one muttered, "On the job anyway," which indicated that the gossip was alive and spreading.

McQuade was drunk with tiredness. He sat on his bed at two in the morning. He could not remember a more brutal day, except in the war. There was still the final duty. He knew that the cables would hum across the Atlantic. Theo's widow would be weeping quite soon. How fast would the rumors follow, if at all? McQuade knew that the weekly airplane went from Vila Lobanda tomorrow afternoon, or, rather, today as it now was. She must have a letter from him, his own personal sympathy that must exclude any tiny hint of anything but duty. And it must be on that plane today or she wouldn't hear from him for ten days and by then it would be too late for sympathy. Dear Suzé. No. My dear Suzé. A girl at a party six thousand miles away. The sweat dripped on the paper and

226

he tore the sheet and screwed it up. Dear Suzé. A car, some soldiers, unfortunately, a curfew, an accident, a passenger too. Duty. We loved him and he was brave on our behalf.

In another hour or two they'd take the elevator seventeen floors up and ring the doorbell to wake her—if it was that time of day. No flowers. Killed on duty. Make the evening papers in New York and Toronto, tomorrow morning's in London, Paris, Düsseldorf, Istanbul, Lisbon . . . If the item was of sufficient interest . . . The slaughtered lay in bits and pieces around the coffee beans drying in the fitful sun, and the lieutenant sat on the wall and wanted to weep. The iron, greasy foul smell of blood, rotting bodies lying by the jeep among the mango trees. The insects crawled and drank themselves drowsy in the blood. The villagers ran from the flaming huts, their skin alight, because they had been caught in the logic of war. Dear Suzé. Small and dark and anxious. She'd know. He wanted to weep because he couldn't prevent it. If he neglects his duty I'll be suitably angry. Also killed was Miss Lilli X, aged eighteen, who was a passenger in the car. Very interesting. Of political value because, however distantly, it would knock the moral integrity of the United Nations and to do that had value, literal value in money.

The rain fell on the dead heads and arms strewn in the apple trees, but this was of no interest because it had no financial value or philosophical content. Very faintly, with pity almost theoretical, but which caused the water to run down his face meaninglessly, he remembered Jane D. Brown, the blood bank and the garlic on the gangster's breath, a hand holding his at a party and a voice hurrying for pity, knowing he had to apportion his time, for there were too many . . . Dear Suzé, he wrote. Love is forgiveness. Forgive me because I failed you . . .

11 ▪ ▪

AFTER THREE THEATER outings, four dinners, a walk around Saks Fifth Avenue, four movies in the cold afternoons, a frozen half hour at the top of the Empire State Building, and an unsuccessful evening in Greenwich Village, Bill held her hand suddenly in a taxi. It was as if they had to experience a number of pointless things together to earn a status: friendship; they were friends.

It was a release of tension, at last something declared—an end to mere companionship, a higher risk in the more personal needs of friendship . . .

"You're a hell of a nice person," Bill said.

It sounded a little dull. Kristan could have maintained that status without having her hand held or the knowledge of his face waiting to plead close to hers.

She found response difficult. He now grasped her hand with the awareness that it weighed whole ounces. "Hell, I'm not as nice as all that," she responded, as usual conscious that this wasn't the way it went in the magazine stories, with their four-color illustrations. Never a dull moment or a doubt with *those* characters. She laughed gently at herself so that Bill suggested, "Share the joke even if it's on me."

"I was just thinking how badly I compare with the girls in the magazine stories."

"They make love seem so easy—"

"Love?" she questioned, alarmed.

Bill qualified, "Exploration of character. It's the same in the novels. No one *cares*. They trot around and leap into beds, and you're supposed to presume sexual maturity or something."

She inquired whimsically, "And you're trying to understand my character?"

"I do understand it."

"Oh!" she said, startled.

"You're sensitive and shy and you have a conscience."

"All that?"

"Don't you like to talk about it?"

"It's silly. And I don't believe it! I'm just dull and why the hell you bother—"

"And you have practically no conceit."

"You're prejudiced in my favor," Kristan said like one who has failed in an attempted conversion.

"I'm not disputing that," Bill said.

She asked him into the apartment for coffee, although she felt

228

apprehensive after the hand-holding, scared to face more fervent opinion without the protection of darkness and movement and the claim "You don't know me." The doorman didn't stare; he made a point of not staring. He had made his mistaken conclusion a week before. They stood in the elevator like two people going to see a dentist. She only switched on table lamps in the apartment in a useless prolongation of the night which comforted and no longer frightened her. She at once sensed that this small action to avoid facing Bill in the glare of mere electric light bulbs was an error: he presumed she wanted near-darkness, the atmosphere of love. The fright of this at once showed in her face.

"It was cold out there," she said.

Bill smiled very faintly and chided, "It's gone cool in here!"

She ignored this and continued, "You know, in Canada we had a different kind of central heating when we were first married—a hole in the floor. It was a first-floor apartment."

"And you never fell through?"

"Silly. It had a grating."

He knew she was frightened by possibilities and hurried his coffee.

"Well, I'd better go."

Kristan didn't attempt to stop him. "Shall I phone the man on the door to get you a cab?"

"I'll walk," Bill said grimly.

She fetched his coat. He tried to kiss her, but she moved away, calm now: "You've had enough excitement for one day!" But he was bothered, couldn't be dismissed humorously. She'd have to be brutal if she wanted to be rid of him. He followed her as she took the cups into the kitchen and caught up with her by the refrigerator and a tap she'd left running. It was ridiculous, but he was insistent. She averted her mouth as he kissed her.

"Not your mouth?"

"No."

"Anybody can offer the side of the face—French generals, Russian astronauts."

"I didn't *offer* anything; you took it!"

Bill persisted, ignoring her cowed head, her whole attitude of refusal that waited for him to desist and leave. "For heaven's

229

sake!" she protested, but not quite angrily. In a minute Bill would become angry and would feel humiliated and would leave and not come back. She was fond of him and didn't want that, and after a while lifted her head and insisted, "All *right*, but you shouldn't." It was a concession, he understood at once, a lesser opposition than "You mustn't." It suggested You should not but I cannot stop you if you persist long enough. "Have a drink?" he suggested. "You're so shy." He meant scared and she knew it. Scared of a kiss. "Okay," she said firmly. "You understand me. Now go because this is silly and you'll feel a fool and I don't want you to dislike me."

"Have a drink," he pleaded.

"We just had one. I'm not scared of you."

"He's a long way off."

"And he's right here."

"Have a drink. It's him you're scared of. A kiss doesn't hurt."

"And what about tomorrow?"

"Hell. Sure, I know. But a kiss. Hell, I understand you. You have a conscience."

"More than that."

"But a friend, you can kiss a friend."

"Or a friend could kiss me?" she acknowledged slowly, not wishing to assume more than a neutral position. If things happened *to* her it was different to seeking them out: one could make legitimate excuses: "Oh, he kissed me" was infinitely more excusable than "I kissed him." "Now and again?" she conceded, as if impartiality on these things was possible. "Because we're friends? Now and again? Like children do at night because the dark scares them?"

It was ridiculous, kissing like kids under the mistletoe, hard against a fridge, but it allowed a little sentimentality. "I'll have that drink," Kristan said shakily, half to stop him. "You're red in the face," she told him, giggling, but felt the heat of her own face too.

He was stroking her arms, but moved a few paces so that she could open the fridge door. She had to stoop and his eyes stared and coveted frankly what was revealed of her stockinged legs and examined the body outlined as it bent and tightened the clothes which it lived in. The half-bare arm that stretched to turn off the tap attracted his unashamed disrespectful inclinations. He made no effort to hide from his face the appetites in his thoughts. It was, presumably, a compliment, proof of her desirability. But it was also the middle of the twentieth century, when a woman had to put up with these minor degradations and counter them casually, almost conversationally—the probing hands up a skirt, the fingers at a party pulling zippers to seek the soft pleasures inside, and the assumption that this was your standard of integrity, too. A few drinks, a little darkness and an unknown face . . . It was a world of private moralities: girls worked out their own schedules of what was permissible with whom . . . Kristan did not belong to the older generation who either did not know of or who disapproved with horror of what went on. Nor was she of the young ones who copulated with the indifference of dogs, at parties, in automobiles, anywhere there was room enough and privacy. She belonged to the generation in between, which didn't disbelieve God even though it ignored Him, and accepted the moralities that were presumed to be His.

Bill resumed the clumsy loving by a table, still in the tiny kitchen. It was not God he had to overcome but a long, good marriage. She waited for him to calm down, although she herself was not calm enough to demand it. If she did she wouldn't see him again. It was where morality had got to and what love had become: even lovers were in a hurry; you surrendered the lot or they passed on, for there were plenty of others. Love was a practical business now; it demanded physical stamina and mental adaptation and alertness. Heart tearings and weeping were dead or at least too boring. She was supply and he was demand and it was a customer's market. It was insulting if she thought about it, but she was passing a little way beyond reason. The very deep secret heat had begun to weaken her, so that her legs fluttered and her heart pounded. She wanted a climax, what Shaun gave her now and again. If she could have aroused and completed it alone—even with Bill standing there—that would have been better, but she'd never had inclinations on these lines before and was too innocent to know how. And here was Bill, good friend, tender and courteous normally, he'd held her hand—the first advance in weeks—now in heat like a dog so that she must do something animal with him (that could wreck her marriage in seconds) or she must send him away, the heat of desire diverted to become the warmth of humiliation and hatred. It was absurd and animal; it was shameful but existed. There were no

231

platonic friendships. She should have endured terror alone, any-thing, but not this with all its disastrous possibilities. She had been terrified in the movie house of what she was in acute danger now of surrendering voluntarily. Bill's hands knew the problem, aggra-vated it to the point of madness, not caring what the result was so long as they touched what they desired. They stroked her back, pulled at her waist, smoothed the fabric of her dress and the slen-der rotundity of the buttocks underneath. She was conscious that he was probing like the man in the subway, loving her with his clothes on.

"Bill!" she protested, but he turned her so that he could kiss her neck, and from behind, his hands cupped her breasts and his hot mind knew she was sagging with indecision, was more than halfway to surrender, the weakness and heavy lassitude of the female body that wanted to lie down, its mind too dazed to reason any more.

It was outrageous what he permitted himself to do on the strength of a few kisses—fondling her with an off-hand familiarity, his fingers aware of zippers and the lumpy parts of garter belts, and his whole handling of her, after meeting her ten or twelve times, had an expertise and coarseness that Shaun had had to take two years in delicate exploration to acquire.

"How can you?" she whispered in shock. "What do you think I am? Some sort of tart?"

She was pushing away the hands, although the fluid lines of pleasure trickled down from her breasts to where the legs wanted to weaken and collapse.

"Kristan, don't refuse me," he pleaded. "I'm not a louse." He'd knelt on the kitchen floor and with both hands was stroking her stockinged legs. It was the most humiliating seduction, which she could describe to no one in pride or even shame. His hands were on her buttocks, cold from the street so that she had to qualify crazily, "For God's sake! Your hands are frozen!" He stood up, still behind her, and went on with the embarrassing plea—he was well beyond the point of no return—"I don't womanize. And hell, I'm nearly fifty, almost finished as far as women are concerned. I really haven't a woman friend but you. Oh, yes, I went to the brothel out there, but I couldn't do it because there was no love."

The unconscious implication—that *here* in this kitchen with zip-pers unfastened and a shoe off and her nipples swelling—there *was*

232

love weakened her. She whispered conspiratorially, inquisitive, making comparisons (she was better), "So what happened?" And he could tell by the timbre of the voice and the interest that she was almost his to do what he liked with: she began to breathe heavily, even to pant, as the tiny scratching fingers went on arousing her nipples through the layers of fabric, and then explored within. No opposition now; she wanted this. "Nothing. I didn't love . . . Is it wrong if you love someone? You're fond of me, aren't you?"

"Sure I am," Kristan said, feeling moistures run through her and knowing she must satisfy them unless—but now fear had gone and she wanted someone else to bring the climax. It would be a stunning one, and she knew in a remnant of sanity that she'd weep tomorrow in shame and be very frightened indeed, but now, now the flesh was in charge. She was weeping now, silently, and pleading for him to make the decision, stop, flee from the apartment. "Can't we stop? We'd have nothing to be ashamed of then?"

"Have I got to be *ashamed* of loving you?"

"Do you love me?"

The mind was making excuses.

She, too, was beyond the point of no return.

Think of it, the mind suggested. He's already done things to you that are inexcusable. Why stop? Think of it. Instead of loneliness and fright in the street, the apartment, everywhere you moved and even when you didn't move—instead of that, sheer pleasure, spiced with this madness when his demands became terribly insistent. And all ended quite naturally, with tenderness, no disaster or hatred, when Shaun came back. Bill'd be switched off like a light, never to be thought about. And he wouldn't mind. It would be a bit of fun, the experiment in love that the youngsters tried these days. Or claimed they did. It was insane and she knew it. She'd never had anyone else but Shaun touch her, let alone make love. Her sanity and frigid respectable womanhood and love for Shaun fought hard with the scratching fingers and the pleading mouth and the awareness that the world didn't give a damn. Only your own conscience tore you to pieces. If she could just this once—and keep her mouth and mind shut forever about it; put it down as experience; it was just to see what another man was like, to compare him, see how he failed . . .

"I wouldn't bother you often," Bill said, throwing himself ab-

233

jectly on her mercy, revealing himself, too, in humiliation. "You see, I'm not all that strong. I know I look tough but . . ."

"It's afterward . . ."

"Once, then," he beseeched.

"Even that—"

"You have to."

"All right, all right," she sighed.

And the hands pleasured in her, standing there in the kitchen, and she was hot and glad she'd gone on. And, in minutes, on the bed, light shining from a landing, for even in heat she was afraid he might not love her so well when he saw all of the body he was so eager to couple with. But he delighted in her, slowly at first as he stripped her, and then a little rough, ignoring her frightened cry as he entered. He pounded her hard with his flesh and words that were coarse and alarmed her. But when he pleaded, "Kristan, little slender one, love me like I love you," her final resistance melted and she panted with him in the last seconds and thrust upward until climax burst inside her and she was beyond caring about anything.

Afterward he was tender.

She lay there secretly proud of her capabilities and aware that conscience didn't trouble her. She'd keep a straight face. It didn't matter all that much. The world hadn't fallen apart. Keep a steady nerve and enjoy yourself, she thought, drunk on it, and knowing that she'd do it again.

He slept with one hand possessively between her legs. She knew that he must have had other women and was afraid—afraid he'd go away now that he'd had what had taken him a mere four weeks to obtain. Had it taken longer to seduce the others?

But in the morning, when she finally slept, Bill went out, and just as she awoke, in a terrible panic of shame and alarm, the telephone rang. She answered, knowing it would be him but completely baffled as to what he'd say. Would he sneer now, or laugh, or share dirty jokes, or treat her with indifference, a thing to be used? Bill in fact said gently, "So you're awake? Did you know you snore? I'm coming back in a minute. I'm hungry . . ." And she was glad of the affection. Humiliation vanished, the sordid, embarrassing thought "I wasn't any good at it so he's gone" was replaced by a tiny pride, "I made him happy," and she asked as casually as any competent mistress, "So you want something to eat?"

Bill came with a large and exceedingly heavy parcel which he presented to her. Under the brown paper and cardboard wrapping was the ridiculous brass diver's helmet. She was delighted.

"There's some mail," he said like an admission.

She took it reluctantly. As usual, when she'd forgotten her longing for mail, dropped her guard, a letter from Shaun arrived. She read it with some remoteness, the closeness of events on the bed were nearer. "He's going on a trip to the south," she told Bill. "So I shan't get any mail for about eleven days."

They stared at each other in a conspiracy that was glad to be free from what the postman could bring to trouble consciences and that was ruthlessly realistic and selfish about what its demands were.

Precisely twelve days later—although the significance was lost by then, submerged in a sequence of other passions—Della telephoned. She was one of those who could not have existed socially if this instrument had not been invented.

Kristan had not thought much about her in recent weeks and not at all these last twelve days. It put old friendships into a new and alarming perspective, revealing how little they mattered, how easily they could be jettisoned. Later, thinking about it—still indifferent —Kristan realized that even now Della had not telephoned in sympathy or to assuage loneliness, but in curiosity. She'd heard something. And she had some shattering gossip of her own to disclose. More immediately, she wanted something. Thus she approached a number of things with their perspective and importance in the wrong order so that she could get what she wanted first, stake the claim, then talk . . .

"Where have you been?"

"I seem to have been busy," Kristan told her meaninglessly. It was surprising how easily one learned to defend one's position, to dispute its existence. It was like writing one's own references: one left out that which one didn't want to put in. She had found it quite easy to look straight into the face of the doorman, who was the one person who must know perfectly well what had happened—and found that he still offered the same courtesy . . .

"I feel so guilty," Della confessed. "I've neglected you."

"Don't worry about it," Kristan comforted.

"Are you good with children?"

235

"Don't you mean aren't they good with me?" Kristan countered. "I *like* them. You mean small ones?"

"Fairly small. Same as mine," Della said. "Six to eight. The nice age. No dirty habits, and not much insolence, and what there is, *charming!* I'd be awfully glad of some help on Saturday afternoon with about twelve or fifteen of them. Can you imagine *me?*"

"I have to meet somebody on Saturday," Kristan said promptly.

"Bring him along."

The defenses were penetrated. Kristan couldn't ignore these words, she was too shaken. "How did you know it was a man?"

"Just put it down to intelligent guesswork."

"Della, it wasn't guesswork, was it?"

"Perhaps not. Irene seems to have found out. But don't worry. I'm broadminded. I'm slightly envious!"

"I have seen him a few times."

"And why not?"

"No harm in it. We're both alone," claimed Kristan.

"I'm all for it," said Della. "Does he like kids?"

"I never asked."

"Well, get around to it! Bring him along."

"If he likes kids."

"Everybody likes kids. What's new from Shaun?"

"I haven't heard for ages. He went south into the desert."

"There's been some trouble in Vila Lobanda."

"Is something wrong?" Kristan asked apprehensively.

"It's in today's papers. I thought you'd have seen. Still, Shaun's not there, is he?"

"I haven't read the papers."

"It's about Suzé's husband."

"Suzé? Suzé Alferink?"

"It was on the radio. It was an accident."

Now her heart was panicking.

"For heaven's sake! What was it, Della?"

"He was in a car or something. Theobald, I mean. What a name! Still, he's Dutch, isn't he? I mean was. He was killed. I rang Suzé up. And she said—"

It was a terrible shock, a physical thing that at once started a headache. She was shaky and was filled with the curiously supersti-

236

tious admission "It was my fault," a guilty condition that reddened her face and she acknowledged in her mind, "It might have been Shaun." Shame flooded her so that she at once made the half-hearted decision "It's got to stop. God has warned me." It was as if by stopping adultery in New York she could persuade God to look after Shaun in Africa.

All these absurd penitent thoughts rushed through her mind as her tongue responded, "I didn't know that. You'd think the Secretariat or someone'd tell *me* . . ."

"It's only just been announced."

Kristan had been too full of love to care about what went on in the world and was watched anxiously in print and on TV. The endless stream of words about violence and abuse and scandal and road deaths and foreign disasters were for the lonely and timid people of the world. You couldn't do anything about any of it, but if you had a conscience you at least heard about it and walked the earth sadly, gave pennies and checks to charities and organizations that tried to cope with what the insurance companies wouldn't cover. If you didn't have a conscience you moved around enjoying life and nothing touched you, or you were contemptuous and defied it, or refused to believe it: "It's all lies anyway" or it was a fraud with the usual plea for your money . . . Until finally it hit you. Well, it had just missed this time, but she must walk more guardedly if she was to go on with pleasure. There must be some hypocrisy she could go through, a check to pay someone to keep the world at a distance.

"I can't believe it," she said to Della.

That sad, beautiful, rare, dignified woman, Suzé Alferink; how would she be now? A mess of tears and a face staring like someone sick? What had *she* done to merit the wrath of the world? Again, in herself, the guilt bubbled, an overload, for Kristan knew she had made no effort to see or comfort the equally lonely Suzé, even though Shaun had requested it. She didn't relax easily in Suzé's company—it was as simple as that. And justification was easy: Suzé had made no effort to comfort her, Kristan McQuade.

"Yes, but it's interesting," Della's voice explained into the earphone, like a conspirator in some game of vileness in which all must be made equal. Death in Angolique meant nothing to Della

237

O'Dowd. It was where violence belonged: a long way off. "There was a girl in the car. The papers are making faint implications . . ."

Very distantly but with certainty Kristan understood another implication: that if Della ever really knew the degradations Kristan was wallowing helplessly in—for they'd be degradations, not love, not even infatuation, to a third party, *any* third party—then this was how she, Kristan, would be analyzed along the wires of other telephones. With satisfaction and the pleasure of seeing the dignified and beautiful hurt.

"You mean it was a road accident?" Kristan asked with a sensation of relief—Shaun was safe; the gods wouldn't touch him; it was a mere statistical thing; one in fifteen of your friends die in road accidents over a period of each ten years. She wasn't going to be punished (or punish herself) for the sin on the bed, and the greater sin of love, of wanting it again . . . She could even go on with this tender, burning, exciting and humiliating lunacy a while longer. Ending was in fact difficult to imagine; it was as if Bill had always been here. Had she known for only four weeks this man who demanded, and was willingly accorded, degrees of intimacy which left her exhausted?

"No," Della's voice told her brutally. "He was out after curfew and got shot . . . And this Belgian schoolgirl . . ."

"A Belgian schoolgirl? In the middle of Portuguese Africa?"

"And, you see, I've got Suzé's kids coming to this party on Saturday—"

"They'll cancel that," Kristan assured her.

"No. She's coming. When I phoned—"

"I can't face her," Kristan confessed aloud in panic.

That calm, almost religious, but intensely beautiful face—designed, it seemed, for sadness—would at once identify the shame, seek the evasive eyes, even more immediately than Shaun would, and the disgust would show.

"I'm sorry, Della. I just couldn't take that. She might blame Shaun," Kristan excused herself, willing to lie and to hell with Suzé's suffering, "and become hysterical."

She didn't deceive Della.

"Come on, Kristan. She'll expect you. And so would Shaun. Oh,

238

God, honey, someone's got to help. It's going to be a hell of an afternoon. Twelve screaming kids and Suzé all tense and black but trying to carry on . . ."

"What on earth's she doing at a kids' party when this has happened?"

It was unreasonable of Suzé not to hide away, weep alone, so that on Saturday Bill and she, without being loaded with additional conscience, might . . .

"God knows. But that was what she said."

Kristan knew resignedly and in anxiety that she had to go, if only in terms of cunning and continued deceit. What incredible things love had you crawling around doing. For she must write lies, or half-lies, to Shaun: I saw dear Suzé. She was pale and upset, but had brought the two kids to a little party so that they at least did not have to suffer all the time. If she wrote nothing about Suzé he'd be perplexed. He might inquire, Haven't you seen Suzé? There was something else, the final revelation in this game of self-analysis. One thing about deceptions of this nature: they sharpened the senses and brought you face to face with truth. You recognized some startling truths which you never even noticed in that other, leisurely, comfortable life without lies. And this truth was about Suzé's husband. On Saturday, among the other truths she must keep from Suzé while expressing a horror she only felt in terms of her own safety (love made you realize this kind of truth, too), was the meaning, just realized, of an evening in Suzé's apartment eighteen months back. Theo's kiss on her head, "You're a great kid, Kristan, and Suzé and I love you." She had laughed at this indulgent flattery, expressed in the privacy of a kitchen, but the laugh had been misinterpreted and his hand had smacked her bottom, half caressed it. She'd thought nothing of it at the time. Now she knew it had been the faintest approach to see what was evoked, if anything was. A flick of the eyes, a thickening of the voice, an arrangement of words, and he'd have known exactly the pattern of what might be obtained, circumstances and time permitting. When you walked in innocence you failed to notice these things.

"You're quite right," she agreed now. "I must come to help both you and Suzé."

It could have been a hellish afternoon—kids and cakes and candles and Suzé there in black and Della's eyes curious to note the differences; shameless lies and the longing to simply go away. She was tired of distress. It had no reality. And she was ill with a strange sickness. It could have been like that and despite Bill's presence she went to it shaking with the expectation that it would be. But in fact Suzé was unexpectedly matter of fact.

Kristan found herself crying all too easily, with children staring, and Suzé comforting *her*, as if she was the bereaved. "Don't cry. We knew it would happen, you see."

"You knew what would happen?" Kristan asked, while Bill drifted away, successfully, for there were the shrieks of children being amused.

Suzé sat in a chair with her smaller child, aged two, standing by her knees and now staring with interest at this other woman whose eyes were watering, only without noise, which was quite clever and something she herself couldn't do.

"It was this woman. Four years ago. We went camping across the southern states. It was so hot," Suzé recalled. It was quite impossible to imagine her or her husband outside the environment of Manhattan. *Camping!* "In Mississippi. She couldn't have known anything about us and she told me, 'You'll have another child and you'll have a great loss. The first time you married was in a far country, but there'll be a second time.' It seemed ridiculous at the time, although I remember I was scared for weeks that Theo would be involved in a motor smash."

Kristan felt the huge urge to smile, to laugh hysterically, and her face flooded with color in the effort to resist doing so. She looked hard at Suzé's serious face, where she'd always seen beauty and some female significance she felt she did not have herself. She'd decided years before that it was a European face, a different, more subtle wisdom and another, better sophistication. Now she saw that it was merely a structure of bone and skin. There was no significance in the face; it might even be that of a fool, one whose husband frequently deceived her and who now relied on trivialities to comfort herself.

"So we all knew," Suzé acknowledged resignedly. "Mother and everyone, except the kids. I never told Theo, of course. It was when we visited an alligator farm. This woman was as old as the hills. Colored, of course. They know things we don't."

240

There was no problem deceiving anyone as simple as that. Kristan found no difficulty in the afternoon because it had no reality. She was perhaps ill with a disease, the symptoms of which were a curious increase in both cunning and carelessness. A multiplication in emotions but a limitation in their direction. In this illness you cared for no one but yourself and the other patient. You tried to deceive the rest of the world, pretend you were as before, but it didn't matter all that much. Indeed, there was a slight inclination to boast about the illness. Bill *cared,* and this proved that she was beautiful. She had thought she was nothing, but he was stunned by a passion for every inch of her. He watched her dress and wash and eat, and paid attention to her every syllable. She had forgotten such infatuation could exist. She was forty-three, had led a serious and rather dull life and had been sure that no one cared beyond the superficialities. She had been absolutely, painfully certain of this so that the knowledge had a physical impact: it had dulled her. She had walked about the streets and in shops, attended parties and receptions, *knowing* that she was nothing, not a woman anyone stared at. She was a part of statistics, the consumer market: she used so many bars of soap and gallons of water . . .

Now she was beautiful.

I'm a fool, she'd think in the night and blush with self-consciousness at what she'd been doing and at the terrible certainty of impending recovery from the illness, when it would end with a great smash across the face. She knew she couldn't really hide anything from Shaun. He'd just look into her eyes and know something was wrong . . . I'm a fool of an almost-middle-aged woman who's been seduced. She recognized that this was how others would view it, rather distastefully as if a body forty-three years old should know its place and immorality was for the young if it was for anybody. She was conscious with pleasurable vanity which gave a physical warmth that there was a noticeable improvement in her carriage and alertness and in the new clothes she bought to please Bill or he insisted on buying for her. She used scents more outrageously and sat in a careful but consciously voluptuous manner. When striding, she held her head high and lifted her breasts and was aware of pleasure between her thighs. She even noticed that more men stared in the street in outright admiration and longing, and a few even whistled, and she let them, was pleased, didn't cringe in subconscious fear as before. Love. It was love. However it ended, with ignominious pleas and tears and shouts and other people's scorn and laughter, and pain for Shaun, Bill and herself, it existed now. They couldn't take that away. Once she looked at her own essentially sad dark face in the mirror and cried to God, Oh, please, save me from this madness and give me back the loneliness. But two hours later she laughed over the restaurant table, so that people turned to stare, admire and smile at such obvious devotion at that table.

It was easy, then, to meet Della's curious eyes that wanted to see the symptoms of something shameful. And it was a pleasure to move among small children with their innocence and pleas for sticky cakes and a slide show. Easy to talk to Suzé about the mission of the subcommittee and to advise her what to do now, go back to Holland or stay in New York and find a translating or secretarial job. Easy to stand whole yards away from Bill for hours, scarcely talking to him, so that if anyone was going to make conclusions they'd have very dull evidence here. "He's just a friend," they'd have to deduce, and if that phrase had a sly, dirty meaning it would have to come from their minds, not from actual proof.

She could wait. Time passed in the knowledge of what had been and what was to come. The sly and secretive hands that lay about on lap or arm in the privacy of darkness, real or purchased. Eyes that met now in a room crowded with others who knew nothing, and along the retina's reverse lines a memory of hot rooms and exploratory flesh, copulation greasy with violence, shattering experience subdued later by soaps and foods and radios turned on, metamorphosed back into ordinariness, two people who had conquered loneliness too well . . .

12 ▪ ▪

McQUADE STOOD ABOUT a thousand yards over the border and watched the survivors as they came. He wondered how many had died on the way, adding to the great garbage heap of the primary forest. For it was out of forest that they emerged—a steady trickle of human beings who had found life so difficult or unbearable or terrifying in Angolique that they had struggled through one, two or three hundred miles of the moist, oppressive silence, among the great tree trunks, flanked by buttresses, or standing apparently on giant stilts; had climbed over rotting trunks, trod on a litter of seed pods and marsh and massive rotten fruit; had pushed their way through prickly and stinging lianas. Terror had prodded them on and rumor and some older instinct had brought them to this place where, among patches of grass and little twisted trees and empty circular huts with conical roofs, and a few, more ambitious, with rectangular sides and arched roofs, and all made of grass, leaves and tree trunks—by this evidence of departure or panic and the empty village were huge tents and a compound and (used as hospital and offices) the wooden structure of what had once been a safari lodge.

Here was an outpost of the Red Cross, trying to make amends for what other men had done.

The air was stifling. Ekelund wiped his brow, then his new pair of spectacles, and protested for the third time, "My God, it is hot."

In the distance clouds hung heavily over the mountains from whence these people had come. The mountains had been volcanoes and were still worshiped in the belief that the craters represented the urn in which thoughts were crystallized and the melting pot in which the souls of the dead were resting. How did anyone still believe these things with such an evidence of madness all around?

"It is like this every two or three weeks," said Sister Thérèse. "We do what we can here. They get the cards for rations. Fifty thousand in the last three months here. I'm *tired*," admitted Sister Thérèse, "but if they can get here . . . There are not many today."

There were in fact about sixty of them—mostly women and children. Some had been flogged, or hurt, or wounded—the wounds were appalling and the dressings filthy if they had any at all. A few men had faces and hips burned raw—it could not have been inflicted by anything but petroleum, which meant napalm. But many had not been wounded at all, and were simply terrified out of their senses and had fled from their burned-out village or had heard a rumor about a distant village and had panicked, not without justification. And here these were, stunned, dirty, hysterical, half starved and without the slightest idea of what they could do or where they could go. The children were tired beyond measure and were weeping without the strength to make a noise about it. It was just possible to distinguish the modern men and women of small towns from the warriors and tribespeople not entirely averse to being necrophagous. There were even a few Pygmies among them, disturbed by war and fleeing from their forests. These tiny people lined up apprehensively, swollen bellies and navels and faces of complete bewilderment as if they'd just arrived in hell and were as yet unfamiliar with the routine.

"He will die," said Sister Thérèse in a matter-of-fact voice, pointing to one man who was moving his mouth soundlessly and then looking at the ground. "I can tell now. It is not just the injuries, but sometimes the fear, sometimes the lassitude, the great defeat. It is difficult and useless enough at all times to stay alive; there is no need of a war . . . But you will find no truth in chaos," reasoned Sister Thérèse with unexpected cynicism, "only the truth you choose to believe and that is the one which suits yourself."

She was a small, bony woman, who looked completely unimportant and not one likely to have profound philosophies or be at the end of the earth dealing with chaos.

What she said was succinct enough and needed no explanation, but Ekelund questioned seriously, "You mean that if all goes well the European has civilized them and if it does not then they are incapable of receiving civilization?"

"Exactly," agreed Sister Thérèse. She offered a shrill little laugh, as if Ekelund had been witty, and this caused two men attending to wounds to look around with disapproval. "The degradation of the exploited. Or, if you are Portuguese, you could say that these rebels —for they are rebels if you are killing them and they are cutting your friends' heads off—these rebels claim to be carrying on a great patriotic war, but in fact are sticking your relatives' heads on poles, pillaging and so on. What is the truth?" asked Sister Thérèse. "I will tell you. The truth is that this morning sixty-two persons have arrived. Ten will die of their wounds; ten more of pneumonia—for it will rain on them in the compound this afternoon; two will be killed in the camp—for some of them are fairly

244

handy with bicycle chains and pieces of wood themselves; ten will go back to fight the Portuguese; ten will creep back into Angolique anyway to see if all's well; ten will find relations or fellow tribespeople to look after them in this territory; and the final ten will be looked after by us, sent on a truck or train somewhere."

"Is it possible to talk to them?" McQuade asked. "Do any of them want to talk to *me?*"

"You must not believe them too willingly," advised Sister Thérèse. She seemed a curious mixture of strength, realism, faith and objectivity touched with cynicism. "If they find you are interested they will invent what they feel you'd like to hear and go on for hours. Oh, look. One has pushed a pram. How has he done it?"

A hundred yards away a man was pushing a pram. McQuade had seen many faces these last few weeks, and he recognized this man but could not recall his name.

Ekelund told him.

"Do you see that? Surely it is impossible? It is Cristovão Faure."

It was indeed the quiet teacher from Father da Silva's mission two hundred and more miles south. And with great shock McQuade accepted that it had to be Faure, because in the pram was Father da Silva.

Cristovão Faure had lost much weight and his legs and feet were bleeding. Very distantly he recognized McQuade and great anxiety clouded his face, as if he believed for a dreadful moment that he'd come over the wrong border and here were more Portuguese.

Father da Silva made no attempt to get out of the pram. His feet extended in front of it and his cracked black shoes and bleeding feet indicated that he had walked a very long way before Cristovão Faure had found the pram. Father da Silva had lost a great deal of weight, too, and his face had as many folds as a bulldog's. He was filthy.

He, too, recognized McQuade as someone seen once before in the good times. A friend.

"They killed my dog," he said, in Portuguese. He was quite adjusted to it. He knew it would be of interest, for presumably he had seen its impact on others or had a memory of the importance of the original event. He had dropped far below sanity. It would have been merciful if he could have been shot, for his Order did not love him, nor the Africans, nor the Portuguese—or he would not be

245

here. But he had to go on living. "He will live, unfortunately," commented Sister Thérèse, as if she'd read McQuade's mind, "because he does not have the ability of the *indigena* to sit down and die."

Father da Silva smiled furtively. He was half his previous weight and half his previous mind and he smelled. With horror McQuade understood his secret smile, for Father da Silva had lost control of his functions or had dysentery and didn't care. He really did belong in the pram.

"What happened?" McQuade asked.

"They killed my dog," repeated Father da Silva.

Cristovão Faure explained it. "Some of the people were afraid of vengeance from others if we had a missionary among us. So he had to go. We could not bear to kill him. And when they told him he must go he was angry and said he would stay, so they killed Alfonso, his dog, and burned down the school and church. And they told me to go, too, to take him away. I speak the French," claimed Cristovão Faure, "and here I am. He saved my soul."

"And your pupils?"

Faure looked down at the earth.

"They didn't come again."

Alferink was dead, and somewhere in chaos walked the girl of the photograph, whose body he had admired and coveted. She would be close to death now, in the arrival of chaos . . .

McQuade sat on a trestle with Ekelund all that day, watching and listening and sometimes asking questions. Hour after hour moving his buttocks occasionally on the hard wood and listening to the shaky and angry voices describing that horror or fear or abuse or presumed injustice or inhumanity that had been too much, the final prompting that had set the feet trotting and the heart pounding and the skin, electrified and anticipatory, sweating . . . Private terror and pain had propelled them to seek pity in a sea of chaos: there is no one in the world who has more woe than me; it is not possible. They talked, sometimes, and if they were capable, wept, and bled and groaned with much emotion on this tawny landscape of dreary stunted trees and dust and a meandering river, apparently of mud, which awaited the storm coming over the mountains. McQuade felt a sense of motionless time, mud and thousands of square miles of hopelessness—"a low yield" as the agronomists

246

would say to avoid the more daunting truth that here the white man and the black man had as yet failed.

Sometimes, if they were not too far gone in agony or distress and if they spoke some Portuguese, he questioned the refugees. Their answers were never what the politicians of any color or the newspaper pundits would have desired. Nobody during that day said, "I wanted independence," or even, "I hate the Portuguese and fled from them." They were the victims, the innocent (most of them, although not all) bystanders. "The noise made my heart go too fast" . . . "My baby screamed because of the fire" . . . "I was afraid I would be killed" . . . "Who would do that?" . . . "I do not know, but there has been a lot of killing" . . .

In the nearby camp hundreds stared listlessly from their new safety, or talked excitedly or ate the biscuits handed to them, or slept in new blankets and clothes. In the rooms which were the hospital the doctors—Belgian, French and Italian—worked on those who had walked one or two hundred miles, but whose injuries were such that they shouldn't have even crawled and certainly could not move a yard farther now that the momentum of terror had stopped. As the afternoon spent its strength and the clouds came with a big wind and hot air ran amok like panic, these died.

The torrential rain came, and McQuade and Ekelund drove away thirty miles to the hotel in the small French-built city. With shame McQuade realized that he had automatically stopped sympathy and sought shelter and comfort while these refugees had to stand there in the rain and take it, wounds and all, because there was a shortage of tents, a surplus of refugees and some tents had been stolen. No doubt ten would indeed die of pneumonia.

The storm had not reached the town, but was on its way. The air was stunned and there was a physical sensation, despite voices in the street, of a vast quiet.

They had been interviewing petitioners here, too, but more politically conscious ones, refugees who had moved out of Angolique (or had never been in it) for a purpose. They were politically informed and could talk of the mechanics of police abuse, bribery by officials, the politics of the chaos. Not all of them spoke from experience.

De la Plaza, the *rapporteur* of the subcommittee, was still working on the draft report. It was a hefty business, for they had documentation on education, public health, housing problems, transportation, economics, administration and the Portuguese account of the "disturbances." They also had some albums of photographs.

McQuade was hot and uncomfortable and exhausted. The humidity of the moment was stunning. Nevertheless, he leaned over de la Plaza's shoulder and inquired, "How's it going?"

"It is very difficult to write without prejudice."

De la Plaza was picking his nose in his habitual anxiety symptom.

It was too much. He had done it a hundred times before, but this was once too often.

"Do you have to pick your nose?" McQuade asked, unable to conceal irritation.

"I beg your pardon?" questioned de la Plaza, taken aback.

"It doesn't matter," said McQuade quickly, recovering himself.

"But it surely matters," insisted de la Plaza, in a tone of injustice, red in the face. "I am not in the habit—"

"Then it doesn't matter, does it? I was wrong, presumably," snapped McQuade.

"It was a very odd thing to say, in that case."

"It's not that I give a damn whether you pick your nose or not," said McQuade, surrendering to fury. "It's just that I'd prefer you didn't do it over documents I'm handling."

One of the girls behind them couldn't smother a snigger. McQuade turned on her—it was, inevitably, Marianne—and protested coldly, "What a useless, sour little lemon you are! How you love another's discomfort! Why do you work in this allegedly sympathetic organization, I wonder?"

The lightning streaked close at hand, a theatrical green lightning that was reflected in the hundred windows of the new hotel across the street. The thunder blasted in the corridors of buildings and the rain turned itself on like a hot shower, steam rising from the pavement at once.

Marianne said in a pathetic, punctured child's voice, "I hate working here. It's the most horrible thing I've ever known," and rushed out of the office.

De la Plaza said nothing.

248

McQuade sat down and said, "I'm sorry, it's the heat," to which there was no answer.

He picked up an English newspaper that was lying on a table in the hotel room they were using. It was only four days old, and as rage subsided interest grew, for it was *The Times*, which had full coverage of events in Africa and Portugal. On a middle page was more shock and misery related to Angolique. The first item was small, and for a while the name nagged at him without meaning. Captain Luis Nogar, a deserter from the Portuguese Army, had been arrested in Rio de Janeiro. No journalists allowed. A small cell. His mother, who was a peasant woman of seventy-seven, had sent a personal plea to the President, saying that if her son must be brought back to Portugal and sent to prison—and she said she did not doubt that he was very wrong to desert the Army in its ideological struggle against the terror in Angolique—could she not see him in Lisbon before she died? After a while, through a more vivid memory of other faces and heat and smashed bodies, McQuade remembered sitting in the Trusteeship Council and hearing the captain's voice say, "I know it was a mistake, the authorities really thought they were terrorists"—and his certainty, which McQuade hadn't doubted at the time, "I have the intention now of going to Brazil, where a man may speak Portuguese and still express an opinion . . ." Evidently not.

The second and larger item was much more of a shock. The body found in a quarry near Lupire has now been identified as that of Mr. Brandão, the Minister of Education, recently arrested in Angolique and brought to Lisbon only last Tuesday. He had escaped from custody. Police say there seems to have been no foul play and the body was broken by the fall. But a local peasant who talked to journalists described "something that fell from an aircraft . . ."

It was as if God didn't care. McQuade felt a black sorrow at the obvious murder by the PIDE of the liberal, kind-hearted and well-intended Education Minister. Scarcely ten days ago he had talked to him in Angolique.

"Have you seen this?" he asked, and foolish temper was forgotten in sorrow and mutual depression.

After an hour the storm ended, and McQuade went to find Mari-

249

anne. He grinned sheepishly at her and said, "Come on! We're going out. Drinks on me!"

They strolled around the town. Their hotel was in a square. Outside were residential and shopping streets bright with the red shades of the mango tree, and in other avenues were unexpected lines of lemon, avocado and papaya trees, with hibiscus in bloom. It was a strange mixture, the new Africa: palm trees and concrete, bicycles, the ubiquitous Volkswagens, glass hotels and beggars, the great African throng buying dried fish, a huge open-air market in which were sold stools, chairs, mounds of rice, bananas, wood carvings and masks, drums, batik cloth, fresh-killed monkeys, pyramids of ground manioc, cooking implements . . . After the rain the crowds came out again, most of them African, but quite a sprinkling of Europeans, a few Asians and two solemn Chinese who looked self-consciously aware of being spies or agitators or "technical advisers" to some of the nationalist organizations which had their headquarters here.

By the river—now full again and rushing toward the sea hundreds of miles west, carrying the usual litter of bits of nests, trees, grass and mud—were graceless substantial houses, with beautiful gardens full of red jasmine and half acres of raspberries and strawberries. Farther away were fields of wild flowers and groves of coffee trees. The subcommittee drank cool fruit juice on a terrace café high up overlooking the river and, as the sun went down toward the strip of clouds far beyond the water, watched the elephants from the zoo being led down for their evening bath.

It was life and death, misery and beauty, all accelerated and interwoven in a manner no longer possible in Europe or the United States. In the hotels of this independent African country they still spoke French and served a ghastly parody of French food. Tourists still came, but not many, for this country had had its troubles, too, but enough to give an impression of some holiday.

The crowd nearer the river was interested suddenly in something different, a new entertainment. And some of them weren't enjoying it. Cries of shock could be heard, and throughout the area McQuade sensed fear. Heads turned, bodies suddenly tensed on chairs, doors opened, faces stared from over the river, a hand waved, a woman shrieked, nearly screamed. He knew, or guessed,

250

what it was. The Katuala was moving with increased volume from the hills and bringing down the debris of war.

There were about eighteen or twenty of them—ten close to the riverbank and a few moving faster in midstream. Bodies. All male, so far as the bloated days-old things had any identity. African and Portuguese. Some had terrible lacerations, others carried no visible marks of how they had died. One man, an African, still had his hands tied together. But this atrocity—if it was one, and it probably was—was counterbalanced by the white body in its Portuguese Army uniform, with the head cut off and the hands missing. The bodies had now drifted into the reeds of the riverbank so it was possible to see these details of the evening's entertainment . . . After a while the local authorities came with two trucks and took these things away. People began to laugh and move about again, even to boast about it, as if seeing death had a masculinity. "I saw the ones two weeks ago" . . . "I have seen worse than this" . . . and the cafe-table rumors drifted about: "Do you know, they say that at Maxizico . . ."

It was a little difficult, in the shadow of this tragedy, to go on cheering up Marianne. But they tried. As the sun went below the horizon, fires were lit (supplemented by discreet lighting for the camera users) and the dancing began.

There were about a hundred dancers, including twenty musicians, and they presented a two-act program, with different and colorful costumes for each act. Girls with naked torsos wore masks with sharpened teeth and tightly closed eyes, symbolizing a woman of the tribe famous for amorous escapades. But the men were more impressive. Wigged drummers beat the rhythm, sweat pouring from their faces. Straw was suspended from large false hips in the first dance, to accentuate the movements, and the men covered their faces with the chirhongu masks which were a symbol of masculine force. This dance was executed by some in a crouching posture which represented anteaters with their tongues scouring the soil for food. In the second act the dancers wore banana-fiber headdresses, beaded sashes, the diagonal chest bands popular along the border and skirts of leopardskin; and they carried tiny wooden shields and tall spears. The steps were complex and the leaps into the air higher than many a *premier danseur;* the movements of the torso,

251

shoulders and legs shook the jingling bracelets on their ankles. There was a director who followed their every movement to check the coordination. The drums thundered and the sweat rolled down over the solar symbols on the cheeks of the dancers. Dust rose and could be smelled in the night air. It was not a phony performance for Europeans; indeed, there were scarcely any white faces in the applauding crowd.

Was this the answer to Angolique over the mountains and trees and burned plantations? McQuade still didn't know. Who was right —the *indigena,* the Portuguese, the nationalists waiting on outside territories for the convulsions to end or begin? What was the solution to cannibalism and colonialism, chaos and ignorance, brutality and counterbrutality, corruption and repression, the burned bodies and the decapitated, raped corpses, the weeping and terror of the innocent, and on every horizon the sophisticated with their various motives, none greatly concerned about the *indigena* of Angolique or the Portuguese who hadn't done so badly in many ways?

He did not have to solve the problem, only report it honestly so that resolutions could be passed, and no doubt ignored. But it had to be solved, this problem, whether by negotiation or violence; the nasty little war couldn't run on forever like an open wound. There was no going back to the *status quo.* One could hope for an answer when the regime in Portugal ended, for there was an opposition who had already stated that some degree of autonomy should be given in Angolique. But could it all wait for an old man to die? And was it not true that the other white nations of Africa—Rhodesia and the Republic of South Africa—were hardening their attitudes and drawing Portuguese Africa into their orbit? Rightly or wrongly, the southern third of Africa was becoming the white man's part of the continent. Soon he would be immovable.

In the morning de la Plaza and Ribowski went to the border to see the conditions and arrivals and injuries of other refugees. Asare Johnson, Ekelund and McQuade stayed in the office, and they had a great surprise. The telephone rang, and when McQuade answered in French, a voice asked in excitement, "Can we come to see you?"

"Of course," acknowledged McQuade. "Who are you?"

"I am an old friend of yours, I like to think," the man's voice said—it had an African timbre and McQuade did not recognize it.

"And I want to bring you the most powerful man in Africa—in relation, I may say, to the war in Angolique. Do you know who I mean?"

"I must admit I don't! It is very tactless of me!"

"I am bringing Clemente Matumoza of the *Movimento Anti- colonialista Angolique.*"

"I shall be interested to meet him."

"I shall bring him now in a vehicle. I am sorry you cannot recall me, Mr. McQuade."

Still McQuade could not think who this might be, talking French and yet involved in the politics of Angolique.

In ten minutes he arrived. McQuade laughed in pleasure. It was Mr. Rossio, last seen in a hotel bedroom in Lisbon with the sensuous Glória. They shook hands and half embraced, for McQuade had understood this man's agony of conscience at the time and the other knew it.

"What happened to Glória?"

"Ah, that is another story!"

"A sad one?"

"For me, yes . . . And here is Mr. Matumoza."

He was a man of about thirty-five, moderately tall, barrel- chested, tough, with a big, bearded face and short hair. McQuade had heard of him in the corridors of the General Assembly building —he was something of a joke, a terrorist and a determined politi- cian. He had now an air of self-importance and entered the shabby hotel-room office and picked the most comfortable chair—which was not saying much—and then positioned it so that they had no option but to form a half-circle facing him.

"There is a lot to say," he announced, "so I will ask no questions about the health or the condition of your wives or what is currently the fashionable show to go to on Broadway, where I have been. These things can wait. It is sufficient to say I know the world but give myself and my devotion to Angolique because that is where I was born and it is a country which suffers. You will have heard many lies, but now I will give you the truth."

McQuade made a gesture to Barney, who promptly began to take down the dialogue—it tended to become a monologue—in shorthand. Clemente Matumoza was pleased to see this action.

253

"For my people," he said, "it is the smaller injustices of life that hurt. They can live in the great political injustice because they have breathed it since they were born. They cannot read and they have traveled no farther than two horizons. They know no other world although they have caught the smell of freedom in their nostrils now . . . But if you omit to raise your cap to the *administrador* and are beaten for it; or if you are a chief and haven't produced the full number of 'voluntary workers' and are humiliated for it before the eyes of your people; or if you wait at table and are insolent by another's wide definition; and if you are thrashed with the *palmatoria* or *chicote* for these trivialities and are humbled in front of others, this can be unbearable. And if you are uneducated and live in primitive conditions like a dog then of course you can, when the day comes, use the *catana* to slash open the head that shouted at you. If you have a wife who is pregnant but has to work on the roads and therefore aborts when the *cipaios*, who are the African policemen who smell Portuguese, kick her around, or if you have a sister who is seduced by a Portuguese official in circumstances not far from force, then of course you go mad when the day comes and you cut off the breasts of white women and rape them until they scream to death. This is logical. And it is the man who has been in servility and who at last breaks out who astonishes all by his violent change of character, from dog to mad dog. He must kill all because he knows that if he does not then who survives will ensure a terrible chastisement. This seems to me the philosophy of the atrocities which I have to acknowledge took place in the north.

"What is our program then? What does the *Movimento Anti-colonialista Angolique* intend? I will tell you. Despite these great provocations and countermurders there will be no discrimination against the European in Angolique. As you know, investment there is substantial and healthy, by Germany, Israel, America and others. We must ask for and will obtain self-determination for the people. We shall ask and obtain political amnesty for the hundreds in prisons. We must have civil liberties so that we can exist, and to ensure this the armies must go. Then will come the round-table conference between all our parties—there are ten but only two or three of real account—and Portugal . . .

"We of the *Movimento* have done much work. Politics, as you

254

know, is hard work. We went to a conference at Casablanca with all the parties from the various Portuguese colonies in exile. A permanent secretariat was set up. Appeals were made to the leaders of Afro-Asian states to bring their influence to bear to end the war. Then in New Delhi we met again to report progress. Moral and material help had been given. Ghana banned Portuguese ships and aircraft from her harbors and airports. Indonesia recalled her ambassador from Lisbon. There was much lobbying and pressure in the United Nations. We have a massive program in terms of survival and information as well as the original business of politics. We try to prevent disease and we distribute medical supplies to our armies and our refugees, the essentials of food and clothes to people who have been driven out of villages and have nowhere to go but still want to fight. We have to distribute thousands of leaflet instructions among the villages over the border or, frankly, they'd go dry on us in their miserable conditions. We ask in return for reports, for money, for unified opinion. Nevertheless, although we are safe here in this town from the napalm, there are Portuguese activists and professional spies of all nations over there in Leopoldville, and corruption has occurred in other parties via the Portuguese Embassy there. There has, I fear, been prevarication and lack of unity."

"This seems to me the great weakness," said McQuade. "I have met some of the others, and they operate remote from each other, as if no other party existed or was equal. I met Mr. Bajune, for instance—"

Matumoza laughed, a big, happy, likable laugh. "I have issued a communiqué to the press repudiating Tando. Bajune is a neurotic bum. And the NWALO Party. You have heard of it? I repudiate that. Quissanga has been to Lisbon and will no doubt present scholarships to the young in Vila Lobanda! He has pestered Lisbon and Washington and the UN with much correspondence of a cultural 'proof' that Angolique is not a part of Portugal. Well, we all know that without writing to Salazar about it! Then there is this clown Gomais of the ANP. He has also been to London. He negotiates with the UN, which never acts upon resolutions even when they're passed."

"*These* are from the UN," Rossio reminded him, winking at Mc-

Quade as if to say, He, too, is a bit of a clown, but bear with us: he is a means to an end . . .

Matumoza laughed hugely again, unpenitent, and admitted, "I am new in politics. I talk to so many people I forget who they are and put my foot in, yes? Gomais is nothing. He has a reputation for killing Portuguese, but is no politician. There were many hundreds from Angolique in Leopoldville when I arrived there, and they gave me a banquet," claimed Clemente Matumoza, as if this constituted election to something. "We must analyze the facts. And the facts are that I am now recognized abroad. This bum Gomais is a racist —he is working for the superiority of his own tribe. I am working for Angolique. This is acknowledged in New York and London and Paris"—he bowed toward Rossio—"We have worked hard, too hard, to provide the documentation for different African organizations and delegations to the UN.

"Sixty thousand Africans have been killed, gentlemen. And many of the Portuguese soldiers are to stay as armed settlers in Angolique. It is a policy such as Fascist Italy had in East Africa. We have to act soon or it will be impossible to act at all without other nations and a bloodbath. It is a race between the complete Portuguese occupation of Angolique and the emancipation (whether by negotiation, which is refused, or by violence, or by a third party such as yourselves). There are neutrals and cowards on this issue and I regret that there is lack of cooperation between some of our own parties and there is even fighting between a few. But do not underestimate the immense capacity that Africans have for forgiveness. Thirty-two of us were shot two days ago in the courtyard of the Vila Lobanda prison. My brother was betrayed in a big error. He was in Swaziland with our organization. Several members there, not being susceptible to Portuguese invitations to come back to Angolique, were almost the victims of a plot—indeed, my brother was a victim, for my people killed him. You see, letters were sent by the PIDE to these innocent people 'thanking them for their information' and saying that money had been 'transferred to Barker's Bank' in a town in Swaziland. The envelopes were stamped PIDE and naturally their contents caused internal suspicion. My brother was, as I say, killed in the emotional explosion, and money *had* been transferred. That was the awful, con-

vincing thing. But this was typical of the PIDE. But I would negotiate without bitterness tomorrow. The African is an impulsive
sinner, gentlemen, and he therefore understands it in others and
forgives . . ."

Matumoza and Rossio stayed for lunch. Matumoza was recognized and people stared at him in the hotel restaurant. A woman
even approached their table and shouted at him, unfortunately in a
language McQuade did not understand. She was carried out bodily,
screaming and sobbing the whole way. "You see," claimed Matumoza, rather pleased, and completely unruffled, "that my importance is recognized even by fools."

After a while he suggested, "I am going to propose to you that
you come to inspect our army. Rossio will arrange it. Visit a unit of
ours and you will be able to tell the world we are not a rabble or
mad dogs or tribes with rings through their noses and spears in
their hands. We are people, citizens of all sorts, who have decided
it is necessary to fight for political acknowledgment."

McQuade felt an uneasy reluctance settle in his stomach. The
notion of returning into the territory of Angolique again was unbearable. More misery, death or hopelessness to witness. In a few
days' time he was due in Geneva to complete the report. Then,
sweet anticipation, the long flight to New York. But what was his
duty? And to whom?

The serious-minded, logical Ekelund answered for him, "It
would constitute a recognition of your party. We are not here to
take sides but to report."

"But as a private individual?" persisted Matumoza. "Is it more
important to sit in an office and see ten people, or take the opportunity I offer, of seeing thousands, talking to those you care to
select at random?"

That great big pudding of uneasiness, McQuade recognized, that
indigestible lump that had settled in his stomach and bowels vanished as soon as Ekelund offered a reasonable and justifiable excuse. It was fear he had felt. He hated himself for the fear and, to
overcome it, stamp it into the ground, he said (aware that New
York would not sanction it, but also that New York wasn't going to
be informed), "I will come."

"I think it is wrong and quite out of order," argued Ekelund.

257

"There are many spies here who wish to find us," Rossio said. "It will be necessary to move at night and walk for a long way before using vehicles."

"I cannot associate myself with this, which I consider foolish," Ekelund said. "In four days' time we go to Geneva. We have seen all that is necessary, heard all we need—"

"I wonder if that is true," McQuade said to himself.

13 ▪ ▪

THE GUIDE'S NAME WAS Jacinto and he was of the Kimbundu tribe. He wore patent-leather shoes that were a little too large for him, a yellow sports shirt, a jacket that was surely too warm for this climate and a silk tie, blue with white spots. He was sixteen and full of his own importance. "In the last battle," he claimed, "I used a catapult and killed this Portuguese from twenty paces." McQuade did not believe him and his attitude of disbelief was communicated, for the boy said, "I can do the drills, too, the sloping of arms. I have much strength. When the army attacked the plantation at Inhaca I carried a gun."

McQuade said nothing.

There was nothing to say.

He did not like Jacinto, but that was unimportant. They had been walking in darkness for two hours, through the elephant grass and along dirty tracks that were thick with mud. It was hot and utterly dark. The trees in the forest dripped when they went in and the mosquitoes bothered McQuade around the nose and eyes. The fireflies glowed like a man inhaling a cigar. It left the impression that they were not only being followed but preceded by people who were so in command of the situation that they could afford to be careless.

Dawn came through the trees, and the intense light stripped away the anxieties of darkness. It was like having the bandages removed after a guessing game. And he would have guessed wrong. They were in a valley with rolling hills all around. A river meandered through the valley. A mile away was a village of tidy rows

258

of mud-daubed grass huts. A few fires were burning and a dog barked. McQuade saw some vehicles parked in the center of the village and men standing about or loading boxes of ammunition. He had the uneasy feeling that he was already involved too far in things that would take days to struggle free from. Already Rossio and Matumoza, who had organized this trip, no longer took part in it or stayed to assure his safety. His life already depended on the word of Rossio to this youth Jacinto, who seemed to think he was Portuguese. And now others stared at him and, although he did not understand the tongue, he sensed the indifference in their inquiries; in their perspective of things he was nothing, alive or dead. Jacinto was of far greater importance.

The young man sat on a fuel tin and discussed it in the unfamiliar tongue, laughed, looked at boxes, urinated, yawned, ate some food. McQuade was given food, too, and found it most disagreeable.

After an hour Jacinto went to the small vehicle compound and backed out a jeep. He did this with great gusto. He then filled the tank and loaded other tins on board. McQuade climbed in and the boy drove off like a lunatic so that McQuade was thrown into his seat. He was conscious of the laughter behind him.

Jacinto drove for six hours, always at top speed, every yard jolting the vehicle and clattering the boxes and causing McQuade to hold on to things. Dust, mud, ruts, good tracks or bad, it was all the same to Jacinto: the jeep went if you pressed down the right foot, so he did.

They were still inside Congo territory and the journey was taking many hours. McQuade sensed that there were many discomforts to go through yet. In less than four days he had to be in an airplane that took him eventually to Geneva. He had the uneasy feeling that this journey was going to take a day and more, with an equal journey on return. If he merely paid his respects and departed he'd not have much spare time to gather papers and say farewells and board that plane. And he could not expect to travel for a day and a half to stay for a mere ten minutes' inspection of an army. He felt like a young man who has gone to a party which looks like turning into an orgy, and who can't think of an excuse to leave, not yet, and the longer he stays the greater is his involvement.

259

Now he began to feel ill; it was unfortunate, but perhaps inevitable at some time or other in a stay of some weeks in this part of Africa. But he wished it was not *now*. He would have withstood it more comfortably if it had come earlier, at a time when the facilities of the Villa Amélia and the town were at hand. It was humiliating to have to ask Jacinto to stop the jeep while he went into the grass. The sweat now poured down his face and he felt dizzy and weak and this accentuated the uneasy feeling of failure or foolishness, of being lost.

In the late afternoon they crossed the border into Angolique on a dirt road. There was now no white man within a hundred and fifty miles. Ten miles inside the border the track ended in a village of the familiar grass huts, and here was a compound under the trees—stacks of boxes, a row of jeeps, trucks and guns—here was the outpost of Clemente Matumoza's army of the *Movimento Anticolonialista Angolique*.

McQuade was not expected, evidently, but the papers Jacinto handed over must have been impressive, for at once soldiers dashed from place to place to fetch people. By now McQuade felt very weary and ill and wanted to lie down and groan, but this would not have been understood, so he walked about with excited young officers who showed him around the depot—the huts and the flagpole with its green MAA flag, the trucks and the mortars and the communal kitchen. He was given food as he sat at a long trestle table; he felt sick and it was a great struggle to eat. He drank quite a lot of their *aguardente* and this revived his body, although he knew nature would punish it later on.

He had almost forgotten what he was doing and felt so ill he had lost initiative. It was a shock to find himself given a guide and many handshakes, and the handshakes were those for a man who is leaving the safety of a base to go to the fighting. So confused did his illness make him that McQuade was relieved to be on the way. He wanted to hide his physical distress from his enthusiastic hosts, and if stumbling off into the forest in darkness was the way to do it, then he accepted that.

The second guide was a young man named Mauricio. He was quite the opposite of the bumptious Jacinto. He was dressed in khaki shorts, was barefoot, and was loaded with rifle, grenades

260

hanging from a belt and a knife. He had a gentle sort of rounded face and McQuade knew that he was scared: an honorable sort of fear that would vanish when the fighting began. He treated Mc-Quade with the courtesy reserved by soldiers for people who are prepared to come out of the big talk into the dry mouths of the battlefield. He knew the paths which were completely meaningless to McQuade.

In the darkness two hours later McQuade heard the click of a rifle bolt and thought wearily, Oh, God. His skin crawled, antici-pating noise and panic. But Mauricio spoke in Kikongo, and the sentry, if anything, seemed relieved.

He was standing outside a grass shack a hundred miles from anywhere, and he even had a desk. It indicated organization on an impressive scale by the MAA. He flashed a torch on Mauricio and McQuade.

"Passport," he demanded.

He looked at McQuade's Canadian passport meaninglessly, a little impressed. "I keep this," he said. McQuade knew he desired it to play with—he could not read; it was an interesting toy, a war trophy. Protest was useless. In pitch darkness in the sweating for-est, scores of miles from anywhere, the young man with his Portu-guese rifle was king of the world. Useless to argue that "I may not return this way." The long processes of civilization that had brought McQuade to this moment meant nothing to the Bakongo sentry. He was there to exercise authority. He had not done so for three days; now there was something to do—he would do it. Argu-ment would arouse pride and bombast; a bullet in the chest would equally be duty, and all the pious horror in the world wouldn't find the body tossed into the bush. It was one of the many differences between theory and practice, talk about freedom and the process of obtaining it. McQuade knew this and shrugged.

In the second dawn they joined up with a larger group of the *Movimento,* a long column moving along a wider track, carrying boxes on their heads and armed with submachine guns and rifles. They were singing and occasionally one at the front would shout a joke which would be repeated all the way down the column of about a hundred and twenty. There would be giggles and laughter and a counterjoke propelled forward. These people did not seem to

261

be the ones who had cut off breasts and gouged out children's eyes. They were just soldiers, going off to a fight, singing because it was companionship and the companionship was the only good thing, they knew, as all soldiers know, in the terror of what is to come.

The rain came through the trees capriciously, sometimes in a fine spray, sometimes in a mean streak of water as if a tap had been turned on. This was a war to daunt the heart before the fighting began, a war against humidity and the rain and their bare feet in the mud and the indifferent forest and vast distances, and the other enemies—dysentery, malnutrition, trachoma, superstition and yellow fever. The vultures waited for the blood to spill, the bodies to drop; they flew sluggishly above the small trees and bushes and the elephant grass miles away, aware already of the arena of death.

They sang because they were frightened. If somebody could have provided a reasonable excuse they'd have all gone home—except that there were no homes to go to.

It was pitiful and ridiculous and courageous and probably useless. McQuade was there to find out things, but it would have been insulting to question them, "Why do you sing?" . . . "Why do you go to die?" . . . "Do you fight for independence?"—as ridiculous as asking the Canadians at Dieppe, "What are your war aims?" or the bomber crews back from the Ruhr, "Do you feel this is a good strategic conception?" It had nothing to do with that. It was the end product of other minds, noticeably not here in the flesh. It was the young men who marched, and this was because it would have been shameful before others not to. The moist mouths of the politicians and intellectuals talked of the freedoms and autonomies; no one ever mentioned them in the area of casualties. It was part of the condition of man. It was absurd and it was dignified. The *voluntarios* enlisted for Angolique because this was proof of manhood and in a good cause. Hadn't they heard the awful stories of crucifixion and rape? They, too, somewhere in the misty *cassimbo,* were edging about with tightened skin, submachine guns with the safety catches off.

McQuade had tired quickly because of the diarrhea and his stomach pains and because he was forty-seven years old, but he identified in himself the new layer of strength that ignored the conditions of himself and the day. Unwashed, with a stubble, soaked in sweat, he remembered that the first condition of war was dirt and exhaustion. In the holocaust of tanks and gasoline and 88mm. shells that went straight through Canadian tanks, such was their velocity, and set them on fire with the friction of their passage, in the rubble and noise that shattered all previous conceptions of noise was the tiredness. Presumably you were trained so hard so that you went through the right motions mechanically when your real desire was to sleep or scream . . . It was the exhaustion of the battlefield. Fear made you realize that what you thought was exhaustion in normal society was just the beginning here—there were whole reservoirs of strength to absorb and use up yet, and then still more when they gave you Benzedrine to cope with a situation that had gone sour. That kind of exhaustion hadn't begun here yet. In theory he was visiting the field headquarters of a political organization, but a pinprick of terror acknowledged that he had been waiting for this day and had been afraid of it since he had been appointed chairman. He was angry with God—for want of anyone else—who gave him the white dry tongue and the nauseating numb tiredness that accompanied whatever illness he had, which took away initiative, so that he plodded on with Mauricio, willing to leave the result of the day to itself. Wasn't it enough that he was forty-seven while all *these* were sixteen and twenty? He wished he had allowed Asare Johnson to come too, for Asare had pleaded to do so. He was so lonely he could have wept in sorrow for the whole senseless world. Kristan's anxious face, cool and white, stared at him in his mind, and he pleaded to God, Let me get back to her. I'll give you an arm, a hand, an eye, even a leg, but let me get back to her. I am her world and she is mine.

Presently the *cassimbo* lifted and the great heat struck down, enjoyable at first but soon exhausting and sweat sucking.

They passed through a village of deserted huts, some of them burned out, and the trees and grass around had been shriveled by gigantic heat and there were black long scars along the ground showing how extensive was the tongue of the napalm. The singing had stopped. They were not likely to meet Portuguese soldiers this far north, but they weren't completely sure, and some of them had their rifles at the ready.

They reached another grass shack in the trees, with its table for a desk and sentry with his clipboard. This one was from the town and wore glasses and a lightweight jacket. "You shouldn't have left the passport," he reprimanded mildly, a rifle tucked under his elbow and inevitably pointing all over the place, mostly at McQuade. "You will never get it back from these comics."

Two more sentries checked the column and then they arrived at the military establishment. It had been a coffee plantation and it showed how much in control of the ground the MAA were: they'd been using it for six months. "We had a village camp, but the rains washed it away," explained Mauricio. "But we are cautious. We eat and sleep in the buildings, but the ammunition and guns are stored among the big trees so that the pilots won't see the boxes."

The house had been of white stone and had had extensive wings. Some walls had split and the pillars on the handsome porch were peeling. Weeds had cracked the steps. The main house and the barns, warehouses, hospital and what had been the smaller houses of the staff had all been damaged by fire in the original capture. McQuade saw the fissures and black stains and broken glass; termites and creepers crumbling the stucco and the beautiful wood; doors and windows hanging with a kind of uselessness as if conscious that these new occupiers wouldn't use them . . . Weeds grew in a terraced garden and lizards lay in the sun. On the lawn surrounded by the weeds and bright flowers a group was receiving machine-gun instruction. McQuade flinched as a pupil fired with splendid disregard for safety regulations.

The column was directed five hundred yards beyond the mansion to where the forest had been halted half a century or more before. McQuade saw them unloading the boxes. For half a mile among the massive trunks he could see the hard oily gleam of mortars and rifles, and the orange wooden boxes of ammunition.

Rossio sat on the terrace with some young men who were, perhaps, officers.

"You are tired," he said with the sympathy of the fellow *civilizado* who has gotten mixed up with the exhaustions of battle. "How do you fancy an iced beer?"

"Jesus!" said McQuade with feeling.

He sat drinking it, feeling the ache of his flesh throb into the wicker chair which had known other people . . . The young officers were introduced. They had been south on patrol and had rested during the night. It had been the usual clash of small groups, and two men had been lost—but four Portuguese had been shot. It was good arithmetic, their grins implied.

"At first we had no cohesion," Rossio told him. "It would have been quite possible for two of our patrols from different villages to clash. Now we have a few radio contacts and some planning. We acknowledge routine and tiredness and morale. There are many places like this; some are villages and some camps. And these are interwoven with smaller units, ten or twenty men in a jungle village, sentries in huts and so on. It is the air we fear most of all. We have no retaliation except machine guns. Oh, hell!" he commented expressively, for somewhere whistles blew and in the same acoustic instant the jet engine boomed over the hills. The men ran from the lawn into the trees. Others fled inside buildings. Rossio and the officers didn't move. "What is the use?" he asked. "It is a fighter. The visibility from his cockpit is not all that good. It is movement he looks for."

This opinion seemed justified by the vicious noise diminishing among the hills. "Let's go and eat," suggested Rossio. A long way off they heard the brisk drumming of cannon fire.

They ate quite well, and McQuade, listening to the voices instructing in drill and gunnery, the occasional laughter, felt a bit better. He was able to wash afterward. Rossio showed him the communal kitchen in which girls and old women worked. In the hospital twenty Africans lay on beds or on mattresses on the floor. Some of them had appalling injuries. There was one doctor. McQuade suspected, because of his extreme youth, that he was or had been a student. He was learning fast in a grim practical manner: there was a bit of everything—grenade wounds, bullet wounds, "normal" diseases, and three men who had been in a village burned by napalm. The young doctor had nothing except jars of ointment and penicillin tablets. There were two girls doing the nursing. They, too, had an indefinable air of being keen rather than well trained.

"It is not easy," admitted Rossio on the lawn. "They send us ammunition from Tunis and machine guns from Dar es Salaam and sometimes the two don't match; but we don't find that out until we try them together. Sometimes we have thousands of bullets for one

265

weapon and dozens of rifles with a mere ten bullets apiece. Logistics are our anxiety, but supplies are gaining momentum. Strategically, it is also worrying. For how do we advance a thousand miles and occupy such a country with this pitiful logistics and these shortages of medicine and an almost total inexperience with and supply of vehicles? There will have to be outside help, an invasion from the Congo, or Tanzania, or Malawi or from the sea, and who is prepared to take that great risk for *us?* Clandestine supplies and technical advisers in a half dozen camps are one thing, artillery and bombers altogether another . . . Only the enthusiasm is high. All the villages are with us for hundreds of miles, so no Portuguese live here, and their patrols don't come too far from the roads where their convoys are led by bulldozers. We have mined the roads in fifty-two places," claimed Rossio. He laughed boyishly. "We can hear the bangs in the night sometimes! And in the jungle fighting we are at least as good as they."

They were watching mortar instruction when the whistles blew again and three aircraft circled around with unmistakable intention some miles off. People began to run to the trees. The aircraft were Canberras, old jets, but they were without opposition. In the tick of seconds, as their engines sucked at the warm moist air by the ton with an alarming rasp of noise, McQuade saw their bomb doors opening. He, too, began to run, and he found that he was not exhausted at all: he could fly—that was just the laziness of inactivity he had experienced earlier. The seconds moved slowly, allowing quite a lot of movement as the bombers separated, and McQuade saw girls running into the trees with saucepans, and men fleeing with their rifles.

The first bomb exploded and the Canberra seemed to send a draft over McQuade's scalp as he reached the trees. It was ridiculous to stay by boxes of ammunition among the trees—a hot belch of napalm along the ground and the trees, gigantic though they were, would blow up. He wanted to get farther into the forest. It was the logical thing to do—a hundred yards even. But the others were too frightened to move. The trees were certainly enormous and would indeed save them from observation or fragmentation bombs, but any delayed fuses or napalm and they were done for. The Africans sheltered among the massive roots of the trees,

266

crouched in the clefts as if these could save them from blast. The vicious thumps went on at intervals as the bombers circled. They flew so low that the sound of the engines was terrifying. Smoke drifted and someone was screaming and McQuade recalled that these, too, were the properties of battle. Please God, he prayed, no napalm. It would be too vile. Some of the boys were weeping. He could see them shaking, with their mouths open and their fingers either twitching or clenched tight. On the ground a machine gun was firing back, but the horrible business went on. It was the buildings they were after. There was no red cross on the roof of the little hospital so the Portuguese pilots didn't spare it. The main mansion was now burning.

Suddenly the noise ended, very abruptly, as if all the jet engines had failed. The Canberras had in fact dropped below the next hill and, just as the young Africans relaxed, began to grin, "I am alive. See, it is nothing; I am brave," just then the motors rolled back a great wave of sound and were gone.

There was a horrible mess, but not many had been killed.

The patients in the hospital were all dead, presumably, under the rubble, but the doctor and nurses came out of the trees self-consciously. Five had been killed in a shed, and there were ten injured with shards of metal, but shock hadn't reached them yet. They bled but stood on their feet grinning. The doctor had taken his meager supply of penicillin tablets and his few instruments when he'd fled for shelter, and he began work on the lawn. Everyone else wandered about, hopelessly, but rather pleased with themselves. Giggles and good humor were in order. But the training stopped for that day and no patrols went out.

After a while the *cassimbo,* which might have spared them, came back, and as the sunlight faded the heavy rain came. The sleeping quarters had been destroyed, and so had the kitchen, but there was no irritation or frustration. They had lived without brick and stone buildings and without the white man's taps before, and they could do so again.

McQuade hated to have to mention his return, but Rossio's mind was one which acknowledged timetables. McQuade had not slept for several days and nights and the illness burned hot within him. He was glad to rest for some hours in a shed. Sleep wouldn't come.

He could hear the voices talking all around and smell the smoke of the burned-out buildings. The rain beat on the corrugated iron above his head and there was a hot smell of something fetid, something that had gone sour. But in the end exhaustion claimed him.

Someone shook his shoulder hours later. It was still dark and the rain still beat on the tin roof. He felt terrible—stunned and drained with tiredness and a pain now in his head and neck. Rossio's voice said in the darkness, "I am coming with you. We will have vehicles within two hours." And very distantly McQuade realized that he was on his way home to Kristan. He would reach the airport at Brazzaville and thirty hours from now begin a journey to Paris and Geneva. After four days in Geneva a Boeing would take him in seven hours to Kennedy Airport.

He stumbled for two hours along a muddy path, through wet elephant grass, fell once into a stream and finally gained a momentum which took him along with Rossio and a guide, another boy very anxious to please and instruct. In an hour the dawn came, cold and humid and dirty. McQuade had not looked in a mirror for a very long time and would have been startled at the tired, filthy face he would have seen in one. He was too dulled by fatigue to be aware of his clothes, muddy and torn.

They reached a village where there were huts and great rows of ammunition boxes becoming useless in the rain. They ate sausages and some cheese and drank some of the local *pombe*. The villagers seemed in good humor. Just how or what they ate or what work they did in the chaos of war and with the Portuguese departed was difficult to say. Perhaps the *Movimento* provided supplies. Certainly they were going nowhere this day; obviously they intended to hang about and attend to the comings and goings of vehicles, which weren't likely to be numerous in this weather.

McQuade sat in the back of a Soviet Gaz jeeplike vehicle with its canvas roof up. The ride was quite comfortable on the balloon tires. Ten miles and they'd be over the Congo border. He began to relax and think about the report and the Boeing from Geneva.

After a long silence he asked Rossio abruptly, "What about the prisoners?"

Rossio counterquestioned apprehensively, "The prisoners, Mr. McQuade?"

268

"I saw no prisoners. Are any ever taken?"

Rossio said uneasily, "I doubt it. In a clash there is killing and then one runs."

"And if the clash is successful?"

"We leave their wounded."

"I was not asking about the wounded."

"Mr. McQuade, how could we look after prisoners? We do not have proper camps ourselves. We have nothing like barbed wire and no surpluses of food."

"They get murdered?"

"No, assuredly no, Mr. McQuade. It may have happened in the Bakongo atrocities that people were murdered. But *we* are an army. Every report I have seen is of a brief clash, and we have enough difficulty bringing our own wounded back. For there is no Red Cross and there are no stretchers . . ."

McQuade did not persist. He doubted if the niceties were observed by either side in the jungle; the terror and stress on the individual were a little too much . . .

After another hour McQuade's bowels troubled him and he had to ask, "Would you mind stopping?"

Rossio laughed.

McQuade went a little way into the trees. He was conscious of Rossio urinating in the grass by the road and the boy still sitting in the vehicle. He felt most horribly tired and dirty and wondered what time it was in New York. Was it raining there, too?

The boy's shout meant nothing because it was in the Kikongo tongue, but he heard the thrash of Rossio's feet in the grass, the frantic propulsion and squelch, and then, deafening and totally unexpected, the blast of a submachine gun and shouts, the smell of smoke, and then, for long moments, a terrifying silence. A Portuguese voice sixty feet away asked in anxiety, "Did you get him?" and a breathless answer, "Yes. And the driver." The first voice said, "There may be others," but another voice qualified, "There is only the one jeep."

McQuade was a hundred miles from anywhere, exhausted, and wanted to throw himself on their limited mercy; so great was his exhaustion that for long dull moments while his heart thumped the earth he believed that all he had to do was speak up, in Portuguese, and he would be cared for, taken away; he might still get that jet from Brazzaville. Then he thought of another possibility and when he had done so he wished God had not put the thought into his head. He had no strength in him so great was the willpower needed to decide. He could hear them, the kick of feet against the vehicle, a bitter comment "It is one of those Soviet things," and the first of the voices, "There is always someone against God."

McQuade's feet fluttered in fright and he shouted in a shaky voice, in French, "I am unarmed."

The silence was electrifying.

The second or third voice asked, "What did he say?" and the first voice, presumably the officer, said, "He says he has no gun. What a pity! He is white by the sound of it." The other voice asked, "Do you think he is wounded?" And the answer, in Portuguese, was "No. Just frightened"—"Shall I kill him?"—"No. See what it is all about."

Another quiet and then the officer's voice, in classroom French, shouted in the rain, "Stand up and reveal yourself."

McQuade stood up and put his hands in the air. He looked and was frightened.

He just had time to see the three of them when one fired. The burst of bullets thrashed the grass around McQuade, who fell on his face in shock. Then, as he recovered from this, the running feet booted him. This was just caution. He stood up.

There were two Portuguese jeeps seventy feet away and eight soldiers with one officer. Five of the soldiers were Africans. All were brittle with the shock of the encounter. Rossio was dead, doubled up hideously in the grass by the side of the track, and the boy was dead, half spewed out of the vehicle. Soldiers were searching the vehicle and the bodies.

The idea had crawled into McQuade's dulled brain and lodged itself there, extracting the final ounce of idealism. Prisoners. He had asked Rossio and knew the African answer. Political. He was filthy. He did not look like a Canadian diplomat in a lightweight suit. He had the exhausted, filthy appearance of someone involved in war. A mercenary or a technical adviser. Someone these would hate. The label of his suit might confirm their hatred. It had been bought in Montreal, but the shop had a French name.

270

All he had to do was say, "I am from the United Nations. I have just completed a tour of Angolique and have now visited the *Movimento Anticolonialista* to hear petitioners." Mention a few names and these men would not dare to kill him. They would be daunted by the names of the politicians. They would feel a little dislike, some respect tinged with loathing, but no more; a delay in the journey to safety, but not much. These men would see him to some calmer place; he might even catch that airplane . . . But no. He had committed himself now. It was the one thing he didn't know. No one in the world knew what happened to political prisoners of the Portuguese in Angolique. The human being and husband in him wanted to weep, and even now he hoped that these soldiers would insist on some circumstance that would enable him to go to Geneva.

The officer was small and heavy, had gray hair. He had large eyes, but was not romantic. Not today. He was a captain who should, by virtue of age, have been a major or higher. What had kept him back?

The captain asked the shaking McQuade in French, "Are there any more, pig?"

"No. Just the three of us."

The captain struck McQuade so violently across the face that his nose bled. "I'll kill you first if there are."

McQuade said, "You are over the border, in Congo territory."

He received a hard kick with a heavy boot for this, and the officer shouted at him, "I will decide where I am and what I'm doing." Nevertheless, he said in Portuguese to his sergeant, "He says we are over the border. Back then. Two dead and this pig and the earlier ones are enough." He switched back to French, lumpy in his fury. "See what you are doing, pig? Killing them and killing us."

He referred to a man soaked in blood in the area of the hips who lay, rolling in pain and moaning in misery, on one of the jeeps, the spare wheel and various tins having been removed. McQuade wanted to cry for Rossio, whom he had loved. "What are you teaching them for, pig?" the captain shouted, rage reddening his face. "What is the sense in it for a Frenchman?"

"I was not doing that."

"Then what were you doing?"

271

Silence, because McQuade was too exhausted and shaken to think up a satisfactory lie.

The captain said grimly, "It is political, eh? Well, we will take you to people whom you will find interested in politics."

This took a long time—about twenty-one hours in fact, much of which time McQuade spent in jeeps, or standing in one of two camps. Once they heard gunfire and grenades in the forest. This was before they reached the first camp. When they did reach it, McQuade stood about in the open, under guard, and people stared at him and the captain passed him into another jeep with a different officer. While these things were attended to and time passed, he saw rows of wounded—about thirty in all—writhing or lying still, stained with blood. They had obviously just come in from the fighting. And his eyes saw that the Portuguese Army doctor was giving equal attention to black and white, friend or prisoner —it was entirely a question of the injuries—and he was moved and would have wept if it had not been likely of the false interpretation of self-pity. He saw trucks being loaded with terrified refugees, clutching their children and pitiful, useless bundles. Again he felt the sorrow for all of them and the uselessness of wars to interpret the ideas of people—usually men, for no woman was prepared to start a war—thousands of miles away. Very faintly, despite illness and utter exhaustion, he was glad he had chosen to come back to this troubled land, and remotely he wondered if he could succeed in what he intended.

In the long journey beyond the second camp, with the smell of the sea in his nostrils in darkness, he slept fitfully and no one interrupted him. In the dawn of the second day the jeep came into a small, attractive coastal town and went across a causeway and onto an island of palm groves and white sand. There were sentries and parked vehicles and an impression of many things going on somewhere. Then they came to the fortress. McQuade had recognized the small town and knew therefore that this was the political prison of São Damba. Fright lay in a heavy lump in his stomach because pain and death might be here.

The morning sun touched the fortress and its white old stone hurt the eyeballs. It was a vast square with immense high walls; there were octagonal towers at each corner, with openings set at the

272

angles, and there were scrolled buttresses. The fortress was exceedingly photogenic there among the palm trees and under a fierce blue sky. But there were no windows on the side they approached, not even openings in the stone, and the young officer, who had been quiet for hours because he spoke no French and was dozing anyway, said, unaware that McQuade could understand his language, "Good luck to you, soldier. You must have done something terrible to come to this place."

There was a colossal stone entrance with two towers, a lion and a golden fleece on one side and carved on the other the instruments of the Passion. The sun and moon decorated each end of the door lintel. But the door—there were two halves of it, one above the other—was of steel. In a courtyard were cars and trucks and a few soldiers.

The officer waited to hand over McQuade. The first guard telephoned and after a few minutes a civilian came, yawning, surprised, and interested, but with reservations. It was as if he had a day's work planned and had just begun it and now *this* . . . He looked unpleasant but clever, not likely to be amused by flippancy. He had an air of belonging to this place and of having much authority inside it. He looked at McQuade—the tall, dirty, exhausted white man, believed French—and identified something different that had passed unnoticed by the officers in the area of battle.

"Any papers?"

"No," said the junior officer who had brought McQuade. "Just a watch, the wallet with the money, these keys."

This was true by accident. The sentry had taken McQuade's passport and, in civilized need, McQuade had used Rossio's paper of introduction and identification for the purpose which had spared him Rossio's fate.

The civilian, who was almost certainly of the PIDE, asked in French, "Who are you?"

McQuade didn't answer.

"I am talking to you," shouted the man. McQuade said nothing, and the PIDE man, unruffled, said, "Very well. You wish to be nothing. You *are* nothing and will be treated as such." He said, "Thank you," to the Army officer who departed, and then flicked a finger. A guard seized McQuade and pushed him inside the fort-

273

ress. Here, in an area of stone floor and hanging electric lights, were desks and a few clerks on duty. The PIDE man sat at an empty desk and filled in a form. He wrote down rapidly the circumstances of McQuade's capture.

"Name?" he asked in French.

"Does it matter?" said McQuade.

The other looked up. "Oh, so you do speak? Do you wish your relatives to know you are here?"

"I have none."

"Suit yourself. What I meant was, if you should die here, in what manner would you wish to be buried?"

"I shall not die here."

"You think it impossible?"

"Unless you murder me."

"Then let us regard that as a possibility."

"In which case I would like Protestant burial. With flowers."

"You shall have it," said the PIDE officer with grim humor, "if it becomes necessary."

He instructed the guard in Portuguese, "All right. He's yours. No beatings. This one may be important. Let him stand for a while, eh?"

A second guard joined the first. One preceded McQuade and the other followed. Both were armed. The vast labyrinthine interior of the fortress was impressive: it was like a cathedral given over to secular works. The smash of impious booted feet on stone. The musty smell of centuries. Cobwebs and moisture: it was even cool once they'd turned a corner. At first, on this side of the fortress, the long beams of the sun, shining through circular barred windows the size of coffee tables, threw shadows like cartwheels on the opposite wall. Some of the vast arched ceilings were moldy. Light diminished as they went deep into the interior. Up steps that led to other corridors, some illuminated by naked electric light bulbs, keys jingling, the boots still smashing on stone at a regular pace and McQuade's own shoes pattering at a different, irregular nervous step. And then he heard voices hollow in air that was damp and the voices were so distant they might only have been in his mind; they seemed to come from under his feet. And from the same sort of distance, he smelled as uneasily as suspicion the fetid odor of— what? Sweat? Dirty flesh? Suppuration? Old bones? It was as if the

274

thick walls had been soaked in something far too long—dry rot and dead insects and blood. At the junction of two corridors were, unexpectedly, some statues, neglected, forgotten, chipped and mildewed, hundreds of years old—Christ with His hands tied? A warrior who had failed? A saint who was a bit of a masochist? It was difficult to decide. Valuable, no doubt, by New York standards, but here they gave no hope . . . Some of the metal corridor doors were new and had labels, names and meanings. Wires ran along this damp wall to illuminate some dark corner or power some foul equipment. A groan now, real and not in the mind, echoed uselessly along endless vaulted corridors, seeping out of keyholes. And suddenly they came to a circular cistern put to some sinister purpose—a brick hole in a stone floor, a black cavity that looked like an indoor well. Out of it was funneled a smell of slaughter and pain, airlessness and death, bodies lost to the maggots, not necessarily of this time but frightening the nostrils nevertheless.

The first guard hung a hooked ladder and motioned McQuade to descend. This McQuade did, going down into blackness that had the viscosity, it seemed, of syrup. He did not think the guards would follow. Fifteen feet down his feet touched slimy stone. Rats ran away from him. There were the smells of blood and feces, five hundred years of them . . . He was astonished to hear the roar of the sea somewhere. And there was a faint current of air. But it was impossible to think of either except in terms of rumor and what Costa had said—"I think they drop them to the sharks . . ."

The guards also descended, the one holding a flashlight as he came down, shining it on McQuade so that the second one could shoot if necessary. Then, when both had reached the lower floor the man with the light shined it on a stout door, which his companion unlocked. Now other feet echoed along a corridor that was slippery with moisture and mold. The voices were clearer and human enough to laugh. Around a corner were the two guards of this underground gallery, who had been waiting with interest. The four of them now talked, shared cigarettes. Somewhere someone cried out, and the guards eyed McQuade to see his reaction. A door of steel slammed a long way off. Something was being dragged somewhere. It was coming this way. McQuade felt uneasy.

Two men came past, dragging a sack of potatoes along the stone

275

floor. Then in the gloom McQuade realized in fright and horror that it was not a sack but a human being too beaten and enfeebled to walk, and so lugged by the ankles with the head rubbing on the stone floor and now and again bumping where it was uneven. Whoever it was had been beaten or tortured to the point of unconsciousness or fainting. Keys jangled and one of the dungeon doors twenty yards away opened. Then, heard distantly, there was the thump of the body thrown and after that the slam of the door.

A telephone rang with startling noise and a guard ran to grab it off a corridor shelf.

The guards with bloody hands were African. The conversation was a macabre experience in racial equality.

"Did he talk?"

"Yes, but not what they wanted."

"The Frenchman next, did they say?"

"No. Let him sweat."

"He has to stand."

"The old fool next, with his dignity."

They all giggled at some private joke. Someone went to fetch the "old fool," and with distress McQuade recognized the voice. It belonged to Colonel Unguanda, last seen shaky with fear in a house of keys and locked doors eight hundred miles away.

He did not sound frightened now. His old voice protested defiantly—but wasted—to these men who guarded him, "Do you think louts like you can frighten me? I have lived my years. I can die."

The guard who was bringing him said in irritation, "Save your breath, old fool, for your screaming. If we want you to talk you will be glad to."

"What is there that scum like you would understand?"

Blows, grunted breath, a hiss of pain, and the guard's satisfied question, "How do you feel now, old hero? Talkative?"

They came into sight, the colonel scarcely able to walk after the blows in the kidneys and the prompt booting, but he was trying—God, how he was trying.

McQuade did not suppose he would be recognized in his present filthy condition and in this place. He did not wish to identify himself yet, but could not let the old man go to the hell prepared for him without a word.

276

He called out in French, "Take heart, colonel. Their day is almost over."

"I know your voice."

"Then do not tell them who I am."

That was as far as the dialogue went before two of them booted McQuade and the Africans hit the Colonel again.

It didn't help anyone. With horror McQuade heard the voices hiss in surprise, "This one knows the old fool," and a protest, "You see, the old one was in with Leopoldville." And boots hurried along the stone to inform others of this.

Nevertheless, nobody did anything about the receipt of this exciting information for a long time.

The guards separated and went to their various duties. Two of them took McQuade into a small room empty except for a chair. One guard drew a chalk circle with a diameter of about two feet on the floor. He pointed to this and smiled. "Stand here," he said in Portuguese. "You are a statue."

McQuade affected not to understand, and some blows and a kick or two persuaded him.

One guard now left and the other sat down, rifle on his lap, held lightly but directed at McQuade.

McQuade knew that this was the statue punishment/torture, known to the Germans during the war as the *Stehzelle*. He had heard that it was more effective as a punishment than mere standing might seem, for the blood went into the feet and with mere intervals for food and no sleep allowed, after many hours or even days the feet swelled up, the pain was immense, the prisoner passed out and there was a tendency to feeblemindedness, stomach illnesses and other surprises . . .

But he was already ill and after two hours collapsed.

This happened twice more and as it was obviously not pretended the guard consulted a senior guard and McQuade was taken to one of the dungeons, half walking and half supported. They threw him inside and he landed painfully on the stone floor in pitch darkness.

He lay down in pain, too enfeebled to move for a while. The air was stale and musty and his bowels troubled him. He explored the walls with his hands and found that the cell was about three feet wide, seven feet long and higher than he could reach with extended

277

arm. When he found the massive door he banged on it and shouted —in French, although the urge to surrender to Portuguese was strong in these humiliating circumstance. No one took any notice. Perhaps they could not hear, and in the end he had no option but to submit to the demands of the illness in a corner of the cell.

Many hours later they brought him food, but slammed the cell door at once so that he had to find his way in the utter darkness along the floor and eat the food with his hands. It was fish and bread, both stale. It strengthened him for a while and enabled him to sleep, but when he awoke his bowels made their humiliating demands again and he had to surrender to them like a dog locked up in error.

Two days later—it felt like a week to McQuade—the same two gallery guards came for him and took him along the corridors to one of the steel doors. After the total darkness even the faint illumination of the corridor hurt his eyes. The guards were disgusted at the smell of his cell and shouted at him in rage and thumped him— perhaps they would have the job of cleaning the cell . . .

In the small room on the other side of the steel door was a desk and two chairs. A plump, middle-aged PIDE officer sat smoking and drinking coffee. He motioned McQuade to sit down and dismissed the guard. He bit his lip and considered McQuade.

"You do not look well," he said sympathetically, in French. "Is anything the matter?"

The sympathy made McQuade tremble. After a while he answered calmly, "I do not know."

"Can we now talk?"

"Is there anything to talk about?"

"Oh, yes. A few things. What is your name?"

"It is not one you would know."

"Can we be sure of that? Tell me and allow me to judge."

"It is not one of importance."

"You mustn't be modest. They tell me you have met Colonel Unguanda."

"I have met him socially."

"How is that possible?"

"In the normal manner."

"He was the Governor General of Angolique and you say your name is of no importance?"

"It was at a party perhaps."

"He was associated with Leopoldville, was he not?"

"I am sure he was not."

"Who do you think were his associates?"

"I think he is an old man who had the courage of his convictions."

"Whatever they were—"

"He had an opinion. I doubt if Leopoldville would particularly like it."

"You are well informed for a nobody! Especially about what Leopoldville likes! Is that because you are from that city?"

"I have never been to Leopoldville."

"You met the colonel socially?"

"Yes."

"Where?"

"In Angolique."

"What was the nature of the meeting?"

"We had dinner together."

"And conversation?"

"Yes."

"What was that about?"

"The train."

"The train?"

"Yes. He was expecting the PIDE to come on the train and arrest or kill him."

The other man looked puzzled, even disconcerted. He recognized that the absurd mention of trains had a ring of truth in it. This meant that this prisoner *had* met Colonel Unguanda and in the last three months. It was a peculiar situation—two men in a room that smelled of stale cigarette smoke and damp walls and breath exhausted by suffering, neither of them knowing the other's name and having nothing in common, but engaged in a careful, polite meaningless duel of words, with the death of one a possible result.

"And what else? What was said while you ate the cheese?"

"I cannot remember. About his flowers perhaps."

"Who else have you met—socially?"

"Nobody you'd know."

"You are a liar. You were with this traitor Rossio."

"Not exactly socially."

279

"And not talking about flowers either! You are very frank! But not truthful enough. You meet Colonel Unguanda and you meet Rossio and you think you do not need to tell me your name! Are you a fool or something? Clearly you are a spy of some sort. Why were you in a jeep with this man whom we know was a traitor?"

"I am not prepared to tell you that."

"You act as if you had rights here! Indeed you act as if you are in charge! You realize you will be shot as a spy, whether with a name or not? Start talking, fool, or I shall be obliged to have you persuaded. Start talking about places and names and shipments and plans."

"I have nothing to tell you."

The officer said, "We do not wish to hurt people."

"Am I to disbelieve what I see?"

"You have seen nothing. A few kicks and bruises. What are those? I repeat, we do not *wish* to hurt people—it is degrading to us, too. But it is certain that in the conditions of this war they must tell us what they know. This is logical on behalf of Portugal, who would otherwise be anybody's fool."

"I saw a man being dragged. He had been tortured. I saw a guard kick and thump the old colonel."

"Oh, I do not dispute that things happen here. We employ people who are very good at it—"

"And you believe that you are personally absolved because you sit behind a desk and talk politely?"

The officer flushed in anger. He struck McQuade across the ear and then, discontinuing, sat down again, a little out of breath.

"You seem to be in search of logic. Who are you to imply exemption—you who were caught in a jeep coming from some killing or other? You do not even have the courage to do it yourself—you incite others with words, or train them in areas of safety, or use your white skin to spy safely on Portugal. Is it logical for every country in the world, including your own rebel apparatus in Leopoldville, to ask questions with force but not *us?* You are French?"

"I speak French."

"You fought in Algeria?"

"No."

"You believed in that cause while France was engaged in it?"

280

"No."

"You did not believe in France?"

"Not in her policy in Algeria."

"Obviously you are a second-rate Frenchman!" sneered the officer. "But still, you are French. And you know what tortures went on there? In Paris itself? You know that Algerians were drowned in the Seine in the autumn of 1961? You know they were guillotined in the courtyard of the Santé prison after questionable legal proceedings? You know of the tortures by the French in Indochina? And of the trial in Madagascar in 1948 when the innocent were executed? And of the suffocation of forty-one suspects in a cellar at Ain Isser in the department of Oran, where 101 had been incarcerated for a night? You know of the Algerians hung in the woods around Paris? And you talk to *me* about Portugal?"

"I know that these things and others like them obtained no result in the end—"

"Listen!" said the officer angrily. "Let us stop the intellectual clowning. I am the servant of Portugal. You are either an enemy of Portugal or a spy. I am entitled to ask you questions. I will do so again. If you do not answer then pain will be inflicted to make you. The option is yours. Consider it. It is not an atrocity or maliciousness that Portugal or I wish to inflict despite the provocation by slaughter and vileness inspired by Leopoldville. The option is *yours*. You can spare yourself misery. There is no disgrace, for assuredly you will talk with the pain and therefore can talk before experiencing it. You are not sending any friends to death. They are, I presume, a thousand miles away. Is this logical enough for you?"

"I do not wish Portugal any harm. It is *you*—"

The officer hit him in the face again.

"Stop that trash logic. Do not try to talk me into a position of immorality. You have the option. What is your name? What is the big secret about it? *My* name is Captain Bravo and I am not ashamed of it. I am a patriot and Portugal is not going to be driven out of Africa by criminals if I, her servant, can help her, even in this dirty business."

"I believe you," said McQuade sadly.

"Then talk sense. You are a Frenchman, not an African or a Chinese agitator."

281

"There is nothing to talk about."

"We shall see," said the officer grimly. "But be clear. You were given the choice. The pain is of your choosing. There will be pain, you will talk, and tomorrow you will be shot."

He walked out of the office, red in the face.

The guards came in and smiled. One pulled McQuade by the hair.

"This way, pig, to the butcher. You will see how your Africans treat pigs."

"It seems you were very brave," said the other. "Marvelous with the talking."

They both laughed.

Then one tripped McQuade and they both booted him for a moment. It merely made him angry and he struck one hard in the face. But the other merely clipped his offending knuckle with a rifle butt so that his hand bled and he almost fainted with the pain.

In a cellar of great size two Africans were scrubbing a table. The table was bloodstained. The smells of blood and other miseries and humiliations were very offensive. McQuade wondered why they were scrubbing the long plain table which was perhaps used as a bench. It would, he presumed, be so that the degree of bleeding of the next victim could be identified: after all, they could hardly buy a new table for each prisoner.

Several Africans and *mestiço* guards were standing around in an attitude of Who's next? They were supervised by a Portuguese officer. Here was a place where the color bar did not quite operate in terms of money. McQuade knew that nothing was going to spare him the pain. He had long since forgotten the point of all this: the wish to understand the miseries of the *indigena* by identifying himself with those who expressed political opinions and were caught doing so . . . There was no use in saying anything. The interrogations came afterward, if at all, on the basis of Do you feel like talking now? He was deadly tired, with some illness that made him feel sick already and had weakened him. Further, it wasn't really his war; that is, he had no hatred with which to defy the pain. He was an impartial observer, loaded with pity which was useless here. So he was very frightened although he was a taller man than most of them here.

282

And certainly it was something to be frightened about. On the floor, like litter to be taken away, were three of those who had been tortured. All were bleeding. One was moaning. Two were black men and the third was white. McQuade had yet another shock, for the white man was Captain Luis Nogar, supposedly in Brazil.

The officer looked at his watch and strolled across to the two guards and McQuade. He was fat and barrel-chested, and had an immense head and neck, but absurdly self-conscious blue eyes with bags under them. Under other circumstances he might have been a good worker—a farmer, perhaps, in a small way, known for being bloody awkward and driving his workers a bit too hard, but no worse than that. Here he was king: they all suffered the whims of his jurisdiction.

"Who's this fellow?"

"The Frenchman."

"Big, isn't he? And wearing a tie! A French gentleman! All right. We'll take the bounce out of him. Take these two away. Not that one. He hasn't agreed to talk yet. Any more this morning?"

"No. The old fool has died."

"I am sorry. He tried so hard. It was so funny. We should finish early, then?"

"Will you be swimming this afternoon?"

"It depends. I may have a date."

"Phone me later."

"Ah, yes, after I've phoned *her!*"

The guards dragged away the mess that was still, but only just, Captain Luis Nogar, and the officer considered McQuade.

McQuade was shivering with the consciousness of the first physical contact, like a girl held down for rape. He had no advantages at all.

"Blindfold him," instructed the officer.

Two of the Africans, in shorts, their smooth strong chests sweating from their earlier exertions, ran to obey. It was noticeable that both had erections. Instinctively McQuade resisted. They enjoyed this because it gave them permission and scope. After a while the one sat on McQuade's stomach and the other was busy tying his ankles together. The first one then got off his stomach and tied his wrists to the ankles. All this was painful and exhausting. For a

283

foolish moment McQuade thought it was all over, but in fact it was beginning. Trussed with his elbows slightly below his knees Mc-Quade was rolled backward a pace or two by one African while the other fetched an ordinary automobile tire. They inserted him into this so that he was wedged in a posture of a baby in the womb. He could breathe only with shallow gasps. He was handled with roughness, as if he was an irritating piece of furniture: he was just a job; no gentleness was needed; it wasn't valuable furniture. He was in darkness behind the cloth over his eyes and his skin was tight with the expectation of kicks or prods. Perhaps they'd roll him until he was dizzy.

They didn't do this.

They stopped up his nose, none too gently, and his fright was that of the hospital patient who knows these people mean well, they have good intentions, but how it hurts . . . A tube was put into his mouth, continuing the parallel, and, unexpectedly, cool water shot to the back of his throat in a jet. For one instant it gave him relief, then it flooded and the choking sensation began. He wasted a lot of breath trying, absurdly, to scream and protest, to ask them to stop, didn't they know what they were doing? His stomach, compressed, like his lungs, in the posture of discomfort, soon protested, and began to spew backward. A great roar of pain and suffocation and choking filled the world. It was unbearable but had to be borne. Unconsciousness came without mercy but rather in a dizziness and faintness of the heart.

It was all very undignified.

He was sick when he regained consciousness and quite willing to lie on the floor when they'd eased him out of the tire.

"On here!" he heard the fat officer instruct.

They took the covering off his eyes. He was soaked in sweat and water and unable to do anything for a long while but gasp for breath. He knew he was now lying on the table, for he could smell the soap with which it had been cleaned.

"Take off his shoes," the officer ordered.

McQuade wondered what little task he saved for himself—or was everything done by the two African hearties?

But no. The officer was performing his daily task—not too strenuous and no loss of dignity in a scuffle.

284

He was beating the sole of McQuade's left foot with a *palmatoria*. McQuade had heard of this instrument and had not been very impressed. A paddle with holes in it didn't sound too vicious. One hundred and forty-seven blows, a refugee had said. For insolence! And certainly the refugee had walked with a limp. But could he really count that far? After the water torture mere blows on the foot were a luxury. But after a while McQuade decided he had formed a premature opinion. There was much to be said for the *palmatoria* if you persisted, if using it didn't tire you. For some way past the hundredth smash on his left foot the holes in the *palmatoria* began to suck out welts, and he writhed and groaned and ground his teeth because not to do so would be to scream or plead and that would give pleasure, and he had no wish to afford satisfaction to these things. Indeed, his impartiality on these citizens of Angolique was so removed that he would have killed them if he had had the means to hand.

It was this rage that saw him through to the fainting.

No questions were asked, not even a statement requested. It was as if they'd lost him officially in some governmental idiocy of red tape. There was nothing to do but continue until somebody came back from lunch, or found a chit in the "Out" tray which should have been in "Waiting."

It ended with the clock, because the guards and their officer, incredibly, had an appetite and wished to eat.

The two gallery guards came, and McQuade was rolled off the bench. He fell three feet to the floor and that was what made him cry. They did not even respect him for what he had endured.

He tried to stand up, but fainted. The guards, as with others, pulled him by the ankles, and his mind, still working faintly, instructed his body to lift the head so that it wouldn't graze the stone floor. But the neck, although willing, just couldn't support such an attitude and so the head was dragged along the corridors.

McQuade crawled into a corner—no one had cleaned the cell—and slept for some hours. Then he awoke, vomited, and slept again. He awoke a second time, very conscious of pain, all nerve ends working fully, and the left foot throbbed; he knew he'd limp for the rest of his life—however long that might be. And he waited for the next performance of pain with shaking terror and prayed that no

285

more would be inflicted and that, when the time came, he would make himself understood.

The time came in the next dawn when the two gallery guards came to fetch him.

"Walk, pig," the one shouted.

McQuade found that he had the power to walk despite the blood and suppuration on his left foot. It was better than being dragged.

They went along galleries and out into a courtyard surrounded on three sides by an attractive stone balustrade. There was a beautiful view of the sea and, two miles or so away, the town. But the tremendous light was more than McQuade's eyes could at present bear and he fell down and covered them with his hands. The headache thumped and he felt old and too dirty to be alive, too far gone to become normal again, make a speech, eat with a knife and fork, drive a car, make love to Kristan.

Then there was the violent noise of a shot and he found he was shaking and desperately interested in staying alive. Life was sweet and beautiful on any terms.

They'd just shot one wretch in the skull and now a third guard was removing a grating some yards away. He then dragged the body to this hole in the courtyard. Many seconds passed before the splash. McQuade's mind was occupied with the minor problem: why shoot the wretch anyway? Did they believe he was strong enough to swim two miles and fight sharks on the way?

Another guard was literate and was reading a newspaper. He had put down his rifle to do so, but the half dozen prisoners here were too enfeebled to do anything.

McQuade watched through his fingers how the man came back from his task by the grating, applied his rifle to the base of the skull of the next victim, who whimpered. The guard turned his head to one side. He actually closed his eyes. He didn't like this part of his work! It was incredible! Nevertheless he squeezed his rifle trigger. Again the deafening bang. There were five more to be shot, including McQuade. He knew it wasn't a trick to frighten him into talking. In as many seconds as it took the guard to get around to him he would be killed.

He beseeched in frantic Portuguese, "I am a Canadian. I am chairman of a United Nations subcommittee—"

The one reading his paper looked up and laughed.

"It seems a very good reason to shoot you!"

He saw that they meant it. In seconds he would be dead.

"I know Colonel Domingues."

"Don't we all?"

"Phone him—Captain Bravo. Say I speak Portuguese as you hear now—"

"God!" said the one who'd shot the two prisoners. "How communicative he has become!"

"Look in your paper!" shouted McQuade frantically. "There is a United Nations diplomat missing. McQuade. A Canadian."

The ones who were about to die shuffled about, looked with sad, useless eyes at McQuade. Hurry up and complete the useless pleading. We are tired and afraid too. Don't delay death now that we are adjusted to it . . .

If there was nothing in the newspaper . . . If the guard refused to look . . .

But he did look and something was there.

"You want to make a statement?" he asked doubtfully.

"Yes."

"To Captain Bravo?"

"Yes."

"I will see if he wants to hear it."

This guard went away.

McQuade said in Portuguese, "What are your names? Tell me."

Only one was able to answer. He said "I am Armando Maúa." It was the last thing he ever said, for the guard steadied his boot on his throat as he handled the rifle. Again he looked away. The deafening shot, the trail of skin and blood, the splash. McQuade wept in shame.

Captain Bravo sat at his desk. He was embarrassed but coldly angry.

"You wish to make a statement to me?"

"I would like to try."

"So you are not a Frenchman? You are a liar? You speak Portuguese? And now you are near to death you want to tell me something?"

"I never claimed to be a Frenchman. I merely spoke in French."

"Talk quickly. Save your evasiveness for God."

McQuade told of the circumstances in which he had been travel-

287

ing and captured. He did not reveal the whereabouts of the *Movimento Anticolonialista* camp and was glad that he didn't in fact know it.

Captain Bravo said, "You had better drink some brandy."

McQuade did this, but at once passed out.

When he had recovered he was given coffee. He found he was as weak as jelly and trembling.

Captain Bravo said, "I am offering no apologies. I do not understand your intentions. Perhaps you wished to acquire prejudice. I accept that this is a place in which to do so. But I am at war. All of Portugal is at war and many of our enemies smile and are sophisticated and talk politely and go away to tell lies. It is none of my business what you do. But note this. I could have you killed here and now. It would spare Portugal the great embarrassment you are going to inflict on her. I shall not have it done. We only kill our enemies. The people who fight us here in Angolique spare none of us. They take no prisoners at all, or, if they do, God knows what happens to them before they are killed. So we are a little rough here in our determination. But only here. Do not believe these stories that every prison in Portugal and Angolique is a facsimile of a Gestapo camp. I would have neither questioned you nor had you hurt if I had known who you are. If you had been killed no one would have been aware of it, for we ourselves would not have known whom it was we had executed. You opted for this strange foolishness yourself. I cannot expect you to go away without prejudice and no doubt you will go away with hatred . . . I shall now telephone the Governor General for instructions. Perhaps he will apologize. I shall not. Meanwhile, whatever comforts we have are yours . . ."

Four hours after this McQuade was in the office of the Governor General. Colonel Domingues was startled at McQuade's appearance. He was nevertheless understandably cautious.

"We regret the mistake very much," he said, no doubt truthfully! "It was naturally considered that you were a spy or mercenary hostile to Portugal. I am told that your subcommittee did not wait for you but went to Geneva. Nevertheless, they were understandably anxious, with one man having been shot in vulgar circumstances and now their chairman disappearing." The colonel smiled very distantly. "I am told that they were divided in their opinions as to the rights of what you had done. We were surprised ourselves at such a prejudiced and foolish action. And we were worried for you, knowing these Leopoldville criminals as we do, although you had left our territory. I shall see to it that, as soon as you feel strong enough to leave, an aircraft will take you directly to Geneva. I am sure you will feel quite safe there to talk to the journalists who will, of course, be only too anxious to hear what you have to say."

"I do not wish to go to Geneva or talk to journalists, Colonel," said McQuade.

"You wish to go to New York?"

"I am going to Lisbon," announced McQuade.

After an hour and a half Dr. Pessanha sighed.

"We live in a sick world," he confessed. "And you look tired now, telling me about it."

McQuade liked the Minister for Overseas Boundaries, but he had not yet persuaded that gentleman to change his mind. Perhaps he did not really know *how* he could change it and Portugal's policy in Africa with it.

They had both been very frank indeed.

It was true that McQuade was tired. Talking soon exhausted him. Everything did. He was very weak and had an inclination to sit and stare at nothing.

But he persisted, "Did you know Mr. Brandão?"

Dr. Pessanha looked wary.

"I never met him."

"I did," said McQuade. "I talked to him ten days before he was pushed out of that aircraft."

"Oh, come, Mr. Minister. You believe the sensations of rumor and the press?"

"On this occasion, yes," affirmed McQuade briefly. "I knew what he was doing. He half expected arrest. What shame you should feel about him and Colonel Unguanda."

"I have done nothing to be ashamed of."

"I mean your apparatus of PIDE, that kills the well intentioned. These men were among Portugal's best—"

"You are not likely to favor our police or jails," pointed out Dr. Pessanha.

"He said a good thing, did Mr. Brandão."

289

"He also gave papers to illegal and hostile persons."

"He said that the problem of Angolique could be understood only by an understanding of Portugal."

Dr. Pessanha gave one of his courteous little seated bows.

"That is undoubtedly true, Mr. Minister."

"And it can only be solved in Lisbon," continued McQuade. "Not in Leopoldville, New York, Dar es Salaam, Salisbury, Capetown, Lagos, Addis Ababa, Conakry or London. Only Lisbon can solve it without violence and misery."

Dr. Pessanha disputed, "We cannot and will not walk out of Angolique because a lot of immoral journalists and African politicians decide that we must do so on the basis that *they* have decided what is right and wrong."

"That is not precisely what I had in mind," said McQuade. "You feel that most violence and unrest is instigated from places such as Leopoldville and Dar es Salaam?"

"I *know* it is," affirmed Dr. Pessanha. "And so do you now, Mr. Minister."

"I agree with you that some is," accepted McQuade. "Why are they fighting and killing coffee growers and old women?"

"Because they trade on fear and chaos, sir."

"They claim to be struggling for freedom, don't they?"

"What is your point, Mr. Minister?"

"If the *indigena* in Angolique who are not engaged in murder were given a measure of political power, these others would have nothing to fight about, would they?"

"It sounds like play with words, Mr. Minister."

"No, Excellency. I am a man who—within reason and without any authority—wishes you well. Do you seriously think you can end this struggle under the world limelight by a victory of arms? I mean on a long-term basis? You may and perhaps will achieve the victory of arms, but Africa and Europe are against you. So is the clock. Is it such a valuable territory? Will it retain such value as it has if the world boycotts it? Is the difference between provincial autonomy and what you had before the fighting—but won't recover —so great? Is it not a matter of dignity, prestige and face? If it is, *now* is the time for you to overcome yourselves and act generously, while the United Nations gives you the opportunity."

"The UN is detested in Lisbon, Mr. Minister, as you know."

"Then do these things that are necessary without the United Nations. I have not come here to be a hero of the time. I am not going to talk of what you did to me to obtain sympathy even for my organization. I just want a solution without burning villages or decapitating old women. Are you going to drag on this skirmishing and slaughter in jungle and on plantations and the misery of terror to achieve a victory on the statute books? Or to keep a few rich families in Portugal and foreign investors happy? Are these your motives or is it the belief in your national dignity, the humiliation of bowing to other opinions? The British, French, Belgians, Dutch and Italians have bowed, graciously or not. If there were provincial autonomy in Angolique would not the Portuguese still be in charge? Would not the economic and political and even the educational ties still be with Portugal? Do you think Ghana has the merchant shipping to do you out of business or Great Britain is going to muscle in with her export of automobiles? Consider this, too, Excellency. I went as a private individual to see Mr. Unger at the Baixange hospital. He was ill, his friend said, with burns—"

"Who is Mr. Unger? Is this really relevant?" protested Dr. Pessanha.

"You must decide the degree of relevance," said McQuade. "My brain is still weak from the illness and unpleasantness. Mr. Frischauer said his friend Unger had burns. He had. They were severe radiation burns. I never saw him. He had died that morning. How do you get severe radiation burns in a copper mine? Unless, perhaps, you are fooling about with uranium. Still, it is a matter that could be cleared up by inspection of factories and ships. Naturally, I must consider whether to report such a triviality or even mention it to my colleagues—"

"Are you saying, Mr. Minister, that Mettallic Angolique is exporting uranium to West Germany?"

"I did not say a word about Mettallic Angolique," pointed out McQuade. "Or West Germany. I am very tired, you understand, and may be suffering from hallucinations after my experiences . . ."

Dr. Pessanha smiled very faintly and with respect. He considered these matters.

"There is our friendship with Rhodesia and South Africa to consider," he said.

"Quite," agreed McQuade.

Dr. Pessanha protested, but a little weaker, "If we granted some autonomy, there are ten parties, all of which would want the central power, and they would quarrel and murder and there would be the chaos and bloodbath that took place in the Congo."

"Not if the Portuguese were still in charge and it was a provincial autonomy."

"But they'd soon say it was a fraud—mere attendance at meetings. They'd claim they didn't have any real power. And by infiltration it would merely become that much easier to have the revolution, to let in the armies from across these other borders."

"Not if you said there would be a referendum in a few years."

"For a Canadian," said Dr. Pessanha, "you have become a pretty shrewd African! Go to Geneva, Mr. McQuade. Join your friends. Make your recovery and your report. But don't damn us too hard and don't complete it for a while. I can promise nothing and these things cannot be hurried. But I will talk to others and one in particular and see if anything can be set in motion. Stay in Geneva for three or four days, will you? And read the newspapers."

McQuade smiled cautiously.

"I will be very quiet," he promised, "and do just that."

He was hopeful.

The taxi sped down the Rue de la Servette in the rain and zigzagged its way through to the hotel in the Quai des Berques. McQuade was tired but exhilarated. At last he was in a free country—in this cuckoo-clock land of mountains and clean towns. Geneva was not as crowded as in summer, but nevertheless the streets were filled with lunchtime strollers. Many of these who walked so lightheartedly would be UN diplomats, translators, secretaries and stenographers, for in this city, in the parks to the northwest, was the European headquarters of the organization, with, behind it, the peaceful slopes of Collonge and Versoix.

It was a very fashionable hotel in the American style, with coffee bars and dance floor and on the fifth floor a restaurant with fountains. As the elevator took McQuade and his new case up to the seventh floor he saw through the glass panels of the fifth floor the members of his subcommittee. He realized that it was a reflection in a huge mirror that he observed and he, too, felt as unreal as a ghost. He was a man back from the dead. And he realized from the mirror how untouched they were by their experiences. For they were laughing. He had not returned yet to the condition of being capable of laughter. The blurred reflection of Barney's wide mouth and good teeth and de la Plaza's uproarious profile touched an edge of irritation, and he felt the urge of the sick and wounded man to snarl. Had they so soon forgotten the mud and the vultures and the napalm and the depressing cool *cassimbo?* Could they eat rich food with appetite undiminished by memory of the limbs strewn among the apple trees and the refugees, shaking with terror and gashed with the marks of steel? He was too upset for a while to go down the two floors to meet them, although, absurdly, in the taxi his heart had been accelerating with the pleasurable anticipation of surprising them.

As he finally walked into the restaurant—the smell of food from somewhere making him queasy and even slightly faint—some of them evidently saw him in that same long mirror. Asare Johnson came rushing through crowded tables, bumping waitresses with trays, in the haste to greet him.

A cable had been sent to tell them that he was safe, but they stared at him now, some standing, some still seated, curious to see what he looked like. What had happened to him? Had he suffered? What had he seen? Why had he flown to Lisbon? And they were all a little ashamed because they had been so ready to believe him dead and fly here to the safety and comfort of Geneva. They'd agreed on the signal that had been sent to New York and this had excused *them* from any participation and pointed out hastily that their chairman had taken his decision in spite of their disapproval . . .

"Sit down," urged Ekelund. "Have some brandy. My God, you look exhausted. You have lost a lot of weight."

"I collected some illness," said McQuade. "Just as well, too, for I happened to be in the bush when Rossio and the driver were shot."

293

"In which territory?" asked de la Plaza. "There are rumors that it was in the Congo."

"I'm not sure," said McQuade uneasily. "I am certainly very tired."

"Did they harm you?"

"They certainly asked a lot of questions. They believed I was a French mercenary."

"But did you not tell them who you were?" asked Ekelund. "You are the only one of us who speaks Portuguese. I would have thought—"

McQuade had not expected cross-examination.

"There was a misunderstanding."

Ribowski, putting down a glass of milk, said ominously, "You talk like a man who has been brainwashed."

There were protests from the others. "He is tired. Do not bother him with questions" . . . "Do not be so stupid and rude."

But Ribowski persisted. "You have been beaten. I can see that. It has happened to me in my time. What are you afraid of in Geneva?"

McQuade flushed angrily.

"If I am afraid of anything it is prejudice," he told Ribowski. "I am therefore saying nothing until this report is written. How far have we got?"

Ekelund protested, "This is a little odd—"

But de la Plaza answered the question. "It is completed. We are all agreed and when you see—"

Ribowski now interrupted, "I can see that you have learned to love the Portuguese, Mr. Chairman. I expected better from one whose country was under the colonial yoke for centuries."

This caused some outright laughter of contempt, which aggravated Ribowski's point of view, for he sensed that they were all hostile. "And these others are sheep who talk of what they call 'fairness' as if we play a game, but it is what I believe to be cowardly hypocrisy to please the State Department."

There were protests. People looked around from other tables and a waitress who had been approaching turned away.

De la Plaza questioned angrily—he had had to do most of the physical work of writing the report—"Then why the hell didn't you say so? You were consulted at every stage of the business."

294

Ribowski said, quite calmly, as if he had maneuvered into a position intended and only courteous departure was now necessary to those of the previous position, "I cannot and will not go along with this report. It is too meek. It is unbearable, all this slaughter and filth. Has not the world and Africa had enough of it? And we only saw a thousandth part of Angolique. The Portuguese must concede something. It is monstrous and insulting that they should feel any doubt about it. They must be thrown out. I regret, Mr. Chairman, that I cannot continue, even in this final stage, to be a member of this subcommittee. I must ask you to accept my resignation so that the world can see that I and my country are not identified with this swindle."

"I think they will give some ground now that I have talked to them," said McQuade.

He regretted the words instantly.

"You?" sneered Ribowski. "What have you got that is so special?"

"Do you speak for yourself when you so bravely offer your resignation?" asked McQuade, stung to angry logic. "Or are you also a sheep who has had instructions from his government to resign?"

Ribowski flushed. "That is my business."

"Don't these instructions seem dishonest in view of what we experienced? As Gregorio just said, you've been consulted all along. I will consult you later when I have read the report. What else do you require?"

"I am the servant of my country, its delegate."

"I realize your position and have some sympathy," said McQuade. "But will you do me a personal favor?"

"That remains to be seen."

"I will accept your resignation in four days' time if you still wish to offer it."

"That is a long time to wait."

"But will you do it?"

"Very well, Mr. McQuade. But as I asked before, what have you got that is so special?"

"I am not sure," said McQuade, "but I think it's called lack of prejudice."

"This is nonsense talk," protested Ekelund. "We are all free from prejudice. That is our job."

295

"Mr. McQuade," asked Asare Johnson. "What did you say to Dr. Pessanha?"

"That, too, will have to wait three days."

"But we leave for New York tomorrow," pointed out Marianne in disappointment.

"Now that I have resumed my duties as chairman," said McQuade, "I find it necessary for us to stay three more days."

"I wish that you would take us into your confidence as readily as you do the Portuguese," said de la Plaza with anger.

"What do you want to eat?" Ekelund asked, for the waitress had now returned.

"Nothing," said McQuade, and they all sat there uncomfortably until they could reasonably separate.

The reunion was very unpleasant and not as McQuade would have wished. But he was sure that each member of the subcommittee and the two stenographers would be shocked into more prejudice if he told them exactly what had happened to himself and what he had seen—Ribowski for political reasons, Asare Johnson at what was happening to Africans, de la Plaza and Ekelund in terms of humanity, and the girls in terms of sensation. All would be conditioned and would say so in loud and indignant voices. They would put these personal matters into the report, no doubt justifiably, and would talk with loathing of all things Portuguese around the corridors of the UN and embassies for the rest of their lives . . . Another man might have thought that his own pain, inflicted in this manner, was the most relevant and important factor encountered since he'd departed from New York, but not McQuade, although the temptation was very great, for he was hurt by their rage and could have enlisted their absolute sympathy in as many seconds as it took to utter the words. His experiences had been very unpleasant and would give him suffering and weakness for months yet. But if, via his silence, a result was possible unimpaired by shock and hatred, that would be the worthwhile reward.

And so for three days they hung around in an atmosphere of disbelief and mild dislike and minor embarrassments. There were long silences, and people walked out of the bar or office or, in the case of Ribowski, sat at a different table in the restaurant. There were stares of irritation from Marianne and no doubt sour remarks for other ears and whispered questioning in corridors and elevators. And all the time, for McQuade, there was a terrible but decreasing exhaustion. The agony in his foot was so great that he could not walk as far or as fast as they did, so sat around in parks or by the river and lake—and this was regarded as sullenness, for the group knew nothing of his pains. And, to add to increasing anxiety and a useless urge to sit near the telephone, a letter from Kristan, ten days old, said that she was lonely and was flying to Europe to see Peter. She might be within two hundred miles of McQuade right now, but he had no means of finding her. She had disappeared as completely as he had. By now she must have seen Peter and moved on to Paris as she said she intended. But there was no address in Paris to write to or indeed fly to. Since writing her letter Kristan must have heard of her husband's disappearance and also—for it had been in the papers—of his safe return. Yet cables across the Atlantic were unanswered and she did not arrive in Geneva although he expected her and longed for her to come. Once he rushed across the street, dodging trams and taxis, to a woman who looked like her, and was very nearly involved in a row with policemen. The physical activity of this short dash caused his foot to give him agony, but it was the disappointment that caused him to hide his face in the effort not to weep.

These days, which ought to have been full of relief and personal happiness, were very frustrating. He was sought out several times a day, elbowed into privacy in bars or bedrooms, and beseeched, "Shaun, do be reasonable. Can't we finalize the report and get the afternoon plane? What is it we're waiting for?" And the answer, more and more difficult to believe in himself—perhaps he had misread Dr. Pessanha's implications—"No. We must wait" . . . "But we are doing nothing" . . . "Is that not pleasant for you?" . . . "It is ridiculous and the signals from New York increasingly say so."

Finally, when on the morning of the fourth day there was no signal from Portugal, no relevant headlines in the morning's newspapers of any nationality, he knew that Dr. Pessanha had failed to persuade others. It wasn't a bad report they were taking back, but it wouldn't alter the world. It would be just another UN report, words, words, words, and like the endless articles by journalists

297

would be read and only blood pressures would be affected. It would be ignored by those who wanted to ignore it, regarded as truth by those interested in the truth but equally impotent to alter it, and as prejudice by those who were committed to other prejudices. For a foolish few days he had believed that he, a Canadian delegate, could alter the world, succeed where others had failed and often failed because of prejudice. He had thought he could spare the thousands of innocents who were inevitably and always the victims in wars and uprisings, spare them what would now come because the world insisted on a violent solution. It was the way the world functioned: it only learned in pain . . .

They were standing with suitcases in the lobby of the hotel, waiting for the doorman to find a taxi to take them all to the airport, and waiting, too, for Asare and Barney, the only two who had enjoyed these final few days. McQuade felt too weak to stand.

Then he saw Asare and Barney coming in a hurry out of the bar fifty feet away, and Asare was pulling her by the hand. Both were very excited. McQuade was touched and again he felt that foolish urge to weep. In the end it is not the great principles and the resolutions but love in the human heart that makes anything at all bearable. The peasant women hacked to death after the many abuses of their bodies in the orchard and the big house had stayed by those they loved and had died with them. The peasants working in the fields could bear it better than the intellectuals thousands of miles away with hatred in their hearts, so angry on their behalf, so ready with indignation. It had been possible to bear the pains of the water torture and *palmatoria* because, a long way off, Kristan waited and he was loved. Seven or eight hours from now she might be there . . .

Asare threw his arms around McQuade's neck, nearly knocking him over. It was a gesture of love, not to be restrained by the porters and old women standing with disapproval by the elevators.

"Mr. Chairman," he cried, full of laughter. "What did you say to those Portuguese?"

McQuade's heart thumped about excitedly. He felt faint and weak, but good—oh—he felt good all of a sudden.

"Oh, I just said they were rather wicked in the old colonial style."

298

"You said it very persuasively," Asare told him. "The midday newspapers say—" But he was too full of emotion to speak. Barney said it for him, "They're going to allow nine members into the Angolique provincial legislation. They're going to grant an amnesty for political prisoners. They promise no victimization of those who return to the territory. There's going to be independent provincial autonomy in two years and a referendum in five . . ."

Asare gave a great shout of joy and embraced McQuade harder. "Mr. McQuade, you're a *real* white man!"

McQuade still felt this foolish, feminine, emotional nonpolitical urge to weep. It was silly how a little pain and tiredness and sympathy made you as weak as jelly. How absurd to be drunk on words!

"You're not so bad yourself," he asserted, "for a big black cannibal. Show me this nonsense they've put in the midday papers."

Asare was still rolling about, drunk on joy. For him it was that much more real. It wasn't just a theoretical problem, part of work, a charitable exercise in how to love the black man, an interesting tour overseas in pursuit of evidence. For Asare the African was the real man and it was his duty in New York that formed the tour overseas, the unreality in which to work . . .

Ekelund and de la Plaza insisted on shaking McQuade's hand, too, and the two girls kissed him, Marianne whispering in his ear, "I'm sorry I was a bit of a lemon. I really don't mind if you squeeze me!"

"This is absurd," protested McQuade, too late. "What am I supposed to have done?"

"We don't know," said Ekelund. "It's your secret. But you did it very effectively."

Even Ribowski smiled, joining the group.

"Mr. Chairman, I'm glad I didn't go away. I might even, despite my stomach disturbances, attend a party if we should postpone our departure half a day longer for that purpose!"

Asare grabbed Barney by the hand, went through a private dance, and continued the pleasure of the day. "What a lot we have to celebrate! Tell them all the other news, this trivial social nonsense." And when Barney blushed and remained silent he cried, "We're going to be married!"

Barney said through her teeth, "Who says so?"

299

"I say so! Didn't you agree it was a good idea?"

"I said it wasn't a *bad* idea!"

"Then let us put it to the vote," insisted Asare, bubbling with confidence.

Everyone laughed and there were cries of "Resolution adopted!"

"If there is a party," said McQuade, "I shall give a toast to Miss Barney Widener, who on this journey has withstood more than the rest of us, but finally succumbed!"

They canceled the taxi and stood in the bar offering toasts. Mc-Quade looked out of the window at the bridges along the quai and across the Rhone to the statue surrounded by tall poplars on Rousseau Island. In the lake, farther away, the Jet d'Eau had been turned on and the water spurted in a high column. The rain had ended and there was superb clarity so that he thought he could see Mont Blanc in the distance. It is done, he thought, duty is completed. For a while, until the next time, I can experience joy . . .

He was the man who perhaps had been the one who had finally influenced the Portuguese to surrender to the pressure of years. But he had his sorrow and misgivings, for all that. There was no political problem in the world that could be solved without hurting someone or creating a secondary problem. The UNO delegates and Secretariat officials would be elated, for it constituted a triumph for the organization even though the Portuguese statements made no mention whatsoever of UNO. The intellectual journalists would write gleefully of how Portugal had heeded *their* wisdom. The Chinese advisers and strange collection of armies in Tanzania and elsewhere would have to go away, and the nationalists in exile there and in Leopoldville would now begin to experience the tiresome frustrations of the responsibilities allowed and achieved in place of the excitements and chaos of war and expectation. But in overcrowded Portugal, with its poverty and stony soil, the peasants wouldn't even have the possibility of going to Angolique to find land to sweat on. They'd have to suffer. And no one was going to offer loans to European Portugal, because it would not be fashionable to do so even if her pride had allowed her to ask for help.

Despite her secret police and political limitations Portugal was a country—one of the last—with conceptions of dignity, bravery, honor and hard work on the soil. It was a beautiful country, a powerful plea from the past against the vulgarity of the machine,

300

money, the world that had taken "freedom" too far, so that there was nothing to believe in . . . The *barcos rabelos* sailing silently down the rivers lined with terraces of vine, and the oxen pulling carts loaded with the great wine barrels: these had the dignity of a longed-for past. The sandy crescents of small fishing villages: bright small houses and nets spread out to dry. Yokes of oxen still sometimes used to haul the colorful boats up the shore, the women in felt hats and wrapped in long black shawls, the fishermen dressed in plaids, all chanting in the great silences of the *praia*, unbroken except by the surf and themselves . . . The vines ripened in the schistose soil of the Douro's upper valley. The peasants swarmed over the green fields and gray rocks of these vast amphitheaters of terraces and in the stifling motionless heat of vintage-time carried the wicker baskets to the proprietor's *quinta*. And when the vats were full the vintagers trampled barefoot on the piles of grapes, gripping each other around the waist and dancing to a slow rhythm while the cold juice oozed between their feet. And later, when the liquid had been fortified by brandy, the ox-drawn basket carts took it to the coast and the warehouses and the senseless agitated world that knew better . . .

A country of better days, always hard, fierce, full of faith. The Romanesque doorways and the decorative motifs of the medieval tombs. The Manueline architecture that made buildings look like sculpture, slender and vertical in contrast with the heaviness of Spain. The fountains in the squares of mosaics and the old women and children in black moving in the crippling heat toward some cathedral. Belfries, palaces, gardens, the pilgrims climbing stone steps in the stunning warmth with the scent of riotous flowers heavy as the day. No African had ever conceived anything as superbly beautiful and complicated as the retable of the high altar of Coimbra cathedral. Nor, McQuade realized, had any Canadian or North American . . .

The storks flapped by over the painted sails of the fishing boats on the river. Portuguese girls bent their backs in the ricefields and black pigs wandered in the fields not far from Lisbon. But the world was not interested. It was too frightened. For it was the age of the giants. It was the era of nothing or "everything." All men were free, or none . . .

During the next twenty-four hours shares in Mettallic Angolique dropped 25 per cent in value. Less noticeable, shares in forty-two associated companies, many larger than the African one and none of them in Portugal, dropped between 15 per cent and 4 per cent. The financial pulse of the world evidently still had doubts about Angolique and the black man.

14 ▪ ▪

THEY ARGUED ABOUT IT for days. It was something to talk about. Bill pleaded with the angry persuasion of desire and the wish to continue what had gone before, the inability to admit any reasons against the idea (for him a necessity in any case). Kristan scratched around among logic and morality and there obtained many good excuses to cover the truth, which was fright. It was the enormity of traveling to Europe with him, thus committing herself absolutely if any one person in the world recognized them, which terrified her.

But it was not logical to argue that love-making and dining out in the New York area were less likely to be noticed, so in the end they compromised. She refused to travel except with her own money, the ramifications of guilt admitting that if she allowed Bill to pay hundreds of dollars she was truly compromised, had been bought. She finally found a legitimate excuse, exciting and, it seemed to her, so reasonable that she could even write to Shaun about it. She would visit Peter, who was at a Royal Canadian Air Force airfield in France near the German border. She conceded financial help from Bill from that point on—for he was proposing to take her to Rome, which he had to visit briefly. He would stay out of the way in the hotel in Metz, the city nearest to Peter's airfield.

They flew over the Atlantic at night. The Boeing was packed and hot and strewn with blankets and people's jackets and empty cigarette cartons. The rear half was full of American troops, who stared at her and grinned. The soldiers played cards and then, after eating, slouched down to sleep. Kristan was too scared to sleep. She hadn't flown the Atlantic before. When Shaun had been at the

302

Embassy in Paris, they'd traveled from Canada, and returned to it, by ship. The night flight was Bill's idea, so that he could plunge straight into work—an interview, she gathered—an hour or two after his arrival in London. Then they'd be free to enjoy London for a day or so before flying on to Paris. Now Bill snored by her side, the sweat gleaming on his face in the faint light. Kristan was sure she was the only person either scared or awake out of the hundred and fifty, but when the Boeing ran into clear-air turbulence and shook itself and the illuminated "Fasten your seat belts" sign came on, the click-click-click of scores of belts sounded like someone shuffling cards. Proving what? She smiled and confidence rose.

The predawn came over Ireland, with thick cloud far below the Boeing. Over southwest England the light came and shone on rivers, an estuary and small towns. It was such a small country that the Boeing was losing height all the way across to land at London. Now, over the countryside, was pure white gas lying about like cream poured over porridge. It was beautiful, but a stewardess talked solemnly of problems ahead. Ten minutes later they came screeching down to the dirty mist and thousands of lights and apparent chaos. The unexpected roar of the engines power-braking scared Kristan, but all of a sudden they were there. It was some crazy hour like 8 A.M. in England. They walked the glass corridors and went through the customs, and outside the London airport was the confusion of rush-hour traffic, the tiny vehicles being driven by lunatics.

Fifteen miles in a taxi—it cost Bill a fortune—through miles of ugliness and this terrifying traffic that seemed so dangerous compared to New York's—tiny frail cars that were used on the road as if it was a race track—and they came into the sort of London she had expected to see. It was small compared to Manhattan, but the variety of buildings fascinated her.

The hotel was unimpressive outside. In fact she didn't even notice it. But inside was an old-fashioned lobby, large, full of people shouting and laughing and throwing confetti. The porters on duty leaned against the wall and watched this tail-end of a wedding party with amusement.

Kristan followed Bill up a few steps to a lobby where, behind a

303

glass partition, three girls were already doing clerical work. They were smart young women with that appearance of sophistication on their faces, the special knowledge of humans acquired from hotels. One talked with what seemed like arrogance into a telephone. Nevertheless, they themselves exuded an atmosphere of extreme respectability as well as the cynical awareness, and Kristan turned away, feeling that they could identify her. A high-class tart? A silly Canadian woman with an equally silly American oilman? Kristan didn't know, but all three girls had that English attitude of amused superiority and it made her uncomfortable.

Bill was saying, "One room. Two nights, I think."

"You're American?"

"I am."

"Can I have your passports?"

Kristan stood there, scarlet.

Bill said dully, but without embarrassment, "Oh, sure. I see what you mean. It's not as bad as it looks, miss. We were married two days ago. My wife still has her Canadian passport."

"Not to worry," said the girl with a very tiny smile.

They were given a bedroom on the fifth floor. It had an old-fashioned stale smell and appearance. Net curtains. A view of pipes and chimney pots. A slightly seedy room with a cheap chest of drawers and lampshade. Across the corridor was the strangest old bathroom with a vast lavatory on a kind of throne, its seat of old wood and the china cracked. In the bedroom the paint was a prison green and it was flaking. The wash basin, like the lavatory, was old. "Royalty slept here," Bill said. *"When?"* asked Kristan. For some unknown reason there was a window, or flap, open on an *inside* wall of the room, and Kristan, dazed with travel and strangeness and guilt, heard the pling of a telephone being lifted, and a boy's very English voice saying all too clearly in the next room, "Hello . . . Rodney here . . . How are you? Mummy and Daddy have gone down to breakfast. They'll be *ages* . . ." A dog began barking right outside the bedroom door.

Rain began to beat on the window. Jets screamed overhead on this west side of London, and the boy was trying someone else, with even more enthusiasm: "Hello, *darling* . . . Rodney here . . . I say, you are with it today . . . Not a terribly good party

304

. . ." And a quick knock on their door and a Spanish girl's face and explanation, "I come back later."

"Liberty hall," Bill commented. He shut the corridor flap.

"I feel a bit sick," Kristan admitted.

Bill was the sort of person she could say this to. He didn't insist that life was pure enjoyment, love a sort of drunkenness without any hangover. It was still possible to be scared or ill . . .

She was in fact overcome by guilt and uneasiness. She was downright nervous, too tired to go out and face the day but too self-conscious to stay alone in the hotel while Bill did. So she dumped the problem in his lap.

"Do you mind if I make a few phone calls?" he asked. "You take it easy for an hour or so."

"Sure," she said, and smiled gently at his care.

She watched him in his shirt sleeves, stained under the arms from the heat of travel, waving a hand about and nodding his emphasis when he agreed with some arrangement on the phone. She felt warmed and tearful because he cared. How beautiful that he should care. For at forty-three, she knew life, she was sure; she was aware with cold certainty that no one cared. Other people were not interested. They would talk to her if she happened to be present, write to her if she wrote first, would listen to her providing they did not have to alter their lives or opinions except in terms of their own pleasure. But that was fundamentally the limit. She was only as important as a hairdressing appointment, a canceled ticket, an arrangement of guests. That was all. Her death would be fascinating for a day or two, a shock tingling with the interest of a problem: why? what now? It was a brutal truth to face—the slow deterioration of beauty was proportionate to the amount of love and care offered. But Shaun cared, she knew in shame, for the very weaknesses of bones and flesh. He had pity in his love.

And now, these last few weeks, Bill, attentive, amusing, tolerant, fascinated . . . He cared passionately, without pity. It was, she felt, ridiculous, but equally it was too tempting. She couldn't bear to throw him away, plead safety and the rules; you can't care. It had been easier to say (or think), You can care a little but don't admit it. People would—if they ever found out (and two of the three American friends already had)—condemn her, say with a snigger or with scorn, "Doing *that* while her husband is in Africa risking his life in idealistic purpose." But while the affair existed she did not care much about what they said or thought so long as they said it somewhere else . . .

Nevertheless, it was a bad day. Other people existed.

They went out in the middle of the morning.

"Like to try a London double-decker bus?" Bill asked as they stood in Knightsbridge.

This seemed an amusing idea, and they had time to spare before Bill's appointment.

The bus was fairly empty. It took them through parts of London which Kristan recognized from photographs and books.

Bill wasn't quite sure where to get off and stood up rather suddenly, saying, "We've just passed it. Come on!"

They moved toward the platform of the bus behind two youths who themselves were nudging an old lady forward. What occurred then happened so very quickly that Kristan was never quite able to examine it in her mind without doubt. The conductor of the bus began to come down the steps from the upper deck. Kristan remembered the sound of his boots later. The two youths evidently hadn't paid their fares and now they laughed, elbowed the old lady out of the way and leaped off the bus, which was still moving at perhaps fifteen miles an hour. They ran for a hundred yards before slowing in contempt and indifference and despite cries from the bus. The old woman lost her balance and fell from the bus, but in the convulsions of her hands caught the lower end of the rail. She was dragged for some yards before the bus stopped.

There were cries of protest from passengers.

"It was those two louts."

Some passengers were now standing on the pavement and pointing down a fairly empty pavement to the two long-haired leather-coated youths who turned, laughed and ran out of sight around the next corner.

Kristan helped the old lady to her feet. Her knees had trickles of blood. She was small and light and with a gentle face. Not strong, was what leaped into the mind at once.

Kristan asked, "Are you all right?"

"Oh, yes, I'm all right."

The old lady lit a cigarette, commented with remarkable impar-

306

tiality, "It is the strong, you see. They are not interested in the weak."

Shock hadn't reached her yet.

"Shall I get you a taxi?"

"Me? A taxi?" The old woman laughed, "I haven't been in one since my husband's funeral!"

The bus conductor asked, "You okay, ma'am?" and then she said, "Sure I'm okay; this is society, yes? To get knocked down. Is it not so? It is the strong. We are weak. It is the day of the hooligan."

The conductor said, in a hurry not to become involved, "You said it, lady," and rang his bell.

The bus began to pulsate with the increased impatient engine noise—the driver was, like his conductor, more concerned about timetables than hooliganism. The passengers on the pavement climbed back into the bus with haste, as if it were a game and one of the rules of the game was that you gave what sympathy you could, but only if the circumstances gave you no excuse to avoid doing so; if they did you took the excuse.

This game seemed to be accepted by the old lady, too, for she made no protest.

Bill said, "Come on, honey. It's nearly eleven o'clock."

Kristan could not have been more surprised if he had knocked her down. All her anger and frustration was instantly switched to Bill. He was walking away and she followed, hot with complaint.

Bill was conscious of her anger. After a while he said, "There was no point in getting involved. You can't be a witness in a court if the two accused haven't turned up."

"Very logical," she said with fury.

They separated while Bill went to his appointment. Kristan walked about and looked in shops and smoldered with anger.

It hung between them at lunch, through an afternoon on a river ship and in the taxi back to their hotel. She answered his questions, made comment at times because it was irresistible not to, but was acutely conscious all the while of this thing that was now between them and had to be settled.

In the dreary hotel bedroom Bill asked, "Where shall we go after dinner?"

"Nowhere."

307

Silence. She could see now that he was struggling with irritation. Then he said, "It was that old lady, wasn't it?"

"It's *nothing*. I happen to be tired after a night in a plane and a day walking around."

"Oh, Kristan, don't be stupid."

"I certainly didn't like it."

"What did you expect me to do?"

"Nothing. It's just your attitude."

"You want a little hypocrisy or sympathy for the old fool so you can feel you're still clean?"

"Shaun would have at least *said* something."

"Oh, sure. Shaun's a great committee man."

"That's not a very smart thing to say."

"You asked her if she was okay and she said she was. She lit a cigarette and her hand didn't even shake."

"Okay. So I'm not to be bothered if old ladies get knocked off buses. It's society, like she said. Normal. I look forward to my old age with people like you around to protect me."

"Oh, Christ, honey, stop making a big deal of it."

In the next room the telephone plinged as it was lifted and the boy's voice said almost at once, "Hello, Patricia . . . Rodney here . . . I thought so, too, but you know Colin . . ."

Bill whispered, "Come on. Time for dinner."

Kristan snapped, "Do you think I feel like sitting around *eating?*"

"Oh, to hell with it. I'm going to," Bill told her, angrily, and went off to do so.

She was too tired to move, go away, show independence or unconcern. All she wanted was an admission of humanity.

It came at one in the morning: "I'm sorry, Kristan. It was all a bit too quick for me. That's about it."

She unwound the anxiety that had frozen her all day, the fear of him being pitiless and complained now, but tenderly, "You fool of a man! Why didn't you say that in the first place?"

In Paris it was better, and it was not until the day they moved on to Metz by train that uneasiness and conscience began to take away her appetite again; but this was only in terms of being "found out"

308

by her son, Peter. There was little shame now in her actual frailty. Rather, she clung to it as one who knew the world would take it away. This was illogical, her mind told her, for the world delighted in lovers. It was impossible to see a film or read a novel in which the lovers were regarded as the guilty in the theme. Always it was normality that was mocked or despised, the cuckolded husband or wife who was the fool or the detestable character, and the ramifications of infidelity were examined with loving care, as if they were the parts of a new faith. But the experience, Kristan now found, was not like that. It was loaded with its own failures and the shame of betrayal. She could not so lightly throw off the feeling of guilt, even of impending punishment. This put her on the defensive and caused her to cling to her infidelity, to justify it in her mind, to intensify the various aspects of it . . . And much of the emotion was genuine enough, the feeling of love real, so that she outstared the French clerks and old women who were examining her, the foreigner, with what she felt to be more than acceptable frankness.

Bill was reading a British newspaper, but he stopped very abruptly and whispered, "Come into the corridor."

Kristan followed him and leaned against the dirty wood, stared outside at the dull countryside, with its touches of industrialization that made it dead.

Bill said, "They're worried about Shaun."

She was startled. "Who are?"

He showed her the tiny item. "Anxiety Over Missing UNO Delegate . . . subcommittee which had been visiting Angolique and was now . . . Had gone to visit the HQ of the rebel nationalist group called the *Movimento Anticolonialista Angolique,* the exact whereabouts of which was not known . . . Overdue by twenty-four hours . . . Mr. McQuade, a Canadian, aged forty-seven . . ."

Kristan swayed with the train as it took a long curve. She was terrified, swamped by the news so that she wanted to surrender to somebody, give up. God was angry with her, would show her that it was evil to enjoy this sordid love. She fought down this absurd but powerful sensation and was merely frightened. Then she felt the sullen anger of the guilty: Why don't they leave us alone?

"What do you think?" she asked.

309

"They don't watch the clock like we do."

"You mean he's probably all right?"

"Almost certainly."

"You're not trying to comfort me?"

"No."

"It takes the edge off things, doesn't it?"

"Yes," Bill agreed. "It makes you feel they can prove you're doing something lousy."

"Do you think we are?"

"Not in itself."

"But in relation to others?"

"If you love someone it's bound to be at the expense of others."

"Sounds logical, but I feel terrible. What do I do?"

"We read tomorrow's papers."

"God, I hope he's safe."

Bill looked at her and said nothing.

The hotel in Metz was far dirtier than the one in London, but Kristan didn't even notice. They took separate bedrooms because of the possibility of Peter coming to the hotel. The clerk stared at her just as suspiciously as if they'd asked for a double room.

After an hour she telephoned the airfield. She was glad of the remoteness of the telephone. They found Peter after a while. His calm young voice came along the wire. No, he had no further news of his father, but seemed optimistic. It was, after all, he told his mother, a political visit arranged by politicians. They were not exactly on the telephone out there . . . Kristan's spirits rose a little.

He was waiting for her by the cathedral two hours later, and with him was the girl he had written about.

Peter was as tall as his father, but had his mother's dark features. Friends said to her, "He looks like you," but she didn't believe it, had always disputed, "No, I think he looks like Shaun." This was because she wished him to do so. In nature and temperament he was quite different from both of them. His career in the difficult and (they thought) dangerous business of flying, his absorption in the RCAF, had removed him to a life in which they could not be involved. There was therefore a slight remoteness in the relationship. Every time Kristan saw her son she felt how serious he was, and how extraordinarily calm, considering the work he

310

did. She was conscious of the approach of middle age and the inferiority of the nontechnical person who feels inadequate in the presence of one who flies at 1600 m.p.h. and yet dismisses it as a mere job and is prepared instead to listen to small talk about Della O'Dowd or traffic jams.

Peter embraced her—a bit unusual, this—and said gently, "You look tired. Don't be upset. I'm sure we shall hear he's safe in a day or two." And then, stepping away and grinning, a bit sheepishly so that, very faintly, Kristan recognized the boy of twelve she'd been able to scold, to reprimand in terms of using more soap and eating rather less hastily, he introduced the girl.

"This is Yvette."

Kristan was disappointed. She acknowledged tiredness, alarm and, of course, the shame that Peter knew nothing about. But in her mind she had for weeks carried the impossible picture of a French girl, taken from *Vogue* and a distant memory of diplomatic parties ten years before . . . Yvette was neither tall, slender nor sophisticated, but a plump girl of medium height, with pale hair that wasn't fair enough to be remarkable, a round, absolutely untouched face. And she worked in a pharmacy. And she had projecting ears. Why do girls with bat ears, Kristan wondered in irritation, invariably fail to hide them? On the contrary, they always seemed to loop their hair behind these projections and show them off to the world as if these were ears to be examined with fascination!

Yvette said with a voice that struggled through the translation into English, "I am sorry that you have this anxiety about your husband. I do hope all will be better."

Kristan looked at her and thought, Oh, the fool—meaning Peter. To be able to fly jets and yet in all the world find only *this*. To take this girl seriously, to introduce her to me . . . Oh, that vacuous mouth and those cow eyes. A supple body, but too much flesh. Legs too short, no elegance. And dressed like a waitress going to a friend's wedding. My God! She's not even wearing gloves. And such big hands. She saw in her mind the fashionable women she met in Manhattan at the delegates' dinners and parties. Even the girls showing people around the UN buildings had a look of intelligence and poise. *This* was disastrous, for in Peter's letters there had been the unmistakable hints of reciprocal affection and plans. This

311

girl was just for breeding purposes. Of *course,* she concluded. He's such an innocent boy, so involved in the Air Force, and she's let him sleep with her and he's so overcome by it he thinks it's *love.* But she felt the hot beginnings of a flush, for she was estimating and criticizing from a moral position which she had jettisoned . . .

Peter took them to dinner. It was dreadful. The girl was serious and obviously had a kind nature, but she was so *dull.* Kristan could see in her mind the scorn in Della O'Dowd's eyes when *this* girl was introduced as Peter's fiancée or wife.

She was exhausted by the day and therefore unable to conceal disappointment when the girl had gone.

"Who is this Yvette?"

"Oh, she's a girl, as you saw. No more than that. Didn't you like her?" Peter asked.

"I mean who *is* she?"

Peter said lightly, but fully aware of his mother's opinion: "Like someone said, or should have said, a girl is a girl is a girl . . ."

"Don't be tiresome, Peter."

"You're not a snob, are you, Mother?"

"You mean there's something this girl doesn't have, but I must like her anyway?"

"Oh, I see," sighed Peter. "So you didn't like her?"

"I can see her attractions."

"You sound like somebody judging a beauty contest, but very reluctantly."

"Isn't that what it is? Isn't she just a face and figure?"

"What are you worrying about, Mother? What do you *want?*"

"She's a nice girl, but isn't she rather provincial for a jet pilot?"

"All right. So she's a simple, ordinary girl who happens to have several diplomas useless in society. She's not sophisticated. Nor are all jet pilots."

"It wouldn't do to take her seriously, Peter, that's all I'm saying. A friendship, yes. An exploration beyond friendship, if that's what's done these days. She has, hasn't she? She's allowed it?"

"She has *not!* Christ!" Peter protested. "What do you think I am? And she's a Catholic—"

"You're too important," Kristan claimed, but the words felt cold and meaningless on her tongue. The argument was remote, part of her defense against herself, her "proof" that she hadn't altered. She had just been disappointed in the girl, that was the truth. Yvette was pleasant enough, if she failed to be startling. "Too important to me."

"I might be important to her," Peter argued. "She's fairly simple on ideas like that and might not understand it if I said I was too important for her."

"Oh, you're going to be silly over it. I'm sorry, Peter. Let's go and have a drink and talk it over."

"I think we have talked it over," said Peter. "And I'm not allowed to drink because I'm flying operationally tomorrow. Will you still be here the day after?"

"No, Peter, I have to go back to Paris."

"I'll see if I can be taken off tomorrow."

"It doesn't matter. I'm sorry, too. But you don't have to prove anything to me. If you love the girl—"

"I do, as it happens."

"Then forgive me for being a snob and a fool," said Kristan, and burst into tears.

Kristan strolled alone by the Tiber, which seemed completely motionless today. Every now and again she looked at her wristwatch. The traffic roared by with Rome's everlasting rumble of tires, squeal of brakes and rasp of scooters that at times startled her. How beautiful this city was! Here, a few hundred yards away, were the aged stone arches of a bridge that crossed the river to Castel Sant' Angelo. She considered whether to cross, but distances were defeating and tiring her, and she would be in danger of wandering too far and getting lost. Therefore she stood watching the traffic crossing this perfect Ponte Sant' Angelo, insulting it with practicality. She stared to the horizon beyond the immense fort, to a skyline of modern buildings, square and forthright, but still intruders in the miles of stone, the sea of domes, the endless pale gray ancient walls. Under a grim wet sky of early spring and above the rumble of tires, bells began to acclaim something—God, the hour of day or of particular prayer, the uselessness of sin, the inevitability of death. Whatever it was, they were all aware of it: convents, churches, basilicas . . .

It was a rather oppressive day. Her mind had tired itself out and

313

she awaited events, no longer made decisions. She would see what happened and then decide—when it was too late. Nobody stared at her very hard. Perhaps, she thought in pessimistic analysis, I have resumed the dull posture of the defeated. For it was certainly as tedious as marriage, this love affair, and was attended by all the symptoms of collapse. Events were just not going to allow it to continue. She saw that bitterly.

She returned to promenading by the shops. A quarter of an hour later she stood outside the office building, in a stance which indicated miserably that she was waiting and was not interested in affecting to be doing anything else.

Bill came out of the building. He was hurrying and was no sooner beyond the glass doors than his head turned this way and that to see her. This caused her to feel weak with foolishness, for it meant that he was as dependent on her as she on him, and this was what she wanted.

"Are you all right?" he asked, taking her by the shoulders and looking into her face. "You've got that sad look again."

"You like that?"

"It attracted me, but I'd prefer you to look wicked, not morally disappointed!"

"I can do this?"

"You can look very wicked and splendid!"

"And how was Mr. Callaghan or whatever his name is?"

"Fine. He wanted to take me to lunch. But I said I had an attractive lady to meet."

"Was that wise?"

"Hell, Kristan, who cares?"

"No. I mean in regard to the job."

"That! I got the contract."

"What does that mean?"

Bill said, "Let's find an American newspaper."

She hurried by his side.

"Well, what does it mean?"

"A job in North Africa in a few months."

"What about the other job?"

"If I don't pick up my option—"

"I see."

314

She waited for him to say something else, but he didn't.

"North Africa sounds fine," she prompted.

"It is," he agreed. "The best part of Africa. Just like the Mediterranean countries, only cheaper."

They found a newspaper kiosk and stood near it skimming the big news for the one item. Unlike yesterday, which had given nothing, and the day before, when the news had still been that Shaun was long overdue and the main party of his subcommittee had flown to Geneva, today there was a small item to say that he was safe, had had talks with the Governor General of Angolique and had been taken at his own request not to Geneva but to Lisbon. This last meant nothing to Kristan.

She just stood there, exhausted and relieved, her conscience, irrelevantly, lighter.

"Thank God for that," Bill said.

Kristan said fiercely, while people walked by to lunch and rain began—rain had seemed to follow them on this journey—"I love you. You know what I mean? I love you."

"Sure I know. You mean you couldn't have done so if Shaun hadn't been safe."

"We haven't much time," Kristan said. "Or have we?" she asked, hoping for some answer that would at least go through the motions of saying "forever" or "As long as you wish." She urged in Bill's hesitation, "Let's be happy. This is a lovely city. We've had a miserable trip so far. How long have we got? Three or four days? Let's make it pretty important, Bill, in case they hate us too hard when we get back."

McQuade sat in the taxi as it took him from the East Side Airline Terminal. It was early morning in New York. He felt weak with excitement and sentiment. A pale blue, rather feeble-looking sky spread over Manhattan. The island was shrouded in tissues of smoke already, as if it was breathing badly. The watery sun climbing over Queens sparkled on the glass in the concrete stalagmites and on the sidewalks still wet from rain in the night. Through the open window of the taxi he could smell other people's breakfasts.

The taxi moved rapidly beyond the endless lines of parked cars —so clean and enormous in comparison with those on the streets

315

of Vila Lobanda and Lisbon. He remembered that morning when Father Jorge had joked about the mud on the Land Rover and the Fiat. There was not much traffic yet, but the traffic lights were slowing the taxi, and every second was frustrating, although she might not be there. But there'd be something—a message of love, the smell of her scents and clothes, letters, things he'd forgotten in a matter of weeks . . .

Then he saw her walking along 96th Street.

"Stop!" he shouted to the taxi driver, who skidded with the protest, "Jesus, friend, have a thought for my coronary." McQuade stepped out of the taxi laughing at the quick comment.

Kristan had hesitated, had turned to see why a vehicle should skid in an empty street. She now stood still, as if aware that this might be for her.

They ran to each other and embraced. Kristan said fiercely, "Oh, God, I was so scared."

McQuade laughed with sheer pleasure. "You were scared? I was *paralyzed!*"

He had carried her in his mind, but his mind had deceived him, overlaid the memory of his wife with other faces—Barney, Marianne, the French and Belgian ladies whose names he still didn't know, the vain pathetic Lilli with her superb but selfish face . . .

"Christ, how beautiful you look! I didn't realize—"

It seemed absurd and even insulting not to recall how beautiful one's wife was! "You've bought new clothes!" he said in good-humored accusation. "That's what the trick is! And you look so happy!"

She even walked in a new way, it seemed to him, with an exciting grace. He was in slight awe of her as if she were a new person he'd have to woo . . .

"What are you doing," he asked, "walking about at eight o'clock in the morning?"

She hesitated. "Didn't you get my letter? I've just come back from Paris and Metz."

"You mean you've just flown the Atlantic?"

"Yes. I was at 34,000 feet! Where were you?"

"Higher than that."

"It's a small world," Kristan said with slight anxiety. "And you didn't see me at the Airline Terminal?"

316

"I wasn't looking."

"You look awfully tired," Kristan told him with worry and a curious guilt, as if she ought to have shared the pain. "You're limping. Have you hurt your foot?"

"Where's your case?" McQuade asked suddenly. "You've left your case in the taxi."

"No," Kristan said. "They lost it. They say it'll turn up. Three other people lost their luggage, too. You think I care about a case this morning?"

"Tell me about Peter. Did you call and see the Soutters while you were in Paris?"

Kristan answered with a rush, "Yes, but they were away. I saw Margaret Barton."

"I don't remember her."

"I'm not sure you ever met her. Oh, Peter was fine. He calmed me down, said you'd be safe. This girl's called Yvette. I can just see her in Quebec. She's very nice and sensible."

"Get any photographs?"

"Well, no. I didn't bother to take my camera."

"You know something?" McQuade said with pleasure. "I feel hungry. That's something I haven't felt for a week or two."

"I'll look after you . . ."

Kristan was shy and evasive and delightful all day. He couldn't keep his eyes off her or bear to be in a different room, and he followed her about, touched her as if questioning the reality . . . He was brutally exhausted but eager to make love when night came. And she was still shy, passionate but difficult, and excitingly different: she did *not* turn the pink light on and had a new way of stroking his forehead. "So you really missed me?" he questioned in pleasure. Once in the night her feet rubbed against his damaged left foot and he cried out in agony. In the morning she insisted on seeing what was the matter with it. When he allowed her to look, she went as white as paper and wept hysterically. She ate no breakfast. "I can't take food after that," she said. "And you weren't going to say a word." She insisted on applying ointments and bandaging the foot with delicate care.

After a while she went out to do the shopping. "There's a lot to do," she said, "so you mustn't limp around with me. You stay in bed today."

317

But he couldn't do this and wandered about the apartment, picked up the newspapers with their headlines about himself, looked out of the window at the traffic.

At about ten o'clock the telephone rang.

Would he be the guest of honor at the AAAA dinner on June 7? The AAAA, explained the male voice in answer to McQuade's ignorance, was the Associated American-African-Asian Culture Group.

It depended, said McQuade.

Ten minutes later the instrument rang again.

Would he agree to write one of the seven articles in a symposium to be entitled Africa: the Politicians Speak? The fee would be around five hundred dollars for, say, six thousand words. The symposium would be under the direction of the well-known traveler and writer Clara G. Bueno.

McQuade said that he was very tired at the moment, had many duties to attend to, and was not sure that Clara G. Bueno was truly impartial. The voice disputed this along the miles of wire, tediously, if politely, until McQuade put down the instrument.

Five minutes later a TV studio rang. They wanted him for a discussion on sex throughout the world.

Two minutes after that a public-relations man offered his services, which, he felt, would be useful in order that McQuade might fully exploit his position.

The phone rang again. The voice seemed familiar and was eventually recalled from the night of the party the subcommittee had held before leaving for Lisbon and Angolique. "You have done a foolish thing, Mr. McQuade. Many thousands of shareholders will suffer, including Canadians in the Toronto area—"

McQuade replaced the phone on its cradle and decided to ignore it. But he couldn't really do this, for the Ambassador might call, or Kristan from some shop . . . A quarter of an hour passed and the thing rang again.

"Oh, shoot!" protested McQuade.

He was irritated and therefore caught completely off his guard.

It was an airline—not the Swiss one he had used to fly from Geneva, but the one which had brought Kristan west over the Atlantic. A girl's voice, calm and impartial, said, "We're pleased to tell you that Mrs. McQuade's baggage has been found."

318

"Good," said McQuade. "That was quick. Where was it? In the Atlantic?"

"It was put on the wrong plane from Rome," the girl's voice explained, "so it missed the connection in Paris."

McQuade, the delegate and diplomat, the husband and idealist, said unhesitatingly, "But Mrs. McQuade went to Paris, not Rome."

It meant nothing to him.

It was merely words.

Tickets. Words in the wrong arrangement.

"Well, no," disputed the other voice, equally concerned only with the truth of words on bits of paper. "Mrs. McQuade came back from Rome on Flight 9372 and the case was on Flight 9390. Do you want me to check that?"

"It doesn't matter," said McQuade, with the overwhelming knowledge that it mattered very much. "Is the case being sent on?"

"Yes. There are no customs problems."

How did it matter?

He sat and thought about it and the phone left him alone to do so. But he was too tired and too certain of Kristan to care—or, rather, to absorb any implications and suffer.

When she returned he opened his mouth several times to say, "Your luggage has been recovered," but couldn't do it. He preferred to let it go, not to know about it, whatever it was. Almost certainly she was scared of telling him that she'd spent a lot of money. She said not a word about Rome and wasn't too at ease talking about Paris.

Two days later he went to see Suzé. He went on his own, Kristan qualifying, "It's better if you talk about it alone. She won't want me around."

Suzé was still in the apartment seventeen floors up, overlooking the Hayden Planetarium and the park. The rooms seemed to be at a junction of the central heating, for they were unbearably hot. It was three o'clock in the afternoon and Suzé was drunk. Not frivolous or weak on her feet, but determinedly not sober: alcohol was her anesthetic. In a few weeks it had coarsened her face slightly. The place was untidy. A man does not normally notice that, and least of all if he's just back from the chaos of Angolique, but it was obvious, it proclaimed itself. Even the small child crawling on the floor wasn't quite getting the attention she required.

319

Suzé greeted him in a hard voice, "I guessed you'd come. Why didn't you do it over the phone like the others?"

"I thought you might prefer to see me."

"Sit down," invited Suzé. "You look a bit beaten up yourself." She walked about while McQuade couldn't resist seating himself; it still hurt to stand or walk.

Suzé said shrilly, "I haven't wept for him yet. He doesn't merit it. But the shame of it hurts. They all pretend he died on duty."

"He did die on duty."

"Oh, don't *bother*," she protested. "What's the matter? Are you scared of the truth? Or do you think I am? Or are you so dumb you don't know it?"

"I came to apologize—"

"Oh, Jesus Christ! *Apologize?*"

"I did make a promise."

"Who cares? You kept it, didn't you? You weren't there, were you, when he was shot with this hepped-up schoolkid?"

"Yes, I was there," said McQuade. "I'd just returned from the east, and there were many things to attend to despite the curfew and I sent . . ."

Suzé sat down by him, on the arm of his heavy chair. She put a hand on his shoulder and, to his concern and relief, he felt the warm spots of tears drop on his neck. "Shaun, it's true, isn't it? He died the way he lived—with a woman. In the middle of the night. He needn't have died."

McQuade persisted with the untruth calmly, for he saw that there was a possibility of her believing him. She *wanted* to believe what he said. "He was sent in the car by myself," he continued, willing to take the eventual hatred, the endless condemnation and questions. "There was a curfew. This kid he had in the car had run away from school. She was slightly crazy, the headmistress said—"

"Don't pretend to me," Suzé pleaded, hovering on belief. "Not you. They're all lousy. Theo never thought about how lonely I was. Certainly I have the kids and that takes care of Suzé! But what the hell can you do seventeen floors up? And they're all rotten. What am I talking about? People. The husband over the corridor, the political friend who wanted to take me out because I was lonely. So I go, I trust. And he wants to touch me. They have to get half

320

drunk and then try to kiss me here. A bit of fun, they say. Don't pretend to me, Shaun. You're an honest man." Suzé smiled grimly. "I can see you've been kicked by something harder than boots, too. Don't be too mad with her. She was scared. Not a nice feeling though, is it? How did you find out?"

His hands trembled and the great shock hit him in waves. His heart thumped so fast he had the feeling of faintness, the physical choked sensation of the water torture.

"Find out what?" he asked at last.

"Oh, sorry." Suzé giggled. "Take no notice. I'm drunk."

"What have I to find out?" he pleaded. "I want to know."

"So do I," Suzé claimed, "but you won't tell me."

"There's nothing to tell. Theo was cheeky and his charming self to our stenographers, but that was all."

"I haven't anything to tell you either," said Suzé.

She didn't need to.

All the implications of the baggage that had gone temporarily astray were there to understand if he wanted to. It was difficult because so hopelessly out of character with all previous knowledge of Kristan, and he didn't want to hear about it . . .

"Where will you go?"

"Back to Holland," said Suzé decisively. "You don't think any normal person wants or can afford to live in this city, do you? My kids belong to Holland, not this ridiculous organization. And the genever's cheaper in Amsterdam . . ."

He left her. When Kristan asked "How was Suzé?" he answered briefly, "Drunk."

It wasn't believable even now, but he could not quite hide his alarm, nor she her guilt. His duties began to claim him. But a week later he came home and found her note which told him "May be late back." And while he waited for her to come back, the beautiful face to look away, to blush at certain words, to hesitate, to worry when the telephone rang, he searched the house. He was looking for her bankbook. When he found it he could have wept with shame and relief, for the recent withdrawals indicated exactly the sort of money which she would have needed to fly to Paris and travel to Metz. He was ashamed of his suspicions; it was the pain and torture . . . But as he replaced the bankbook his fingernails

321

caught the edges of an envelope, buried under all sorts of odds and ends. And the letter inside was recent and was written to someone called "my dearest secretive one." It was signed "Bill." It could still have been a letter concerning other people, although he knew it was not. And in the three long paragraphs that proclaimed love were the damning words "these perfect days in Rome and Paris" and, far worse and hurtful, "You say he is a good man. I know he is, but a good man and an idealist cannot be a lover. There is no poetry for diplomats or absent husbands . . ."

McQuade sat on the edge of a bed and wept.

Part Two ▪ ▪

Far away,
For the last time,
I heard the scream,
The scream of terror
The voice of loneliness
Screaming for love.

1 ■ ■

IT WAS UNBEARABLE but had to be borne.

It was silent and not even acknowledged, but it existed and was killing both of them.

And in the end it exploded into admission, and, as is the wont with bad days, other things burst upon them and that day was shattering.

McQuade came home at six o'clock in an early summer evening, after an empty day, nothing had happened, the world was hushed, waiting for the next convulsion. He arrived full of love, unable to bear the silences and fears any longer. He would say, "I know all about it because of your suitcase that went astray and a letter I found. Tell me the truth and let us see if I can bear it." And he knew he would have to bear it and forgive, for when you don't want to lose something you are ready to surrender to almost any circumstance. He had always presumed that, in the theoretical possibility, quite impossible of existence, of unfaithfulness on the part of his wife, he would do physical, violent things to the man and to Kristan. But he found that his heart was full of misery and appeasement, and he did nothing, was afraid to speak of it, allow it to exist, lest by its existence it separated them. And small things gave him hope—her obvious mutual distress, the fact that she hadn't left him . . .

Thus, he came home willing to talk, to concede and forgive, to weep with her, to begin again. The brutal truth was also that his recovering body wanted her. He loved *her* and to hell with it, and he ascended in the elevator believing that there would now be a reconciliation in tears and physical passion. It wasn't the real Kristan who had betrayed him. She would have left if she felt love for this other person . . .

Having thus arranged things in his mind, he expected her to be there. She had been there, evasive and miserable, for the last fifty days. But today Kristan was not there. Instead he found a letter

325

which simply stated, "I have to go out. Will be back rather late. Love. K."

In his condition this was too much to stomach. He was very touchy these days, near to anger and loathing and self-pity. He was very much in danger of going sour and becoming a completely embittered man. The frustration now was hard to bear. It had to be channeled out in some manner, but could not be, so it was contained as rage. He fulminated. He kicked the waste-paper basket across the room. The bloody cow! Telling me of her appointment with this bastard!

There were some letters.

McQuade was still receiving some strange mail. Some of it was unanswerable. Some he passed on to the appropriate committee or organization to play with, in words. Here again, today, were some envelopes carried across the world to Mr. McQuade at the United Nations, the Canadian Mission and the Committee of Twenty-four, and some unusual stamps: Swaziland, England, Leopoldville . . . And the contents were stranger still: "A leader of Tando in Swaziland known as Mr. Henrique Assunção. He had a girl friend by the name of Miss Dias. There was a PIDE spy in the town who owned a taxi service, and he made friends with Assunção soon after he'd escaped from Angolique and took him to restaurants. On June 3 at 7 P.M. Mr. Bordalo, who was the PIDE spy, took my friend Mr. Assunção with him to translate when he 'went to see a witch doctor at Manzini.' A day later Mr. Bordalo gave Miss Dias a note in Portuguese saying that Henrique Assunção would be away for a few days. Bordalo was seen talking to the PIDE man Silva in an hotel. Assunção has not been seen again. Miss Dias knows Assunção has come to harm because he does not write Portuguese. *Question.* How could the vehicle used for this abduction have taken Assunção back to Angolique without British connivance? For there were two roadblocks to pass before it could get out of Swaziland. *Question.* In this connection it is pertinent to ask about the activities of British official Mr. Gannet . . ."

And sentences in others caught his attention: "A white South African Afrikaaner also visits Dar regularly, posing as a member of an antiapartheid organization, but recently we lost two members and we know now that this man is a security-police agent of the

South African Government . . ." "He was accused of trying to overthrow the Government at a time when he was in prison . . ." "Thrown from a six-story building by the mob . . ." "Can you tell me if any of them reached safety? As you know, the lake has half its waters touching South Africa and half Angolique, but in the middle is this narrow channel to Swaziland . . . I jumped and was able to get ashore because I had learned to swim on the beach at Lourenco Tomas, but some of the others . . ." "We got as far as the tree at Ibrahimo, which is the crossing point for refugees and members of the MAA, but were dispersed by firing. I saw Jesus Pinho shot here. Later we had to leave the women and children because of wild animals and the lack of food. We lived on berries and rats . . ." "Please see that drugs are sent to us. We are still doing our best, and our hearts are with these people, although our nurses have to sleep on the floor and we lost Doctor Artur . . ." "There are German squadrons in Portugal . . ." "Saw three trucks loaded with corpses . . ."

It scarcely touched him today.

Black bastards. They love it.

It was lies. Lies. Because there was no God or justice or love, so why should there be truth? They thrived on chaos. They loved it. To hell with them. Man was a fool, a raving lunatic. He wasn't an imitation of God because there was no God. If there was a God, He was an impotent fool and that canceled the proposition automatically. Man was a pig of an animal, an endless list of justifications he trotted out to prove he had a soul. The poor clown! It wasn't true. Man didn't have a soul. He just had a brain and a penis. There were rules about the use of both, and he ignored them. And woman? Woman was Eve. Woman was a whore, eating asparagus in a restaurant and admiring herself in the mirror across the room and wondering how much was in your wallet.

He laughed to himself in deep, angry, bitter amusement. Right, you whore. If that's the way you want it. He kicked a chair over. The telephone rang but he ignored it and went out.

Love. A girl, anyone, this one in the elevator, panic flushing up her neck because she identified some ruthless property in his stare, the contempt that stripped her. Love, his heart and body cried. If I could begin again. I want it too. If one could go back to innocence.

327

Did I make a mistake? If so, can it be corrected? Is that what *she* is trying to do? Trying to go through life again with the wisdom of experience and middle age?

The first thing to do was betray her, get to an equal status and see what the perspective was from there. He was entitled to that. The law of reciprocal experiences allowed him to screw one girl. One of these hot children you saw walking around flaunting their properties, who threw a challenge when they looked at you, not caring if your wife was with you: I'll let you screw me if I find you amusing . . .

He'd never betrayed Kristan in his life, not by a kiss or a pat on the buttocks.

Black, he thought with bitterness. It has to be a black girl. Just so I can feel I've really contributed to a multiracial society. See how she likes *that!*

The bar in mid-town Manhattan was almost empty. There was a delivery of bottles, and a barman was carrying boxes of ice about and chipping large lumps into pieces of suitable size. It wasn't the right sort of bar anyway; it was too masculine—black leather benches, hard wooden stools, stuffed fish in cases.

The barman was colored. He was hard, a face of ebony, emotionless, the properties only of ruthless survival writ large upon his face. The fast buck and to hell with everyone.

McQuade drank down a whiskey and asked, "What do you think of Portugal?"

"I never been there, mister."

"Ever been to Africa?"

"No, can't say I have."

"Don't go. They'll kick your face in."

"Somethin' botherin' you, mister?"

"What are your politics?"

"A nigger don't have politics."

"Some of 'em have too much politics."

"Not me, mister. I keep my mouth shut."

"You sound like a creep," said McQuade with indifference.

"You're looking for trouble awful early in the day, aren't you, mister?"

"Where do I find a black woman?"

328

"I don't know. Downtown, I guess, in the Village."

Two hours later McQuade sat in the corner of a packed bar, half dark, full of smoke, talking to a Negro. Both were drunk, talkative and embittered.

"And you know who did it?" McQuade asked scornfully. "Africans."

"Friend, the world is a troubled place," agreed the Negro, whose name was Frank. "I been kicked around myself. You know who stole my wife? My best friend. Chicago, that's my town." He drank beer in a long wet sip. He was dressed in a dark suit and, absurdly, had on a tall faded trilby hat with a wide brim so that he looked like a cowboy. A small black one. "Sometimes I go back. Once I went back to beat her up. You know that? I beat up my own wife. That's politics!"

He laughed in a curious titter. "My turn."

McQuade had long since lost the point of the exercise, but now, looking around, he caught a girl's eyes: they shone, catlike, in some tiny corner of illumination.

Frank came back with beer.

"So what do you do?" McQuade asked. "I guess you must be lonely."

A sly smile altered Frank's face from simplicity and defeat to vanity. "Me? Lonely? I'm never lonely. I like people. You know that. Women. I've got me a cat or two."

"Two?"

"You hungry or something?"

"I might be," said McQuade, but cooler all of a sudden. Frank's "cats" would probably be as ugly as Frank himself. If you were going to betray your wife it had to be worthwhile—with someone at least as beautiful.

"There's a lot of girls where I live," claimed Frank. "Come on. I'll show you."

It was raining outside, but they walked along in silence, heedless. McQuade had long since forgotten where he was. Frank said, "I'll arrange it for you," and McQuade felt some relief: money was involved. If he didn't fancy one, he could insist on another. The smell of cooking belched out of doorways. Traffic going to better places swished by, throwing dirty water. They passed bars and res-

329

taurants that were full. A woman tried to accost them, but Frank pushed her off the sidewalk. Music conditioned the night, tried uselessly to make it beautiful.

"Come on in," Frank invited.

It was a tall apartment building, crumbling, dirty, old, and on the porch a woman protested "Oh, it's you." She was a Negro, small, fleshless, her interests narrowed down in the entire world to here and now, *this,* doors and keys, people, comings and goings, dirty bed linen, payments. "There's a letter for you."

"Jesus, I'm important," claimed Frank sourly. He looked at the envelope with its Chicago postmark. "That woman betrays me and wants money. Still wants money."

McQuade asked, "Got any kids?"

"Kids? Oh, sure. I'm capable. Three kids."

"You ought to send money."

"You criticizing or something?" Frank asked belligerently. "You understand it all? Let *him* look after the kids. I got no money anyway. This isn't my town. Chicago's my territory."

They were climbing the stairs. The walls smelled of dirt and age. Frank had a key in his hand.

It was a large sour room, with a greasy carpet, a double bed that wasn't made up, two chairs as dirty as the sheets on the bed, a sort of cupboard-*cum*-dressing table, and things lying on the floor—a suitcase, crates of beer bottles, sex magazines, a bottle of milk. On a shelf were glasses, plates and some cutlery.

Frank said, "Help yourself. I'll go see who's in."

McQuade poured himself a glass of beer.

Frank came back from wherever he'd been in an attitude of conspiracy, things achieved. He had the sly expression on his face again.

"It'll cost you five dollars on account of Mrs. McKell downstairs. Eileen's in. She's okay. She's Chinese. You ever tried a yellow-belly before?"

"Can't say I have," admitted McQuade.

A Negro girl came into the room and complained at once, "I thought you said— Who's this guy? What a mess this place is in. Don't you ever do anything?"

"Shut your big lips," said Frank. "You act like you're married."

The girl giggled.

"What a brave one you are when your belly's full of beer! If you think I've come here to be thumped about because you've got a big wife who's too strong for you!" They both became hilarious on another kind of drunkenness. "And who's this guy? Is he important or something?"

"He's come to see Eileen."

"Then what's he standing around here for?"

Frank nudged McQuade to the door and whispered, "Five dollars, see. Room seven. I'd better have the money then you'll have no problems."

McQuade handed over the money. Frank looked regretfully at the wallet which obviously had a lot more than five dollars in it.

"What's he bought?" the girl shrieked. "The whole district?"

In a room along the corridor there was, sure enough, a Chinese girl. She heard McQuade's shoes as he approached and stood behind a part-open door like someone in doubt. A radio or phonograph was on behind her, and the concussion of hot music, the mood, you had to be in the mood . . . Time and darkness, money changing hands, the senses stunned by alcohol and music and then, only then, could you probe the other body, fluid and waiting to be entertained. Love. God is love, he thought with a bitter snigger, seeing the tall girl's face peering, Oriental eyes examining him, a friend of a friend, anything was permissible. Democracy or something. The journalists worked hard on it. And here it was. Would there be a brief technical dialogue about the merits of rubber goods as compared with the pill?

She was in fact rather beautiful. Beautiful but poor, with a touch of something that didn't belong here—a student who'd rejected society or parents or gone on the drugs. Untidy but shiny long black hair. The eyes had sadness and hatreds, were beautiful, too, but dragged down a little by the pouches of debauchery or late hours or poor food or illness . . . She wore a pink blouse and black skirt. Carpet slippers.

"You Frank's friend?" she asked.

"Sure. You're Eileen?"

"Come on in." She didn't yet ask his name. "You like the music?"

"I'm satisfied."

"Are you in a hurry?"

331

"Not so's you'd notice."

"You can't stay all night. She complains. Technical stuff. Lights and laundry. Besides, I have to go out. You don't look like— Have you got problems?"

"Wife problem," he acknowledged.

"You look different."

"Different from what?"

"Oh, just different. What's your name?"

"Shaun."

"Irish?"

"No. Canadian. I went to Africa," he explained hopelessly. "She got lonely, I suppose."

"Africa? Why didn't you take her with you? I'd have come."

"There was a war of sorts."

"There always is. Who cares?"

Eileen sat on a stool in front of a dressing table and brushed her hair. It was a tidy bedroom. Radio, linen basket, table, two cupboards, a rug, two pictures. Outside, among the corridors of concrete and glass, a police siren howled. As usual, it was impossible to decide in which direction it was or where it was proceeding: the sound was weird and disembodied among the skyscrapers.

She asked, "Do you like me with lipstick or not?"

"I don't mind."

She had a small mouth, but attractive. Lipstick didn't do it any good, but he didn't say so.

"A friend I once had said he liked it because it's kind of slippery . . . Why don't you relax? Take your coat off or something?"

He sat on a chair.

"Were you born in China?"

"No," she answered, shaking with laughter. "Jackson Heights. I got as far as Maryland. You know. Working. Making airplanes. Not for me . . ."

"You mustn't think I'm peculiar," he said. "I have this wife. I love her," he explained as if this merited apology: it was shameful to love a *wife*.

"Relax," Eileen instructed. It meant nothing to her. "I hope it's not peculiar to stare at me. Okay? Is that logical?"

She wasn't insulted, just adroit, and amused, but he apologized promptly, "Sorry."

"Oh, relax. I know all about it. You think I haven't been kicked around? I studied economics. But not hard enough. I got put in pod. Oh, a lot more to it. You don't want the whole story. Too dull."

"I'm still sorry."

"I can see that. But stop worrying. Take a drink. We're friends. I don't get you. You're not scared, but you don't fit. Not with Frank anyway. Haven't I seen you somewhere?"

"Maybe."

"Don't tell me," Eileen pleaded with a smile, "Don't disenchant me. Let me kid myself you're a movie star."

"Politician," he told her.

"Africa. Ah, well. I like you, Shaun."

She stripped off a few things—the blouse and skirt, wriggling quickly free. "Don't you want the Scotch? It's not extra. We're friends."

"You too?"

"No. Wait a minute. Don't drink yet. Want to dance?"

"I'm not very good."

"You can watch me."

She was feather light, moving on stockinged feet. It was a contact, hand to hand, shoulders touched, but it was better to stay apart and watch, she was so graceful to witness.

"I don't get it," he admitted. "What do you do?"

"I work in a restaurant. What don't you get?"

"You act like a human being."

"Not a tart? My God, where've you been since you went to college? No. Let's not quarrel. I'm always *arguing*. I gave up trying. That's the story of my life. And any friend of Frank's—"

"It doesn't matter who I am?"

"I'll tell you something," Eileen said. "You're lousy at dancing! And you're real political, asking too many questions. It doesn't matter. I can tell. I looked, didn't I, through the door?"

"You can tell that quickly?"

"Sure. You're too modest. You're not a peculiar or a creep. Do I have to know you for a year? Life's too fast. And too lousy. And you've got a kind face. See? Philosophy. Frank really studies the economics half of it."

McQuade felt the wish to comprehend, a little stronger than the urge to betray and soil. She was *human,* standing now in a slip. She understood things about him in a glance. She was Chinese in complexion, American in nationality, shared the language and the city, but was more remote than the girls of the Kimbundu tribe; he hadn't the slightest idea of what made her tick. And he wanted to know. He cared about the wastage.

She suggested, "Have some gum? It takes the smell of booze off your breath when you're necking."

"I don't understand you."

"Is that startling? How long have you been here? Ten minutes. I don't get you either."

"You seemed to."

"At least I know what you want!"

She sprawled back on the bed, gave him his money's worth of spectacle—legs and pants—and yawned. "I won't go out. I'm tired. If you really want to stay—"

Her slender sallow sensuality stirred him, but he was doubtful. His mind had become more inquisitive about her than his body. There was something he had to understand.

"You're pretty slow," Eileen complained. "Be a little friendly. Nobody's watching. Does my Chinese skin bother you?"

"Your face is beautiful."

"Oh, thank you."

"Too beautiful for this."

"Can't you make that beautiful, too?"

He knew what it was. The man walked in the rain and answered the telephone, groaned under the *palmatoria,* but existed, couldn't be disputed. McQuade had followed him for years. Believed in him. And now the man was lost. It was impossible to find that man, explain it to him, seek his advice: do I go on, pull the pants down, sweat with her, five dollars worth, great fun, go home, wash, sleep soundly, have fun? *Why not?* There is no God, no wife, no— For the man was a better man than McQuade. No. This wasn't the argument. Then what was? Find the man, ask him, he was here in the room . . .

He sat on the bed, loosened his tie, leaned over Eileen, began necking, still chewing gum. She was frenzied, boiled up eagerly, soon panted, but he was tender, careful, because it was here somewhere in this room, stalking about.

334

"There's nothing left," he said.

"Don't be sad," she pleaded. "For God's sake don't be sad, sad, sad. I can't bear it." She kissed him, pulled at his neck, wrapped a thigh around his. She, too, was chewing gum. Peppermint was breathed and pounded around his nostrils. Her hips had been against his, willing to be explored. Her knees had been up in the air, the stockinged legs in a posture which invited tactile exploration. But she sensed it wasn't enough and wrapped the warm thigh across him, forcing herself into exploration. Her shoulders were bare and he had only to flick a finger to expose her breasts. Her body writhed about, eager to give whatever he wanted, but her brown Oriental eyes stared into his in anxiety.

"What's the matter?"

"You're beautiful."

"Oh, sure."

He pulled the strap off one shoulder to prove she was desirable, and the nipple in the ocher breast was already swollen in pleasure. It was like a quarrel from two mistaken viewpoints. He touched the breast tenderly, but knew it was not for him. He ran his hand along the stockinged leg and it moved for more and he was hot with it. But the man walked around the room, the one man in the world he respected, the one thing left. And that man was himself. That was what was left besides a God who tried you too hard and a wife who betrayed you.

Himself.

He'd almost forgotten.

"This is a funny party," Eileen complained, perplexed.

Her face stared at him, the sad, defeated face, her hair was lank with sweat and so was the skin under her eyes, and now, desiring climax in haste, her delicate fingers were on his trousers and knew it was some other failure, not in his body or hers. She was stung, jealous, determined to win, drag him down to the level of the world; and the fragile touch was feeling around and had reached the zipper. In seconds she'd have the flesh and he'd be lost.

He moved away violently.

"To hell with you," he said.

She was angry, justifiably, he knew, humiliated, sweating, panting and in heat like a dog for a man who was a politician and had been to Africa and now refused his five dollars of pleasure . . .

"And to hell with you!"

He tried to take hold of her tenderly, but she was wounded, dirtied in front of a witness, smashed, and kicked at him.

"You get back to your office and your big bank account and your holidays in Bermuda and Italy. Just go away. I don't want your advice or your sad eyes looking at me like you know better."

She was shouting now.

He was horribly sober and sorry about it.

"What do you do it for? It's not the money, is it?"

She raged at him, "What's it got to do with you? Do I have to explain it to you?"

"I liked you too much—"

"Oh, sure. I could feel your sincerity right there between your legs."

"Don't you want any friends in the world?"

"I've got friends. Real friends. Just go away. Stop lecturing. I know you creeps. A Bible in one hand and what you really want me to do—"

He slammed the door as he went out, but felt sorrow for all that. There was some tender quality in her which had been brutalized not quite beyond recall. He found he was still chewing gum.

That seemed enough for one day, but it hadn't even started . . . He walked away in the rain and after a while laughed. It was ridiculous.

He no longer felt drunk, merely amused—a tolerant, contemptuous amusement, superior to all these other fools who walked in the rain, and vastly holier than his wife, who left notes to say she was having afternoon tea with her lover . . .

Nevertheless, there was nothing left to do and he went home to 96th Street.

He was rather pleased with himself. Not happy, but satisfied that he had found a place in the world, fairly high up, from which he could look down on the fools and cowards who did not have personal integrity—who crawled to money, sex, politics and all the other rubbish that influenced a man's life.

He stood in the elevator, tired now, but quite certain of himself. If he had been asked what he would be doing tomorrow he could have listed the items with confidence and contempt—the meetings, the luncheon, the flag-raising along the Plaza of some silly little nation.

He would have been mistaken.

The elevator was quiet, as indeed was the whole building. But in the apartment a Kristan not far away from some sort of hysteria bothered him straightaway.

She said in a rush of breath, "The Chinese have just invaded Angolique."

McQuade laughed.

"I've just been with a Chinese girl. We had chewing-gum together. She didn't mention invasion."

Kristan identified the tail end of the drunkenness. She was alarmed and went behind chairs, almost cringing, her eyes never off him, as if he'd gone mad and she expected to be beaten up.

"The Portuguese say thousands have been killed and farms and five thousand square miles—"

"Shall I tell you what I think of the Portuguese?" he said loudly. "And the dear old Africans? And the knock-kneed British and the Chinese, French and Americans? The whole damn lot of them? Shall I tell you what you can do with them? Shall I start by telling you what they do to each other? The nice old African cuts off the penis of the Portuguese farmer and—"

She seemed pleased at his reaction. This baffled him.

"What's the trick?" he shouted.

"They want you," said Kristan. "You won't go, will you? Not again. It wouldn't be fair."

"Go where, for Christ's sake?"

"To Angolique. Mr. Cannon said—"

"Is that his name?"

"What?"

"His name? Your lover. Is that his name? Mr. Cannon! Take off your boots, Mr. Cannon!"

She shook with the impact of his loathing, began to shake and weep silently, and said, "On the phone."

"Did you have a good time?" he shouted.

"What do you mean?"

"This afternoon. You went out."

"I don't understand."

337

"You went somewhere," McQuade raged. "Did you have a good time? Yes or No. If I've got to be miserable at least let it have some use for somebody."

"I went to the hospital."

"You're in pod?"

"Don't be vile."

"It figures, doesn't it? It can happen to a Chinese student of economics. Why not you?"

"To see Irene."

He put on the diver's helmet which she'd brought into the place while he'd been in Africa.

She stood there, pleading.

"He's one of the Secretary General's aides."

"So he is!" acknowledged McQuade. "You did very well. But it'll have to stop, of course."

"*Please,* Shaun! Talk sense. Take that off. I can't hear you."

He took the helmet off and rolled it across the room. Kristan trembled at the noise and the gesture.

She said uselessly, "He's going to ring back."

"Tell him I'm drunk."

"Don't go," Kristan beseeched. "Not again. I was so scared."

"Why do they want me to go to Angolique?"

"He said something about a transfer from the Canadian Mission to the Secretariat."

McQuade was shocked into sobriety. "Say that again about the Chinese."

"They've invaded Angolique. From Tanzania."

"Ah!" he said. "But why me?"

"He said he'd phone again. It was vital. You'd have to go tomorrow."

"*Tomorrow!* It'll take days to transfer me to the Secretariat."

"I was so scared," she admitted. "They must find someone else. You've not recovered. *Please,* Shaun, don't go. I was nearly silly last time—"

"*Nearly!*" he protested.

"You know, don't you?"

"Yes."

"I was so scared without you. I'm ashamed."

"But you still meet him?"

She was silent.

He was exhausted. The doubt had kept him going. Now there was nothing left. He was finished as a human being. No. He disputed that. There was this man, himself, drained of strength and love, but not destroyed. He knew he'd go.

He looked at his wife and she was far away, a small voice pleading for nothing.

She recognized it.

"Don't go. Tell them you're ill. They'll send someone else."

"I can't avoid it."

"If you don't refuse I can promise nothing," she tried to threaten.

There was nothing to say.

"I was frightened," she confessed. "I was terrified. That's why it happened . . . I couldn't bear it."

He was moved. He understood. He wanted to weep for her.

The telephone began to ring.

"There's the whole damn world," he said.

"Don't be silly. It doesn't depend on you."

"Perhaps it does," he said.

"Maybe," suggested Kristan, "you'll find they're not as grateful for what you did as you'd like to believe."

It was a shrewd but cruel remark.

"You know it's my duty to go."

"What about your duty to *me?*"

"Have I ever neglected that?"

"You don't care . . . All right," she raged in despair. "Go! If it's all that matters. If you don't bother about your marriage any longer."

"Is there any left to bother about?"

"Don't play with it," she cried. "You know there is."

"I'll have to answer anyway."

She wept as he took the ten paces to the telephone. He wanted to cry out, too, but the voice talked into his ear and he accepted what it had to say. It was not a proposition he could avoid, for the voice of Mr. Cannon, a man McQuade had scarcely heard of, placed the responsibility of the whole world onto McQuade's shoulders.

2 ▪ ▪

MCQUADE REPORTED THE following morning at 9:30 in the Secretariat building.

The express elevator was full of people who talked about the world rather as if it was their property and world government had indeed arrived. All of them had American accents.

This impression and the uncomfortable, unexpected feeling of strangeness—the new boy at a school of too-clever people—was continued in the office of Mr. Humphrey Cannon, although Mr. Cannon was down-to-earth and did his best to reveal that he was approachable, a man of the people.

But first McQuade encountered Mr. Cannon's outer office, with its spaciousness that allowed two desks to stand yards apart, a floor of beautiful wood, flowers, paintings and silence . . . The silence was perhaps the most impressive of the surprises for McQuade, who had to sit for five minutes and wait. For on every floor except this, the 38th, and in all areas of the General Assembly and conference buildings, there was movement and noise, often hullabaloo. Here, however, was a distinct feeling of separateness, possibly on Cloud 7. There were just two stenographers, who, at 9:45, hadn't gotten around to their day yet. Both were superbly beautiful Eurasian girls. (There was a tendency, probably related to the building's geographical location, for the girls to become progressively more beautiful with each floor one ascended.)

In Mr. Cannon's office the first impression was of light—the sky through the enormous window—and then the view, which was magnificent. The Secretariat building stood to one side of Manhattan and from this 38th floor was perhaps the most impressive view in the world—the man-made world anyway. The eye was bludgeoned by it, couldn't take it all in. Straight ahead the Pan American building caught the eye, then the Chase Manhattan Bank, the Chrysler Building, Rockefeller Center and Radio City. McQuade could see right downtown, past the Empire State and the Woolworth buildings to tiny tissues of smoke from the ferry going across to Staten Island.

Mr. Cannon stood beside him and commented, "Not beautiful. You couldn't say that. But strong."

In his office were plants and a superb carpet, a bookcase full of books about the UN—other people's views of it or a delight in self-concern, for the UN had this tireless interest in itself. There were two bronze medallions in frames on a wall and cute ornaments and trinkets from far corners of the earth: to prove he'd been there and knew what he was talking about.

Mr. Cannon was in shirt sleeves. He switched on an electric razor and began to shave himself. Presumably he had spent the night here, looking after the world. He sat at a fine desk and put his feet on it.

"Have a cigar?" he suggested.

McQuade refused.

Mr. Cannon lit one for himself.

He got down to business.

"The Secretary General thinks very highly of you and wanted you on his staff. He's gone to Michigan, but he was very anxious to have you." Mr. Cannon gave the very distant impression that the Secretary General was sometimes like this—he got carried away and didn't consult Mr. Cannon. "But he spoke to your Ambassador, who is, as you know, agreeable to a two-year transfer. We were in such a hurry," he conceded, smiling, "we almost forgot to ask *you!* The Secretary General was impressed by what you did in Angolique. He felt that you'd make a good Secretariat man."

"I hope so," said McQuade.

He still felt as if he was with the headmaster, or at least a housemaster, of this new school.

"This," continued Mr. Cannon, "may be the most embarrassing thing we've ever encountered—and we've had a few! For here we have Portugal—of all countries—appealing to the UN, complaining of military attack! And we can't ignore such an appeal. Portugal is a member of the UN which has lately heeded our recommendations." She is one of the good boys now, Mr. Cannon might have said. "And yet this is not—if it exists at all—just an attack on

341

northeast Angolique. This is the attack organized by friends of the UN—no doubt impatiently—who are members of the Organization of African Unity, and the thrust is intended to go through Angolique, Rhodesia and maybe get to Capetown. This may not suit Wall Street or the city of London, but it is an action with which in principle we agree, although it would be very embarrassing to support it in action. So you must go and assess it, Mr. McQuade. Is it important? Give us the facts so that we may make our evaluation and advise and act accordingly . . ."

McQuade was a little startled at the difference between Portugal's claim and its reception up here.

"My wife said that on the telephone you said, or somebody said, the Chinese—"

"Sure," said Mr. Cannon. "We all know the OAU is supplied by the Chinese."

"Not *me*," qualified McQuade. "I'd heard rumors, but— Surely, then, Portugal has a right to complain?"

"Within limits," said Mr. Cannon.

"I don't follow you."

McQuade was shocked by something he couldn't as yet define.

"What don't you understand?" Mr. Cannon asked.

"It sounded as if different standards applied here to the Africans and the Portuguese."

Mr. Cannon looked at McQuade. He knew the Secretary General was in error. He'd picked the wrong boy. This one was bothered about the unimportant things. His first thoughts were not for the school.

"They do," he said, "although not in the records. We are susceptible, Mr. McQuade, to pressures, like everyone else. And the Afro-Asians have a good deal of pressure around here, and sometimes with the State Department. Portugal has none. Furthermore, there is no political hope for the African in Angolique unless we help him. Do you think there's going to be a great political change in Portugal when the present regime ends? Do you think the PIDE is going to disappear overnight any more than the KGB is in the Soviet Union? Or that the opposition is going to put things right in Portugal or Angolique? They're too inexperienced! They are only able to talk about their experiences in prison! And the place is stiff with

342

German and Spanish advisers. Do you think the émigrés in New York, London and Paris—dining out on disaster and having love affairs to pass the time—are going to have the dynamic quality for governing Portugal when the time comes? This little war on the edge of Tanzania has been going on for years. Why complain about it now? The Portuguese have been having the best of it. What goes on, Mr. McQuade?"

"You seem remarkably well informed since both the UN and the Western press are not allowed near this war," commented McQuade. "I can't think why you need me . . ."

"Because this is your hot potato, Mr. McQuade. You got us into it. Now get us out! And they know you, don't they? Both the Africans and Portuguese met you. They trust you."

"I wouldn't go so far as to say *that!*"

"Well, you go and assess it, Mr. McQuade. The Portuguese may feel they've embarrassed us by their appeal—it's due this afternoon. We have the uneasy feeling that almost every nationalist has now been trapped and is under surveillance and at the slightest justification—in terms of *us*—the Portuguese will arrest the lot. Some of them have quite high positions now. These, too, would go within the same justification and we'd be back to square one and Portugal would be stronger in Africa than ever and it'd be permissible on the statute books here. This organization would lose all of Africa and Asia's confidence. We'd be out of business . . . Assess the situation, make the UN's presence felt, send a signal to tell us what it's all about and if troops are needed for stabilization, and by the time you do we'll have an army ready to fly in . . ."

Mr. Cannon seemed ready with the fire and sword, the napalm and helicopters. His language was that of cuckooland and the editorials. McQuade knew it had no relationship whatever to the reality of Africa. He looked at Cannon in contempt. A great fat slug of a man, too heavy from too much sitting down. A massive body and an enormous head which was formidable in shrewdness and layers of cunning. But when the face turned to look out at someone crossing the street from 42nd, an ant down there in the rain which had begun, the profile was interesting, for among the folds of flesh and the craggy brows of middle age was a boy—and McQuade could see him, thin and earnest and clever with talk, bad at sports, half

343

despised, only the second-best girls for him . . . Well, here he was in charge of the world while the Secretary General was making a speech somewhere. We'll have an army ready . . .

"You may find," continued Mr. Cannon, confirming himself to McQuade's satisfaction, "South African or Rhodesian troops fighting with the Portuguese. We particularly want to know about that. There are so many hot potatoes in Africa you can't win, to be frank. You are going to hate it."

"No," said McQuade. "I'll love every minute of it."

Cannon sensed the double meaning, but let it go.

"You did extremely well last time," he acknowledged. "Beginner's luck? I hope not! And, Mr. McQuade—no more private deals. You're not a Canadian now. You're a sworn member of the Secretariat."

"I'll give you the truth," McQuade told him, "and I'll be interested to see what you do with it."

"Good!" said Cannon, ignoring what was meant as an outright insult. "I'll tell you the most important thing of all, Mr. McQuade. There is one thing the UN cannot afford and must not do if there's fighting. And that is, lose a battle. Not one. We have too many enemies and we represent too much to be able to afford many more defeats."

Mr. Cannon was an executive assistant who was empowered to make high decisions. During the day McQuade met other people close to the Secretary General—British, Swedish, a Nigerian, a Pakistani general, five or six Americans, all of them principal advisers. They talked to McQuade calmly, reasonably, not pressing any particular point of view, but he listened with a detachment bordering on contempt. For they were, he considered, bought men, yes-men, who in a long sequence of words and pressures took orders not from the nations of the world but the State Department of the United States and, if it suited the State Department, from countries like Britain which went cap in hand to see the American President when they had problems that only the brute force or enormous economic pressures of the United States could deal with. This sour view of the Secretariat was certainly not disputed by what he heard this day, and many of the telegrams he saw on important affairs of the world were quite different from the information supplied to enable the delegates in the General Assembly to be adequately informed for discussion and decisions to be made and voted on, even if they weren't carried out . . .

The advisers talked all day and McQuade listened to them with good-humored indifference. How they could talk! What a lot they knew! Unfortunately, the one thing they had not done was visit Angolique to see if their strong views and indignation were justi-fied. Not one of them. He had.

All men were fixed except him.

All men were conditioned and had no honesty, or had to surren-der honesty to an allegiance, whether it was marriage, or work, or an editor, or even this ridiculous organization.

He would give them the truth, the burning hot truth, and see if they could bear it, or talk their way around it, or put it into the sausage machine and churn out Secretariat sausages with a differ-ent, sweeter flavor . . .

The truth was that political existence in the UN was conditioned these days by the triangle of pressures exerted by the United States and its allies, the Afro-Asians, and the Soviet Union and its bloc. At one time American influence had been so strong it needed no assistance, but currently it had to exert itself a little to make a proposition work and to obtain some Afro-Asian support. This was not too difficult in terms of loans and financial pressures and busi-ness help, and the United States Government's policy still coin-cided with the UN's decisions.

In the Secretariat also American influence was supreme. This was partly due to the very position of the buildings in New York, but more especially was it due to the high proportion of Americans among the permanent staff. The Secretariat had long since been purged of known Communists and even White Russians, and the American citizens, who far outnumbered the other nationalities, were likely to identify loyalty to the world with loyalty not exactly to America but certainly to the American way of life.

Thus, in the councils of the United Nations and in the Secretar-iat, the pleas of a small, unpopular country like Portugal were rela-tively meaningless unless shown to have some bearing on the United States. This, McQuade acknowledged, was a generalization, and the human mind, including the American human mind, had a capacity of give and take, a sense of humanity and fairness—but only if the truth reached the minds to be influenced. And often it didn't until it had been through the sausage machine and acquired the prejudice. The process was all very natural and realistic in terms of the real world of power balances and the human capacity for self-deception and the convenience of an idealistic label for a particular stratagem, but was indeed a far cry from talks to schools and debates about democracy in universities.

Mr. Cannon was so in love with his own sophistication and the sausage machine that he'd forgotten the simpler issues. Africa was starving. Africa was nine-tenths illiterate. Africa wanted food, not votes—millions of Africans didn't know what a vote was. And Africa was by no means as hot and bothered about so-called freedom as was the white man on its behalf. Some of Africa wasn't enjoying the independence acquired. The new nations tended to be regarded by the UN as adult countries, one of *us,* problems over. But the real problem for the emergent African nations was the thousands of slightly educated but disappointed young people, full heir to their predecessors' problems. And therefore the young man might be angry with his grandfather, who was the politician who'd gained independence for him . . . There were big problems of juvenile delinquency. Some countries had set up Ministries of Sport and Youth in answer to this problem. Improved health services and schooling escalated the birth and survival rates, but brought the near-disaster of a vaster population demanding work, but not organized for it. Perhaps the problem was, fundamentally, how to develop a society which would calmly grow crops in a proper manner and do so when it was increasingly disappointed and frustrated by it knew not quite what . . .

Further, the sneer of some South Africans on that Boeing to Vila Lobanda—what a long time ago that seemed!—was not without considerable justification. The "one-man, one-vote" formula had in many cases drifted into the "one-man, one-vote, one-party" of dictatorship, with its economic *dirigisme* and alarming symptoms of megalomania—the hangings, beatings, murders and massacres, the military parades and the "spontaneous" popular demonstration, the pictures of Christ and the leader, and the sudden departure of the dictator's old friends to prison and death. Opposition could not be tolerated. Political talent was short; half of it could not be wasted in opposition! And, of course, dictatorship was easy because the machinery tended to be all in one place. Grab the radio station, the few newspapers, the palace, the barracks and you were at once in business! And half of your tribe took high office immediately! From that point the corruption and bribes began, the sycophants crowded around, people disappeared and other opinion came to an end.

Africa was in turmoil. It was like Europe in the Middle Ages. Cars were shot up for no reason at all in the Congo and mercenary armies moved about doing what they liked. Saudi Arabia bought vast quantities of sophisticated military equipment from Britain and America. Egypt was armed to the teeth and Radio Cairo blared hate over thousands of miles in scores of languages. Thousands were massacred in Zanzibar. In Nigeria democracy was comic and painful: the riot-wrecked vehicles and the police firing on the marketplace; the hundreds of dead and the chicanery and the rigging of the elections cheerfully accepted as normal. The votes were stuffed into loaves and smuggled into polling booths and there was manipulation with the lists. Polling agents were beaten up and the tribal gangs were out around the countryside with axes to substantiate their opinions, while the intellectuals sat in prisons reading English paperbacks. The refugees of the Kuku tribe flooded into Uganda by the scores of thousands from the equatorial province of the Sudan, and their welcome was doubtful. There was a contrived silence about the fate of Christian Negro refugees and the Sudan African Liberation Front talked in vain to the Organization of African Unity—which didn't want to hear that the black man had racial problems of his own—about the atrocities it had suffered: the thousands of burned-down houses and the shootings and floggings and the popular and fatal torture of tying a victim's head in a bag of red pepper. Tens of thousands of Tutsi were slaughtered by the Huta in Rwanda. And in all these maneuverings there were no rules at all—for Africa didn't yet read the liberal newspapers so anxious on its behalf; it was still the continent of realism—giant in weather, landscape, animals and blood. So the prisoners were tortured or killed at once and missionaries and nuns suffered indifferent brutal death if in the way. It was only 5 per cent

347

of Africa, this violence, and the rest of the country worked for mere existence on a difficult earth, or taught in schools and worked in banks. But 5 per cent was enough. And the white man waited his turn. Scores of thousands of the Spanish Foreign Legion waited, hot with impatience, in the Spanish Sahara. What for? South Africa manufactured French military aircraft under license ready for the day . . . A US Air Force general sat in an office in Madrid running the Spanish Army. There were German aircraft in Portugal and Portuguese Guinea. The hotels of every capital city from Cairo to Capetown, Elisabethville to Dar es Salaam, Algiers to Villa Cisneros were full of men with heavily laden, hard-worn leather briefcases full of maps and diagrams and photographs of the effectiveness of their equipment—it penetrated steel and smashed brickwork—and the talk over dinner was of calibers and impact and credits, aerial cameras and mines, machine guns and bazookas, and the smaller but necessary items of clubs, barbed wire, handcuffs, grenades . . . Espionage, murder, torture, massacre, corruption and disappearances, and all of them under an indifferent, vaster, merciless and more efficient sun . . .

At eight o'clock McQuade went home, comfortably exhausted by the hours of talking and listening. In less than thirty hours he would be in Lisbon. He wanted calm for a while, but there wasn't any.

There was silence in the apartment. When he called out her name hesitantly, Kristan answered, "I'm in bed."

She didn't look well.

"What's happened?" he asked.

Kristan began to cry.

"I feel awful."

"Haven't you seen the doctor?"

"I couldn't be bothered. I'm too tired."

"I'll phone him."

"No. It doesn't matter. You look tired, too."

"I am. I have to fly to Portugal tomorrow."

"Oh, Shaun, *please*. Do you have to go?"

"It's all arranged," he said uncomfortably.

"Don't be silly. It doesn't depend just on you."

"Perhaps it does."

348

"Oh, God," she cried. "You don't care about me at all."

He knew then what her illness was—the wish to stop him.

"I feel so ill," she whispered in confirmation.

"I'll get the doctor."

"No. I'll be all right in a few days."

"I'll get him anyway. If it's serious I can't go, of course."

He was perplexed by the feeling of relief and hope in himself.

Kristan stared at him sullenly, aware that he had decided not to take her excuse.

The doctor came an hour later. McQuade didn't stay in the bedroom. He talked to the doctor afterward and smiled grimly at the man's embarrassment.

"I can't find anything seriously wrong," the doctor admitted. "Is she nervous? It could," he told McQuade with a rush of words, "be psychological. Has it happened before?"

He was blushing, which was decidedly unusual for a doctor.

McQuade asked with brutal frankness, "You mean it's something on her conscience?"

"That's a possibility," agreed the doctor.

"Then I'm the patient?" reasoned McQuade.

"That is not for me to say," the doctor qualified stiffly.

It was a bad night.

"He says you're all right," McQuade told Kristan.

"Good!" she said with rage. "So now you can go and be a hero again with a clear conscience."

"It's my job to—"

"I'm ill and you don't care."

"Yes, but nothing serious—"

"How do we know without X rays and things?"

"Honey, I can come back if it is serious. You know that."

"You don't want to come back."

He said with irritation, "I don't get it. What are you so unhappy about? You had great fun last time I was away."

"I want you to care," she shouted. "I want you to forgive. I can't stand the way you sit in a chair and look at me."

"I still love you. What else do you want?"

"I don't know."

"I have to go, but I'll be back."

349

"I'm ill and you don't care," she repeated sullenly.

"I'm sorry and I do care."

"You don't. Look in the mirror and see. You look like a kid who's in danger of not getting his new toy."

"Don't you believe in anything?"

"Yes," she shouted. "The almighty dollar and the ICBM. That's me. That's *real*. That's the truth. Who do you think you're fooling in that sanctimonious building? It's just jobs for the boys, that's all. Sure it looks good. Sure the speeches are fine. But do you think *that's* preserving the peace of the world? It's the Bomb, big boy. All those Minutemen in the silos and the DEW and all that stuff. They'd have been tearing into each other fifteen years back if they hadn't known that'd be the end. It's a nice building, Shaun, and they do fine work on sanitation and swamp drainage and bandages and mealie-meal and powdered milk for orphans in their own chaos. It's a great place for those who've got the urge to be a do-gooder—especially on the lecture platform. But it's not really the Big League stuff. Those decisions are taken elsewhere."

"You cheap cow!" he bellowed.

From then on it was silence and tears and anger all night . . .

During these hours the General Assembly adopted a draft reso-lution, submitted by Portugal, South Africa and the Netherlands, calling on the governments of Tanzania and other states to respect the system of government in Angolique and to refrain from action calculated to change it by force, at least until a special representa-tive of the UN, with his staff, had been to ascertain the facts and attempt a reconciliation. The Portuguese delegate said that coun-teraction had to be taken in defense of what was still sovereign Portugal and in protection of innocent Portuguese and African farmers. He said that about four thousand square miles of this part of Angolique had had to be evacuated, but made it clear that Por-tugal would be glad to hand over the military situation to the UN if the Security Council would make arrangements to protect the peo-ple of Angolique from violence while the territory itself was under-going political changes in respect of and in accordance with the UN's wishes.

It was a crisis.

Not a very important one, but any crisis might precipitate a larger one and escalate the world into war. The world adjusted its chessboard accordingly. Feet hurried along corridors; armorers loaded fighter aircraft; naval vessels refueled or changed course; men were recalled from leave; the editorials of newspapers were altered; the five hundred strategic troop carriers of the Military Air Transport Service of the USAF stood by; the rockets were aligned, checked, the operators deep down in the silos inhaled their menthol cigarettes more carefully. Papers were burned and espionage agents risked telephone calls and caught unintended trains. People were arrested who had merely been under suspicion. All over the world computers and cybernetics machines with the speed of ten million minds stood by to cope with problems. Thousands of fingers unfastened safety catches and reached for the triggers. Millions of people were scared, millions prayed . . .

And the prayers and wishes in a thousand languages depended on one unhappy man with a pain in his left foot, one unhappy man who was tired and embittered and couldn't sleep because his wife's body was tense and warm with misery beside him . . .

The world knew now that he had been appointed.

One and a half miles away from where he lay in bed, three journalists of a newspaper whose thinking had been conditioned by companies and finances associated by about sixteen links with that of Mettallic Angolique in Africa and Germany were discussing McQuade.

"He must have a weakness somewhere. It's not human to be infallible. We'll find it."

"He's a bit of a bore, that's my complaint. Lousy copy," said a second journalist.

"I think he's a good man," affirmed the third.

The other two turned around in astonishment.

"How *young* you are! And how firmly on the orange juice!" said the first.

"If he isn't corrupted by money or women or little boys," suggested the second, "surely it's because he's past them and it's power."

"If he's corrupted by a longing for power," said the first shrewdly, "he doesn't know it. It is possible that he's a man who believes in what he's doing."

351

"Don't we all?'"

"Has anyone dug into his past?"

No one had.

"That might be worth doing."

"What for?" asked the youngest man. "Why do you want to destroy him? Why do you hate everyone who's trying to do something good?"

"You should get a transfer to *Reader's Digest*," suggested the second one.

The young man didn't want to lose sophistication in the sight of his colleagues. He passed on a rumor he had heard. "They say his wife's a bit hot."

"That really is interesting."

"We might get a photograph."

"We might indeed!"

"A photograph," the first journalist suggested to the idealistic young man, "is truth. Agreed? Here's to truth, then, and, of course, to freedom of publication."

Two boys were flying a kite near the river. Small urchins, they knew the nature of the landscape better than Peter or Yvette did, and they sniggered, worldly wise, at the age of ten, aware of others who strolled along this path to the woods, littered half a mile on with contraceptives and cigarette packs and bits of paper. But this view of the world was only for those who wanted to see it.

Peter and Yvette didn't look at the ground, but at each other, a tenderness that all the sophisticated encouragement of that view couldn't alter. Love. It still began somewhere; it wasn't a course one took at a college. A girl like Yvette rarely saw the magazines that instructed her in the importance of sexual love, sleeping around. She had begun months ago in exploration as delicate as breath, and her thoughts ran even now in terms of hands touching, his variation of facial expression, and, when excited or exploratory in half-sleep, she considered marriage in practical terms and regarded Canada as the romantic half of hopes and expectations.

Peter's view of her was inevitably, at times, in thought, more sensual. If there was opportunity to stare at her bended knees, her body as it maneuvered within clothes to open a door, enter a vehi-

352

cle, climb stairs, he took it. He did not like her to know that he stared and had not the slightest idea whether she ever caught him doing so and, if she did, what was the nature of her opinion or shock. Otherwise he treated her with extreme tenderness, claiming little more than was permissible by the strictest moral standards. It was not easy to be alone. Doors and people in restaurants, boys along a path, other lovers in woods and on a hillside, a crowd in a party at the officers' mess, all prevented isolation . . .

"What's the matter?" Yvette asked.

She knew him well enough to identify apprehension despite easy chatter.

"Nothing. Nothing much."

"But something?"

"Yes, but not serious."

"Tell me."

"Not now."

"You will tell me?"

"Oh, yes. Let's find somewhere."

"That's a problem!"

"It's a weekday," Peter pointed out, meaning that other people were at work, children should be at school.

They were already two miles out of the city, but still the leaves and grass were dirtied by coal dust and the wind carried the unpleasant smell of a tannery. It was agreeably hot. They walked on tirelessly. The horizon of trees and river seemed to stand still; feet were powerless to alter it. He identified some of the landscape and it was frustrating to realize that he crossed it in the Starfighter as quickly as the flick of a switch—in flying terms what they now covered in an hour was nothing in the jet, the bat of an eyelid.

But finally they found a place far away from people. There was just one man a mile away in a field, going back and forth in a tractor. The boys' kite could no longer be seen. Very faintly the air rumbled with the workings of a colliery, but the wind in the grass was louder. They lay on the coarse, smoke-touched grass, face to face, hot in the day, sweated into each other's faces like less discreet lovers. Opportunity was too good and rare to waste. They caressed for a long time, until in fact they were out of breath and too hot.

353

Her eyes were inches away from his and staring hard, full of love.

"You were going to tell me . . ."

"I have to go away," Peter said.

The collapse of her facial expression, the flood of panic, were the most perfect proof, if proof was what he desired, of her devotion, her thoughts in terms of permanence. The large blue eyes were at once shiny with the approach of tears and the soft mouth trembled.

"Back to Canada?"

"No," he hastened to reassure her. "Nothing like that. It's what's called a Middle East reinforcement exercise. Just a few weeks. Perhaps only two. We fly in exercises with the British and Netherlands Air Forces. We'll be using an airfield in Tunisia."

"You'll come back here?" Yvette questioned anxiously.

"Of course."

"Peter, when do you go back to Canada?"

"Oh, years." He asked suddenly, chancing everything, "Will you come with me?"

"What do you mean?"

"You know what I mean!"

"Yes, but say it!"

Peter found he couldn't.

Yvette rested on one elbow and looked at him. "I might come," she said, but she was teasing him. He could see that she was shaken with the joy of it. She kissed his left ear. "I think I'd like that very much!"

He pulled her down onto himself. Her breasts were warm through her summer dress. He kissed through her dress and his hands stroked her arms and buttocks. "Take it easy!" she said, sure of herself, easily in control. He persisted a little, rolled her, protesting, on the grass. But it was the mere touch he wanted, like a man who'd just bought something sought for years and thinks, Is this really *mine?*—and touches to be sure.

"Come on," he insisted and pulled her to her feet.

"Where are you going?"

"Before you change your mind—"

"I shan't do that—"

354

"I'm going to buy a ring."

"Peter, you don't have to."

But he was insistent and she walked lightly with him toward the ugly coal mines, the miles of railway yards, the slums and the thick belch of smoke from engines, toward a horizon that was, for both of them, beautiful . . .

3 ■ ■

LISBON AGAIN, in summer now, 95° in the noon sun, crowds along the hot shuttered avenues, Americans swallowing magnesia tablets in the restaurants to settle their stomachs and lifting their dark glasses like visors to inspect the delicate fish foods.

It felt like home to McQuade.

He had a feeling of belonging here. It was real and not the property of words. His left foot hurt and he sat for a long time in the botanical gardens, content to absorb sun for the few hours left of this day. Eventually it became irresistible to walk about. The sun was boiling hot and the sweat rolled out of him and soaked his hair. People sat under trees on the grass. The heat in the Avenida da Liberdade was stupefying; he wandered without purpose under its influence. As ever, there were dozens of good-humored touts, the symptom of poverty: shoeshine boys; an old man who wanted to do a caricature of McQuade. Several times young men approached with a conspiratorial *"Pssst!"* and tried to sell him a "gold" watch, ignoring the one on his wrist. "Automatic," they claimed, with an enthusiasm for the word which the clerk in that mortuary in Canada had not possessed . . . The American girls on holiday stood out noticeably because they were so tall and fair and consciously sensual. People stared at them with slight disapproval. There were notices on the pillars down by the Praça do Comércio, beginning to fade in the strong sun: "The soldier who fights in Angolique is serving the integrity of Portugal."

The Mercedes taxis, absurdly cheap to hire, skidded in the tramlines and on the gray mosaics of the little roads that climbed up to

355

the castle. McQuade's sad eyes took in the superb views from the castle grounds—looked over the pannen tiles of incredibly complicated roof structures in the narrow tortuous streets of Alfama and beyond to the center of Lisbon and the Sea of Straw and the French liner this side of the new Tagus bridge. He walked down from the castle in the poverty, among the dwarfs, cripples and old women, the crippled family who sat on an Alfama doorstep in a street as narrow as an alleyway and played cards and smiled as he went by. The taxis hurtled past with their content of visitors too rich or too lazy or too hot to climb on foot. Take the photographs from the castle grounds and then hurry back to the world of restaurants, theaters, what to do tonight . . .

This time there had been an accident. In a row of crumbling, beautiful little shuttered slum houses, with birdcages hammered onto some of the outside walls, which here and there had picturesque tiles embedded into them, a boy had fashioned a swing. So limited was space that he had opened the front door and used its lintel as the axis for his arc. The automobile, coming down the hill too fast and with the usual bad brakes, had hit him in the outer half of his arc. Old women stared sadly from ground-floor windows. Men and young women in black had come out of little shops and doorways, silent in accusation. He wasn't dead, but smashed. He'd join the numbers of limping cripples with pale faces and haunting eyes who hung about at every public center in Lisbon.

McQuade dined alone. He was too unhappy and close to rage and despair for chatter. Lisbon softened him a little, but he was conscious of the need to avoid conversation which might betray his condition. On the menu was printed the item "little white fish in despair" and this at least made him smile. And sure enough, he was served with two small fish coiled up and looking miserable with their own tails in their mouths!

He went to bed early, for he had had no sleep for two nights. The young tireless foreigners, mostly American, crowded the foyer of the hotel at 9:30 P.M., ready to recommence the day, bombarding the desk with questions: "Where is Maxim's?" "Isn't there a night club here?" "Get me a taxi?" "What about my shirt?" The pitilessness of youth and health and money and eyes that didn't see . . . McQuade was tired and unhappy, but could not sleep.

356

Hot air blew through an open window. The traffic was a distant rumble, but near at hand gargantuan music belched its way across a dusty piece of ground: "Deutschland über Alles," with roaring voices and cheers, and then, in complete contrast, "Tea for Two," played very sweetly in the cha-cha manner. The smells of hot foods drifted out of lower windows—and long past midnight the endless crash of cutlery and crocks being washed the same two floors below.

It was no use. He had to surrender. He sat up and wrote the brief letter. What do I say? I love you. What else matters? What more is there to say? I have to do this or I cannot feel human, but never doubt me. Pray for me, for I need someone's prayers.

At once he slept and didn't stir until nine in the morning.

He sat in the lounge of Lisbon airport. It was too noisy, so he went upstairs to the concrete terrace. A South African Boeing was taxiing in. The screech of engines was tremendous, and heat waves billowed from the huge machine like heavy breathing. McQuade went restlessly downstairs again into the symptoms of slight panic: people coming through for departure, a clatter of cases, forms to fill, anxiety, clocks ticking, harassing, the tremendous shriek outside from the Boeing, and the South Africans came in—young, most of them, like athletes, and in high spirits, a very long way from defeat. A colored girl's face shone with humor and she looked intelligent and wore good clothes and laughed with white people, ignoring the theories and hatreds of the world. Silence now, and people scattered, empty tables, dirty ashtrays, and the mechanical voice talked in Portuguese and then English; "The next airplane to arrive will be the Pan American from New York." His heart thumped absurdly and he went up the steps again to watch it come in.

And then, from a hundred yards away, to his astonishment he recognized Marianne among the crowd. She walked with the others of his staff, whom he did not know yet—his deputy, an Italian, Raffaele Franzo; the finance officer, a Brazilian named Juan Sáenz Ecchegarri; and the military adviser, an Irishman, Brigadier Michael Fermoy. So great had been the haste to get someone to Lisbon that McQuade had not met any of these Secretariat men before. He was touched by a tiny warmth and hurried down and half

357

embraced Marianne, a Portuguese gesture, for he knew she had volunteered.

"Didn't expect *you*," he said. "I thought you'd had enough last time."

"I'm a masochist," suggested Marianne. "And the place sort of gets you," she added grudgingly, presumably meaning Angolique and Africa.

Franzo was a pleasant, gentle-looking Italian of about thirty-five. McQuade resisted with difficulty the thought, What does he know about Africa, recognizing the raging disturbances within himself. Ecchegarri was about forty-five, plump, pear shaped, serious in disposition. He looked a little lost, like someone who'd never been to Lisbon before, much less Africa. Brigadier Fermoy, also nearing fifty, stared around and said, "Let's get out of this damn place," which did not endear him to McQuade. McQuade thought Lisbon's airport attractive, with its gong for announcing the departures of aircraft and the dignified Portuguese girls, who looked blank when fat Americans became impatient about delays and merely explained with calm, "We must not fly until the airplane is in order, agreed?"

In the late afternoon McQuade went with Franzo and the Brigadier to see Dr. Pessanha, the Minister for Overseas Boundaries.

They sat in the same room as before. The windows were open in the summer day and distantly trams clattered, whistles blew, cars accelerated, while near at hand thousands of feet tapped the dry pavements and voices laughed.

"I am not happy," affirmed Dr. Pessanha. "Mr. McQuade, you surely recognize that Portugal surrendered much of her integrity in Africa and the world to satisfy the United Nations, which claims to represent the world.

"We were and still are prepared to surrender considerable power to the *indigena*. Some of them are judges in Portuguese Africa now. Others are Ministers. They work with the same equality as does the peasant alongside his fellow peasant who has a skin of a different color."

"I don't like the word 'peasant,'" observed Brigadier Fermoy, who was sitting in an attitude of disbelief, of waiting for the blarney to conclude.

358

"I think the word has great dignity," claimed Dr. Pessanha. "Portugal does not equate morality and dignity with a high standard of living."

"No doubt that is a comfortable observation from an armchair," remarked the brigadier.

Dr. Pessanha was startled by this rudeness and looked at Mc-Quade as if to ask, What kind of lunatic is this?

McQuade said with deliberate courtesy, "Excellency, we have come to observe the military situation. My mandate does not exclude me from talking to political figures and even achieving a settlement, although it is the military situation that gives the most anxiety. But I shall certainly see leaders of the Tando, ANP, MAA and NWALO parties with a view to confirming the situation Portugal has given us in the United Nations."

Dr. Pessanha observed, "The ANP is in Dar es Salaam. They are the party using that territory for every adventurer in Africa to soldier. They have Chinese advisers, equipment and possibly some troops."

"It's a long way from China," pointed out the brigadier. "Logistics must be difficult. I shouldn't worry too much, Excellency."

"I find your partiality disturbing, Brigadier, for one who has come to seek an impartial truth," said Dr. Pessanha.

McQuade said woodenly, "And the other parties, Excellency?"

Dr. Pessanha told him, "The Tando Party is in effect working with Portugal. Gomais and the ANP are in Tanzania, as I said. Quissanga of NWALO and Matumoza of the *Movimento Anticolonialista* are both in Lourenco Tomas. They are quarreling with each other and with us, but not seriously. It is a ridiculous situation. It is also a tragedy. All of Africa is," asserted Dr. Pessanha. "And it hurts me that the English, who once understood Africa, now fail to see it. The intellectuals still howl for our total departure from Africa. We have conceded to the UN what it requested despite our misgivings, but this for the theorists on paper is not enough. It is viewed by the extremists of black Africa—and the white meddlers in London and New York who have never been to Africa—with glee as a sign of weakness. They can't wait for the processes they desire in hatred to materialize, so they urge the armies in Tanzania forward to kill.

359

"The idealists cannot have it both ways," continued Dr. Pessanha. "In England, again, they have an archbishop who advocates violence in the right conditions. By that I presume him to mean for justice, law and order. But it is precisely law and order that Portugal has always been fighting for in Africa—at first against the chaos and terror organized from Leopoldville and, more recently, the military force from Tanzania. The amusing question in England is, Who responds to this cry for violence from an archbishop? The pitiful few who still go to church and still believe in God? No, Mr. McQuade—not them, but the intellectual pack of the left, the meddlers on paper. We in Portugal see the tragedy in our oldest ally, England. We see this once-great nation split to pieces—the young and the old, the immoralists and the moralists, those who remember war and the Empire and the great past, and those who grow up caring nothing for it. It is tragedy to see the young divert their idealism and great vitality to mistaken, selfish and dirty ends, to destroy themselves faster and faster, with suicidal frenzy, not heeding the old or the wise. The intellectuals lie on the ground outside airfields and submarine bases. They howl against the use of nuclear arms at all and conventional arms in Vietnam and against the horrors there. But when it comes to the orderly societies of Rhodesia, Portugal and Angolique, that's different. They can't get the helicopters and napalm there fast enough. God preserve me from the hatreds of the intellectuals," concluded Dr. Pessanha fervently, "for theirs is the most vitriolic of them all."

Brigadier Fermoy observed in the silence, "I have to admit a certain tiredness from travel. Could we perhaps leave the intellectual aspect for some other time, Excellency, and consider now what you believe to be the military situation?"

The words "believe to be" were meant to be offensive and McQuade flinched. But Dr. Pessanha walked over to a map on the wall and suggested, "Have a look, Brigadier. This is *miombo* country—a brutal landscape dominated by the tsetse fly. There are almost no roads and the water is either foul or saline, and it is drying up now anyway. It is a grim place to die. But there are a few very small villages and settlements—here at Vila Metumba and Marrula, for instance. A main road comes up from the south as far as Nova Olivenca. By 'main road' I mean, of course, a wide dirt

360

track. But adequate for trucks. And we use two tiny airfields there and a major one built in nowhere, which we call Concrete One."

Brigadier Fermoy commented, "If you've only just been attacked, how come you already have a concrete airstrip suitable for jets?"

"I will ignore your rudeness," said Dr. Pessanha calmly, "and inform you that previously there was infiltration into Angolique from Tanzania along the edges of Lake Nyawi. Now there has been a buildup because of the urging on by the intellectuals of the West: the black man can do as he likes; he has the moral sanction of the United Nations and the West."

Franzo asked, "What is the scale of the fighting, Excellency?"

"It is terrible country, of course," said Dr. Pessanha, "and logistics would prevent armies of hundreds of thousands. It is fought by small units. It is a miniature Vietnam. The enemy have a forward base in Tongea and infiltrate fairly conspicuously through the village of Tchukiu—in trucks, in fact, and by canoe along the shores of Lake Nyawi. Marrula is almost cut off, and you may be distressed to hear, Mr. McQuade, that two Canadian clergy and a nursing sister, Miss Pogson, are in this situation with about a thousand Portuguese citizens of black and white skins. Many Africans —they are of the Nyanja tribe—have fled from the area altogether and have gone into the mountains or to Tanzania or across the lake. Farming is tremendously difficult in this area anyway—impossible in most of it—and many farms now stand empty. Once again we are subjected to foreign-inspired and foreign-trained violation. This time we have the right to appeal to the United Nations."

"Do we have free access to any part of the area?" asked McQuade.

"You do," said Dr. Pessanha. "And you have free access, Mr. McQuade, to any person in Portuguese Africa you wish to see. Black Portuguese or white Portuguese. In opposition or not. In prison or in office."

"Thank you, Excellency."

Outside, by the great pack of parked cars, in the heat of Lisbon's summer afternoon, Franzo commented, "I thought he was very sincere."

361

Brigadier Fermoy sneered, "He just wants help in a war he's losing. He has a lot of sweet talk."

McQuade said in irritation, "So would you have if the whole world listened only to the prejudices against you."

"I find that a curiously prejudiced remark in itself," observed the brigadier with a bit of a laugh.

"Then you must see when you get to the fighting."

"I suppose you know all about that, too?"

"I was in battle with the Canadian Army and know rather more than an Irish brigadier who has been confined to maneuvers," said McQuade loudly, giving way to anger. "And in future perhaps you'd leave the political dialogue to myself or Mr. Franzo and confine yourself to the military."

Brigadier Fermoy was shocked, but he knew at once that this was a good moment to withhold an angry reply; it would place McQuade in the wrong. Calm would give him the advantage. He would remember. He would be in the right. He could quote these words of McQuade's when a situation arose, and he would see that a situation did arise.

He said slowly, "Willingly. If you wish to sit through that sort of pap, I'll leave you to it."

The chances of success for the mission had now diminished, because these two men hated each other with that deep, instantaneous loathing that corrodes the soul.

They walked the hot streets in silence, an anxious Franzo aware of the possibilities of disaster.

4 ■ ■

VILA LOBANDA AGAIN. It was a Portuguese Boeing this time, and in the late afternoon it floundered around just inside the *cassimbo*, with the sun going down into the sea in a massive incandescence. Again the grim landscape around the airport, the red hostile earth and the solitary eerie baobab trees like huge wooden bottles the size of a small church: the red dusty empty roads and the Katuala seen far below for a hundred miles. Were the Bakongo still slaughtering down there in the most formidable landscape in Africa? Or had they given up because Portugal had surrendered positions to some *indigena* in the courts and legislative assembly in Vila Lobanda—a town beyond their comprehension in the forests from which they'd never moved?

The small crowd of Portuguese businessmen, priests, students and spies (every aircraft that flew in the whole of Africa had its quota of priests and spies) walked across the dry earth into the airport buildings. And there, as before, was Mr. Hermano Costa— the same lightweight suit, the same style of haircut as before, even the same tie, McQuade was sure.

He greeted McQuade and Marianne with something like affection, and this automatically incurred Brigadier Fermoy's dislike.

"The Governor General and the Minister of the Interior will see you this very evening," he claimed with the pride of one who had achieved a miracle for these foreigners.

The same drive through the same suburbs of open spaces, bungalows, miniature skyscrapers, the tin huts of suburbia where poor Portuguese and African lived together. Past the Villa Amélia and the convent and the Lycée, where Lilli no longer studied. They had rooms in the Hotel Marromeu, still clinging to its claim of being the Hygh Note of International Society. There were no unpleasant Belgians in the bar when they got to it—just two Rhodesians, some Portuguese aircrew and an old American couple who were going around the world the hard way.

They dined at Government House, which was rather agreeable considering the last occasion upon which McQuade had seen Colonel Domingues. The Minister of the Interior, Tamagnini de Oliveira, was there, and they weren't very far beyond the soup course when his dislike of Brigadier Fermoy's attitude began to boil over. It was almost funny for McQuade, who loathed the brigadier already and hadn't cared for the small but powerful Minister —almost funny, but not quite, for it was part of tragedy.

Colonel Domingues was explaining how agitators and saboteurs still tried to enter Angolique despite the surrender of some sovereignty by Portugal in heed of the UN's wishes.

363

"It's quite sophisticated," he explained, "and very difficult to stop altogether here or in South Africa or indeed anywhere in Africa. For the so-called nations north of us do not want it to stop and are well supported by American money, Commonwealth Preferences, UNO and a vast apparatus of espionage and sabotage trained all over the world."

Brigadier Fermoy interrupted, "Do you not feel you should qualify, Excellency?"

"I don't quite follow you."

"It is, surely, a matter of opinion, all this, not fact. Your opinion, Excellency, not necessarily mine."

The Governor General said evenly, "Certainly the dead cannot speak in evidence. And the explosions are not entirely of the volition of the chemicals; someone has to press the plunger. Nor are the agitators silent. They do open their mouths. Fortunately, it is not easy for them to speak Portuguese! But as I was saying, Brigadier, for your interest rather than your persuasion, the sophisticated spies come in the airplanes, but the saboteurs often try to come straight through the border and customs posts. Often they do it in the guise of being part of the crowd. All of southern Africa has seasonal movements of workers across borders, for some of these other so-called nations cannot, even assisted by US and British money, support themselves. So the workers come in thousands to Angolique and South Africa to work in factories and refineries and elsewhere.

"And our immigration and customs men haul in a dozen gunrunners and saboteurs a week. South Africa catches more. The girls come through with jars of cold cream which even smells and tastes like cold cream but is in fact plastic explosive. Beer bottles are suspect, and there are far too many jars of plastic strawberry jam! Then they bring along battered old suitcases tied up with rope, and the rope happens to be lengths of cordite. Their papers may be in order, but they are ignoring your resolutions just as much as they defy our hospitality and law. And not all come across the border through customs posts, I need hardly add."

"It is, one presumes, an expression of opinion," suggested Brigadier Fermoy.

Mr. de Oliveira asked slowly but with loathing, "If you have

364

come with a prejudice that is contrary to the supposed impartiality of your inquiry, why do you come at all?" For once McQuade agreed with the sentiment of the question. Oliveira concluded bitterly, "It is not a parody we are going through, but a reality in which Portuguese lives are taken. You have been given the freedom to go where you like and to talk to whom you like. Lisbon has asked for your help in a war that is unnecessary. Go to that war, Brigadier Fermoy, and learn the truth. Do not abuse the hospitality of the dinner table to quote the rubbish and prejudices of journalists who have only one eye."

He stood up, a small old man who gave his all to Portugal. And in rather dramatic support of his gesture all the lights went out. It was pitch-dark in the dining room. The Governor General said, "Do remain seated," and groped his way to a window. Outside, the lights of the entire city had gone out. Even the air conditioning was silent. It was possible to sense the astonishment of people in the street and even the drivers of automobiles. Somewhere out on the sidewalk a girl laughed. In a few minutes the lights all came on again and Oliveira was standing there as if he was operated by electricity, and he now moved out of the room.

"Forgive my colleague's rudeness," apologized Colonel Domingues. "He is a patriot, that is his excuse."

"And forgive my associate's ignorance," said McQuade, who was furious with Fermoy. "I have no idea whom he serves."

For the rest of the meal conversation was very difficult indeed and limited to the timetable of their itinerary. They would be leaving this part of Angolique in about thirty-six hours.

Part of the next day McQuade spent with Manuel Bajune and a few senior members of the Tando Party. He took Franzo with him, but said coldly to the brigadier, "This will be a political conversation. I shall not need your advice, and you will not wish to listen to pap . . ."

On the way in a taxi Franzo ventured anxiously, "This is very worrying, Mr. McQuade."

"What is, Mr. Franzo?"

"This quarrel with Brigadier Fermoy."

"Do you think I am being unreasonable?"

"Neither of you is being tactful."

365

"I think it's got beyond that point," agreed McQuade.

"Be most careful, Mr. McQuade, I beg you. He has access to important ears."

"I am only concerned with the truth. It cannot hurt Africa or the UN."

"It's not as simple as that."

"Well, perhaps you are right to remind me."

"You will not quarrel with *me* if I point things out that seem to need pointing out?"

McQuade stared at him. "Oh, come now, Franzo. Am I as unreasonable as that?"

"I fear this quarrel may get worse, Mr. McQuade."

Bajune and four members of Tando talked to McQuade and Franzo in the back garden of a bungalow. It was like high politics in suburbia. From over two wire fences an African neighbor, a plump housewife, stared, retreated, giggled, ventured back and forth to have a look. Chickens squawked and Portuguese and *indigena* children played in the dust; there was the comfortable smell of heat and goats.

McQuade half embraced the little Bajune, with his saucer glasses and honest voice and curious respect for the London School of Economics. He introduced Franzo and the other four there shook hands and all was agreeable and relaxed in the hot afternoon. There was no excitement or hatred, just conversation.

"And how are you getting on?" McQuade asked.

"Well, as you know, I am now the Deputy Minister of Education," said Bajune. "So the answer to your question is I am getting on quite well and rapidly!"

The others all laughed gently—an African joke.

"We are all members of the legislative assembly," said a second African. "Outnumbered three to one, but we are there!"

Again the good-humored laughter.

"Do you find the Portuguese agreeable?"

"Oh, yes, they are all right," said Bajune.

"Not many quarrels—"

"Some are good men, some are not."

"They still don't invite us to their homes," said one African. He shook with amusement. "But, then, I don't invite them to mine!"

366

"I have been to the house of Hermano Costa," said another.

"I would not go to drink wine with Oliveira even if he did ask me!" commented another.

McQuade and Franzo joined in the laughter over this remark.

Bajune said, "The Tando Party still exists. Many Africans hold a little power now. There are judges and even high police officials. But that is for the moment all."

McQuade argued, "You must be reasonable and patient. You do realize that your own education wouldn't get you anywhere near as high a position in Europe or America?"

"You phrase your remark badly and suggest that I am an ignoramus," disputed Bajune.

"I'm sorry. That was not intended."

"But of course this is the way it must be done," agreed Bajune. "Like the British carried it out. Learning, acquiring and taking over gradually and without hatred. That is why I am prepared to work now with—and not, I feel, merely *for*—the Portuguese, who have been most reasonable, always excepting Mr. de Oliveira. Gomais and Matumoza hate me for this, but Tando is in accord, I feel, with the world which does not want violence."

"Is there still fighting in the north?"

All of them wanted to speak at once.

"I have heard that the Bakongo are defeated . . ."

"It depends what you call fighting . . ."

"Matumoza left the north and went to Lourenco Tomas . . ."

"I have seen wounded in Vila Lobanda . . ."

"If it exists it is not the *Movimento Anticolonialista* which has fallen apart . . ."

"I have heard from my cousin who says trucks and guns . . ."

"My mandate is to find out what is happening on the borders of Tanzania."

They knew nothing about that.

"It is nearly three thousand miles away," pointed out Bajune.

"It has long been said," remarked another man, "that all of Africa concentrates its violence in Dar es Salaam and is trained there and supplied by the Chinese and others."

"That is exactly what I have to confirm," said McQuade.

They stared at him sadly, in as much ignorance as he was, and he knew in his bones that he would have to hear the guns and see the dead before he could report the truth to the Secretariat.

Long before dawn they were at the airport, and, to McQuade's astonishment, Vila Lobanda airport was crowded. There was a great agitation of feet and conversation, much embracing, tears and laughter. Priests moved about urgently with a crowd of students, most of them white but some black, all teeth and laughter. There was the clatter of cutlery and hiss of steam and smell of things cooking; a lavatory door opened and closed ceaselessly; an increasing line of cases stood on a platform; paratroops with submachine guns strolled in pairs. The radiomen and press of Vila Lobanda were seeing off an important football player. The commotion had nothing to do with war at all!

"It's going to be a packed Boeing," complained Marianne.

The great gong boomed in the departure hall and the pace intensified, the tears and the touch of hands. But it wasn't a Boeing and it wasn't crowded. It was a rather old Super Constellation, and the long, fiery red line of the dawn shone on its silver metal. Only thirty-two people were flying from this part of Angolique to the other, from west Africa to the east and southeast. The machine did not seem to be very "super"—the brakes had a job to hold it and as it took off the long thin wings with the petroleum pods at each end seemed to flap and creak visibly, and McQuade, sitting by a window, saw what appeared to be an oil leak in the hydraulics of the ailerons or flaps.

A priest went around conversing with the Portuguese passengers —perhaps reassuring them about the oil leak!—and stared at McQuade and his party with that slight uneasiness of the priest in Africa who has good cause to be suspicious of the sophisticated. The attractive, dignified Portuguese girls hurried around with the breakfasts of omelet, bread, cakes, coffee and orange juice. The brigadier sat two seats away from McQuade, emanating hatred. Marianne stared out of an opposite window and took photographs. Ecchegarri looked a little anxious and air sick and closed his eyes.

The Super Constellation climbed slowly above the dawn. The *cassimbo* hung about in shreds but, not far below, McQuade could see the waters of the Lower Bompopo Scheme. He recalled Ekelund's whispered remark months ago when he had stood down there —"It is nothing." He had half agreed at the time. Now he wondered. The Valley Irrigation and Settlement Scheme was a worthy project. And Angolique had made it on her own, for Portugal in Africa received no financial help from anywhere in the world. One-seventh of Angolique's income had, for some years, been poured into the Lower Bompopo Scheme, and there now, down below, it could be seen. A road and railway went across the irrigation barrage to use it to the full. McQuade observed the Katuala River, the protective dikes which prevented flooding of the irrigated area, the distribution canals and even the white lines of the raised concrete flumes which carried the water to the crops. Settlement was, he knew, open to black people and white people, and the red tiles down there were on the neat semidetached houses of both. They came with nothing and were given an ox cart and a few acres and they got on with the work. It was peasant-style farming, to suit the poor of southern Portugal and the *indigena*. The villagers there met in the village and farm councils and there was often the remarkable situation in which the secretaries and treasurers were Africans because they were *more* literate than the Europeans. But this was something the world did not want to hear about. It was important that the white settlers all over Africa should be betrayed by those in the capitals of Europe who hadn't been to Africa and took their evidence elsewhere . . .

The Super Constellation soared over the wet, hot mountains and the broiling forest, over small rivers like tightly coiled silver wire lying on a beach from which the tide had long receded, over the great rivers looped in an endless series of capital "Ss." It went over vast landscapes of brown earth with burned black patches like slates on an infinity of cocoa dust. It hastened at its meager 350 m.p.h. over other, slower meandering rivers and their lagoons, crowded on this dry morning with the water birds, the flapping wings and the opportunists' eyes of the storks, herons, geese and fish eagles. It passed over escarpments the color of a lion's skin and over the flat featureless distances of the drying-up mudpans and their thousands of flamingos. It navigated its way safely over the desert which told the navigator nothing, the great sand-filled basins where strong winds blew and there was great variation in tempera-

369

ture from day to night. The pink oxide dunes, touched here and there with spiked shrubs and big hard acacia trees, rolled over the world of the desert like an enormous sea, the waves of which were a hundred to five hundred feet apart and often almost straight for miles, each with its crest of stiff grasses.

It flew over open country and thickets, bush and square rock boulders that weighed thousands of tons. It went with the slow perspectives of great distances over the bush and woodland and the floodplains drying out now in a year of exceptional drought, but still, four miles below McQuade's eyes and Costa's sad face, there was some grazing and water for the hippopotami, buffalo and waterbuck; and sometimes from the dense woodlands the sables and roans ventured out to join the eating. The Super Constellation, with Brigadier Fermoy smoking and full of hatred, and the calm, kind eyes of the stewardess watching for fear, illness, hunger or need, followed its course above the short-grass pasture and its congregations of the great herds of wildebeeste, eland, gemsbok and springbok. It flew without heed over the north of Bechuanaland, over rivers drying up but still quite full of crocodiles which had their human victims each year . . .

High above the earth it flew, high beyond the great dramas and tragedies of Africa, over wide soda lakes with their millions of flamingos, and it crossed from land which was in part moist or saturated to a world which was baked dry. Some of the damp country —and, indeed, some of the dry—was disturbed by wars and intolerance and upheaval, and no longer received the care needed to combat those elements likely to hurt man.

In these politically distraught areas the flying locusts were no longer sprayed, for the white man had gone. And so the great swarms regained their existence. A fair-sized swarm of locusts would contain a thousand million insects and it would eat its way through three thousand tons of green food each day. Successive generations of these odd insects might multiply into many swarms, and the same damp air currents that controlled rain moved them in hosts that darkened the sky. When they settled, their sheer crawling mass of weight broke trees and crushed plants, and living animals could not bear the physical contact.

Another of Africa's huge dramas, beautiful and cruel, was evolv-

370

ing down there below the Super Constellation. The lakes and the rivers and even the dams of Africa not yet bothered by drought were choked with the alarmingly multiplying, beautiful water hyacinth. It had brought lake fishing here and there to a standstill, and African fishing villages were empty and the truckloads of fish no longer were carried. The hyacinth formed mats on lakes and reservoirs, and these grew with terrifying haste—in months 75 square miles would become 200, and even the small lake steamers would be in danger. A change of wind moved the beautiful mass, and if a man was stranded in his little fishing boat, he could neither swim nor row through the mat—he had to wait for a change of wind.

In the nearly three thousand miles McQuade traveled from west to east, here war was a triviality, for here was taking place the greatest tragedy of them all.

The earth of all Africa was, it could be said, determined by its rain. Five inches of rain in the year and it was desert; with fifteen, it was grass steppe with acacia and other bushes; with fifty inches, it would be either forest or savanna, according to whether the rain fell in one season followed by a long drought or whether it was well distributed through the year.

The pattern was fascinating.

In the areas of low rainfall the grass tended to be dominant, for its great mat of fibrous roots was able to make more use of the meager rainfall than were the widespreading roots of trees. When the sun burned and smoked the land dry the leaves of the grass withered, but the roots and growing points remained alive. But trees and shrubs could not do this, having to maintain the water content of their twigs, and could not resist using water through the long arid days even though they shed their leaves as a man might shed his vest and waistcoat but still go to the tap . . .

The cattle and sheep came and ate the grass and the trees began to win back supremacy. The suppression of natural fires also helped trees to gain in the natural struggle of balance between trees and grass. As the grass was eaten too close by domestic and wild animals—a particular culprit was the zebra—it withered and died in the semiarid land, erosion came, the bush became thicker and the land lost its pasture value to man . . .

But nature also worked an opposite pattern. The great fires of

371

summer could burn trees as well as grass. The trees standing alone or in small numbers in a vast sweep of grass ten feet tall could not withstand the fires and burned with the grass, exploding in crisp eagerness. After fire came the erosion of the topsoil, now too shallow for the great trees, and when rain came grass grew, supplanting them, changing the nature of the land. Another vast process went in parallel. The heavy eating of the trees by giraffes and the four-ton elephants which knocked the trees down destroyed the growth in areas which had rain. And when many trees were torn down the grass took over and grew tall and lush. And, similarly, over landscapes in which there was not sufficient rain for agriculture and much of it was infested by the tsetse fly, there could be only limited grazing. The rainfall might be erratic or the drought severe and the grass could not grow tall, nor were the fires severe—for there was nothing to burn. And in such a world the trees could not grow big and they stood only twenty feet tall.

But now came the worst of a sequence of droughts, and even the wild animals died. For, normally, wild animals can often live with less water than domestic and do not die in drought. In the bushveld areas of Rhodesia, for instance, the wild animals use the vegetation very efficiently, need no veterinary care and are immune to harm caused by the tsetse fly and several diseases. But this drought was not normal. Half of life was dying or would never be born. The wildebeeste in their calving grounds had conceived before the drought, but they now abandoned their babies, for they could give them no milk. And since they themselves would die or would not be able to conceive, another calf crop would be lost when the next season came . . .

Central and eastern Africa was burned dry and starving. From Ethiopia to the Cape each country took its dreadful turn. The rains failed in area after area. The rivers and the wells dried up and the crops did not sprout or else shriveled on the stalk. First Somalia, where three-quarters of a million people starved. Then the coastal plain of Ethiopia. And then Kenya, Tanzania, and all the way through Matabeland to Basutoland, Swaziland and Bechuanaland. The charitable agencies and the League of Red Cross Societies struggled hard. The South African Government sent maize to Basutoland, Bechuanaland and Swaziland. The United States drew

372

upon its grain surpluses. But the gestures could not defeat the giant scale of events in Africa. And the sour truth was still that all financial aid to Africa was less than 1 per cent of the national incomes of the developed countries. Further, and more deplorable, 80 per cent of the aid given was "tied aid" and had to be spent in the donor countries. This tended to direct the aid to buildings and cities, hotels and offices, restaurants and motorways, and the dire need for village development in an agricultural society was ignored; and the millions of the rural populations of the continent, as usual, already lacking the physical stamina, literacy and technical understanding, were left to face drought when it came . . .

My chickens have died because there is no chaff. There is no chaff because there has come no grain. My dog which I loved has died because I could give him no tidbits from the cooking pot. I had two goats and they have died because there was no rain and no leaves stayed on the trees for them to eat. There has been no rain and no grass has come and so the cattle of my people have died. And my children die and I must stand and watch and do nothing and the tears which I and my woman shed will not make the grass grow or the leaves come. The two-year-old baby of Europe weighs twenty-eight pounds but my baby boy here is two and he weighs only ten pounds and the flies cluster around his face and he cannot find the strength to raise a hand and brush them away. I have another son by the same woman who cries here, and he is three but weighs only twenty-four pounds and he can be carried in one hand. And my little girl of eight, who is buried in the dust down there, weighed only thirty pounds. My woman and my children and myself have swollen bellies and sores on our legs and my baby is going slowly blind. Bring me not freedom or votes or armies. If you are so clever, man, make it rain! Make it rain!

Eastern Africa was parched. It was a landscape of dust, cracked hard earth and bleached bones. Cattle herds died, the grazing land died, softwood trees by the million died, and this caused damage to water-cache areas. And when the water was thus able to flow quickly off baked land, the surface was burned up quickly and serious erosion was inevitable. And a change in the pattern of what rain there had been also caused chaos, for sometimes the total fell in a few days where it had been expected over a longer period, and

373

so crops germinated rapidly and sent up shoots which were now shriveled. In some cases the cattle died even though water was there to drink, for the sun had burned up the grass. The carcasses of the dead lay among the living, which stood mournfully around the lakes of Bechuanaland and watched the vultures and maribou storks gorge on the dead, and their solemn eyes knew that this end was coming for them, too. The dry wind howled and stirred up columns of dust . . .

The shanty towns and villages of the eastern half of Africa were full of starving, destitute, workless people. And the bony cattle sat down with sorrow in their faces and died. All across Bechuanaland, Swaziland, Kenya, Tanzania, Rhodesia, Basutoland, even Somalia and Uganda and some parts of Angolique, the earth and the people and the animals were undernourished, erosion was aggravated and grazing limited. The pack animals in the mountains were too weak to trek and fetch the necessary food which that small part of the world sympathetic to such disasters had tried to give through governments and voluntary organizations. Hundreds of thousands of people were in misery and cattle died by the half million: a third of this nation's, a half of thats. Scores of thousands of acres could no longer be grazed and such grazing as existed was diminished by the inevitable invasion of other stock. Milk yields were low from animals which survived. Foot-and-mouth disease stalked hand in hand with these other woes. Cattle ventured into the forests in hunger. Laborers demanded wages in food. Squatters were stealing to live. The rainfall had dropped year by year from perhaps twenty-six inches to nine . . . There was, too, bitter truth in the cry of a Kenyan minister that the officials of the United Nations Food and Agriculture Organization should get out of their plush chairs in the Rome offices and see what was going on in the world; that the FAO headquarters there was a hive of paper industry; that too many "experts" were of poor standard or were too elderly or frail for their work. The great drought was left to voluntary organizations and the Red Cross and to African governments who fought against starvation and disease, and these were assisted in their hour of need by the much-maligned South African and Rhodesian authorities. The UN tended to form more committees and advise . . .

And all the great rubbish heap of civilization that thought so well of itself, endlessly preening itself in a mirror of words and scratching its sores with satisfaction, all it could think of on behalf of this man standing in the dust and longing for rain and food, all it could suggest in its great superiority of wisdom was that he must have a vote, he must be free (or have a freedom conditioned by US loans, or Commonwealth Preferences or the purchase of grain by Communist China); he must join in the big talk; there must be a huge killing on his behalf to bring his freedom to pass . . . The dust stirred on the cracked, dry riverbeds and God must have laughed with great bitterness . . .

All these things passed through the mind of McQuade, whose heart was hurt and body tired, but who still wished to spare the innocent of the villages the tragedy that the men of words and intellectual hatreds wished to impose on a continent which needed no help from them in terms of disaster.

After more than seven hours the Super Constellation swept down over a city in the sun. This was Lourenco Tomas, one of the most attractive cities in Africa. Like Vila Lobanda, it formed a grand crescent on the edge of the sea—fine modern buildings of Portuguese and European style, the evidence of a holiday city, sophisticated in the warmth of a kind Indian Ocean sun. But it was also a city big in other terms. The Super Constellation crept in over miles of shipping, oil refineries and long, broad, residential avenues. Again, as in Vila Lobanda, there was an area of boxlike constructions of tin and wood which from the aircraft had the appearance of a honeycomb, but were, McQuade knew, where the poor lived—the white poor, who had arrived from Lisbon and Oporto with nothing, and the *indigena,* who shared these huts and corrugated-iron homes with them.

The aircraft descended over plantations and rows of neat houses in some outer suburb. Its wheels touched the ground and started to roll, and McQuade relaxed for a moment, withdrew his gaze from the scene outside.

It was a mistake to relax.

One of the tires burst after the Super Constellation had rolled a few hundred yards and the sensation was very alarming. Marianne was not the only one who gave a cry of fright. A few passengers had not fastened their safety belts and now fell sideways.

The wheel thrashed the burst tire to ribbons and then ran on its

375

hard rim. The pilot's struggles for control were superb but not appreciated at the moment by the passengers. The Super Constellation ran off the concrete runway and swung about in a very frightening manner but came to a stop with only a slight tilt.

There was laughter of relief, the sharing of a dangerous event, but it, too, was premature. Running on its rims had worn hard at the undercarriage structure of the port side and now it collapsed and the port wing smacked down onto the grass. Now there was screaming and something of a rush to the exits.

The Portuguese girls called for calm and opened the emergency doors, and all the passengers had to do was jump or crawl or hang and let go their hands and drop perhaps seven or ten feet to the ground, depending which exit door they used.

McQuade and his party waited for the other passengers to leave first. He then sat on the edge of an exit and launched himself off. He landed on his left foot, which hurt and collapsed under him.

Half a mile away a man on the restaurant balcony took photographs of the passengers. He used a 600mm. telescopic lens so that in effect he could well have been a mere ten feet away. This man was a Greek who normally took photographs (from an inconspicuous distance) of sophisticated people in semiadulterous postures or in attitudes that might be regarded as lecherous. A trivial playboy prince might be sitting at a table in some outdoor restaurant in this city (which was used quite a lot as a starting point for comfortable safaris), and he might glance down at the half-revealed breasts of the woman with him; at that moment, at some high vantage point a few hundred yards away, the photograph was taken. And around it went to the international magazines which specialized in this sort of titillatory gossip. On this occasion the photographer had been asked through a chain of about five conversations, three letters and a local telephone call to see if he could take McQuade's photograph in an unfortunate position or with an expression on his face that could be interpreted throughout the picture magazines of the world as vulgar, angry or silly.

And here to start with was a photograph of McQuade collapsing like a man more than half drunk, and in any case with loss of dignity. The rest depended on distribution and a careful but malicious caption. The photographer was taken ill a few days later,

376

but by then the photograph of McQuade in a ludicrous position had reached Germany, and copies had moved on to Belgium and France. A day later one New York paper and two London dailies were carrying it, and Mr. Cannon and many others had it thrust before their eyes.

In the same few hours Kristan, walking along 96th Street with Bill Dardick, was stopped by a man who said, "Excuse me, aren't you Mrs. McQuade? I'm from—" and he acknowledged the newspaper which employed him. Kristan said angrily, "I've nothing to say to you," and Bill looked embarrassed, for it was a mere 9:30 in the morning. As she stood in an almost stationary posture of anger and anxiety, a photographer took a picture. That, too, made the newspapers with the apparently meaningless caption "Mrs. McQuade, wife of UN diplomat Shaun McQuade, who is negotiating the flare-up in Angolique, seen with oilman Bill Dardick this morning on their way to do shopping . . ." This newspaper and its associated magazines inevitably reached the desks of Mr. Cannon and hundreds of UN delegates, journalists, cynics, admirers of the UN and businessmen who did not like it, and implanted cynicism and suspicion among thousands, even millions, of ordinary people who always assumed that the press guarded their interests and knew what was "going on."

The smear, in fact, had begun.

Lourenco Tomas was a city of vivid architectural designs and colors in its miniature skyscrapers and long boulevards parallel to the Indian Ocean. Villas were pleasantly arranged among lines of palm trees, and there were many attractive outdoor cafes full of people chattering, drinking coffee, sampling the *piri-piri* or jumbo shrimps or dancing inside. Many of the offices were decorated with mosaics—even the National Bank had one a full hundred feet long. Most startling of all, on one of the main avenues from the harbor and city, the headquarters of the PIDE was fronted with blue and white glazed porcelain panels showing fisherfolk at work and play. The PIDE in fact didn't take the slightest notice of McQuade or his party; not a case had to be opened.

The war which worried New York, London and Peking and Mr. Cannon and the liberal journalists was a thousand miles north of

377

Lourenco Tomas, and the people of the town weren't disturbed by it. "Oh, yes," agreed the hotel barman, a boy from Goa, with a shrug and a smile, "there are troubles in the north." Not *ours,* was his implication.

In the city was a new church in the bizarre design of a paper hat. It fitted in surprisingly well with the Manueline-style public buildings, the inevitable fort by the harbor, the bright sails of small boats on a burning blue sea, the Africans strolling, light with laughter, across the larger *praças* inlaid with mosaic-tile pavements. The rich Jews from South Africa strolled out of the one ugly hotel in the town. There was laughter and haggling among the leopard and zebra skins, carved heads and handworked ivory for sale in the open-air market. The children of all colors shrieked with laughter, but nevertheless knew that the strange new building was a church and crossed themselves accordingly.

It was not the atmosphere of war, nor did it contain any of that anxiety of Europe and North America in the gray rain. The mood was easygoing, undaunted, tolerant and happy. White visitors from South Africa and Rhodesia on holiday strolled about self-consciously in the manner of the English in Italy, rather startled to find others more than capable of building a fine city by the sea and quite able to survive happily without any need of taking their perspectives from London, New York or indeed Johannesburg . . . The Portuguese men sat relaxed in the outdoor cafes and watched these strangers with their skin burned red who strolled about—even though they themselves lived in Africa—as if expecting a riot or some bizarre erotic experience to overtake them. Priests walked purposefully with knowledge of belonging here and being of use and even importance in a way no longer possible in Regent Street, Fifth Avenue or perhaps Commissioner Street, and the few Army officers who walked about had the same air of pride and belonging, of being where army uniforms were not associated with the dregs of society . . .

The Portuguese and Africans drove cars fast, and other Africans strolled about or rode on bicycles, laughed, held hands, stared in shops, and no one kicked them out of the way. On the contrary, any conversation in the street had its quota of *indigena.* There was no atmosphere of tension at all. So here they were, the oppressed

378

indigenous population, hurrying along the broad avenues to the north end of the town center, where on red dusty earth a fair was in full swing.

The hotel was full of South Africans, and these, too, defied the headlines: they were likable and human. It was proof again that much of the hatred of the world was on paper or in the ideas of people faraway.

At 3:30 in the afternoon the shadows were already long and the sun came through the colorful trees into McQuade's eyes. Soon the lottery and shoeshine boys flooded the crowded city streets and haunted the sidewalks to sell newspapers to the South Africans, not their own Portuguese. And what was worrying South Africa today? Nothing except the sports results! At half past five, as in Vila Lobanda, a hot, strong wind stalked through the town, the sun finally went down in a sky half streaked with pink and the ships anchored in casual pattern along the miles of harbor were illuminated. The restaurant and cinema lights came on and the city relaxed.

The South Africans at dinner filled the restaurant with laughter, and children made the usual pleas for sweet and sticky foods. The African waiters spoke English and posed for photographs. Talk of war completely baffled them; they had work to do, children to provide for. War was far away, a game played in the bush by people who liked that game. They, it so happened, didn't.

In the morning McQuade went with Franzo to see André Quissanga of the NWALO Party. He found him in great distress standing on the sidewalk of a broad avenue in a crowd controlled by policemen. Smoke billowed out of a second-floor window in the last stages of a fire. The crowd watched with great interest; indeed, they filled the tables outside a grocery shop across the road and sat down to watch it! Diagonally across the way, at a minor road junction, a road gang were at work, waist deep in a trench, their black skins shining with sweat. They were not supervised but only stopped working with picks and shovels to laugh. They all thought the efforts of the fire brigade enormously funny. They wore trilby hats and split pumps, but McQuade noticed a watch on one wrist.

It took half an hour to isolate Quissanga. He was very upset, and quite understandably, for the offices of NWALO had been broken into at four in the morning. It was not burglary, although type-

379

writers, documents and even the telephone had been stolen. There had been no secret about it. Thirty *indigena* had done it, and these, as Quissanga was now telling some press men, were members of Clemente Matumoza's *Movimento Anticolonialista,* which was now allowed on Portuguese territory and, oddly enough, still retained its name that was hostile to Portugal. Members of Quissanga's staff stood about in despair; a typist was weeping.

The raiders had been driven off by Portuguese police who, Quissanga claimed, had arrived *two hours* after being notified. This caused Quissanga to cry out in the street, "We have been betrayed. The police are in the pay of Matumoza, who is in their Government. But the people will not be deceived. I shall not sit down with any member of the *Movimento.* They have destroyed the records of my party; they have betrayed the African in his efforts to achieve a status. What for? To become important. But we are not deceived. It was not a *coup d'état.* Matumoza represents nothing. He has trained baboons in the forests of the Congo but here among sensible people these tactics of monkeys will not survive."

It took time to calm Quissanga sufficiently for any dialogue. He was so upset he didn't know whether to be angry or pleased about discussions with representatives of the United Nations.

"We are betrayed," he insisted. "I negotiated with Lisbon when these others were killing in the bush. And with Washington, which is now as silent as a corpse. And who gets the power which I obtained without violence? These traitors to Africa, Bajune and Matumoza. They are made ministers while I am offered the post of a mere clerk because, of course, I am not dangerous; I do not need to be placated by big bribery and power—"

"What about the war?"

"Ah, yes. Gomais has the right idea. Talk from strength. Kill Portuguese. Throw them out of Africa. But I am *here* and I and my party are watched. What can I do?"

"My mandate allows some negotiation as well as observation."

"Does it? Well, put it to them, Mr. McQuade. I do not set fire to people's offices or slaughter Portuguese farmers. Nor am I to be disregarded. I am the leader of a hundred thousand people. Portugal and Washington made promises to me."

"It is unlikely that Lisbon can ignore Bajune or indeed Gomais,

380

even if he fights with armies now. He will have to become part of the African's power here if there is a war and it is to be stopped by negotiations."

"Oh, there is a war all right," claimed Quissanga. "And I cannot hold my people here in restraint forever if I am given no promises or they are not fulfilled. But sit at a table and talk with a lunatic like Matumoza? Never! He is a disgrace to Africa. No wonder the white man still laughs. All the black man wants in your world is status. He dislikes being used as a puppet or regarded as a fool."

"This I know, sir," McQuade acknowledged. "Although he does indeed have some status. Nearly half of the General Assembly of the United Nations is African."

"He is allowed to talk and vote, certainly," agreed André Quissanga, "but when the big events come, these things mean nothing and the white man's money and pressures shape the destiny of the world and even of Africa in the manner he desires. That is why it is so pitiful and stupid to do *this*," he claimed bitterly, pointing an arm at the smoke trickling out of the broken windows . . .

Where was Matumoza?

McQuade was due to fly to Tanzania to see Gomais the next day and therefore had to talk to Matumoza today if at all.

McQuade discovered that Matumoza was on holiday at a lagoon a hundred miles north of Lourenco Tomas. There was nothing to do but drive north and see him. McQuade hired a car and took Franzo and Marianne. Brigadier Fermoy wanted to come, but McQuade refused and left him behind, a very angry man.

The road wasn't crowded. It was lined with cashew trees for miles beyond Lourenco Tomas, and Africans wandered barefoot among the trees, ignoring the possibility of snakes. There were bags of cashew nuts along the side of the road. By a river women washed blankets and clothes and their arms and breasts; nearby, children climbed a fence to watch African police cadets drilling in the hot sun. On the river the miles of hyacinth drifted, and McQuade could see the tunnels of hippopotami in the reeds. Small boats with canvas roofs, packed with laughing workers, were propelled through the hyacinths to a dairy farm. Along the riverbank were thatched huts, and a woman came out of one and emptied a bucket of dust as a European housewife might empty a bucket of water. Black goats wandered about, and long-horned cattle sometimes filled the road in a cloud of dust. Boys fishing from small boats waved at the car as it passed. One hauled up a big crab and held it high for approval. All along the road for the entire distance small processions of women walked with boxes on their heads; McQuade saw one girl carrying a long axe laid flat upon her hair. All were in brightly colored frocks and had bare feet. Some had bare breasts. They and their children and the old men sitting on the roadside and the young ones perched on gates or fences or high banks waved and grinned.

They drove out of the bush into grassland and saw a wider horizon. Melancholy long-horned cattle were being driven across the earth by a little boy perhaps eight years old. Still the figures walked along the roadside and smiled or waved. Where were they all going? Many of the women were fetching water. Occasionally they could be seen queuing at the iron wheel of a pump. And back they would walk for miles with calabashes on their heads or, perhaps, with the help of boys they would roll water barrels which had long handles and looked like the garden rollers used in Europe for rolling lawns. The landscape, hot in the sun, was now like southern Italy: tiny villages centered around a service station and cafe, the occasional small school or church . . .

They found Matumoza in a bar. It was, incredibly, in a hotel run by South Africans and right beside a beautiful lagoon. A few South African girls in bikinis played on an almost empty beach of white sand and palm trees, with sunshades and tables and waiters yawning in the sun. There, in the comparative cool of the attractive bar, was Mr. Clemente Matumoza with his wife. Beyond the lagoon the sharks waited . . .

"Well!" he greeted in astonishment. "What a capacity you have for coming back from the dead!"

There were introductions and they all drank iced beer.

"We have made some progress," claimed Matumoza. "For this we owe a tremendous debt to you and to Mr. Rossio."

"I am on my way to the area of Vila Metumba and the fighting," explained McQuade. "No one seems to know what the position is. Why is anyone now fighting the Portuguese at all? I have seen Bajune, but he and Tando know nothing."

382

"They *are* nothing," argued Matumoza. "I repudiated Tando many months ago. They do not exist except as puppets in the Portuguese administration."

"And I have seen Quissanga and he believes there is fighting. He is angry with you."

"With me?" Matumoza laughed. "This toady of the Portuguese is angry with *me?*"

"He thinks your people burned down his office and official records."

"He thinks I and my people did that? The evidence will refute that suggestion. Then, I suppose, he will think the Portuguese did it. That will be fine! He will kill a few Portuguese and then they will kill him, and that will be another clown out of the way!"

"Surely only cooperation among parties can possibly hope to obtain power?"

"I have power," claimed Matumoza. "I have an army, as you saw for yourself. It still exists. Its other leaders are still in Leopoldville. I have only to give the signal and the killing will recommence . . ."

McQuade wondered if this was true or whether it was merely a statement to cover up an embarrassing truth, that Matumoza had abandoned the military struggle for the limited power of a minister.

As if in explanation Matumoza told him, "I am the Minister of Transport in Angolique. I thus hold the most important post. For if I give the word Angolique comes to a stop, trains cease to carry coal, oil, copper and diamonds."

"Do you know what the position is up north?"

"There is fighting."

"Is it Chinese inspired?"

"It is the continuing struggle of the *indigena,*" said Matumoza. "It owes nothing to the Chinese except"—he laughed—"except money for the arms they send! It owes much to the wishes and inspiration of the Organization of African Unity. The OAU is going to throw the white man out of Africa. Oh, yes, Mr. McQuade. Out of Vila Lobanda, Lourenco Tomas, Salisbury and Capetown. The feebleness of armies and the great distances slow it down, but such a will cannot be denied."

"Africa is one-seventh of the world," argued McQuade. "No

383

other one-seventh except China denies the existence of black and white and yellow nations."

"I would dispute that," Matumoza said. "Asia is also tired of the white man's colonialism and soon may be independent of him financially. And what does that prove except that his wickedness has come to an end?"

"With respect and regret," said McQuade, "and even though you have paid for the beer, I think it proves that the color bar and racial prejudice operate in two directions and not one, as is claimed."

"This may be so," agreed Matumoza. "In which case, when the great convulsions have ended and each can say of where he lives, 'This is mine,' then, surely, we can begin again as mankind and explore a new relationship in terms of equality?"

"In the meantime," pointed out McQuade sadly, "we have the world as it is."

McQuade began the long drive back to Lourenco Tomas before the afternoon light faltered. He drove fast on the narrow, dust-bordered road, past the bright green landscape of sugar plantations, along roads raised above irrigation ditches, past farms and small neat Portuguese buildings, narrowly missing buses piled high with workers who even sat on the roof. People waved as they had done before. Every time a vehicle came the other way, it, too, came at maximum speed. McQuade could sense Marianne's tension as she sat beside him, for it was dangerous; each vehicle charged past the oncoming one all right but went straight into a cloud of red dust. Once, McQuade had to hurl the car into the loose sand on the side of the road and it slid out of control for long seconds.

The sun dropped like a big red ball onto a horizon ahead consisting of bush and brittle trees. It was marvelous to behold, for as the sun neared the horizon it seemed not to be in the sky at all but to have become a red-hot sphere which had settled on the soil a few miles off. It broke and bulged and was gone. For ten seconds afterward there was the extraordinary, strong blue-green light where it had been, and then a yellow too fierce for the eye; and finally the sky turned crimson and night came.

The fog of dust was worse at night and far more insects spattered themselves on the windshield than during the day. Fireflies

384

and other insects glowed phosphorescent in the headlights. When the oncoming trucks' lights met McQuade's the glow of insects was like light snow falling. The trucks neither dimmed their headlights nor moved to one side, and many times McQuade swerved onto dust and ruts, and the car—it was a diesel Mercedes—crashed and shook. Marianne at last protested, "Just supposing we survive the drive, drinks are on you! You're scaring the life out of me!"

McQuade smiled, but was unafraid. He looked down the headlights to where, even in the dark, the African figures walked along the side of the road in a world of bush and huts and no streetlighting whatsoever and knew he was safe. His destiny was not here.

Dar es Salaam was another attractive African city, built by the Germans and English on a coast which had many of the conditions of the archetypal tropical beach: palm-fringed sands, coral cliffs and the Indian Ocean breaking its brilliant blue on sand of pale gold. The city itself and its harbor were attractive. The white buildings stood vividly against a deep blue sky, and although it was a commercial port, it was equally a wide turquoise lagoon fringed with coconut palms and not far away was the vivid green of tropical vegetation.

It took hours to get there, a short flight from Lourenco Tomas to Salisbury and then a long one from Salisbury to Dar es Salaam, flying at night over the area where the war was supposed to be. But during all the hours of flying, between dozing, McQuade saw not a single light or flash across yet another four thousand miles of Africa.

The taxi was driving past the old German and British buildings and internationally built concrete offices in the tree-lined Azania Avenue when it stopped because a crowd was in the way. The crowd was hostile, which was meaningless, for how could anyone know who was in the taxi? A vehicle came out of a side road, and McQuade's brain, dulled by travel, realized that they were going to collide. This they did, with more noise than damage. The second machine backed in haste; its driver reengaged a forward gear and came forward and rammed the taxi again. "Don't get out," said Brigadier Fermoy. "That's what they want you to do. Reverse, you fool!" he shouted to the taxi driver. The crowd was now dispersing and the driver of the other car drove it violently around the nearest corner. He was, McQuade saw, Chinese.

The African policewoman put her head into the taxi and inquired in English, "You having a good time?"

Marianne answered, "I wouldn't have missed it for the world!"

"Anyone want to complain?"

Nobody did, not even the taxi driver.

McQuade ignored this bizarre incident. He just didn't know what it meant or was intended to do.

After lunch and a rest they walked around the town to find Ernesto Gomais and the ANP. Some verandaed bungalows of the British regime remained, but there were many more blocks of multistoried flats. The Ocean Road Hospital, half German and half Spanish in style, was still there. There were a few movie houses, a theater and the African markets, where crowds looked at crocodile, lizard, zebra and lionskin handbags, baskets and mats, seashell ornaments and wood carvings. A litter of small boats made the harbor look like a poor man's Cannes. On the streets walked all sorts of people—Arabs, Ismailis, Hindus, Sikhs, Africans from all across the center of the continent; men in long white *kanzus* and with red fezzes on their heads; Asian girls in brilliant saris; tribesmen from upcountry who had earrings in their ears and bangles on their arms and legs and little more than a red blanket for clothing, strolling among the vehicles from England and Germany and carrying spears. The street signs were still in English although there were few white faces here now. The same black policewoman in peaked hat stood directing traffic on the corner near where the taxi had been rammed.

The Parliament of Tanzania met in the Karinjee Hall, a modern building with Oriental touches. It was positioned near botanical gardens, which were full of a variety of tropical trees. But Gomais was not here. He had an office in the building of the Organization of African Unity. All other visiting heads of state, or persons who claimed that they expected to be, were provided with office suites and automobiles, and could get down in comfort to organizing war or propaganda against Portugal, South Africa or wherever took their fancy. One of the facts of life the British Government had avoided for years was the use of this Commonwealth territory by many politicians and even armies dedicated to removing the white

386

man from Africa. Thus, if Portuguese farmers were being killed and their farms burned down in northeast Angolique, as was claimed by Portugal—and even Mr. Cannon assumed that "it had been going on for years"—then the British taxpayer, unknown perhaps to himself, had been paying money and granting Commonwealth Preferences, not to mention loans, to a territory used for attack upon their NATO ally Portugal. This splendid irony had been going on for years because British officialdom leaned over backward—and possibly forward—to accommodate the howls of African nationalism, supply it with money and retain its friendship and the survival of a parody of a Commonwealth at the expense of Portugal in Africa, Rhodesia and eventually South Africa. These curious liberal sentiments were complicated by the parallel wishes to be popular in the United Nations and at the same time do big trade with Portugal and South Africa if not with Rhodesia.

Ernesto Gomais, who had once studied to become a priest, had once been, like Bajune, to the London School of Economics, had claimed to be negotiating with the UN, was still aggressive and suspicious. He was not pleased to see McQuade. He was no longer a suppliant. He was, or believed he was, a powerful man in an organization that was going to see that the continent of Africa was taken over by the black man, and no other circumstances or reason interested him. He had found out that the white man was fallible, even a fool sometimes, and when killed looked just as dead as anyone else. Gomais had the scent of victory; concessions or a new approach to multiracialism by Portugal meant nothing to him.

He asked brusquely at once, "Why are you back in Africa? To snigger at the black man?"

McQuade was not as calm as he had been before; he had been tortured by black men and betrayed by a white woman; God was not interested.

"To stop you making a fool of yourself," he answered promptly.

"So now I am a fool?" said Gomais loudly, and his African secretary turned from her typewriter to stare, as if asking, Who are these white people who come to be rude and interrupt our important work? "I do not giggle, Mr. American."

"Canadian."

"In what manner am I making a fool of myself?"

McQuade said, "Why are you fighting the Portuguese when they

387

have surrendered a good deal to the *indigena,* who now hold considerable power in Angolique?"

"You believe that?" questioned Gomais. "You have been talking to that sycophant, Bajune. Oh, yes, I can become a member of their legislature in Angolique. But I must abandon my party and this organization."

"But surely the ANP was formed only to obtain precisely what the Portuguese now offer—a share in government?"

"We fight, Mr. American, because the African must fight or he will be tricked, deceived, betrayed. The pressure must go on here in Africa and in the United Nations until the Portuguese go, and not only the Portuguese but the South Africans and Rhodesians, too."

"Is the African so unreasonable he will not negotiate at all?"

"I did not say that, although I hear of no pleas for negotiation from Capetown—"

"I am here to observe the situation, but my mandate allows some negotiation."

"With me?"

"With you and the Portuguese."

"I do not negotiate with the Portuguese."

"That is nonsense and contrary to the spirit of the times and the UN."

"So now you say it again. I am a fool?"

"It is the Portuguese you *must* negotiate with or allow me to do so on your behalf."

Gomais said angrily, "I have been betrayed by the African, by neurotic creeps like Bajune and people like Matumoza who can be bought. I will not align myself with these, nor will I negotiate with the Portuguese and dissipate my strength. The point is that I am recognized by the Organization of African Unity. I am part of it. The OAU does not view Matumoza favorably any more. Bajune and Quissanga it regards as nothing."

"What, then, do you expect?"

"I shall have what I want, Mr. grinning American."

"Canadian."

"I shall have Angolique. All of it. The OAU wouldn't give this office to one who wanted half measures. The Portuguese will be driven out—"

"That is force. I am not here to countenance force."

"I do not much care *what* you are here for. You betrayed us last time. You traveled with Portuguese, you even talk it. You are for the white man."

"I suffered torture for the black man," pointed out McQuade, "and obtained a result. Perhaps I was wrong to do so. But the rest of the world watches, Mr. Gomais. It does not admire threats or the refusal to negotiate."

"We have been betrayed too often," claimed Gomais, "but now we are obtaining satisfaction. Great things are afoot about which you seem to know nothing. It is the white man's turn to be afraid and to squeal."

"I do not think you show the sense of a politician or the dignity of a statesman," said McQuade.

"The door is behind you," said Gomais. "And who are you to presume what you think has value? You still have the ingrained arrogance of the white man who believes he is superior. I *am* a statesman. You are but a straw in the wind and it will blow you away."

On the other side of the door Brigadier Fermoy protested, "What a mess you made of that. You got his back up straightaway. And you say I must keep my nose out of politics?"

"He will have to negotiate," said McQuade, but he was shaken for all that. "And so will his organization. They have not yet taken over the world, nor have they laid down a new set of rules which the rest of us must abide by."

"I hope you report your conversation accurately," suggested the brigadier, "and allow the Secretary General's office to estimate for themselves."

"I shall give them the truth," said McQuade. "They will then do what they think right."

"What you think right?"

"I didn't say that," snapped McQuade.

He regretted the remark instantly, with its near admission of contempt for the Secretariat.

"You mean," questioned the brigadier, "that the two things are not coincidental?"

"I didn't say that either," McQuade pointed out, but he could

389

see the thought processes going on behind the brigadier's face, and he wondered if this enemy would in fact interfere directly, for he, after all, had many friends up there on the thirty-eighth floor in New York, and they might like to have news from him directly about a man who held them in scorn but acted on their behalf.

5 ▪ ▪

EIGHT HUNDRED MILES north of Lourenco Tomas and three hundred north of Nova Zeira, where they had picked it up, the Land Rover followed in the dust of five Portuguese Army trucks. Squashed in the Land Rover were McQuade, Marianne, Franzo, Brigadier Fermoy, Ecchegarri, communications officer Jean-Louis Barbu, a tall young Frenchman, and Mr. Costa. In the back of the vehicle was a litter of cases and equipment, including the Telex machine picked up at Nova Zeira with Barbu.

As Dr. Pessanha had forecast, the nearer the column of vehicles came to the area of war, the more hostile was the nature of the territory. They were still on a road, but it obviously would end soon, and no doubt the Minister of Overseas Boundaries was right and the water would be foul and drying up anyway. Along a small brown river McQuade saw in the same mile women washing clothes, children paddling and splashing about, goats excreting as they drank, men fishing, a man urinating, a queue of girls and women at five in the morning waiting for water and obtaining it from a pipe so positioned that it produced gravity flow. He could almost see the myriads of insects and bacteria in the water. But it was not a question of lack of hygiene; the stream represented all the water of any sort for forty miles and there would be no rain for months.

The trucks and the sweating humans left the roads and the tiny towns and the smell of civilization and entered one of the greatest expanses of uniform vegetation in the world—the *miombo,* which was a sour kind of savanna. For a while there were tracks of a sort and the vehicles zigzagged through the monotonous landscape, with its soil leached almost white and acid, where nothing useful could

390

be grown and no humans cared to live. Sometimes there was impressive stunted, gnarled, thick woodland along a cool ridge six thousand feet high with miles of moss. But where the water ran along the valleys the earth was now drying and the tall sour grasses and the acacia trees had a dreadful similarity relieved only now and then by the termite heaps, tall fibrous hibiscus, purple flowering shrubs and the syzygium tree along the soggy acid swamps. It was an area of hundreds and thousands of miles of small woodlands with grass under the trees. But the oscillation of the sun was at variance here with much of Africa and was at full strength high above in December, not June as in most of the continent, and so while half Africa starved and died, the *miombo* had rain. Now, as McQuade came, the leaves had fallen and the sour grass withered and fire crept through it. The grass became black and the trees were bare in the violence of the sun and it was the most depressing landscape in the world.

The drought came and the water reserves were shrinking now in the deep sandy soil. The days were cloudless and there was no wind to bring dust and obscure the sun. It was very hot and it was dreary and the air was motionless and stifling. The leaves burned in the fires and much of the earth was black.

But now and again the arms of old rivers, cut off for centuries, had become perfect lagoons which mirrored their fringes of large trees, and although these still waters were drying out, the animals concentrated to obtain water. On the second day they passed such a lagoon and saw big herds of buffalo and hippopotami.

By day the hawks, the vultures and the eagles stood in the sky, searching for food, anything from insects to the corpses of large beasts. The diurnal birds of prey hunted by sight, and at dusk so did the owls; but in the pitch darkness of the African night the owls hunted with their asymmetrical ears and facial discs that reflected sound, and their own flight was absolutely noiseless and in it they pinpointed the rustle of the invisible victim. Their sense of smell, like that of other birds, was negligible, so the corpses lying in the dark were cleaned up by the hyenas and jackals . . . In the *miombo* the chimpanzees were coming more and more out of the trees to kill in the open savanna, and many a small antelope died at their hands. Once McQuade saw a chimpanzee push a stick into an

391

active termite heap and lick off the insects like a kid with a lollipop.

It was a wilderness where the infertile soil excluded man and in which the tsetse fly kept out domestic animals.

In this dry season man could soon be lost and die among trees of similar size and kind in repetitive pattern on an earth without water. The animals trod carefully, each in its proper place; the sable antelopes and roans tended to stay in the wooded country along the water courses. Among the inselbergs, which were prominent bosses of hard black rock, one of the few features by which man could at times orientate himself, lived the leopards and baboons, the hyraxes and klipspringers. The Africans slaughtered the zebras and antelopes, and the lions and leopards preyed on all, taking care only of the great horns of the sable and roan. The attractive black-bordered orange charax butterfly and the masked yellow weaverbird, standing on loops of grass for all the world like scaffolding as they completed their nests, were the rare touch of bright color except for the pitiless persistent blue of the sky.

The sunset glowed over the endless woods and bush and when dark came the freckled nightjar began to call and the hyrax cried in alarm . . .

On the third day they reached a mighty river, the Bueda, and here the water ran fast and blue over smooth rocks. Plovers, herons, storks and kingfishers stood in thousands on the banks, and in the backwaters the wattled crane lived.

The area was magnificent and untouched by man, who could not defeat it, but beyond this river the soil was sour again and the grass pale and dry. Soon they were driving—and they had long since left roads of any kind—through the harsh monotonous impoverished landscape of the *miombo* again.

In the afternoon of the fourth day they came to Lake Nyawi and the tiny town of Vila Metumba, one of the most curious towns in the world. A couple of seaplanes and a gunboat on the lake were all so old that unreliability rather than enemy action was surely their greatest risk. There were a few long wooden huts, four or five small, old, tiled cottages, a few buildings by the lake and on its shore some cattle standing sadly, thousands of flamingos in graceful, stationary posture in green slime, and a little collection of fishing boats.

392

Portuguese soldiers strolled about and children ran in the dusty street. Here, as in Lisbon, as in Vila Lobanda, was poverty, a curiously undaunted poverty which was happy because it did not have the world of the color supplements and TV interviews to appreciate its own condition and become unhappy. Five miles away was Concrete One, an airstrip nearly two miles long, and a handful of old bombers. Not far away was war. Twenty miles, ten miles, or five hundred yards? The monotonous *miombo* did not reveal; and it could have hidden an army if any army could survive the conditions it imposed or the vast distances in appalling terrain necessary to overcome to get to this place. It was an arena, not for the tanks and impressive lines of field artillery, but for skirmishes and miniature slaughter, the cruelty of knives and grenades. Ten miles away the war was unknown and man tried to catch fish or grow a few things to eat in the leached sour soil.

They were not expected.

People stared at the white Land Rover as if it had come from outer space. The Army trucks they identified and understood. These went into a compound where there were other vehicles, some of them under repair after damage by mines or the brutal nature of the *miombo* in which they had to operate.

After a while two Portuguese officers came from the compound. They were marked with the strain of battle and the limitations of the area. They weren't by any means filthy, but had that slightly scruffy appearance of people in the battle zone. The lightweight suits and fresh haircuts and Marianne's New York summer dress and the well-fed faces of the Secretariat party were quite a contrast.

The Portuguese officers introduced themselves as Major Miguel Cordeiro and Captain Mário Maia. They were pleasant and courteous over the matters of quarters, food and rest, and at first were startled by Marianne, but soon became talkative and amusing. They had a slight and natural tendency to assume that the group had arrived with sympathy for their situation and discomfort, and it was Brigadier Fermoy who introduced the note of discord.

He asked, "What is the nature of the fighting?"

Mr. Costa translated for him.

"Oh, that is under control," responded Major Cordeiro. "You must not believe your newspapers! These boys really come to steal

393

cattle, not fight. Occasionally we encounter the ANP from Tanzania. But our fellows have it in hand."

"That is for us to judge," suggested the brigadier.

The major looked puzzled but made no comment. He assumed a mistaken translation by Costa, although the quality of the brigadier's voice was disturbing.

McQuade pointed out—in Portuguese, which the brigadier did not understand—"You will appreciate that we have come to assess the situation in response to a plea by Portugal at the UN."

"It is not serious," said the Major, "except in what it represents."

"How am I to know anything if you do not translate?" demanded Brigadier Fermoy.

"Then why the hell do you come at all?" McQuade snapped irresistibly, if not very logically.

The major and the captain stared at these two men, sensing the hatred although they did not understand the language.

Costa explained to them—and how bizarre it sounded here in the stifling heat and endless, indifferent monotony of the *miombo* and the little unpaved street and a small gathering of children, "These gentlemen are very important and have seen all the Ministers in Lisbon, Vila Lobanda, Lourenco Tomas, New York and Dar es Salaam."

Major Cordeiro said with a smile, "It sounds very impressive. Then why do they come here?"

"To assess the military situation and report—"

"Will someone have the courtesy to translate?" Brigadier Fermoy pleaded angrily, but McQuade ignored him.

Major Cordeiro's smile spread and he said, "We can give them the opportunity to do that. I am indeed pleased that the politicians of UNO have the courage to move out of their preoccupation with words and see what in fact these lead to."

Costa translated this for the brigadier, who responded promptly, "Tomorrow, then, we'll go to the forward area."

"Not tomorrow," said the Major to Costa. "That is not possible."

"Does this fellow have a superior?" the brigadier asked Costa. "Do I have to chatter with majors about when and what I do?"

This was duly translated and the major's smile vanished and he told Costa, "This is my small area and I am responsible for the conditions and lives within it. That includes this man's. He may travel to the battle zone the day after tomorrow when conditions allow it. I would be happy to offer these people the facilities of the officers' mess, but there is no mess and there are no facilities. However, I will have beer and food sent to their quarters."

With this he turned and with Captain Maia walked away.

They ate tinfoil cheese and drank bottles of beer and waited in the stifling heat for the sun to go down.

McQuade went to the shore of the lake as the sun stood above the horizon like a fiery ball in milk. The few *indigena* who were fishermen were setting out in their dugout canoes with large conical nets. There was no moon and they would lure the daaga fish into the big nets with lanterns. There was a dead mule among the slime and grasses at the edge of the lake, gashed by war and rotten now, and it gave off an offensive smell. But still McQuade stood with Marianne and Franzo watching the water, which lapped around the grasses. Far off hyenas began to howl and something stirred the papaya trees. Then, far out on the lake, disregarding the war, the lanterns came on, about thirty of them, but reflected in the still water so that they merged with the stars and only the movement betrayed which was which.

Behind, the sheds, huts and tiny houses were pinpricks of light in a world of complete darkness. Marianne took McQuade's arm and she whispered, "I'm a little afraid for you," and then, when he made no comment, counseled more earnestly, "I'm your friend. And I'm scared for you. Don't hate that stupid man too hard. He's a bad enemy to have."

The morning sun came through the open door. McQuade sat at a table writing messages for Barbu to transmit on the Telex machine to New York.

There were four children outside watching him—two very small *indigena*, a Portuguese boy of about seven in shorts, and a *mestiço* girl of ten or eleven, and they giggled and retreated every time McQuade looked up.

395

Finally the oldest of them, the *mestiço* girl, commented in Portuguese, "You write very rapidly."

"I have to," McQuade told her, "although this does not make for neat writing."

"I can write quite well," said the girl. "I can write in English."

This was improbable a few score miles from the border of Tanzania, on the Portuguese side, but why should he doubt what she said?

"Can you read this?" he asked.

She came into the hut which they were using for everything—eating, working, arguing, living within yards of each other's hatred. She was untouched by the atmosphere, however faint, of cities faraway, the lineup of bombers and the voices pleading with loathing and in ignorance of her. She was barefooted and shabbily dressed, but had an alertness, eyes that looked around quickly, and she had a face already beautiful, as *mestiço* children's and women's often are. No one would ever know about her. The debates and editorials, the tides of opinion, would roll on like the sea on sand, but the world would never know about this small girl. Some Portuguese soldier, perhaps, if the Army stayed here that many years, would marry her, take her away with pride. Something touched his great bitterness as gently as a butterfly's wing, something faraway and lost in the words and the Boeings and that other war, and he was afraid.

She read it very slowly, but proving her claim was true: "Fighting on a very small scale. Expect to visit area tomorrow. Information is that refugee camp at Mindi in Tanzania also used for guerrilla training. Suggest OAU inspection invited. No force required here except perhaps for maintenance of local confidence. Will report further when visited fighting. Considerable use of mines by guerrillas in hit and run. Words not wars wanted."

McQuade smiled and agreed, "You read it quite perfectly! Can you understand it?"

She stared at him and asked, "Have you come to save us from something?"

Again he was touched by the terror of uneasiness. The "war" was a few miles away, and the whole world was indignant, but she did not know if it existed.

396

He knew that in these matters it had to be proved to exist before it would be attended to. No one did anything until there had been a good deal of killing. It had to be proved over and over again how pointless and terrible violence was. Appeals had to be made by the Pope, strange eccentrics in England and the United States and by interested parties in China and elsewhere. Students had to run through the streets and embassies had to be smashed. Further, proof of existence had to be on specific terms or it was not allowable. The TV cameras had to come and prove it existed. If they did not come, then it did not exist and could be disregarded. If it could be proved to exist on TV, then it existed and only then could consciences and prejudices fall into the preconceived patterns like minds put into slot machines, so that the result could be predicted before it began. It was as if man operated by particular smells, like a dog, and was incapable of responding in any other way. But when the TV cameras had shown the smashed buildings and the dead and the dogs caught the smell, they'd begin to howl. Then, and only then, when it existed, could the issue be divided up among editorials and channels and experts and reissued as "truth"; only then could negotiations by people thousands of miles away begin without loss of face. But how did one explain to a child of ten that she must lie bleeding and screaming on the ground—so much human garbage—before the world too late even tried to care?

She said now, "My uncle used to live in this house."

"Used to? Where is he now?"

"He went to Nova Zeira."

"We came from there."

"I have not been. Is it pretty?"

"It has a nice harbor."

"Shall I show you the letters I have written to my uncle?"

"That would be interesting."

"I will bring you a drink of coffee."

He knew that whether it would be made with milk or water it would be riddled with diseases, but he would have died rather than refuse her.

"Where do you live?"

"That is my house," she told him, pointing across the dirt road. She lived in a tiny square house painted white, but crumbling,

397

the walls flaking, but nevertheless having an attractiveness, with its old red pannen tiles in the sun.

"You live there with your mother and father?"

"My mother."

"No father?"

"No," she said frankly, so that he blushed slightly. "My father went away to the war and he didn't come back," she said without fuss—this was life—and now McQuade was humbled.

"Portuguese father?" he presumed sadly.

The child did not answer directly. "Why do you not come to my house and see my books and the photograph of my father?"

"That would be most pleasant."

He thought she meant some other time, but she was intending in terms of the moment. He walked across the baked earth that was the street, the other children jumping about with the excitement of this important event.

In the small room on the ground floor of the house, among religious pictures and ornaments, old photographs on a wall, and the oil lamp on a heavy table, the girl pointed to a photograph of a man in Portuguese Army uniform—a peasant's face, but kind, strong, interesting—and said with pride, "That is my father." Not that *was* my father, McQuade noticed, and was moved and disturbed again.

"These are my books."

They were a very peculiar collection—children's stories, religious stories, a few magazines, most of them old and almost sour.

"This is my favorite."

It was so old it was falling apart. It was called *Great Works of the World,* and had been published in Lisbon in 1935.

"Who taught you English?" McQuade asked.

"Father Poulter. He went to Marrula."

"What is your name?"

"Cándida," she told him.

"That's a nice name."

"Look. Here are the letters I am writing."

On a long piece of lined paper were written five short letters and she had begun a sixth. There was just a space between each letter. Dear Uncle Antonio, Dear Auntie, Dearest Ema . . . Cándida explained, "I write to everybody I know and send the letters in one envelope to Uncle Antonio. This way it saves money."

"Where is your mother?"

"She has gone to clean the engines," Cándida said meaninglessly.

McQuade presumed this to mean some work for the Army.

"Do you not go to school?"

"Sometimes."

"Not lately?"

"No. I have to look after them."

She referred to the smaller children who stared up under McQuade's chin.

"Will you write to me?" the girl asked.

"When I go away?"

"Yes. And tell me all about America."

"And you will write to me?"

"Yes. I shall begin now."

"But I am still here."

"Yes, but there are many things to say and the man is coming to fetch you."

Franzo came into the small house and said, "There is a small airplane ready at Concrete One to fly us over the battle area. The pilot is here."

The pilot was a young man who introduced himself as Lieutenant Narciso. He was tall and tough, good humored, and had curly red hair. "You would like to have a look at the fighting?" he asked.

McQuade and Franzo said that they would. Brigadier Fermoy came out of the office. At one doorway stood Marianne and at the other, across the way, the child Cándida and her companions, silent and interested.

Lieutenant Narciso took the driver's seat in a jeep. McQuade sat by him, refusing to be contiguous to the brigadier. The lieutenant drove off with a jerk and McQuade knew that if he drove a jeep like this he would probably fly between trees. He smiled, wondering if the brigadier's stomach could take it.

He was thrown forward as the lieutenant stamped on the brakes. A truck had come out of the compound in front, two African soldiers in it, both roaring with laughter and not looking along the dusty track for other traffic. Lieutenant Narciso hooted the horn of the jeep to show his displeasure, and the truck, as if prompted, went ahead at an increasing rate. It broke the crusty hard baked soil and dust rose behind it. The lieutenant dropped back a hundred feet.

It was a military track which took them the five miles to Concrete One. Already McQuade was sweating in the nine o'clock sun, and the dust began to coat his face. The bush was formidable and revealed the appalling nature of the terrain in which the soldiers fought a few miles away.

The explosion was violent and unexpected. A shard of tin flew past McQuade's face, part of the truck's door. Black smoke stood in a small cloud. A hot wave went across their faces. The truck had tipped over. It wasn't burning and it wasn't totally destroyed.

They stopped, shaken, and went to see what had happened. The mine would have smashed the jeep if those two Africans had seen the officer and had hesitated for him to pass.

One was dead and the other was split into strips but still able to scream. He thrashed about in the mess of his own stomach and legs and soon died.

Lieutenant Narciso said, "That is the nearest yet. My God, they must be near. We haven't had a mine within ten miles before."

McQuade asked, startled at the way his own voice trembled, "Isn't the road checked for mines?"

The lieutenant admitted hopelessly, "They're Soviet plastic mines. And the soil has traces of natural ferrous deposits which would make detection difficult anyway. And the Army has no mine detectors in any case," he concluded.

They drove on toward the airfield, proceeding very cautiously and watching for traces of freshly dug earth which would reveal where any mine had been laid.

Within half an hour they took off in a single-engine reconnaissance aircraft. The red-haired lieutenant sat at the front; behind him sat Franzo and Brigadier Fermoy, and in the rear sat McQuade in a mess of straps and aluminium bars. The aircraft had a radial engine which was very noisy and the pilot's window was open, which didn't diminish the racket. It was a very old airplane, heavily stained with oil streaks, but nevertheless it lifted easily off the concrete and at once the world was beautiful, God's, not man's . . .

They flew along the edge of Lake Nyawi a few hundred feet above the still water. Birds flew off in clouds as the engine noise pulsated the air. There were long edges of brown earth, where the lake level was shrinking under the evaporation of the tremendous sun, and small sour estuaries, where the water had gone altogether. The bush was sage green or gray, and here and there was black, where fire had wandered at will.

Lieutenant Narciso had earphones on. He turned his head and shouted "Marrula," and ahead and to one side McQuade saw the neat holdings and the three or four rows of small white houses and the red tiles, and a crowd of people who stared upward.

The horizon tilted as the pilot turned, and now he went very low over the bushes and trees. Hot air shook the machine and McQuade was amused to see both Franzo and Brigadier Fermoy press their feet sideways to defeat the uneasy sensation of loss of centrifugal force. Ahead was another stretch of water, drying up in the drought, but still miles long and glistening in the sun. It was the pale brown of a cup of tea, and a few hundred feet below, hippopotami wallowed in it. Nearby were two villages of round thatched huts and between them a rise in the ground, and on the rise McQuade saw two elephants standing in the shade of trees.

Ten minutes later Lieutenant Narciso turned to shout again. "Tchukiu," he pointed out. "They infiltrate from here."

Sure enough, two hundred feet below was a truck, and men scattered. One or two were firing at the airplane with rifles. They didn't use tracer bullets so McQuade knew in uneasiness that they in the airplane would never know what hit them.

"Another look?" shouted the Lieutenant, and took assent for granted. He banked the machine around so violently that McQuade was thrown over. He had a blurred crazy impression of bush above his head, and by the time he'd orientated himself the lieutenant had completed the circle and there was a bullet hole in the rudder.

The stink of oil and the sensation of aerobatics were now making McQuade feel queasy, but he refused to admit it in the presence of the brigadier. Franzo suddenly banged the pilot on the shoulder in a rare moment of level flight. Franzo had turned green. Lieu-

401

tenant Narciso grinned, but was sympathetic. He motioned to Mc-Quade, who saw that there were paper bags in front of him. He passed a few to Franzo, who groaned as he used them.

"Go home?" shouted the lieutenant, and McQuade shrugged.

Back in Vila Metumba the girl Cándida waited in the heat of day by the door of the office hut.

"There was a big bang and I was frightened," she said.

McQuade didn't know what to say. At last he comforted her with a smile. "I was frightened, too, a bit."

"I wrote you a letter," she said, giving it to him.

"Why did you do that?"

She told him with the shattering simplicity of a child, and the innocent far away from the sophisticated world, "I will love you forever and you will be my friend, and when I come to your house I know that you will make me welcome."

He turned away quickly so that she should not see his eyes. He felt ill. The airplane, he tried to believe, but knew it was not so. He began to tremble in a moment of truth, and he saw himself sitting there in Mr. Cannon's office, full of biting scorn for these little people who were trying to run the world and whom he despised for even trying; he, full of loathing for all men, knew better. The voices whispered in his ears. You think I haven't been kicked around? I studied economics. But not hard enough . . . I want you to care. I can't stand the way you sit in a chair and look at me.

"What's the matter?" asked Cándida.

"Nothing."

"You are angry with me?"

"I have been ill," he explained oddly. He turned to her and promised earnestly, "Listen. I am your friend. I am your friend forever."

She looked at him and saw the strange convulsions and she was a little afraid, not understanding them, but knowing that she had been their cause.

Just before dawn McQuade heard someone groaning. It was a little startling, for it was only yards away. And then the voice—it was a man's—sobbed in a kind of protest in a language McQuade didn't know.

402

He drew back the dirty curtain and there on the horizon was the tiny filament of light, but it was not yet enough so he lit an oil lamp and walked a few yards.

"What's the matter?" he asked.

Ecchegarri's voice pleaded, "Fetch a doctor. I am very ill."

"There is no doctor," admitted McQuade anxiously. "What is the matter?"

"Don't come in," insisted Ecchegarri.

There was no need to enter. The smell told McQuade all he needed.

Outside, a vehicle broke the silence of the dry earth and air. It was the truck that came to fetch the women who worked at Concrete One.

The Army had a doctor and it only took half an hour to get him. His diagnosis was brief. Despite the bottled beer and the food kept in tinfoil Ecchegarri had food poisoning. McQuade had to leave him in the doctor's hands, and in the care of Marianne and Barbu, knowing that he would be taken away before he, McQuade, returned from today's mission. He'd never see Ecchegarri again. It was callous, but the day's duties didn't allow anything else.

It was not yet hot and outside now the sky in the east was pink. Before they left under the guidance of Major Cordeiro, Marianne separated McQuade from the others.

"He's sending messages in contradiction to yours," she told McQuade in a fierce whisper.

"How do you know?"

"Barbu told me."

"Do you know the content?"

"No."

"All right, Marianne. Leave it with me."

They weren't late despite Ecchegarri's illness. The soldiers were still loading boxes onto the small gunboat. It was appropriate that the Portuguese, the last colonial power in Africa, should use a gunboat! This one was small and the iron looked old and the 30mm. cannon behind metal shields also seemed old, although from hard wear, not neglect or time.

The flamingos lifted gracefully off Lake Nyawi in clouds as the gunboat moved off. The Portuguese soldiers, black and white, sprawled on deck in the increasing heat of day and examined with curiosity and indifference these foreigners, people who did not belong to the real world, and the real world was this—the still slimy green water and the flies, the rancid smell of old vegetation and the rotting corpse of the mule, the grim hot bush and the bleached grass and burned-out trees, the plastic mines that killed them . . .

McQuade stood on deck and read the child's letter: "I am ten years and seven months old. My real name is Cándida and my father is a soldier. Father Poulter said that if I prayed . . ."

It was touching, but today, like forgiveness, a concession by God for the softening of his heart, across the same *miombo* in a Portuguese truck and before that in airplanes and other vehicles, something even better had come. A letter from Kristan, written the instant she had received his plea from Lisbon. "I will pray for you. Do you think I don't care? Let us see what we can repair when you come home."

He said to the brigadier in a tone of reasonableness, "What signals have you been sending to the Secretariat?"

But the Brigadier was merely shaken that he should know, and did not notice the conciliatory tone.

"About the military aspect."

"You have seen my signals. Am I not to see yours?"

"These are about military matters and wouldn't interest you."

"I am sorry you think that."

Brigadier Fermoy stared at him, recognizing the wish to begin again, work together, but he mistook it for the plea of a weak man who was frightened of signals sent behind his back, and he mistakenly despised McQuade for thinking that he would indulge in petty personal matters when he communicated with the Secretariat.

They both stood by the rail within feet of each other, but as faraway as ever.

Lake Nyawi was beautiful. It was neither big nor deep and it was what was called a soda lake.

The great heat came and the water shrank from the edges of the lake, leaving acrid yellowish bands of earth. As the water shrank and its salts became more concentrated, it became too bitter for animals. The fish died, even the zebras and hippopotami could die. Then the sun burned feverishly and the bottom of the lake, too,

404

was warmed, and the minute diatoms and algae multiplied until the lake, or some of it, turned the slimy alkaline content a pale soupy green, and there was a bird which could select this rich food which had come, could eat it without swallowing the lethal fluid. And this bird was the flamingo.

McQuade watched in awe as the gunboat passed a half million of them, two or three miles along the shore in a band fifty yards wide. They stood in the water at the shore's edge and ate, sweeping their heads from side to side in a scything selection. The water was calm or they could not have fed.

In the distance two men were paddling a canoe and their panic was obvious. They had rifles across their shoulders. They were agitators or infiltrators on their way south.

A shout from the bridge, a cannon revolved, and there was a deafening noise which made McQuade's skin crawl and he jumped in shock.

The burst of shells splashed hard, sawed a way across water and shattered the canoe. Bits and pieces spread. Something exploded.

With a great blaze of rich pink, the flamingos rose, the whole half million in a tremendous flash of color and slow beating of wings. On their long legs some of them had developed the small hard balls of soda masses which would eventually drag them into the mud and kill them . . .

Cormorants and migrant ducks played about near reeds and bushes and the great white pelican soared on thermal air currents to high altitudes, flapping his wings to maintain height. In the cool of evening he would come down.

In three hours they reached the landing stage at Porto Metamhane.

There was great excitement. They were welcome. The captain of the shallow-draft gunboat and various Portuguese officers on shore talked animatedly.

Brigadier Fermoy couldn't keep silent. "What do they say?" he asked in frustration.

Mr. Costa told him.

"Marrula has been relieved. Or, at any rate, the road was cut and now it is restored. A convoy has gone. Soon we will chase it by ourselves or with other vehicles."

405

The heat of noon was tremendous. Everything metal hurt the hand. Boxes were unloaded by Portuguese soldiers, and army officers walked about with urgency. They all had the toughened untidy appearance of people who fight hard, have lost sight of words and talk simply in terms of ammunition. McQuade and the others sat about self-consciously, drank beer and ate more food from tinfoil. They strolled off the broken planking of the landing stage and up and down, up and down, apprehensively, by the few white huts and broken trucks of Porto Metamhane. Africa stretched forever all around.

At two o'clock they piled into a jeep and followed three Portuguese Army trucks, each with ten soldiers; most of them relaxed, but at least two in each vehicle had weapons pointing to each side.

McQuade did not suppose they would catch up the previous convoy, which was by now three hours ahead of them. It was only forty miles to Marrula, along tracks. But in an hour, after twenty miles, they came up behind it.

It was tough country.

In the stunning heat of afternoon the earlier convoy was moving at walking pace. Men were in fact on foot exercising themselves.

The grass had flowered at the end of the previous rains and in the great heat a little of it had shriveled. Some of it grew four feet high. But here and there was the interesting and obvious area where two rainstorms had overlapped and, giving a double quota of rain, had offered greater survival and a greener world . . . The bees swarmed around the leguminous flowering trees. The acacia trees here were mostly medium-sized and armed with the hooked thorns on long spikes which protected the older toughened growth from browsing animals. The softer trees were eaten in the great hunger. Sometimes the acacia was inhabited by colonies of small ants, which were sufficiently irritating to discourage the eating animal.

The grasses and the herbs had to seed copiously for survival in such an area, and the seed-eating birds ate the abundance. The nests of some weaverbirds hung from the trees in shredded careless style after being weaved. Other weaverbirds made loose globular nests of grass heads and positioned them in the crutch of branches.

The acacia trees dropped a vast litter of spiral pods. These burst with a crack in the unbearable heat. McQuade walked on such a

406

floor of dry pods and they crackled, absolutely dry, under his shoes. The acacia trees here were in fact bush and did not have the great height or the hundred-foot umbrellalike crown or the solitary dignity of those near the desert.

The engine of the jeep was boiling hot in the heat and because of the slow movement in low gear.

What was the delay?

It was not delay. It was a deliberate pace and it was conditioned by the need to find the mines which might have been laid on this, the only track to Marrula. The pace was set by five prisoners who were walking some distance ahead of the entire convoy, and these prisoners were stamping the ground, high stepping in the manner of drum majorettes. They were in fact not only looking with their eyes for the freshly turned earth which would betray the laying of a mine, but were being made to stamp the ground and set it off in case its possible existence could not be seen.

When Brigadier Fermoy saw this he was incensed. Inevitably he directed his anger at the person he hated most, McQuade.

"Now what about your Portuguese and their dignified peasants?" he inquired bitterly.

McQuade said nothing. The brigadier was in theory absolutely right to be angry, but McQuade remembered the Bakongo and he wondered what awaited the brigadier's eyes in Marrula.

Mr. Costa looked ashamed, but claimed, "It is a harsh and bitter war. This is nothing to what happens to Portuguese prisoners."

McQuade had walked four or five miles in the enormous heat. Now he jumped back onto the jeep.

"Cigarette?" Franzo asked.

"No, thanks."

Franzo lit his own cigarette and flicked the match over the side of the jeep. Costa said in shock, "My God, that was a reckless thing to do, Mr. Franzo."

It was too late.

His remark was justified within five seconds. Lines of flame ran along in little bright trickles in two directions. The grass and the hot seed pods crackled crisply, and in ten seconds a tree was on fire. It ignited with something like an explosion, and flames ran amok in the grass. Other trees thirty feet away crackled into vio-

407

lent, noisy fire and flames leaped twenty feet up. Nests and branches flared and birds shrieked and flew off. A cheetah ran across the road behind the convoy.

The Portuguese soldiers in the trucks shouted and at the front the pace quickened. The prisoners trotted, but soon collapsed, exhausted. They were picked up and tossed into a truck, and the whole convoy raced off with boiling radiators.

They were scarcely fast enough. At one side an area of a hundred square yards was on fire, and now the terrifying bright lines raced across the track like molten metal and other trees grasped the lines and exploded crisply into flame.

Franzo had started a savanna fire. Miles of land would be burned black and animals would die . . .

Two miles outside Marrula were the scattered corpses of soldiers, black and white. A few heads had been hacked off, but it was the marks of the teeth on the bodies that caused McQuade to feel sick.

Marrula, like Vila Metumba, was nothing, nothing in intellectual minds far away which thought in terms of cities taken and retaken. It was made up of at most twenty long white huts and a bit of a church, square in design, and five small red-tiled houses. Some of it had been battered by grenades or mortar, but the buildings, relatively speaking, did not matter. The dead lay in rows along the one street, near two wrecked trucks. Some were women and children and there was part of a white priest among them: Father Poulter presumably. There were no bestialities; they were just dead because the other Army had driven many frightened scattered people into this small haven, and in the accident of some attack on a "position" they had been killed.

The nursing sister, Miss Pogson, with heavy eyes that blinked so fast they were out of control, talked hysterically to McQuade.

"Canadian? A Canadian? So am I. Winnipeg. Why the hell did I ever leave it? Did you bring the medical supplies?"

"We're from the United Nations."

"I don't care where they come from, only—"

"We're observers—"

"God Almighty! Who wants observers? What use are you? I must have bandages," urged Miss Pogson. "And a pair of small scissors. I can't find mine." She began to shake and weep. "For the love of God, why doesn't someone *send* something?"

"We came with the trucks—"

"There was nothing."

"I mean the second convoy—"

"Christ, these Portuguese. They're so *slow*."

There was barbed wire around the whole half square mile, but it was nothing, merely a definition of area; it wouldn't keep anyone out.

The refugees from surrounding districts stood about in a helpless, terrified crowd, about three hundred of them, with no food or blankets or clothes. Babies and children howled, adults excreted or bled where they stood. The trucks would take them back to the lake and the gunboat would take them to the safety of Vila Metumba and areas south, but where they would live or work was beyond comprehension. Now they stood, breathing heavily in terror, mouths open, or wept, or talked to the air angrily . . . A Red Cross nurse was going around with biscuits, all she had . . .

There was a young journalist there. He'd been in the previous convoy. He was, inevitably, British, hot foot from college and the lecture rooms, the theories of what should be done, and was burning with the British urge to tell people how to behave themselves. When he heard that there were United Nations people present he knew he was in business: here was someone answerable to theory.

"May I ask you about the refugee camp?"

McQuade said, "There isn't one."

"Do you feel the arrangements here are satisfactory?"

"No."

The young man was astonished. It was his first war. "You do not?"

"Of course not. There are no shower baths or waitresses. No beds either. Nor any undertaker as yet."

"This seems a curious attitude," the young man pointed out, writing fast. "Would you agree that conditions are appalling? There do not seem to be any toilet facilities at all."

"There aren't any in the bush either," McQuade pointed out.

"The Portuguese don't seem to have any facilities of any kind."

"There are hundreds of people here who were not expected,"

409

said McQuade, pointing out the obvious. "Conditions are not good because there is a war, but no one's going to be intimidated here. The trucks will, I'm told, evacuate these people. It is possible they will succeed. It is also possible that they will be mined or attacked."

"What is your position?" the journalist asked.

"I am here to observe."

"I meant politically."

McQuade refused to answer. He didn't know himself.

The sun went down, but no one slept except the utterly exhausted. The wounded cried and stirred, and Miss Pogson was still at work with the medical supplies which had come. Soon she would collapse, physically or mentally. The cicadas chirped and far off the sky bulged pink as if a strange moon was rising; it was Franzo's bush fire still burning itself in frenzy.

Brigadier Fermoy was naturally anxious to assess the military situation of the whole area, and so was McQuade. Both knew that the dead laid in rows and the three hundred refugees might mean a lot, but equally, in conditions of panic, might mean very little. McQuade therefore translated in a dialogue between the senior Portuguese officer—this one was a major, too!—and the brigadier.

"What are your casualties?"

"In the whole Army? I am only a part of it, but I believe the total for the last three months is about two hundred dead."

"That does not sound like a war," said Brigadier Fermoy.

"Have I said it is a war?" the major asked. "Lisbon gets excited and so do the few journalists who come. And certainly it is now increasing and has passed being tribal cattle raids. But it is not a war of the Vietnam intensity nor even as bad as that fighting months ago north of Vila Lobanda."

"Have you seen any Chinese?"

The major laughed. "Chinese? Do you think the Chinese come fighting? No, sir, no Chinese. They stay in Tanzania and supply ammunition to the camp at Mindi, where these characters we fight have their training. It comes by ship to Dar es Salaam."

"How do you know that?"

"Well, you have me there," admitted the major. "Spies have informed us, so have prisoners, that this is so. More exactly, much of the captured equipment is Chinese or it is Soviet material, we believe, once supplied to the Chinese."

"Do you have any idea of the opposition's total strength?"

"Not personally. Estimates vary. Some thousands. It is accepted that the Chinese and OAU are stepping up the business with the intention of driving the white man out of Africa altogether."

At dawn they began the journey back to Lake Nyawi, preceded again by trucks, this time full of refugees. The convoy stopped after five miles. A gazelle lay in the way. It was dead, torn by the mine which had been laid within the last few hours and upon which it had trodden.

Soon they came to the area burned by the fire caused by Franzo's match. It was unbelievable. It was a parched and blackened landscape for what seemed miles, with tufts of burned grass and millions of blackened leaves, which were now as crisp as the pods of yesterday. Trees were deadened and charred. Nothing moved. All life was still except for the shrilling of cicadas. Here and there were the corpses of animals burned to death. It was difficult to believe anything would ever grow again here, but when the rains came life would try again. Franzo said, "Mr. McQuade, I am ashamed . . ."

They had to wait four hours for the gunboat. The refugees sat on the lake shore silently in the heat of day. Where would they go? What would become of them?

McQuade felt hot and very sticky and dirty. He had had no sleep and it had been impossible to shave.

There were more hours to wait when the gunboat did come. The same unloading of ammunition, and this time, too, forty or fifty more soldiers disembarked.

They had traveled for two hours when the sky to the north was filled with a great roaring: the unmistakable noise of jet engines. This was completely meaningless and unexpected. McQuade had not the slightest idea whose jets these were. They had the grim efficiency of North America rather than the older airplanes of Portugal and could hardly belong to the Tanzanian Air Force or the OAU. Egyptian perhaps? Russian? Chinese? British? French? He was alarmed. The refugees cried in such panic that it communi-

411

cated itself to McQuade's belly and he waited, twitching with fear, for the smash of cannon shells.

As the three jet fighters came in low over the lake, lowering their undercarriages and circling to land on Concrete One—covering in moments what took the gunboat hours—McQuade received the most baffling shock of all: the markings on them were those of Canada.

Brigadier Fermoy said like a confession, "I asked for them. We have to have reconnaissance over a huge area. That little plane's no use. We're in a hurry. We want photographs of everything that moves."

McQuade was confused.

"But they're fighters."

"No," said the brigadier. "They're CF-104 Starfighters used by the Canadians for high-speed reconnaissance."

"Where do they come from?" McQuade asked, although the fright in his stomach told him the answer.

"They're from France," the brigadier told him, "but happened to be near us on a Middle East reinforcement exercise."

McQuade felt the shaky terror, the acknowledgment in his bones, that his destiny was here: all else led to this monotonous *miombo,* a strip of concrete and an angry brigadier. God would soon put the question: Did he care, did he really love humanity, or was he, too, unable to take the crunch? Was he also a vehicle of words, part of the volumes crowding the library shelves of the world?

There on the rotten wooden planks of the landing stage at Vila Metumba was someone he cared about—Peter, his son. And in the small crowd of children who awaited the gunboat was another, Cándida, the *mestiço* child.

It was very strange and touching for McQuade to meet his own son here in the *miombo.* He felt ashamed. Did the misery and anger show? Or was it hidden by the dirt on his face and the forty-eight hours' stubble?

"Well!" he greeted.

Peter's acknowledgment was as brief. "Hello, Dad. Been boating?"

"You can say that again! Would you like to tell me what the RCAF is doing in Angolique?"

"You asked for us!" Peter said, reminding his father of what he thought had been his request.

There were introductions. The child Cándida hung around. With Peter was a squadron leader named Litton. His information was startling. "We have to photograph the whole business. South as well as north."

"South?" McQuade was disturbed. "What the hell for?"

"To assess the Portuguese as well as others, I guess. It's quite easy. Won't take long. Inflight processing. Just shoot the negatives back in the diplomatic bag."

"But," protested McQuade, "this is a Portuguese protest of violation."

The brigadier said, "One with motives that may be questioned."

"Not in my mandate," said McQuade loudly.

Brigadier Fermoy shrugged. He was at last winning.

McQuade was very shaken. The Secretariat was doing things over his head, and he was only informed by accident, although Brigadier Fermoy seemed to know all about what was happening and, equally ominous, what was going to happen. Later he walked along the edge of the lake with Peter and holding Cándida's hand —he was unable to disregard her.

"What do you think, Peter?"

"Oh, hell. Thinking's for you. I just fly the plane."

McQuade struggled out of depression. "What about this girl, Yvette?"

"I'm going to marry her."

"I look forward to the wedding."

"Mother didn't like her."

"That wasn't what she said when I saw her."

"You look tired, Dad."

"We had a rough night over the lake. People are getting killed around here."

"I hope we can stop that," Peter said.

The transport plane with the ground crews and other equipment for the Starfighters was circling the lake to land. Concrete One was crowded. It no longer looked like an amateur's war. The professionals were moving in.

In the shabby hut Marianne whispered as soon as she could get McQuade alone, "I don't like it, Shaun. I smell trouble. Big trou-

413

ble. Have you seen the signals? Something funny's going on."

"I think you're right," agreed McQuade.

"I'm on your side," Marianne stated. "Remember that."

The signal from Manhattan read: "Why disagreement views between you and Brigadier? Bound to accept military assessment of military situation. Reconnaissance aircraft being sent to assess whole area northeast Angolique, south Tanzania. Then talk politics when correctly informed?"

There was almost nothing to say. Mr. Cannon and the thirty-eighth floor weren't seven thousand miles away, leaving him in charge. They were right here in this hut, running the show.

Cándida stood in the doorway, the sun's final strength reflected in the lake behind her. The smells of approaching night and the dead mule drifted into the hot room.

"I missed you," she said simply. "The time went very slowly when you were away. And when the silver airplanes came I was very frightened."

"They are going to take photographs," McQuade explained, but it meant nothing to her. She wasn't deceived. Her fluttering heart in the great roar of noise had told her the truth: these were the machinery of death . . .

In New York and elsewhere discreet pressure was building up on a variety of levels in the United Nations buildings themselves. Various European delegates had already noted the capacity of this unknown Canadian, McQuade, to stir the dust in Africa and persuade Portugal to change her attitude from that of being a white colonial power—these other powers ignored Portugal's claim to be a multi-racial society in Angolique—to that of becoming a colonial nation with a paternalism that now acknowledged the increasing maturity of its *indigena*.

Some delegates' countries had policies and trade alignments in the southern half of Africa which they did not feel should be altered by an idealistic Canadian whose own life and whose country would scarcely be affected. Others had motives and desires related to a political *status quo* and stability in regard to the struggle with communism and the ideology of the Cold War and saw these being thrown into confusion by the United Nations. For a variety of rea-

414

sons, some of which conflicted, it was essential to these people that McQuade should go.

The delegates of these countries began their pressures and persuasions in conversations with the Secretary General and various undersecretaries and people like Mr. Cannon. They also sounded out the Canadian Ambassador to the UN and indeed the ambassadors in Washington and other capitals to find out how relatively hard or soft was Canada's position in regard to its national, McQuade. The arguments they used were of the nature "McQuade is certainly doing his best with a difficult mission, but in doing so he has aroused powerful and unnecessary hostilities in Vila Lobanda, Lourenco Tomas, and among the Organization of African Unity in Dar es Salaam, who, after all, represent most if not all of Africa, and who resent his attitude bitterly. You see what he said to Mr. Ernesto Gomais? I have the cuttings here. They can't *all* be wrong. The most helpful step would surely be to recall him . . ."

Other delegates got to work on the representatives of countries which might be regarded as sympathetic to McQuade's mission. To these—and they included Portugal herself, South Africa, France, the Netherlands and Belgium—the argument was put on a variety of subjects, from nuclear policy, a sympathy for the time being on South-West Africa, or the restraint of a vote on some issue, or sympathy with a new and difficult minor matter cropping up in European or African politics and trade. To these it was pointed out, "We happen to know that our country is on the brink of a reconsideration of policies which would bring our country's attitude nearer to that desired by yours"—desired, that is, by the interlocutor at present embarrassed about nuclear weapons, certain conditions in South-West Africa, the Common Market, or whatever it happened to be . . . "However, one thing is certain, and it is that such a desirable outcome is hindered by the continued presence in Angolique of Mr. McQuade, whose personal demeanor, truculence with the OAU, extreme statements about refugees, apparent indifference to the whole situation, confusion over military matters with Brigadier Fermoy, and whose private life being in undignified circumstances at present, has alienated large sections of opinion in our country . . ."

The representatives' diplomatic arms were strengthened by the files of press clippings they hawked around with them. The fact that some of these countries' "free" press happened to be just as annoyed as their diplomats, primarily because their owners found it appropriate to be annoyed, was known to all parties in the argument, for this was diplomacy and had nothing to do with idealism, although plenty to do with realism. "You can see," echoed a number of diplomats with the same sort of press clippings, "you can see from these cuttings of the last few days only how strongly opinion in our country has been stirred by all this . . ."

And the press clippings—articles written for the most part by people who hadn't been within four thousand miles of Africa or Angolique—did indeed protest about McQuade's "inability to get on with Africans," "temperamental defects," "possible strain of his previous mission," "difficulties perhaps in his private life?" A typical one was syndicated. It thumped its arguments with all the subtlety of a sledge hammer: "And who is this Shaun McQuade who takes charge of a political situation in Africa that could become dynamite overnight? He is a Canadian and was a member of the United Nations Committee of Twenty-four, well known for its busybody activities around Africa, its meddling with affairs it knows little about. . . . The dictatorships are well represented on this pompous body, which trots around the world lecturing nations like France and the United Kingdom about colonialism, liberty and the rights of man. And which countries are represented on this all-knowing committee which takes its evidence outside the countries it presumes to understand and indict, and hears only evidence against, not being interested in evidence *for?*" And farther in the article the paper developed its personal attack, secure in the knowledge that McQuade, thousands of miles away, would never see the paper, wouldn't have the money or inclination to sue a newspaper in a foreign country, and even if he had and did he would be too late: the result would have been achieved. "For why is there a crisis in Angolique at all? It is because McQuade exceeded his brief as meddler before and persuaded Portugal that it would be wiser to heed the UN than its own five hundred years of good colonial administration and racial equality. And now what do we find? We find this interpreted as weakness by that other impotent organization of mischiefmakers, the OAU, who presume generosity to be fear and send in their ramshackle armies to attack northeast An-

416

golique, kill farmers and their families, and ruin thousands of square miles of farmland. And who is sent to deal with this mess? None other than the supermeddler, Mr. McQuade . . ."

The diplomatic effort, even without a press barrage, was certain to succeed in time. The reason was that the strongly held and stated wishes of a great, or even an important secondary power were inherently of more importance than the position of any individual unless that individual was backed with equal strength and tenacity by one or more powers of no less importance. This was why Africa itself, despite all its numbers in the General Assembly, not having the *power*, as distinct from the votes, was still at the mercy of the European and American nations which did.

The Canadian Mission and embassies and the Secretariat put up a strong defense of McQuade that would have surprised him. The arguments for his removal, with the pressures backing them, and the photographs of McQuade and Kristan and the numerous press clippings to add weight, would normally have been irresistible. The UN had already lost many good men in other parts of Africa, a continent with a gift for contentious affairs in which personalities were expended at a pretty good clip. It was the kind of campaign diplomats carried out well and on which they were likely to understand one another best. For it was easier to get agreement on the expendability of personalities than it was on the substance of policy.

But it did not matter this time, for other things were afoot. The arguments for McQuade's extrusion—stretching from Mettallic Angolique and others in Africa and Europe, through angry Africans in Tanzania to the subtle word play in Manhattan and elsewhere— were now on a mistaken, out-of-date basis. They were a mere drop of cotton wool in a furnace about to roar.

6 ■ ■

As DAWN CAME among the bushes and grass in a crimson line McQuade stirred in his sleep, hearing the screech of the jets. This was now normal; it was routine; it had happened on four days in a row. The single reheated air-breathing turbojet engine of each Starfighter shrieked in a new, familiar noise as it came over the *miombo* and headed away on its two-hour mission.

McQuade had been shown one of these pencil-slim beautiful machines, with its pointed nose continuing the pencil comparison. He had been impressed but made uneasy, although as fast as he'd asked questions the pilot, Peter, had answered them satisfactorily. What happened, he'd inquired, if the engine cut out? Peter had explained that a flamed-out engine still windmilled and gave enough power for flying control; and—anticipating the next question—there were batteries to provide an inflight engine restart . . . It was almost impossible to go wrong in navigation even over the uniformity of the *miombo*, for the navigational computer indicated to the pilot his position by "remembering" where it had started. But McQuade hadn't been comforted. Africa wouldn't be impressed. Africa had a habit of ignoring instruments and the cleverness of men. She was so much stronger . . .

Photographic reconnaissance lent itself to the fairly leisurely movement and pace of the African sort of war despite the absence of fixed man-made landmarks. Flying low the Starfighter could take a quick "squirt" with one of its bank of Vinten cameras at low altitude—trucks, men on bridges, columns of mules or vehicles, camps, whole divisions, or, as was more likely here, battalions, were noticeable and they couldn't move quickly. Later photographs indicated the direction of movement. The structured thinking and the sophisticated equipment were almost too good here for what they had to do, and the theoretical analyses of war would have withered in the face of the actual situation if the improvisation and readjustment of technique had not been suggested by the squadron leader.

An aircraft of this sort could, and did, in Europe, flying at from 700 to 1600 m.p.h. at great height, utilizing three cameras in trimegroton and 390-foot film rolls, take photographs of 43,000 square miles in a two-hour mission. Since the altitude of the aircraft and the focal length of the cameras' lenses were known, the interpreter could measure within a few feet the length and breadth of the subjects, and by shadow and time of day and year estimate its height—and in this way he could tell the height of trees, the age of an installation, the type of a steel mill and its capacity and product, or estimate the number of troops at a military base. Camouflage-detection photography used a color film in which all living vegetable matter containing chlorophyll showed up as red on the film. Everything else—even branches removed and used for camouflage, and buildings and equipment painted green to resemble foliage—appeared as a dull gray-green.

This kind of sophisticated photographic reconnaissance had obtained the evidence for the United States of Soviet long-range missiles in Cuba, but it was a little wasted here in Africa. Even so, one Starfighter, flown by Squadron Leader Litton, was taking the maplike photographs using the trimegroton technique—that is, with three cameras arranged to shoot from horizon to horizon, the two outer cameras operating at oblique angles and the third vertically, with a slight overlap on all three cameras. But Peter and a flight lieutenant were flying very low over the bush and taking quick "squirts" at trucks, men, huts, bridges, airfields, tracks, far-off railways and ships, using not only an adaptation of the trimegroton technique but forward-facing cameras which took photographs at an oblique angle as the Starfighter approached. These tended to look like "normal" photographs—but exciting and alarming to McQuade, the parent. The final interpretations of the photographs were made in America, and McQuade was not told what they were. Peter told him of the trucks and small groups of troops he'd seen when flying at less than five hundred feet. His estimate was that as a war it was all very small beer, although he'd shown McQuade photographs taken on a dangerous low run over a camp in Tanzania and a Chinese ship in Dar es Salaam harbor. There had been political complaints about that flight.

This was the routine of the day. At 5:15 in the morning the jets took off. And now at half-past five McQuade heard in the beginnings of day the laughter of women, and their fast meaningless chatter. These were the women who were taken from the village to the airfield of Concrete One where they cooked and cleaned. Cándida's mother was one of them. She was of the Bamakua tribe and was just tall enough to be attractive to European and American eyes. It was impossible to know her age. Twenty-five, perhaps, surely not thirty, despite Cándida's ten years. She had been influenced by the priests and soldiers and Portuguese civilians and was

419

aware of the world she'd never see. She was shy and likable, albeit a little startling as Cándida's mother. McQuade wondered if another Portuguese soldier might not covet her to the point of marriage or support.

The Army truck which came to fetch the women maneuvered outside, and McQuade could smell the dust it left in its wake.

Even in a small war it is fatal to fall into a routine or to assume that one is possible.

At six o'clock the explosions thumped the air faraway and were violent enough to shake the huts. Everybody got dressed and ready for they knew not quite what.

McQuade identified the cannon of the gunboat far off. Then he saw the flying boat in the distance, heading south. Trucks full of Portuguese soldiers went by the hut, and soon there was gunfire, but then came silence. Who had won? The sounds were still a fraction remote and he could smell the coffee Marianne was preparing. Then something sighed outside. The sound was familiar—after twenty and more years he remembered it so instinctively that he threw himself flat on the floor. He would have looked silly if he'd been wrong, but he was right. The mortar bomb exploded a hundred feet away.

Refugees began suddenly to pour into the village. Emotionally this was right, but logically, in terms of offering a mortar bomb concentration, it was mistaken. They were filthy and exhausted, shouting and weeping, dragging children, carrying screaming babies; their attitude was inevitably that of absolute terror and panic. Again the sigh of a mortar bomb and the vicious concussion and this time some screaming, and feet running, scattering. The firing of the mortar bombs was desultory, but frightening because inexplicable, not anticipated by the tens of thousands of photographs. As well, McQuade knew he was old now, not able to endure it so well as those long years ago at Falaise. He had been tortured, which rots the body's fiber, and betrayed, which wounds the soul, and he believed in little. The noises here had not a thousandth of that kind of intensity anyway, but he felt helpless and therefore scared. And not only him. Marianne was under the table and shaking visibly. Even the brigadier was crouching on the floor and had personal anxiety written large upon his face.

420

In a silence McQuade heard the Telex machine typing a message. "What's that?" he whispered. He didn't know why he whispered. Barbu ran across the hut like someone under fire. It was faintly ridiculous. He passed the message to Franzo, who was sitting on the floor by McQuade. What time was it in New York? Somewhere around one in the morning, so what the hell was all this? The typed words told him: "Expect airlift 0900 hours your time. Approximately one thousand troops. Please make arrangements to hand over to deputy and make early visit yourself to New York."

The feeling of alarm and the apprehension about being dragged away from this scene to be criticized were unmistakable; the sensation was as heavy as guilt in his stomach.

He asked hopelessly, forgetting for a helpless moment that he was in charge, "What is all this? I can't go if there's a flare-up. Get a message off, Barbu. Tell them there's fighting and I can't leave."

Franzo pointed out, "Mr. McQuade, those troops are due here in about two and a half hours."

McQuade disputed, "Jesus, that's impossible. It sounds as if Concrete One's being attacked."

Barbu said in alarm, "But the planes of the airlift must be over the Congo or Bechuanaland by now."

Brigadier Fermoy informed them, "Cannon asked me the length of the runway. He said ten thousand feet would be sufficient."

McQuade said angrily, "I never asked for troops."

The brigadier answered, astonishing him, "Don't look at me. I didn't."

"Then what the hell?"

Brigadier Fermoy commented, "You assume the Secretariat doesn't know about this little lot"—he waved a hand to the noises outside—"but perhaps they know a lot more than we do. Perhaps it's we who do not have information."

"The Telex message reads like a request assuming a normal situation. If they want *me* to go to Manhattan for talks—" McQuade said hopelessly.

Mr. Costa made his first remark of the day.

"Portugal has not asked for troops. Who has?"

McQuade said, "I'm going to the airfield to see what the situation is." To Barbu he instructed, "Send a signal that Concrete One may be lost. Where's that coffee?" he asked Marianne.

"In my stomach," Marianne said shakily.

Franzo said, "I'd better come with you, Mr. McQuade."

"I shall have to," affirmed the brigadier.

"Doesn't anyone love *me?*" Marianne pleaded, not entirely for amusement.

"Barbu and Mr. Costa will stay."

Outside, the sun was already strong. There was some litter along the track which was Vila Metumba's one street, and a man and a child lay dead a hundred feet away like an indictment. No one else was in sight. Nothing moved. The firing had stopped. Was there a flare-up at all? No doubt people had either fled or were huddled in terror in their homes. A long hut had half collapsed where the mortar bombs had exploded. There was no sign of the refugees who had come into the village except for the two black bodies.

McQuade took the driver's seat in the white Land Rover. He said, "Let's try the compound first. Major Cordeiro will have been in touch." There was, inevitably, no civilian telephone in the village.

He drove the Land Rover and turned by the wrecked hut and drove slightly downhill toward the military compound and workshops. An African sentry was on duty outside the fence which surrounded the area. He did not welcome the Land Rover, but simply raised his rifle to his shoulder. The brigadier, sitting by McQuade, put his head down—onto McQuade's knees as it happened, which stopped him from changing gear. This was funny, but not as funny as all that. The first bullet hit the hood. McQuade brought his knee up violently into the brigadier's nose, shouting, "Move your bloody nose"—which also was amusing, but not at the moment. The brigadier's nose was in fact bleeding, but McQuade wanted it out of the way. He reversed rapidly—the sensation of having a rifle pointed straight at his face was decidedly unpleasant. The second shot shattered the windshield, but now McQuade drove forward with brutal tire scrubbing and in seconds was behind the cover of the smashed hut, feeling distinctly silly. He was shaken but amused. "Sorry," he said, but couldn't stop shaking with amusement, which did not endear him to the brigadier. "What the hell was the matter with *him?*"

422

The brigadier pointed out, "He believes we are the ANP."

Franzo said, "If he has not seen the Land Rover before—"

"If we go back on foot—"

"No, Mr. McQuade," said Franzo frankly. "I do not think that would be a good political choice."

The selection of words amused McQuade, but it was obviously not going to be an amusing day. It looked like a morning of decision, and already they were floundering.

"Brigadier," he said, "my son told me that the photographs indicated very little threat by anyone. The numbers involved here may be quite small and the airfield in no danger."

Brigadier Fermoy did not dispute this, although he commented, "The flying boat took off in a hell of a hurry. Our duty is to the Secretariat and the Secretariat sees fit to send planes. They must therefore be able to land."

"All right, then, let's see if we can get to the airfield."

"No," argued the brigadier. "If it is taken— Try the seaplane station."

"The flying boat took off."

"It does every day."

Franzo said, "And it means driving past that sentry."

"If we drive fast—" suggested McQuade.

He didn't believe himself as he said the words. It was remote and faintly silly, but the humor was that of possible chaos and the grim little ironies—such as that of UN personnel being shot by Africans —would be for others, later on, far away, to laugh about.

It was one of those decisions that had to be acted on instantly or courage would freeze, so he drove at once around the hut and down the incline toward the lake. The same African sentry of the Portuguese Army this time took fright, ran a few paces, turned when he'd found the protection of a tree and then raised his rifle. But by then the Land Rover had gone past in a cloud of dust.

Down by Lake Nyawi the gunboat was moving off, packed with refugees and soldiers. The few buildings were empty, wrecked. Great heaps of papers were burning on the floor of an office. But there on a desk was a telephone, and nobody had touched it or torn its wires. Franzo and the brigadier walked about on the wooden floor, straightened chairs for no logical reason. It was like viewing

423

a residence that has gone to seed; the previous tenants had been dirty; the plumbing was bad and there was woodworm, and they had left behind a mess of litter, personal and embarrassing, as they'd fled before their creditors. Little boys had broken the windows, as little boys do in empty buildings. The garden needed attention, but the location was desirable and there was a fine view of the lake . . .

On a wall were postcards sent by soldiers from other garrisons in Angolique, São Tome, Macau, Cape Verde, Guinea and Portugal —the little boys had missed these—and military notices going yellow and sour. Among these was a list of telephone numbers. There were a dozen for Concrete One, all in terms of names and ranks. The telephone was splendidly simple: it just had numbers 0 to 9. McQuade took the highest rank—that of a Major Mello e Trovoada (which seemed a name worthy of higher rank)—and dialed his number.

He could hear the phone ringing in that other room, in Concrete One. "I'm in touch!" he shouted excitedly, and Franzo and the brigadier stood close, trying to hear the other voice if one ever came.

One did. A man's voice with an African timbre asked in Portuguese, "Who is that?"

Only in an African war could this happen. The dialogue was bizarre, but useful.

"My name is McQuade and—"

"My title is Colonel Kambezo. Who am I talking to?"

"I am in charge of the United Nations' party."

"This is not a party," disputed the other voice, angry, as if McQuade had been frivolous. "Do not doubt that ANP is real."

"I have met Mr. Gomais," claimed McQuade. "I am not Portuguese. I am a Canadian. I work for the United Nations."

"You know Vorster?"

"I have heard of him."

"Do not prevaricate," the colonel said angrily. "You work for him. Lies will not help you. We do not surrender to such people. We have taken this airfield and the slaughter will stop. Our people will not be cut into pieces and secretly buried or burned with napalm."

424

"I am your friend," said McQuade wildly. "In two hours many airplanes will land on the airfield—"

"That is where you are wrong," argued the voice in rage, but in no hurry to end this bizarre conversation. "Any airplanes will be destroyed. We have fifty prisoners here. If there is any trickery with airplanes we shall kill them."

"I am negotiating for the United Nations. These aircraft are coming from America."

"Do you think these Portuguese lies will convince me?" The voice was bitter now. "The situation is that we have prisoners and will kill them if there is interference. This is not an atrocity. It is part of negotiation with murderers."

The colonel five miles away, a face never to be seen, an anger as unreal as an article in a Sunday paper, put down the telephone at his end and concluded the dialogue. McQuade couldn't leave it at that. He dialed again, but was not answered. He dialed other numbers and these rang, too, but there was no reply

He said, "We'd better get back and see if Barbu's contacted anyone."

They drove full speed past the sentry outside the compound for the third time. Now he pretended not to see them. They didn't exist. There was a crowd of refugees and what looked like king-size hullabaloo inside the compound.

Still the ominous silence and two corpses among the huts and cottages, the atmosphere of desertion. And Barbu's news—the messages typed in this room by hands seven thousand miles away—was, if anything, worse than before. There were two signals. The first one read: "Owing to type of equipment in transport aircraft curvature of earth prevents contact."

"Christ!" protested McQuade. "Then came this," Barbu said, "ten minutes after my own signal." The second message read: "Contacted Salisbury to inform aircraft and allow landing Salisbury airport, nearest suitable. Rhodesian authorities refuse and say any violation Rhodesian airspace by UN will be assumed hostile. No inflight refueling possible. Now imperative you retake Concrete One."

In the stunned silence of this appalling message McQuade heard the noise of jets and his heart accelerated in horror, believing that

425

the transport planes had arrived. But it was a horror much more exquisite and personal. He looked mechanically at his watch and saw that it was still only 7:15 in the morning, and he identified the engines. Two of the Starfighters were circling around, and he went outside in a useless impulse to stop them. He saw the wheels of their undercarriages drop down, and he knew in nightmare that they were going in to land on an airfield which had been taken. And that colonel had been told that aircraft would be coming and had boasted that if there was any trickery with airplanes there were prisoners who would be killed. The third Starfighter now came overhead and down went its wheels as it headed in to land five miles away. One of the prisoners would be Cándida's mother and one of the Starfighter pilots was his son, Peter.

His personal anxiety showed on his face and no one said a word. They stood outside the hut and the engine noises died and McQuade listened intently for the rasp of machine-gun fire or solitary shots of rifles which would indicate the killing. After a while he said in hope, "I can't hear anything," but the faces didn't dare look him in the eye.

As he spoke a mortar bomb moaned over.

Before he threw himself flat on the dusty earth McQuade identified the puff of smoke above the bush a thousand yards away. He knew that Vila Metumba was doomed this morning.

Other bombs exploded. The aiming was poor but sooner or later they'd be on target.

In his mind he saw the thick neck and heard the electric shaver and Mr. Cannon's voice with Manhattan splendid over his shoulder. Must not lose a battle. Not one. We have too many enemies . . .

This one was lost even before the troops arrived.

The mortar—there was only one—kept firing haphazardly, and it felt safer to crouch in the hut, as if that would save them.

Marianne—still under the table; surely she'd get cramp in that posture—said casually, "I keep praying, but I'm on the wrong wavelength and all I get is this talk on apartheid."

McQuade said, "We can't just sit here."

Franzo agreed. "I'll go to the compound. Major Cordeiro must be there."

Fermoy commented, "And what would he do?"

A bomb sighed over the street. It was almost a direct hit. Shards of glass and a cloud of dust blew into the room.

They were quite pleased to survive. They had forgotten this was other people's war.

Somewhere within yards someone was screaming and there was the crisp noise of burning wood.

I will love you forever and you will be my friend, and when I come to your house . . .

He had betrayed her by neglect, simply forgetting her existence as if it was not a war in which she was involved.

Already on this morning her mother had become a prisoner, perhaps a corpse, and it had not penetrated him, the reality of it.

He rushed outside, shocked by the burning buildings and the debris.

She was in there with two of the children. One was dead, the other soon would be, but the pumping panicking little heart was circulating the blood still, and out it poured over Cándida's clothes.

He knew it wasn't worth it. Votes and the pursuit of happiness, compulsory issue, weren't worth this one spectacle, the split black flesh and the small *mestiço* child, more alone than anyone in the world and screaming. What had she done? She was neither black nor white, but the fruit of the love of both.

She was shaking and weightless, a mere small bundle to carry, with the smaller child, who was now dead. In a day or two, if she survived, someone'd have to tell her that her mother had been killed.

Portuguese soldiers were in the village, going from hut to hut, bringing people outside and hurrying these last refugees to a small convoy of trucks. The isolated bombs still moaned over. One mortar was enough for this tiny place.

He kicked the door of the hut open and shouted, "Come on!" and ran with his burden to the Land Rover.

They all sat in the Land Rover and followed the convoy going south. Time ticked away. Those airplanes were perhaps five hundred miles away now. McQuade realized that he had not seen a single ANP soldier face to face, yet he was fleeing with refugees. What he'd endured was merely noise and apprehension. He felt oddly ashamed although it was not his job to do the fighting.

Five miles along the track to Nova Olivenca there were Portu-

427

guese soldiers and other trucks. It was a kind of checkpoint, and here they found Major Cordeiro with other officers. He was willing, despite the confusion of the morning, to have a conference with the United Nations group. Nobody remarked on the child who clung to McQuade throughout. In the stifling heat and standing among trucks, with refugees weeping and shouting in fright and soldiers staring indifferently as they overheard the anxious words, there began the most terrible dialogue of McQuade's life.

At first the talk seemed straightforward as he stated to the major and various lieutenants the facts he thought they didn't have.

"In about one hour UN troops are arriving by air. About a thousand of them. The airfield therefore must be available."

The dialogue had a dreadful slowness as it was translated each way by Mr. Costa for the benefit of Franzo, Barbu and the brigadier.

The major looked doubtful.

"You expect me to attack Concrete One for the United Nations before we are ready to do so? We shall retake it when we're ready."

"But in one hour—"

Major Cordeiro smiled bitterly.

"What are these troops coming for? Why have you asked for them?"

"I didn't," acknowledged McQuade frankly.

"Then why do they come? Who wants them? I do not. Who has asked for them? I have not. Why, then, do they come?"

McQuade did not know. It was an appalling omission on the Secretariat's side. He had not thought about it in the confusion of the morning, and this proved that despite his bitterness, at heart McQuade believed that all the UN's actions had good motives.

Brigadier Fermoy, who perhaps did know, told the major, "They intend to establish a *cordon sanitaire* and fill a dangerous vacuum."

Major Cordeiro disputed the need. "But this we have already done. A strip of land eight to fifteen kilometers wide was created many months ago which more or less follows the border along the River Rovene. All the people on our side in that strip were moved south and the bare ribbon can be inspected rapidly by aircraft. Large numbers cannot move without our seeing them. A few infiltrators, yes, at night, even little groups like these today."

Brigadier Fermoy said, "It is not my decision. But I think my colleagues would agree that Portugal asked for political help and these aircraft are within one hour of arriving. Do you agree, Mr. McQuade?"

"That is more or less my assessment," agreed McQuade.

"Then I must tell you something else," said Major Cordeiro. "I have been on the telephone to Concrete One and a Colonel Kambezo—"

"So have I!" interrupted McQuade.

"Portugal knows Colonel Kambezo," continued Major Cordeiro. "He is not a man one horse-trades with. But he tells me that he has sixty-four prisoners and thirty of them are of the Royal Canadian Air Force and include three pilots. He informs me that he will kill them if I attack the airfield. These prisoners will otherwise go to Tanzania. What do I do, gentlemen, for the United Nations?"

It was the crunch.

The decision was McQuade's.

They all knew it and looked at him with pity.

The sweat boiled out of him in heat and terror.

A hundred and seventeen nations, an organization without teeth and in financial difficulties, half corrupt, silly, fooling about with words, scarcely capable even of moral persuasion, but vaguely, distantly, oh, so confusedly on the side of the masses of the world, the defeated. It was a partial fraud. It was a proposition not as good or inspiring as the God it replaced, but better than nothing.

What to do? What to do? A God who did not seem to care, but watched. A wife, equally loved, who betrayed you. The vast distances and cruel magnificence of Africa, totally indifferent, knowing that, whatever happened, they would win. The black man and the white man, equally wrong. Both with their hopes placed in an organization that was influenced by political and commercial pressures that didn't tally with the ideals and conceptions and speeches.

It was a world without pity, in which no compromise was intended. It was a world of pressures and blackmail and death in which hypocrisy and morality must finally clash. Someone had to win. It was thus a war and in a war the first casualties were truth and love. He couldn't stand aside in anger and sneer. He had to take sides, knowing both were wrong . . .

429

He questioned in a shaky voice, "Are you sure it's a political decision?"

The brigadier said in a voice of pity, "I'm afraid it is."

"And can you do it in time?"

Major Cordeiro said confidently, "Oh, yes. Not much of a problem. It was entirely a question of getting the refugees out of the way."

"Then do it," said McQuade.

He lowered his head so that they should not see him weeping for his son, his hands still touching the child Cándida, but trembling now.

He heard the shouts and orders and clank of equipment and the moving feet and the trucks reversing and even some laughter of enthusiasm, but his aching mind was far away.

Hard over the test area under radar surveillance, heading over Wilhelmshaven toward the North Sea, one eye on M to avoid trailing the supersonic bang over inhabited areas. The unlimited sky and hands and body breathing and on the horizon rushing toward me cloud everlasting. She climbs now in cold thrust at near sonic speed at 40° and the world drops away like a photograph to the floor. Radar instructs alter course 35° and nontoppling fully free gyro systems allow it on instruments only, the sea somewhere behind the right ear. Sound unaltered. At 600 knots push throttle through a dent and up to afterburner position. Dull thud behind as she goes through and the altimeter leaps two thousand feet upward. Pains in ears. Hope they go when we get up to 30,000—but we are already *there!* Mach needle creeps to 1.6. Now *turn* if you dare and see if the structure breaks! The counter clicking off a mile every three seconds. Round in a tight twenty-mile turn, the North Sea (or half of it) and clouds miles below. Visible vortices waft over the leading edges, air banged almost solid, and the girl's face stares, sentimental cow eyes with a little green shadow, badly applied; a reluctant hunger; a little unfashionable, nothing to do with the color supplements, but the tongue freezes; and love confuses the instruments of preconception; it leaps into the heart at the opening of a door . . . Do you have any toothpaste? A man's old voice says from another room "Yvette" and the heart sings in acoustic ownership.

430

Here, thousands of miles from such a moment, Costa's voice said in a sadness that equaled McQuade's own, "Portugal is betrayed. I know it. It is a trick."

Brigadier Fermoy qualified, but not disputing it, "It's all for the best. A little pain and then all will be well."

McQuade did not know what they were talking about. His agony was personal. He believed that the political situation would be over, would be calm, ready for the negotiations, in about fifty minutes. He might not be the one who carried them out, but there was no shame in that. He had done his part.

He whispered gently to Cándida, who had not said a word since she'd been brought out of the burning house, "I will take you somewhere far away where the buildings reach the sky and the streets have thousands of motor cars and there is music and dolls as big as a gazelle." And he felt the rigidity of appalling shock slacken, the enormous fear subside just a little within the love of someone who cared . . .

Far away the firing began and people were being killed. He trembled and said no more. The sun was hot on his face but he couldn't stop shivering. And then the air miles away was vibrant with the roar of many engines and he couldn't withhold the excitement that made him shake with pride. This was the United Nations coming to fill a political vacuum. There were twelve huge multiengined jets, and they went round in a salutory sweep and then broke away into a single column.

He drove to Concrete One, leaving Cándida in the care of Marianne. All along the way in the dust crossed by the marks of tires were the dead. Not many for an occasion of this importance, but pitiful and only worthy of a great cause. Black and white, mostly men, but a few women and children caught in the turn of the tide.

On the airfield among the smashed Portuguese and Canadian airplanes the twelve transport planes had parked neatly in two rows, and out of them were pouring troops, and not only troops but jeeps, light artillery, a helicopter, drums of fuel, tables, tents, boxes of ammunition. The troops were not Canadian, or Scandinavian, or Irish, or Indian, or belonging to any of the "small" or uncommitted nations normally used by the UN to prevent accusations of partiality.

431

They were American.

McQuade felt uneasy. His heart cried, like Mr. Costa, "We have been betrayed," but he couldn't identify it yet. The great silver aircraft had the words "United Nations" painted on their fuselages, and most of the soldiers wore new blue helmets or had painted their old ones the pale blue of the UN. Their shoulder badges had been torn off and the UN one stitched on. But something was wrong. He could smell it.

He was introduced to the general in charge. The general received him very briefly as one of no particular importance and having no further relevance to this situation, which was now his, the general's.

Many of the jeeps were moving off fast, armed with bazookas, and they were moving south.

"Where the hell are they going?" McQuade asked in bewilderment.

"First objective is Nova Zeira," said the general. "Frankly, I reckon four days for that one. After that we'll hit arterial roads and get really moving."

"Are you crazy?" asked McQuade loudly.

"Something bothering you, Mr. McQuade?"

"I'm supposed to be in charge of this political situation, that's all."

The general laughed.

"I wouldn't know about that," he admitted indifferently. "My mission's military."

"And what is your mission?" McQuade asked, stunned.

"You could say to clarify the southern portion of Africa."

"You mean," inquired McQuade, scarcely believing his ears, "you intend to take Angolique by force?"

"Angolique in ten days," said the general. "Then Rhodesia in about two weeks and then South Africa. That might take a month or two."

"Have you gone raving mad?" McQuade shouted.

The general asked sourly, "Are you on our side, Mister? Just so's we know. If not, clear out, boy. I'm a busy man."

McQuade walked outside the office, which the general had brought with him.

432

Mr. Costa had heard other news. He, too, was stunned in a grief that couldn't comprehend. He informed McQuade in horror, "Planes from a British aircraft carrier are bombing Portuguese and South African airfields so there won't be any aerial opposition. With *their* kind of equipment it will be a massacre. But Portugal will fight. This is the biggest betrayal the world has ever known. And for what?"

For what indeed? Somewhere among the thirty or forty corpses being assembled in a pile was that of Peter, McQuade's son.

The American soldiers stood around and looked at the flamingos rising in hesitant clouds and at the monotonous *miombo*. It didn't daunt them. They'd had all the right injections. They were the greatest people in the world. Nothing would stop them. They had no doubts. In the weeks and months ahead they might stand just as cheerfully in the shattered towns—Nova Zeira, Salisbury, Bulawayo, Pretoria, East London, Durban, Johannesburg, Lourenco Tomas, Vila Lobanda, Bloemfontein, Capetown and Windhoek—still firm in the belief that what they did was right, because finally the US and the UN had become one. The good people were at last solid behind the good causes. It had been explained to them in ten thousand TV interviews and a billion words in articles. Integration was essential. It couldn't be managed in American cities but it had to be in Africa. This time the intellectuals were in agreement with the slaughter. This was the big problem of the day—the white man in Africa, his defiance of the good people. Okay. They were the Big People of the world and nothing would stop them. Money and logistics and the PR men would see to that. And if the operation was preemptive in terms of the Chinese, so much the smarter . . .

McQuade couldn't stop them. Nothing that he said would persuade them. Portugal and indeed Africa had been betrayed, but if he shouted it aloud these boys wouldn't understand. They'd laugh, believing he was a nut case ranting in the heat. They were good young men brought up on a diet of democracy, whose sacred cow was the African at present. They were facing south. They were here to adjust southern Africa to the views of the good people of the west and to save Africa from communism . . .

It was tragedy on the gargantuan scale. McQuade beat his fist on the Land Rover in despair.

433

The Africans and Asians of the world would watch in horror and awe and fascination as the white men slaughtered each other, supposedly on their behalf, and left a desert behind them as they did so.

It was as if God and the world had no further use for him.

He sent his resignation along the general's Telex machine, his own having been destroyed. Marianne also resigned, but this was a gesture of loyalty to him rather than disapproval of the UN's policy. Franzo and Fermoy did not resign.

He buried Peter in a mass grave with thirty-one other people. It was his sacrifice to Africa and it had been in vain.

The Secretariat accepted his resignation. This was not surprising since he had been their stooge. No replacement was sent since the situation was for the giants, or those who believed they were giants. After a while McQuade realized that he was hanging around like a masochist, watching aircraft come and go, more and more troops and vehicles arrive.

He took the Land Rover and, accompanied by Marianne, Mr. Costa and Cándida, drove south a thousand miles, exhausting himself each day so that thought came to a standstill, bitterness went away, and after a while he was too numb to care. He just wanted to get home to Kristan, who still loved him and would help care for this child who was one of the early victims of the situation.

In the evening of the second day they sat under the shade of a wide acacia tree and watched elephants and rhinoceroses digging for water in the sand where in a little while the rains would come and create a pool as they'd done last year.

For thousands of miles around was bushland, thorny and often poisonous; acacia, which reached out to tear the shirt or frock, and when he struggled to free himself once he spiked himself on the thorn of another tree. All the world seemed hostile, but it was so magnificent he was thawed. It was greater than the armies. It could only spurt poisonous milky sap or spike the flesh, but it was so vast a bushland it might well defeat the logistics of armies. He smiled in grim satisfaction. It wasn't just Portugal they had to defeat, but Africa.

All the water was bad, either saline or fouled by animals, and was dried up in the great heat of the season about to end. But here and there were the few springs and, great distances apart, the big undaunted rivers.

They drove under the shadows of small rocky hills and whaleback ridges and by the occasional forests, but more usually high ground revealed the original rock on which all else had its foundation.

On the second and third days the heat was unbearable because of the oppressive approach of moisture. Vast cumulus clouds advanced on the third day, under the influence of a gale, and the wind brought with it the smell of wet earth and surviving vegetation. But as the day proceeded and the dust still billowed behind the Land Rover the clouds dispersed.

But on the fourth day the wind blew and the clouds did not disperse. The sky went almost black at noon and the lightning streaked. The rain came as heavy as bullets and in minutes the ground was covered with pools and floods.

The air was full of termites on the wing, and when the rain stopped for a while they saw that other harbinger of rain, Abdim's stork, flying above the wet grassland, a sign for the villagers that the rains were here.

McQuade could almost sense the dry world grasping at the water, the bush anxious to produce a flush of green leaves and flowers to replace its present deadness and grayness, and the coils of grayish-green creepers and the hornlike fronds of prickly euphorbias creeping into hot eager moist existence like a new variety of reptile.

But the weather was dangerous as well, for the rain was not interested in a mere Land Rover. It filled the world with contempt. If it's water you want—here it is, by the billion ton. The heat was now steamy and scarcely alleviated by any breeze. Dry sandy beds of rivers turned into raging torrents, bearing along trees and dead animals; desperately dead, these were, coated inches deep in mud and smashed to bits in the whims of water and nature's violence. The earth, too, was knee-deep in mud, and dangerous, even terrifying when the vicious artillery of the storms moved around. The Land Rover bogged down several times, but McQuade did not care. He was exhilarated and when the rain stopped he fought the mud with pleasure, and each time he and the vehicle won.

And on the sixth day they came to Lourenco Tomas. They flew

435

in a Boeing to Portugal, where they boarded a second Boeing and left for America.

One day, McQuade knew and hoped, he would come back to Africa. When the black man and the white man began anew in friendship and love, on that day he would come back—to the desert and the great swathes of savanna, to the forests and the wide distances; to the flamingos in pink clouds over the soda lakes and the hippopotami dignified and colossal in a river of hyacinths; to the thatched round huts and the bright cities and the vivid sun and the high-hipped African girl striding in the heat with a box on her head. In the meantime Africa would suffer fools and madmen and there was no more he could do except care for this child, this orphan of war, and weep silently seven miles high for all of the great continent.

7 ▪ ▪

MCQUADE CAME HOME in the late afternoon, holding in one hand a suitcase with dirty shirts and a squeezed toothpaste tube inside and in the other the small hand of an African-Portuguese *mestiço* child. He was tired, had a stubble, and felt dirty. He shouted his way through the customs and immigration authorities and, incredibly, went straight through with the girl. There was not one reporter to meet him this time.

Cándida breathed slowly, with care, terrified of the size and the noise. She hadn't let go of McQuade's hand since the Boeing had taken off from Lisbon. She relaxed a little in the taxi, being one step removed from the apparent chaos.

"Do you like it?" McQuade asked apprehensively.

"The people all look angry," she commented.

McQuade was shaky before the impending encounter. Only that one short letter had come to him from Kristan, and he, too, hadn't been able to sit down and write to his wife for a week. He was as weak as jelly and sweating in the elevator.

Kristan wasn't in.

Again he felt the irritating frustration, but calmed it for the sake

436

of the child. Cándida wandered about, interested now, safe, aware that this beautiful high place was home.

There was a newspaper by the desk McQuade used. It was a week old and the headline shouted at him: "UN TAKES OVER AFRICA." He smiled grimly. Inaccurate, as usual, he thought. The smaller words caught his eye, part of the same sensation: "UN Diplomat Sacrifices Son." He began to shake, knowing that Kristan had dropped this paper to the floor when she'd read those and the larger words. She'd gone. He opened the desk and there was the letter, written in such emotional haste that he could scarcely identify the writing. "It's no use. I can't bear what you have done. What kind of man are you who'd sacrifice his son's life for *this?*" Further on was the angry justification "I'm leaving. Forever. You know who with. I tried hard not to get involved and so did he, believe it or not . . ."

It was forgivable. He could imagine her breathing heavily in the shock of the printed words, the fluttering heart and the beginning headache. Then the great rush of tears. And finally the angry pen moving and the telephone call, the plea for sympathy, the last necessary justification for what she'd done. Man, and woman too, liked to be on the side of right even when they were doing wrong.

But for him it was too much. He sat down at the desk, terribly tired. What was the use of it all? What use to live or survive at all? What *for?* It seemed to be man's destiny to be miserable. He remembered the smashed villages and the tanks passing through, the torn bodies on the beach at Dieppe, the mob trotting the streets in India and the women wailing in the hot silence, the flames licking the grass huts north of Vila Lobanda and the abused corpses hanging in a shed. Love. To hell with love, he thought, and the faces stared at him in the mind in vain. He was too tired. He began to weep.

After a long while he realized that the little girl was weeping, too—weeping because he wept. She didn't know anything about anything, but cried because he was unhappy and it was a worrying world of taxis, elevators, buildings that went higher than the clouds, and things that screamed in the sky and explosions that made the heart beat like a captured bird's.

"Don't mind me," he said. "I just had a very sad letter."

She said meaninglessly, "The pipes are hot even up here. That is clever."

He said, "That's the central heating. It's ridiculous really. You know something? You're the only good turn I ever did anyone. D'you follow me? Everything else, completely balled-up. But you. We might do something about you."

Cándida didn't know what he was talking about, but indentified the affection.

After a while he showed her her bedroom and when, half an hour later, he heard her gentle snores, he began drinking. Because, after all, there was nothing else to do and there seemed to be plenty of the stuff in the bar.

He never heard her come.

One moment he was thinking about her, and then there she was, a materialization and continuation of the thought. She looked scared to death, of course. He must look like a wild man.

"I'm sorry," Kristan said hastily. "I didn't know you'd be here. I'll go when I find—"

"Ah, come on," pleaded McQuade. "Admit it. He booted you out. You're a Canadian crumb-bum like me. Nobody wants us."

Very distantly she identified the hopes within this apparent indifference.

"He was quite a nice person," she claimed.

"Was? Where's he gone now? The mortuary?"

"North Africa."

"And he didn't fancy taking you along?"

"Something like that," Kristan admitted. "I think he took fright."

"Well! So you came back here?"

"I didn't know you'd be here. I thought you'd be there with all those smart people killing each other."

"No," McQuade said. "I opted out of that. Oh, by the way, I brought a girl back with me—"

"Oh, Shaun."

"Not that kind of girl. A *mestiço* kid. Cándida. She thinks New York is a mess."

"Well, I'll leave you. I hope you'll both be very happy—"

"Don't go," he said, his shaky voice betraying him. "She's only ten. She needs both of us."

438

"Nobody needs me," Kristan said, tears rolling.

McQuade said, suddenly cheerful and frivolous, "You want me to sympathize or something?"

"You've been drinking?"

"Not celebrating anything, I can tell you."

Kristan said in shock, "You've been crying, too."

"Drunks often do."

"Oh, Shaun, Shaun."

"I'm human, you know. I'm a father and husband and all that sort of stuff."

Kristan put a hand on his shoulder, and he shouted in haste, "Don't touch!" and then, in explanation, "I'm brittle right now. I'd look silly crying again. A big Canadian slob."

"What are you going to do about me?" Kristan asked outright.

McQuade asked, "What do you want me to do?"

"I'm sorry, I'm sorry," she cried.

He said, "Do you think your sins were so very large in the world? If I can forgive *them* surely I can forgive you?"

Mr. Cannon said with an expressionless face, "I regret that the Secretary General could not talk to you himself. He would very much like to have done so. But he had to go to San Francisco to deliver a lecture. It had already been postponed twice."

"An interesting theme?" asked McQuade.

"Very. Moral impetus in new nations."

"I must read it if it ever gets into print," McQuade said. "As I am sure it will do."

"Are you being facetious, Mr. McQuade?" Mr. Cannon inquired, like a man who didn't know and was interested—he, too, contemplated words.

"It's possible," McQuade admitted.

"I'm glad you're taking it all in good humor. Some of them," admitted Mr. Cannon, "have an exaggerated sense of their importance and become very bitter. After all, the result is the thing. I guess you could say you were expendable in terms of a bigger proposition."

"I thought for a moment you were going to say principle," McQuade said.

439

"Well," claimed Mr. Cannon, "you could call it that, but it'd be stretching the point a bit."

Angola
Mozambique
Manhattan
New Brunswick
Lisbon
London
1964/1966